MURDER Duet

MURDER Duet

• A Musical Case •

BATYA GUR

TRANSLATED FROM THE HEBREW BY DALYA BILU

Perennial

An Imprint of HarperCollins*Publishers*

A hardcover edition of this book was published in 1999 by HarperCollins Publishers.

HarperCollins books may be purchased for educational, business, or sales promotional use. For information please write: Special Markets Department, HarperCollins Publishers Inc., 10 East 53rd Street, New York, NY 10022.

First Perennial edition published 2000.

Designed by William Ruoto

The Library of Congress has catalogued the hardcover edition as follows:
Gur, Batya.
[Merhak ha-nakhon. English]
Murder duet : a musical case / Batya Gur.—1st ed.
p. cm.
ISBN 0-06-017268-1
1. Ohayon, Michael (Fictitious character)—Fiction. I. Title.
PJ5054.G637M4713 1999
892.4'36—dc21 98-50456

ISBN 0-06-093298-8 (pbk.)

03 04 ❖/RRD 10 9 8 7 6 5 4

To the memory of my father, Zvi Mann

The remarks attributed to Theo van Gelden in chapter 13 derive from a lecture given by Ariel Hirshfeld in July 1995 in the Music Center at Mishkenot Sha'ananim in Jerusalem.

MURDER Duet

1

Brahms's First

As he put the compact disc into the player and pressed the button, it seemed to Michaël Ohayon that he heard a tiny cry. It hovered in the air and went away. He didn't pay too much attention to it, but went on standing where he was, next to the bookcase, looking at but not yet actually reading the liner notes accompanying the recording. He wondered absently whether to shatter, with the ominous opening chord for full orchestra with pounding timpani, the holiday-eve calm. It was the twilight hour at summer's end, when the air was beginning to cool and clear. He reflected that it was a moot point whether a man called on music to wake sleeping worlds within him. Or whether he sought in it a great echo for his conscious feelings or listened to it in order to create a particular mood when he himself was steeped in fog and emptiness, when it only seemed that this holiday-eve calm embraced him, too. If that was so, he thought, he wouldn't have chosen this particular work, which was worlds removed from the holiday-eve quiet in Jerusalem.

The city had changed greatly since he had come here as a boy to attend a boarding school for gifted pupils. He had seen it transformed from a closed, withdrawn, austere, provincial place into a city pretending to be a metropolis. Its narrow streets were jammed with lines of cars, their impatient drivers shouting and impotently shaking their fists. Yet he was moved time and again to see how even now, on every holiday eve (especially Rosh Hashanah, Passover, and Shavuoth, but also on Friday evenings, and if only for a few hours, until darkness fell), sudden peace and quiet would reign, utter calm after all the commotion and vociferousness.

• • •

So complete was the calm before the music spread through the room, so absolute the stillness, that it was as if someone had taken a deep breath before that first note, held up a baton, and imposed silence on the world. Instantly the nervous, darting, driven looks of the people in the long lines at the ringing supermarket cash registers vanished from his mind. He forgot the anxious expressions on the faces of the harried people hurrying across Jaffa Road with plastic bags and carefully clasping gift baskets. They had to make their way between rows of cars with engines running, whose drivers stuck their heads out the windows to see what was holding up traffic this time. All this was now silenced and effaced.

At about four o'clock the car horns and the roar of the engines fell silent. The world grew calm and tranquil, reminding Michael of his childhood, of his mother's house and of the Friday evenings when he came home from boarding school.

When the stillness descended on holiday eves, he again saw before him his mother's shining face. He saw her biting her lower lip to disguise her agitation as she stood at the window waiting for her youngest child. She had allowed him, despite her husband's death and although he was last of her children still with her, to leave home. He returned only every other week for a short weekend, and for holidays. On Friday evenings and holiday eves, he made his way by foot along the path at the back of the hill from the last stop of the last bus to the street at the edge of the village. People, bathed and dressed in clean clothes, relaxed in their houses secure in anticipation of the holiday. The stillness of the hour would hold out its gentle arms to him as he climbed the narrow street toward the gray house on the fringes of the little neighborhood.

Outside the ground-floor apartment Michael had been living in for some years now, all was quiet, too. You had to go down a few steps to enter it, and to stand in the living room and look through the big glass doors leading to the narrow balcony in order to discover the hills opposite and the religious women's teachers college curving like a white snake in order to realize that it wasn't a basement apartment but had been built on the steep slope of a hill.

The voices of the apartment building's children who had been called inside died down. Even the cello up above, which for several days now he had been hearing playing scales at length and then in a Bach suite, was silent. Only a few cars drove past on the winding street at which he now looked, as he unthinkingly pressed the CD player's button. His hands had preceded his conscious mind and doubts. His act caused the loud unison opening of Brahms's First Symphony to fill the room. In a moment what now appeared to be the illusion of peaceful harmony which he imagined he had succeeded in achieving within himself after long days of restless disorientation had disappeared.

For with the very first tense orchestral sound, a great new disquiet began to awaken and well up inside him. Streams of small anxieties, forgotten distresses, made their way from his stomach to his throat. He looked up at the damp stains on the kitchen ceiling. They were growing bigger from day to day, and changing from a dirty white to a gray-black wetness. From this sight, which pressed down on him like a lump of lead, it was a short way to thought and words. For these stains required an urgent appeal to his upstairs neighbors, a talk with the tall, bleary-eyed, carelessly dressed woman.

Two weeks ago he had knocked on her door. She had a squirming, screaming baby in her arms, and she gently patted its back and rocked it as she stood in the doorway facing Michael. Her curly light brown hair covered her face when she lowered her head to the baby's. Behind her, on the big, bright, shabby carpet, music scores and compact discs outside their boxes lay scattered, and in a big, open case padded with green felt lay the cello, a gleaming red-brown, with a music stand beside it. When he had looked into her light eyes, pale-lashed and sunken, with the dark semicircles underneath them emphasizing their helpless expression, he had felt guilty for disturbing her. He looked inquiringly over her shoulder, waiting for the bearded man he had once seen in the house entrance. Michael had heard him opening the door of the apartment above him, and thinking he was her husband, assumed that he would be talking to him, relieving her of this additional burden. But she, as if in answer to his look, said with pursed lips and lowered eyes that she would only be able to take care of the problem in a few days' time, when the baby recovered from his ear infection. Moreover, the stains had been caused not by her but by the previous tenants.

She had a low voice, pleasant and familiar, yet Michael suddenly felt as if his body was too tall and overbearing. She seemed to shrink and strain, as if wanting to look up at him from below. Her hand moved nervously from the light blanket wrapped around the baby to the curls covering her shoulders, and he therefore slumped his shoulders, trying to make himself seem shorter as hastened to agree to wait.

That was the first time he talked to her. In all the places where he had lived, and especially since his divorce, he had deliberately avoided contact with the neighbors. In this tallish building, too, he confined himself to reading the announcements on the cork bulletin board in the lobby. He quietly dropped his checks for heat, garden upkeep, stairwell cleaning, and emergency repairs into the mailbox of the Zamir family, who lived on the third floor and none of whom he had ever seen. He did suspect, though, from the inquiring and preoccupied looks he got from the short and balding elderly man he occasionally encountered in the stairwell, that he was the building treasurer and also the author of the dunning notices and lists of names of the tenants who were in arrears.

His hesitant knock on his upstairs neighbors' door, which bore a printed card with the name VAN GELDEN on it, for him signaled the beginning of the very thing he had conscientiously avoided all these years. In the building he had lived in before, when Yuval as a hungry adolescent had discovered that there was no sugar in the house and suggested borrowing some from the neighbors, Michael had been horrified.

"No neighbors," he had stated firmly. "It begins with asking for sugar and ends with being coopted onto the Tenants Committee."

"You'll have to do it anyway," promised Yuval. "Your turn will come. Mama's the same way, but Grandpa takes care of that for her."

"If I don't exist, I don't have to do it," Michael insisted.

"What do you mean, if you don't exist? You *do* exist!" Yuval protested in the didactic tone he adopted whenever his father sounded out of touch with reality. He inclined his head with a critical expression, demanding an end to this nonsense.

"If I *appear* not to exist," said Michael. "Especially if I don't knock on doors asking for cups of sugar and flour. It's the only thing, it seems to me, or one of the only things, that your mother and I agreed on from the start."

Yuval, as if afraid of hearing any more about the agreements and disagreements of his parents, hurried to put an end to the conversation, saying: "Okay, never mind, I'll drink cocoa, it's already got sugar in it."

Michael dreaded the troublesome conversation with his neighbor, which he would not be able to avoid because the spreading stains were depressingly redolent of neglect and poverty. The thought of plumbers, ripped-up tiles, hammering, commotion, and general upset, together with the awareness that he had forgotten to buy fresh coffee for the holiday, grew more powerful as the symphony's opening theme continued to build up tension. In order to calm himself, he began to read the little booklet accompanying the disc. He pulled it out of the transparent flat plastic box, looked at Carlo Maria Giulini's handsome face and his shining mane, which failed to hide the conductor's reflective brow, and wondered how an Italian got along with the musicians of the Berlin Philharmonic.

He listened attentively to the music, trying to close his heart to it, to listen to the work for once with his mind alone. Only then did he begin to leaf slowly through the booklet, pausing at the biographical notes in French—of the three languages in the booklet the one the Moroccan-born Michael knew best—and read, not for the first time, about the genesis of this symphony, Brahms's first but completed relatively late in his life, and soon after its premiere dubbed "Beethoven's Tenth." Brahms would work on it, on and off, for some fifteen years after writing the ominous and suspenseful opening. In September 1868, years before he finished it, in the midst of a painful rift with Clara Schumann, he sent her a greeting on her birthday, writing from Switzerland, "Thus blew the Alp-horn today," and below that the notes of the horn theme that would finally ring out years later in the last movement of his symphony. The prosaic words of the booklet, describing chromaticism and what it called the "seal of doom" of the flutes, and analyzing the tension between rising and falling melodic lines, failed to inhibit the overwhelming effect of the music. At first it seemed to him that it filled the physical space around him, and he tried to separate the music-saturated air from his skin, stubbornly concentrating on identifying the various wind instruments and their battles with one another and the other instruments.

For a long moment he stood there actually trembling, wondering at and mocking himself for this surrender to the spellbinding power of the familiar sounds, and telling himself to switch them off or to listen to something else.

But something stronger in him responded to the emotion that was cutting short his breath. The music was full of foreboding, threatening, dark and gloomy, but so beautiful, calling him to follow it, to respond to its ominous gloom.

Michael sat down and put the booklet on the arm of the chair. He thought that one of the ways to dispel oppressive feelings, to put them to sleep and retrieve some kind of peace, was simply to distract yourself from them. Although some people thought that if you did that, the feelings would return and pounce on you from behind, like thieves in the night. ("Just when you're not ready, everything you've run away from stabs you," Maya used to say. The memory of her slender, warning finger landing gently on his cheek, a half-smile on her lips and her eyes looking at him sternly, brought back an ancient pang.) And yet, he thought that it made sense to transfer the source of the emotion from the pit of the stomach to the head.

What was needed was to study the subject, to confront it from the right distance, and especially not to let it engulf you. To fill the void inside, but to understand how it operated.

One could silence the music, and one could also persevere and listen to the CD again from the beginning, paying attention to the nuances, to the softness of the *forte* in this performance, the entrance of the second theme, and even to isolate the transitional passages between the themes.

He went into the kitchen and looked at the ceiling, hoping to discover that the stains had shrunk or at least hadn't got worse. But they clearly had spread since he had last examined them closely, two days ago.

Why did he care about the stains? he wondered with irritation as he stood in the kitchen doorway with the sounds filling the entire apartment. It was the upstairs neighbors' problem, they would have to see to it, and as for the greenish-black patch on his ceiling, a quick coat of paint would soon take care of that.

He looked again at the booklet lying on the armchair, went over to the bookshelf, and pressed the CD player's button. The silence was absolute. The telephone cord, pulled out of its socket and neatly folded, seemed to offer a refuge.

If he reconnected it, maybe the phone would ring. And then? He wondered, Say it does ring, what then? If he let the world in, it might offer him dinner at Shorer's house, or a visit at Tzilla and Eli's, or even an evening at Balilty's, even though Michael had already told him, untruthfully, that he was going to his sister's for dinner tonight.

He had told him this in order to avoid a repetition of the evening of the Passover seder the year before. Danny Balilty had shown up at Michael's door in a festive white shirt, sweating as usual, as if he had covered the distance from the west to the north of Jerusalem at a run. He stood there with his vast belly swaying in front of him as he rattled his car keys in his hand, and with a childish, ingratiating smile, which was not innocent of a certain triumph, said: "We decided that phoning wouldn't work. We couldn't start the seder without you." He had narrowed his small eyes as they focused on the brown armchair in the corner and the yellow circle of light shed by the reading lamp on the green book jacket, and exclaimed in a tone of suspicious bemusement: "So you really are alone on the seder night, and reading Russian literature besides!" The upper half of his body leaned toward the bedroom, and his eyes darted in the same direction, as if he expected the closed door to open and a glamorous blonde to appear wrapped in a pink towel.

"If you had someone here with you at least," he said, scratching his head, "I'd understand. But even then, she'd certainly feel better to be at a seder with a big family and all the fantastic food we've prepared." In recent years Balilty had become an ardent cook. Now he had described in detail how he had acquired half of a lamb, and what exactly he had done with it, and how his wife had made her special meat soup and the vegetables and the salads and the Greek eggplants. He had stood there, looking at Michael with pleading eyes and complaining like a child: "If Yuval weren't in South America you'd certainly come. Matty'll kill me if I come back without you."

And in a moment of weakness Michael allowed himself to be dragged away from the quiet evening he had been eagerly looking forward to all month.

"Why is this night different from all other nights?" he had said to Balilty, who was still standing next to the armchair, and Balilty waved the volume of Chekhov at him (his finger keeping the place) and announced: "Never mind the philosophy. It's forbidden to be alone on holidays. It leads a person to despair. It's well known that for people without families holidays are a disaster."

Michael looked at intelligence officer Balilty's swollen face. He had intended to say something about the threat felt by those who conformed to convention when confronted by deviancy, and that this invitation, which he could not find a way of refusing, had nothing to do with his own welfare. Maybe it could even be seen as the ruthless revenge of the family against a man who lived alone and enjoyed his solitude. He had almost uttered the word "extortion," but instead he heard himself saying, with a little smile: "It's under duress, Balilty."

"Call it what you like," said Balilty firmly, "in my eyes it's a mitzvah."

Then he returned the book carefully to the armchair, and added in a pleading tone: "Why make a big deal of it? It's only one evening in your life. Do it for Matty's sake." Michael held back the words on the tip of his tongue: Why should I do anything for your wife? You're the one who's supposed to make her happy. And if you stopped running after every pair of tits you saw she'd have been happy a long time ago. He went into the bedroom, despising himself for his weakness as he looked for his long-sleeved white shirt. As he felt his rough cheek and wondered whether to shave, he told his face in the mirror not to take itself so seriously. What, in fact, was so terrible about spending one more meaningless evening? When he was young he hadn't been so pompous and pedantic about the way he spent his time.

Maybe he should have bowed to his sister Yvette's pressure and gone to her place for the seder. All this vacillation, he said to himself then, was the result of rigidity, which in itself was a sign of age, and perhaps, as Shorer said, it was also one of the inevitable results of living alone. Like the recurring disappointment of hopes pinned on sitting around a table with a lot of people, and on the empty conversations entered into to kill time.

He was already filling up with the self-pity that would soon lead to anger at himself and his isolation, which when all was said and done was a sign of nothing but conceit and arrogance. "You're no better than anyone else," he had said to his reflection in the mirror, and he tugged at a new strand of gray hair. "Take it easy. What happens out there is often meaningless. The mind is free to wander at will," he said to himself as he quickly dressed. He had even found a bottle of French wine, which he held out to Matty at the door. With a glowing, radiant face she told him he shouldn't have, and after that he sat down obediently among the celebrants sitting around the table for a traditional Orthodox seder.

Between courses he made an effort to talk to Matty Balilty's niece. He remembered that the first time he was there, Danny Balilty had tried to fix him up with his sister-in-law. He tried to mobilize whatever was left of his sense of humor to confront the encouraging looks sent in their direction by Balilty as he ran between the kitchen and the seder table. Matty Balilty, on the other hand, tried not to look at them at all. It was only when he complimented her on the food that she gazed at him with her brown, anxious eyes and asked: "Really? Do you really like it?" As her brother's daughter blushed and played with the edges of her napkin, it was clear to him that it wasn't only the food Matty was talking about.

Michael had presented himself at work a week ago after an absence of two years, during which Balilty had been careful to "keep in touch," as he announced every time he phoned to invite him over. Since Balilty had phoned him just a few days before, he had rushed past him in the second-floor corridor without so much as stopping to welcome him back, only clapping him on the arm and shouting as he passed: "Live it up, Ohayon, live it up. Life is short. Next week you're coming to us for the holiday meal. Matty's making couscous." And so—because Balilty had completely ignored Michael's "But I told you I'm going out of town," Michael couldn't counter Balilty's eagerness with the polite reserve that would be interpreted as supercilious coldness and offend against his sincere desire for a kind of closeness—that morning Michael had disconnected the phone.

Now he looked at the phone cord and wondered why he had put up such a fight. What was so great about his determination to spend the holiday alone, if in any case he was spending all his time agonizing about the ceiling stains and about the note he had found in his mailbox? It was a summary demand to go up to the third floor and receive from Mr. Zamir the Tenants Committee regulations. At the meeting the day before yesterday, which Michael had as usual not attended (the words "as usual" had been added by hand to the typed note), it had been decided that it was his turn to represent the tenants in his wing.

For a moment Michael thought that perhaps he should talk to someone, anyone, before he drowned in a puddle of misery. He picked up the cord but refrained from reconnecting it.

Balilty could come bursting in even if the phone was disconnected, but no one else would dare. If he connected it and phoned Emanuel Shorer, it would end with another invitation to a festive family meal. In any event, they couldn't have a meaningful conversation over the phone. It would only be one more example of Shorer's contention that Michael shouldn't go on living alone.

"So what do you suggest," Michael had asked aggressively at their most recent meeting, just before he returned from his study leave. "Do you want to send me to a therapist," he asked sarcastically after Shorer finished listing the signs of what he called the "deformations stemming from continued solitude."

"It's not a bad idea," said Shorer with a you-don't-frighten-me expression. "I don't believe in psychologists, but apart from wasting money it can't do any harm. Why not?" Without waiting for an answer, he continued: "As far as I'm concerned, you can go to a fortune teller. The main thing is to see you settled down. A man of your age! You're almost fifty."

"Forty-seven," said Michael.

"It's the same thing. And still trying to find yourself. Hanging around with all kinds of . . . Never mind, it's not important."

"What do you mean, not important?" demanded Michael. "It's very important. All kinds of what, precisely?"

"All kinds of non-starters, married, unmarried—above all, the kind of women nothing can come of, even Avigail. . . . A man needs a family!" he pronounced.

"Why, exactly?" said Michael, mainly in order to say something.

"What do you mean by that?" said Shorer, taken aback. "A man needs . . . what do I know? Nobody's found a better solution yet—a man needs children, a man needs a framework. It's human nature."

"I already have a child."

"He's no longer a child. A big young fellow wandering around the world looking to find himself in South America. He's no longer a child."

"He's already arrived in Mexico City."

"Really? Thank God!" said Shorer with undisguised relief. "A civilized place at last." Suddenly he was angry: "You know what I mean, don't try to make me give you a lecture now about family values. A man needs someone to talk to when he comes home. Not just four walls. Not just affairs with women. For God's sake, it's over twenty years since your divorce. It's ten years since you had anything really serious going, if we don't count Avigail. How long are you going to wait? I thought that when you were studying, two years at the university, you'd meet people. . . ."

Michael kept quiet. He had never spoken to Shorer about Maya, and to this day he didn't know what he knew about her.

"I'm not saying you look bad," added Shorer cautiously. "It's not that you've gone bald or put on weight. And it's true that you're a big success with women. All the women around here tell me that as soon as they see you they want to . . ." He made a vague gesture.

"Yes, what do they want to do?" mocked Michael. Again the thought struck him that it was not only concern for his welfare but also simple jealousy that kept his friends awake at night.

"How should I know? They want! It's a fact. Even the new typist. She's maybe twenty-five, but she looks like a teenager, pretty, no?"

He had rolled his eyes. At that moment Shorer reminded Michael of Balilty. He wondered what it was about the subject that made them both talk in the same tone. What was it that suddenly gave Shorer's voice pimplike overtones? Did it have anything to do with a feeling that their lives were over, while he still had untold possibilities before him? In their eyes at least, it might seem so. If only he could speak openly, he would tell them a thing or two about his anxieties, about his despair.

"You've already asked me if I like her."

"Because she asked about you," Shorer apologized. "It's the way you look, tall, polite, quiet, with that sadness, and those eyes of yours. When they find out that you're an intellectual, too . . . they ask . . . right away they want to . . . to make you not sad."

"So, what's the problem? What are you worried about?"

"It's you I'm talking about, not them! Suddenly he doesn't understand what a person says to him!"

"What did she ask?"

"She asked! They all ask, is he married, has he got someone, why not? Things like that."

"And what do you answer them?"

"Me? It's not me they ask! Do you think they dare to ask me? They ask Tzilla. She does her best for you, too. But nothing comes of it. You took your uncle as an example. A bad example. Jacques was a butterfly. Filled with the joy of life. But you take things to heart. And because he was a butterfly, how young he was when he died. The statistics show that men who live alone die younger."

"Ah, the statistics!" Michael spread his arms. "If the statistics are against me, what can I say? Who am I to deny the statistics?"

Shorer snorted. "Don't start with your theories about statistical research."

Michael lowered his eyes and tried not to smile, because something about the way Shorer kept broaching this subject touched his heart. Maybe it also met his need for a father figure, a role Shorer had been playing ever since he recruited him into the police and advanced him rapidly. It showed in the way he had helped him to obtain an extra year of unpaid leave to pursue his studies, and also in the way he scolded him from time to time for what he called his irregular procedures.

"At least if I had the feeling that you were content and happy," grumbled Shorer. "But I can see that you're not."

"And marriage will make me happy? Is it the ultimate solution?"

"As far as I'm concerned, you don't have to marry. Live with somebody. Make an agreement, as long as it's something steady. Not just some girl where it's obvious from the beginning that nothing will come of it."

"How can you tell something like that in advance?" protested Michael. "Chance comes into it, too."

"Really? Chance? Suddenly you believe in chance? Soon you'll begin talking about destiny, too! Pardon me, but you're not serious. You're even contradicting yourself. I have a thousand witnesses who've heard you say a thousand times that there's no such thing as chance."

"Okay, so maybe I really should consult an expert," said Michael with a faint smile.

"I don't believe that people change from going to psychologists," pronounced Shorer, who had failed to notice the sarcasm, "only maybe, maybe if they make an inner decision. Otherwise it's like giving up smoking by external means, without wanting to inside. I don't understand why one lousy marriage over twenty years ago should traumatize a person for his whole life. What's past is past. Nira, her mother and father and all that, may have been Poles, but they definitely weren't monsters."

"Tell me," said Michael, with the irritation that seized hold of him whenever Shorer began talking about his ex-wife, as if he were deliberately exposing a blot on his past, as if he were confronting him again and again with a fatal mistake he had thoughtlessly made in his youth. "Do you think I don't want to find someone, to love a woman and want to live with her?"

Shorer looked at him quizzically: "I don't know. Judging by your behavior up to now? Do you want the truth?"

Michael sighed.

"In the beginning," complained Shorer, "it's too soon after the divorce, and later on it's too long after it, and there are already habits that have been formed, calculations. It's a fact. How many years has it been?"

"How many years has what been?"

"How many years have you been alone? If we don't count your affair with that woman with the Peugeot, the doctor's wife?" Shorer looked aside.

"Nearly eighteen, but—"

"No buts about it," Shorer interrupted him and went back to lamenting Avigail.

Because of conversations like this, Michael had disconnected the phone. They took place most often at his car door on Fridays and holiday eves, when he was about to drive home. Instead of keeping things to himself, as he had always done before, he had begun to respond during them. A note of sympathy and concern had begun to creep into his colleagues' remarks when the holidays came around. He now heard it even in the voices of Tzilla and Eli, who had started out as his subordinates but gradually had also become close friends, who, nonetheless, had always maintained a degree of respect for his wish for privacy. Because of this dreaded note, and because he knew that he would be intruding into a cozy family atmosphere, he avoided picking up the phone. He told himself that there was no point in trying to escape the situation by inventing distractions. On the contrary, it was better to surrender to his feelings until their intensity dulled of its own accord. And so he should definitely listen to the Brahms symphony until the end, because music's consolations were not cheap substitutes. He was about to press the button to restart the music and skip to the second movement when he again heard the tiny whimpering that sounded like the faint crying of a baby.

His certainty that it wasn't the baby upstairs, because that baby's cries never sounded weak, amused him. To think that there was a baby in the vicinity whose crying he knew so well! The sound he heard now was really a kind of mewling, despairing but clear, as if it was coming from beneath the apartment. But since on recent nights his sleep had been disturbed more than usual by the howling of cats in heat, or so it seemed to him, and he had been awakened more than once by what sounded like a baby crying, and laid awake in the dark listening until he was sure that it was the baby upstairs, he now tried to ignore the sound.

But the mewling, which no longer sounded in the least like a cat in heat, definitely had something human about it, gave him the idea that perhaps that black cat had had a litter in the basement bomb shelter beneath him. He opened the door and peeped out, as if to look for newborn kittens on the doormat. There was no cat there, but there was a brown envelope. He glanced inside it. Among the papers—the most recent Tenants Committee financial statements—he found a receipt book, with a folded note between its pages wishing him good luck and Rosh Hashanah blessings for a good New Year. Michael quickly pushed the receipt book back into the envelope, as if it would disappear if he stopped thinking about it. He threw the envelope inside his door, because the sound of the wailing had become sharper and clearer, easily overcoming the noises coming through the closed doors into the stairwell. The stairwell amplified the sonority of a woman's scolding and a little girl's screaming, the television voices, the persistent chords of a low string instrument, the clatter of pots and pans. This medley of sounds did not silence the wailing from below. It was clear to him that he had to act quickly. If there were kittens in the cellar, the sooner he removed them from the building the better, before they settled in.

The closer he came to the bomb shelter the stranger—not in the least catlike—the wailing sounded. The cellar door was wide open, and on the threshold, inside a small cardboard box, on a padding of newspapers covered with a sheet of transparent plastic, and under a shabby yellow wool blanket, a real live baby lay on its back, wailing furiously.

When he took the baby in his arms and carried it into his bedroom, and, after removing the newspapers and unfolded clean laundry, laid it on the bed, he realized that he had not opened his door since midmorning and thus had no idea when the cardboard box had actually been deposited. Nevertheless he tried to work out when he had first heard the mewing. But he couldn't be sure if it was cats he had been hearing on and off for the past few hours or, as it now seemed to him, this baby crying.

The baby now lay on the bed. It looked about one month old. Its eyes were open and baby blue, and a thick down of damp fair hair covered its tiny head. It clenched its miniature fists and waved them in the air, touching its face from time to time but not succeeding in reaching its mouth. Michael took it in his arms again. For a few seconds the crying died down and turned to gasping, and then immediately into a loud, offended scream. Michael pushed the tip of his thumb gently into the tiny mouth, leaving it between the pink gums that clamped tightly around it. He realized that he was holding a very hungry baby in his arms and that he had no way of feeding it.

He leaned over the bed and picked up the blanket, which gave off a moldy smell and shed wisps of yellow wool. But from the baby's smooth face, which was completely wet, and from its neck, he breathed in a sweet baby smell. Even before he laid it on its back in order to remove the garment in which it was encased, he began, on an irresistible impulse, to pick from between its fingers and the folds of its neck tiny wisps of yellow fuzz. The baby wriggled and squirmed in the middle of the bed. Its arms waved in the air and its legs kicked furiously. Michael picked it up again. He laid it on his left forearm, which held the whole body, and pressed his arm to his body. And he did all these things in a kind of compulsion, as in a dream, as if he had been taken back twenty-three years. The very recognition of the distress he felt looking at the hungry baby's face gave rise to another, vivid emotion, which even contained a hint of joy. Unthinking, he heard his own voice talking as he used to talk to Yuval during the long nights of his infancy. He went to the bathroom, the baby clasped tightly to his chest, and let warm water run into the sink. He prefaced his actions by whispering them aloud into the tiny red ear, dipped his elbow into the water, and spread a big, faded pink towel on top of the washing machine. Then he rummaged in the medicine chest for talcum powder, and in a distracted voice informed the baby that he couldn't find it.

He didn't stop whispering into the tiny ear, in the belief that the ceaseless flow of words would silence the baby's hunger. The blue eyes stared at him as if hypnotized. But this fascination, Michael knew, would not last long, for when he finished washing and changing the baby, he would have no means to supply what was really needed, because he had neither a bottle nor baby formula.

When the water was the right temperature, he laid the little body on the towel he had spread on top of the washing machine. He left one finger in each tiny fist. Only later did he wonder at the power of the instincts that had dictated his actions in those moments. The baby coiled its fingers tightly around his. It opened its mouth wide in alarm, its body, exposed to space, began to thrash about, and its lips twisted. Michael bent over and laid his own lips gently on its cheek, keeping up a steady murmur while extracting his finger from the desperate grip of one of the fists. With one hand he undid the plastic snaps of the little garment, bracing himself for the anticipated crying with the thought of a bit of cloth dipped in sugar water with which he could fill the little mouth, which trembled spasmodically in preparation for a renewed attack.

He rummaged in his trouser pocket for a clean handkerchief and tried to make up his mind whether to return to the kitchen now and prepare the sugar water. But his right hand was already removing the disposable diaper, which was disintegrating from its apparent long hours of use. As he folded it he reflected that they had still used cloth diapers in Yuval's time. Then he froze for a moment and heard himself uttering a cry of astonishment before he laughed aloud. He had been so sure of the baby's sex that even the sight of the tiny vulva, which was red and chapped from urine, wasn't enough to convince him at first.

"But you're a girl!" he said and bent over her. "Not that it makes any difference to us," he murmured into the tiny ear, "a baby is a baby whatever its sex. But it's funny how trapped people are in their old perceptions," he went on aloud. "Anyone who once diapered and bathed and fed his boy baby simply doesn't think of a clothed baby as a girl. If I'd known I'd have realized why you don't struggle when you're being undressed, because little girls, they say, are gentler even as babies."

The little body was now completely naked. A network of blue veins stood out on its white chest, red blotches of diaper rash covered the stomach. And before the little legs began to kick again he gathered her into his arms, clasped her to his chest, and lowered her gradually, first the legs and then the buttocks, and lastly his own arm supporting her back and neck, into the warm water. The baby shuddered convulsively and let out a yell. Michael resumed his murmurs and explanations as he laid his hand on her face and neck. He worked quickly as he soaped and rinsed, and very carefully returned her to the towel, wrapped her up in it, and rummaged in the medicine chest again for some cream, finding the white ointment in the blue container which Yuval had used years ago in the army.

The sight of the baby wrapped in the big towel, supported on his one arm, her legs jerking, reminded him of Nira. When he bathed Yuval before feedings, she would stand at the bathroom door, leaning against the doorpost, her hands stopping her ears against the screams. He often had to remind her to hold out her finger to the baby, so that he could grip it in his fist, to save him from the terrible fear of being lost in space. Whenever he reminded her, Nira would hurry to obey, and somehow her helplessness and obedience gave him a feeling of self-righteousness. He didn't like himself when he told her how to behave with her son, but he couldn't stop himself either.

It gave him a strange feeling to dry and powder the baby. When he smeared the thick cream on her abdomen, he examined her red and protruding navel. Suddenly he was afraid that she might have a hernia, as a result of hours of continuous crying. Only a pediatrician could make the diagnosis, and the thought of a pediatrician gave rise in him to feelings of reluctance and fear. A pediatrician meant that somebody else would know about the baby, who would immediately take her away for a medical examination. So he decided to drive the thought from his mind. The pediatrician could wait. Apart from the navel and apart from the diaper rash, her skin was smooth and clear. She began to scream again, making her face red and blue.

When Michael went into the kitchen with the baby and prepared the sugar water, he still didn't know what exactly he would say to the upstairs neighbor. But she was the only quick solution he could think of as far as bottles, formula, diapers, and even a change of clothing were concerned. He couldn't bring himself to put the baby back into her original garment, or return her to the cardboard box. She remained wrapped in the towel, lying in the middle of the bed, a clean handkerchief rolled up and dipped in sugar water in her pink mouth, her lips sucking avidly. Michael built a wall of pillows around her and ran up the stairs to the second floor.

Even when the neighbor stood before him he didn't know what to say. She opened the door a crack. One hand held the handle and the other ran through her curls, trying to gather them up, and then fussed with the collar of her purple man's shirt. He recognized the apprehension, almost the fear, on her face that he had again come about the damp stain on his ceiling.

"May I come in?" he asked. With a kind of helpless submission, but with obvious reluctance, as if she would have liked to deny him entry if only she had an excuse to do so, and because she didn't know how to say no, she opened the door and moved aside until he was standing in the room next to a playpen, against which the cello case leaned.

In the playpen the chubby baby lay on its back, arms outspread and legs apart. It breathed noisily. The cello itself was laying on a little sofa next to a pile of wash and under a big oil painting, on unframed canvas, which at a glance left the impression of a misty landscape in white, black, and gray. The woman coughed and said, still from her place at the door, that because of the holidays she hadn't managed to find a plumber. He tried to say that he hadn't come about the stain, but she went on talking rapidly, apologizing again that because of the baby and her need to get back to work and the holidays. . . .

Michael waved his arm impatiently. "I'm just here to ask . . ." he began, "there's a baby, a little girl, in my apartment now and I don't have anything for her. . . ."

In the seconds during which she looked at him with astonishment, her deep and very light eyes narrowing and wrinkling at the corners, the explanation came to him: "My sister left her granddaughter with me and she forgot all the things."

"What things?" asked the woman. The soft light still coming through the big window lingered on the gray strands in her curly hair before illuminating a smallish blotch on her left breast.

"Everything. Bottles, formula, diapers—all that stuff," he muttered, embarrassed, knowing that his story didn't make sense. Again he panicked at the dawning knowledge, which he hurried to banish from his mind, that he was doing something wrong. "Everything's closed for the next two days, because of the holiday. I can't phone my sister because she's religious. . . . And anyway she lives far away."

Something between apprehension and suspicion appeared in the woman's eyes as she asked: "What? The baby's been left with you for the whole of the holiday? The baby? Do you live alone?"

Michael nodded unwillingly.

"Excuse me for asking," she said quickly, "it's just that . . . Do you know how to take care of her?"

"I think so. . . . It's been a long time since . . . My son's already grown up, but a baby's a baby. I don't think you forget . . ." His voice died away as he heard himself stammering. "Anyhow," he said firmly, "there's no choice now. She's here and I haven't even got a bottle or a diaper, and I thought you could help me. . . ." He gestured toward the baby.

"How old is she? I have bottles and powdered milk," she said on her way to the next room. Michael waited for her to come back, and then watched her as she placed a baby bottle and a can of powdered milk on the round table in the dining nook and stood there waiting for an answer.

"Five weeks," said Michael, responding to an instinct that told him not to give an even number.

"That's a really young baby," the woman said, alarmed. "How could they have left her like that without . . ."

"There's been a misfortune in the family," said Michael quickly, blinking. This lie, he thought, could lead to a real misfortune. Like when he had lied that Yuval was ill, and that very same night the boy had broken out with chicken pox. "I don't have anyone to ask, they're traveling . . . out of town . . . and the baby's downstairs screaming with hunger."

Again she went to the next room, returning with a big bundle of disposable diapers and a pacifier in a plastic wrapper. She paused to think for a moment. Then she went away again and came back quickly with a pile of baby clothes, a cloth diaper, and a round plastic box with a scented paper towel sticking out of it. She pushed all these things together, and then stood surveying the table with her cheek resting on a finger. She glanced doubtfully at Michael.

"He's just fallen asleep, why don't I come with you? I can help you with the first bottle."

"No, no, no," said Michael, alarmed. He could imagine her face when she saw the cardboard box. Then she would understand everything. He knew that he couldn't say he'd found the baby. She would then be taken away from him at once. "I don't want to trouble you anymore. I don't want you to leave your baby alone on my account."

"There's no problem," she said pleasantly, and she began putting the articles she had collected into a big plastic bag. "Ido's just fallen asleep. He'll sleep for a while now. It's no trouble at all for me to come down for a minute."

Michael glanced at the playpen, put his hand on her arm, and said: "I'll come back if I have a problem."

She looked at him doubtfully, but helped him get a grip on the handles of the bag of disposable diapers. "Where are her parents? Leaving a five-week-old baby like that!"

"Her mother's . . . in the hospital. Postnatal complications, and her father . . ." He looked frantically at the wall and said: "He . . . there's no father. She's a single mother."

A look of understanding and concern dawned on her face. "Don't worry," she said. Her full lips, which pouted and gave her a sulky expression around the mouth, broke into a generous smile. "We'll manage with her over the holidays. I suggest you let me help you a little. Ido's almost five months old. Everything's still fresh in my mind." Suddenly, with an expression of alarm, she said: "You left her alone, she must be screaming her head off. Why don't you go get her and bring her here?"

"No, no," cried Michael. The woman's face was now radiant with a smile that completely changed her expression. All traces of disquiet were gone, and her light eyes were wide open, like clear, bottomless pools. For some reason it was clear to him that bringing this woman into contact with the baby girl would mean losing her. Michael didn't know why he was so sure of this. He was merely responding to a feeling of dismay unlike anything he had ever felt before. He thrust aside any attempt at logical thought.

"We need lukewarm boiled water," he heard her call after him as he bounded down the stairs. He was holding the bags of clothes and diapers in his hands and the bottle and other things under his arm. "To make powdered milk you have to . . ." He didn't hear the rest, only the screams from behind his door. Inside, he put the bundles down at the bedroom door, picked the baby up, and clasped her to his chest. The yellow blanket and the pink towel wrapped around her were both wet. A warm wetness soaked his shirt. He put his cheek to her little face. Her cheeks were on fire. For a moment her head jerked back convulsively. Her body struggled, but then her crying stopped and her face muscles relaxed.

For a few seconds the world was complete and at peace, lacking nothing. As if from a distance he heard the faint sound of music. The baby strained and stretched in his arms, and let out a loud scream of frustration. It took a while before he realized that it was the cello again, that the upstairs neighbor was sitting next to her sleeping baby and playing a sorrowful melody. He didn't know what the sweetly heartfelt music was. He bent down and picked up the bag holding the bottle and powdered milk. He wondered how long she had been living here, and why he had never noticed her in the stairwell. He reflected on the beauty of her eyes and smile. If she weren't such a mess she could be really attractive.

He glanced at the instructions for making the powdered milk and sat down so that he could go on holding the baby. While he was opening the can with his army knife and smelling the yellowish powder, he went on murmuring into the baby's ear. How much water did you need to add for a baby girl? For some reason the fact that the baby was a girl made matters more serious, as if she needed more protection and special care than he might be able to provide. Michael measured out the requisite amount of powder, poured a bit more into the bottle just to be on the safe side, and made a face as he smelled the powder again. He wondered how it could possibly taste good to her. He felt the electric teakettle and poured some water into a glass. Since he didn't want to let go of the baby, who stopped crying whenever he whispered an account of his actions into her ear, he couldn't pour a drop of water onto his wrist. That was a gesture imprinted in his body ever since Yuval's bottle-feeding days. And so he dipped his finger in the glass.

"A finger's less sensitive," he whispered into the pink little ear. The baby screamed in spite of his talking, and her screams hastened his movements. "One really doesn't forget," he assured her as he pressed her tightly to his body. "It's like swimming or riding a bicycle," he explained. He poured the water from the teakettle into the bottle, screwed the nipple on with one hand, and shook the bottle hard over the inside of his left wrist. To do this he had to relax his hold on the baby, who screamed at the top of her voice and writhed about on his arm. Drops of whitish fluid fell onto his skin. The temperature was right. He sat down on a chair, set the baby on his lap, and put the nipple into her mouth.

In the profound silence that now reigned, the sound of the cello was heard again from upstairs, full of feeling, vibrant with sweet sorrow. He loved the sound of the cello. How lucky the upstairs neighbor was to be able to play like that on the most beautiful of all musical instruments.

The baby sucked avidly, stopped, and her eyes closed. She seemed exhausted and had given up. Maybe she was too hungry to be fed. But Michael didn't give up. He moistened her lips with the liquid, which came out of the bottle with difficulty, only when he shook it. Suddenly he realized that the hole must be too small. As if to verify his suspicion, the round, pink, perfect mouth opened wide, the head moved in frantic searching movements, and a new scream split the air, silencing any other sound. He panicked for only a moment. Until he remembered how he used to hold the tip of a pin over the gas flame and stick it into nipple holes that were too small. He even remembered the smell of the charred rubber, and how it sometimes melted and made the hole too large. The milk would come out in a big trickle and flood the inside of Yuval's mouth.

"The baby's choking!" Nira would cry, and he would hurry to turn him over. Yuval was a greedy baby. This baby, who didn't yet have a name, or maybe had one he didn't know, looked as if she had despaired of the possibility of being fed, as if she had really given up.

When Yuval was very hungry he couldn't be fed. "Too hungry to eat," Michael would announce, applying his special "method": shaking drops from the bottle onto his finger and smearing them onto Yuval's gums. Patience and perseverance would finally get him to eat. The room would fill with the rhythmic sucking sounds he now longed to hear from this baby.

He shook the bottle hard, wet his finger, and gently inserted it into the open mouth. The inside of the baby's mouth was warm, her gums were clamped onto his finger, and her lips were pursed around it. Then he quickly pulled his finger out and substituted the nipple, which he had previously bitten to enlarge the hole.

Only when she began to suck hard, with a steady, regular rhythm, did he allow himself to lean against the cracked wooden back of the kitchen chair. Only then did he feel how tense his body had been until this minute, when a tremor of fatigue passed through the muscles of his legs.

It was only now that he felt free to examine her face at leisure. With the fingers of his left hand, the one that was holding her, he touched the little button of a nose, the delicate hint of fair eyebrows, the fine, soft down near her ears. Her eyes, which had now been closed for a few minutes, opened, a milky blue. Her tiny mouth was closed around the nipple from which she sucked steadily. She sighed between one suck and the next, and a film of sweat had gathered on her upper lip. Without moving the bottle, Michael rose with the baby in his arms and went to sit in the armchair in front of the French windows.

An ambulance siren wailed persistently in the distance. The sun set slowly over the hills, and the world was still. Only he and the baby remained, sitting in the wide armchair with its threadbare upholstery, the only piece of furniture left him from his married days. In this chair he used to feed Yuval on winter nights. He had listened to the sounds of his breathing and sucking, to his sighs of contentment, and again and again to Schubert's song-cycle *Die Winterreise*. The atmosphere of those chilly nights—Yuval was born in autumn—was with him again. Silence, interrupted only by the sounds of feeding, and a solitude that was not loneliness but a kind of mute and perfect togetherness. The music upstairs stopped, and he had still not succeeded in identifying it. How often did you have to listen to a piece before you could identify it by name?

"We're an autarchic economy," he whispered with his face buried in the soft flaxen hair. The darkness gathered, the bottle emptied, and the baby's eyes closed. Her sighs of satisfaction turned to rhythmic breathing. Her lips parted and let go of the nipple. Michael gently removed the bottle, checked to see how much was left, and put it down at his feet. Then he pressed the switch of the reading lamp. A soft yellow light illuminated her face. The other end of the room was in shadow. Michael picked up the baby and prepared to pace up and down the room. Since he was ready for a long trudge, he was surprised to hear the burp the moment he put her on his shoulder. He smiled with gratification. How little it sometimes took to be pleased! Sometimes it was enough to prepare for some effort and then it was unnecessary. Without making too much of it, the feeling at such moments might even be called happiness. He felt the weight of the little body, limp and relaxed, on his shoulder. He lowered her carefully to his arm, returned to the chair, put the baby on his lap, and gazed at the darkness outside and at the reflection of the lamp in the windowpane.

What now? he wondered. *What do you actually want?* But instead of keeping a grip on his thoughts, he let them wander. At that moment the demons began to surface in the form of the question of how long he was going to be able to keep the baby. He was breaking the law. He knew the procedures. It was obvious that he should have contacted the local police station that shared space with the Jerusalem police headquarters in the Russian Compound, where Michael worked. In his favor it could be said that it was a holiday, and that anyone else, too, would have kept the baby at home or taken her to the hospital. But the truth, the main point, was his wish, his imperative need, to keep her for himself. How brief and flimsy they were, the moments of utter peace of mind and body. One ring of the phone could crumble them to dust. Or a knock at the door, however hesitant. His heart skipped a beat. What if someone was already coming to take her away from him?

This thought had never occurred to him before. Until this very minute, when he heard the knock at the door, and then again less hesitant, and again, insistent. He knew only that he had to keep her a secret. Maybe he should ignore the knocking. But because of the anxiety to which it gave rise, he stood up and looked through the peephole in the door. Complete darkness. Without thinking he heard himself fearfully ask: "Who's there?"

"Me, Nita, from upstairs," said a low voice. Now he knew her given name, too.

"Just a minute," he muttered, and he looked around. He made haste to shut the bedroom door so that she wouldn't see the cardboard box in which the baby had been brought to him as if she were a day-old puppy. Now she had a name, the tall woman in the dark tights and a purple man's shirt, and the dark, plump baby in her arms, its brown eyes gazing at him solemnly. They stood opposite each other in the living room, each holding a baby. Nita's protruding lower lip trembled. She stroked her baby's smooth brown hair, carefully straightened the collar of his one-piece outfit, raised her eyes to Michael, and smiled shyly.

"I only came to bring you a few things you might need," she said, holding out a bag. "Baby soap and cleansing cream and protective cream for her bottom, and a little blanket. I just wanted to see how you were getting along. I hope I'm not disturbing you. . . . "

"It's quite all right, thank you very much," said Michael. They stood in silence.

"Look at us," Nita said with a bemused, ironic smile, "each of us with a baby. What a sight we must make!" Then she came very close to him and leaned over to look at the little girl.

"She's exquisite," Nita said with awe as she raised her eyes. They weren't the same height, and yet her eyes looked right into his. "I see that she finished the bottle. She looks very contented," she said, surprised. "You really managed very well. She's five weeks old?"

Michael nodded.

"You haven't dressed her yet. What's her name?" Nita ran her finger lightly over the naked foot sticking out of the pink towel.

For a moment he froze. "Noa," he found himself suddenly saying out loud, and he bowed his head over the flaxen down as if to apologize for the hasty, arbitrary choice. He took a deep breath and raised his face to the woman, feeling the blood rush into it.

"Ido," Nita announced to her baby, whose eyelids fluttered as if they were about to close, "you have a little friend. This is Noa. Noa was born in the fields." Michael recoiled in alarm, but then she began to hum the tune, and he remembered the popular song she was quoting.

Ido rested his head in the hollow between his mother's neck and shoulder. "I haven't dressed her yet," Michael apologized. "I wanted to feed her first. That seemed more urgent."

"But you don't have to hold her all the time. You can put her down when she's quiet. You can even have a cup of coffee in the evening, especially if you're not breastfeeding," Nita said with a shy smile.

Michael sat down. His arms were trembling. Where, in fact, was he going to lay her down to sleep? He hadn't thought about that yet. He wasn't prepared to return her to the cardboard box. He looked at the tall woman's thin, harried face, at the eyes, which seemed to him at that moment steeped in a kind of blue-green gravity, at the dimple he suddenly discovered not at the middle but at the top of her cheek. He cleared his throat loudly. Anyway, he would need a partner. He couldn't do it alone, he said to himself. Even if only for the next couple of days. He didn't want to think now about the future. But then he wondered what future he was thinking about. Had he taken leave of his senses, or what? What did he want? He stifled these questions and went back to concentrating on whether he should apply to her for help. But what about her husband? "Your husband . . ." he said hesitantly. Her smile disappeared instantly.

"I don't have a husband." Her lips protruded in what was almost an expression of defiance.

"You don't?" he said, confused. He had been sure it was the bearded man.

"I'm not married," she said, this time calmly. "It's not so unusual. You yourself said that your niece is a single mother. It appears to be in fashion, if not an epidemic," she added, and the dimple, which had disappeared, reappeared for a moment.

"Yes," he apologized. "I just thought . . . I saw . . . it seemed to me . . . I saw a man with a beard. . . ."

"A short beard or just unshaven? If he had a beard it was the younger of my brothers, but if he was unshaven it was my elder one. You would probably have recognized him, but he's only been here twice." She said all this rapidly, as if to dispel the sense of oppression that had begun to gather in the room.

"A short beard, or unshaven. I don't exactly remember. Why should I recognize your elder brother?"

"He doesn't have a real beard, he's just not shaved. It's in fashion now. Look, you yourself—"

"I'm on vacation, that's all," he corrected her and slid his hand over the three-day stubble. "I didn't recognize him. Do I know him?"

"My big brother, Theo, is famous. You've never heard of Theo van Gelden?"

"The conductor?"

"Yes."

"He's your brother?"

"My elder brother."

"Van Gelden is a Dutch name."

"Our parents are from Holland."

"And you have another brother? Also a musician? Is he the violinist?" He was searching his memory.

"Yes. Gabriel is a musician, too. Gabi is the one with the beard." Nita sighed. "Anyway, you never saw any husband here," she said with a smile, and added, with embarrassment: "I've come to invite you up to my place. I thought that maybe the babies could sleep and we could have a cup of coffee in honor of a good New Year. Oh, excuse me," she said with a giggle, "what's your name?"

"Michael. Why aren't you at some family meal for the holiday?"

"Neither of my brothers is in Israel at the moment. My father's been alone for some years now. He's too old and ill, and he's not interested in such things anymore. I've already seen him today. We paid him a visit earlier," she said defensively. "And going somewhere just for the sake of going out . . . I didn't feel like it. But I just thought that you . . . I just meant . . ." She fell silent and put both her arms around the baby.

Michael looked at the baby girl. He couldn't really call her Noa, not yet. "We really are quite a funny sight, with both these babies," he said thoughtfully.

"I don't want to press you. I just want you to know that I thought how hard it must be with a five-week-old baby and I . . ." Suddenly he felt that it would be nice to spend the evening with her. She held out the promise of a contact that was neither threatening nor meaningless. Suddenly he felt an impulse to tell her that, and in order to stop himself he said: "First I have to dress her. You can stay down here."

"I'll be more comfortable at home. I won't feel as if I'm imposing myself." Nita smiled with an effort and tugged at the edges of her purple shirt. "And besides, your baby is still easily moved. Ido needs his bed at night, and it's already half past seven." She looked around. "I'll leave this here and go upstairs," she said. She put the plastic bag down at her feet and quickly, furtively, looked around the room again. "Are you coming up when you're ready?"

Michael nodded firmly. Suddenly he wasn't sure. What if she turned out to be a self-righteous busybody? What if she felt a hysterical compulsion to notify the authorities at once? And how was he going to explain his own incomprehensible, embarrassing, and perhaps also shameful compulsion to keep the baby for himself? She might even want to interpret his behavior, to explain his impulse to him, and he would really rather not think about it. What was wrong with acting on impulse for a change? he said to himself. But then a kind of shame for wanting this baby to be his floated up to the forefront of his consciousness and gave rise to a feeling of oppression.

The baby went on sleeping while he was dressing her in the little blue outfit he fished out of the bag the neighbor had brought. Once she shuddered, and once, when he touched her chin, she even twisted her lips, with eyes closed, in a grimace that looked like a smile. He remembered that babies don't smile at this age, that it was nothing but a reflex.

By the time Nita opened the door she had managed to tidy up a little. The pile of wash had disappeared. The cello, shut in its case, was leaning close to the folded playpen against the wall in the corner. On a round copper serving table, in a big Armenian pottery dish, she had laid slices of apple in a ring around a small saucer of honey.

"Come, put her down here," she said, pulling up a baby stroller. "The top part comes off," she explained, "and you can take her home in it later." Because she was standing and looking at him as he laid the baby in the stroller, his movements were clumsy. He was too shy even to breathe in the baby's smell, or lay his cheek openly against the folds of her tender neck. There was something helpless about the way he tucked her in, under what seemed to him the penetrating, suspicious scrutiny of Nita's eyes. When he looked up, he discovered that it was a warm, open look. Now it seemed to him that her eyes were gray and full of an unresentful sadness.

He sat down on the little sofa under the oil painting, and looked at the wall opposite. A large print hung there, a pastel drawing of a stout, bearded man with a thick cigar in his mouth playing the piano. The figure looked very familiar to him. "Brahms," said Nita, who was following his eyes.

"He died in 1897," Michael reflected aloud. "I just learned that today. I always thought he lived a long time before that, at the beginning of the nineteenth century. When he died he was only in his early sixties."

"He had liver cancer, but only spoke of his 'jaundice.' Do you know what Dvorák said about him when he was dying?"

"What?"

"Dvorák was his protégé, Brahms had brought him to his own publisher, and Dvorák was very much influenced by him. He loved and admired him even before he was helped by him. When Brahms was on his deathbed Dvorák came to see him." Nita looked at the drawing and smiled. "Dvorák was a pious man, and when he came out of Brahms's bedroom he said, with wonder: 'Such a noble soul, yet he believes in nothing.' That he had no relation to God. Which isn't quite right."

"What isn't quite right?"

"That Brahms had no relation to God. Of course he did, only not to Dvorák's God," she said in a low voice and inclined her head as if to examine the short legs at the piano pedals in the drawing. "So it was you who was playing Brahms's First? It isn't healthy for babies, that music. It's music of anxiety."

Michael was astonished. "Is that common? To see it like that? Is that the standard opinion?"

She shrugged. "I don't know. I just see it that way."

"I wonder," he said hesitantly, "if music can give rise to anxiety. Suddenly, when I heard it, I really did remember the stain on the ceiling and all kinds of things like that, which normally never bother me. Could it have been the music?"

"Of course it could. It gives rise to feelings, no?"

"What makes Brahms's symphony give rise to anxiety?"

"Well, there are all kinds of things, I think it's there from the very opening." She gathered up her curls. "And also the orchestration and the minor key itself, you know." She didn't wait for his response. "C Minor especially almost has a tradition. It's the key of Beethoven's Fifth and his Third Piano Concerto, and of a particularly somber Mozart concerto."

"The key gives rise to anxiety?" he reflected with surprise. "It doesn't seem possible."

"Well, not only the key. It depends on what you do with it. At the beginning of the Brahms it's the way the string instruments ascend and the wind instruments descend at the same time, and the tension between them, and those pounding drumbeats."

"Mozart's C Minor Piano Concerto doesn't give rise to any anxiety in me."

"Well, okay, it's become background music to all kinds of things. But in a good performance it can give rise to a lot of sadness even today."

"But not anxiety. Brahms's symphony . . . I just want to understand if these things have . . . some kind of objective correlative," he said apologetically.

"It's not so much a matter of keys or harmony as it is a matter of a sound space," she mused as if to herself. "And of Brahms's volume of sound. The opening is *forte*, not *fortissimo*. And the *forte* is muffled and there's something nerve-wracking about it. The drumbeats create a tension that isn't resolved for quite a while, and then, when the music gets fast, there's even more drama. The symphony is filled with frightening events."

"What are 'frightening events' in music? How can you talk about it like that? Frightening events in a musical composition with no words?"

"Of course there are such events," she exclaimed. "You've just heard them yourself. All the transitions and themes, when and how they end, all the dialogue among the instruments—all these things are events, and they can be frightening."

He looked at the cello. "Do you play professionally?" he ventured.

She nodded, drew in her protruding lower lip, and went into the kitchen. "Choose a disc," she called from there. "They're in the cabinet." The only cabinet in the room was a heavy brown piece of furniture, tall and narrow, standing in the corner between the sofa and the wall with the French windows that opened onto the balcony. He got up and stood in front of them, looking out for a moment at the wide street and the hills as if he was surprised to discover that the view was the same as the one from his own apartment. On the cabinet's heavy wooden doors was a relief carving of two angels hovering over a gilt harp. Two bronze hands, one holding the other, joined the doors to each other. He separated them and stood before the crammed shelves. "Like a child in a candy store," said Nita. He turned around and saw her smiling on the threshold to the kitchen.

"Are these in any kind of order?" he heard himself ask. He wouldn't be able to tell her. He didn't know anything about her. He took a pack of Noblesse cigarettes and a box of matches out of his pocket and looked at her for permission. She pointed to the blue glass ashtray next to the telephone and said: "Maybe I should move her into Ido's room. You can also open the door to the balcony, or would you wait until I bring the coffee?"

He put the pack down on the copper serving table and went back to the cabinet. The top shelves were crammed with LP records. The others held compact discs standing in two rows, one behind the other. He pulled out two of them. One was Haydn's *Andante and Variations for Piano*, a work he didn't know. He put it down on the copper serving table, as if to go back to it later, and looked at the other one. On it was a picture of Nita in a black, low-cut evening dress, looking very attractive and holding a cello in her left hand and a bow in her right. Next to her was an elderly bald man sitting at a piano. And then the words "Nita van Gelden and Benjamin Thorpe play the *Arpeggione* Sonata by Franz Schubert." He removed the disc he found in the CD player, glanced at the label, and put it carefully into its box, which held the two other discs of Rossini's opera *William Tell*—a work he also didn't know, except for its famous overture. He replaced it in the player with the Schubert sonata. The sounds that filled the room awakened the hope in him that he would be able to tell her. But after a few moments Nita was standing in the room, her face frozen. She bit her lip and pointed at the CD player. "Do me a favor," she said quietly. "Please turn that off."

He nodded quickly and stopped the flow of sound.

"Where did you find that?" she asked, putting the disc back into its box. He looked at her and stammered: "It was there, in the cabinet. I picked it up by chance."

Her lips relaxed. Now she was embarrassed. "I haven't heard it for ages, nearly two years. Today I'd do it completely differently," she apologized, but this did not seem enough to explain her behavior. "I'll bring the coffee," she said, and she returned to the kitchen and came back quickly, holding a big wooden tray with a glass coffee pot, two cups, milk, and sugar. She put the tray down on the copper serving table and surveyed it intently, but he had a strong feeling that she was somewhere else, that she saw nothing.

"Teaspoons, there aren't any teaspoons," he said.

She smiled as if she had just awakened. "I knew I'd forgotten something," she said, and she returned to the kitchen. The baby in the stroller moved. It let out a weak whimper, and then was silent. Nita stood over her, two teaspoons in one hand, the other hovering over the stroller handle as if ready to rock it. How could he confide in her? She was a total stranger, he knew nothing about her. Even the cello told him nothing. The *Arpeggione* Sonata wasn't a sign of anything. "You have to catch it when it's just starting. Don't let it get stronger," she announced.

"What do you mean?"

"The crying. Sometimes, if you rock them right away, they go back to sleep. Sometimes it doesn't help." Nita sighed. And yet, he did know something about her, he thought. Maybe the fact that she was a stranger would be helpful. He looked at the deliberate movements of her hands as she poured. It amazed him that these hands, which had cut apples into thin slices, were the hands that had played the first notes of the *Arpeggione* on that disc. These hands, big and white, which poured milk and pulled a cigarette out of his pack, were hands that could play a Schubert sonata.

She pushed the baby stroller gently, maneuvering it through the narrow corridor into the next room, where her son was sleeping, sat down heavily on the little armchair, and lit the cigarette.

"And I asked you if you were a professional musician!" He shook his head.

She inhaled and waved her hand dismissively. "Anyone can make a recording," she said hoarsely.

He asked hesitantly if that was her only record.

"There were a few more," she said softly, with downcast eyes. "Don't be so impressed. What's past is past," she pronounced as she raised her eyes to him. There was a firm vertical line between her dark eyebrows. "It doesn't mean anything about the future. It's been a year since I've played or performed."

"Because of the baby?"

She didn't answer. He didn't dare ask her about herself with his usual freedom. He looked at her, wondering what he could possibly say. She put the cigarette down in the groove of the ashtray and held the cup in both hands. The tips of her long fingers touched each other. "After Yom Kippur I have a concert, the first in over a year," she suddenly blurted out. Her eyes stared at the big French windows opposite her. Her armchair seemed too small for her. Nita crossed her legs and leaned her elbows on the chair's narrow arms. It looked to him as if she were contracting her whole body, tightening her muscles to control her trembling. Suddenly she looked at him, opened her eyes wide with an effort, and whispered: "I'm terrified. Maybe I don't have it anymore."

He might have asked her what "it" was, but since he understood what she meant, he only asked: "What will you be playing?"

"All kinds of things. There are two concerts actually. In the first I have a short solo, as principal cello in the *William Tell* Overture. My brother

Theo will be conducting and my younger brother will be in the orchestra, too, as concertmaster—principal violinist—for the occasion, the opening concert of the season." She put the cup down. "And about two weeks later, in the second concert, I'll be playing the cello in his Double Concerto," she said, turning her head in the direction of the drawing of Brahms on the wall. "The other soloist in the concerto was going to be a great young violinist discovered by my brother Theo. Theo is good at discovering young geniuses. Pianists from Italy and violinists from South Korea, sometimes even musicians from here. But the genius got sick and can't come. So Gabi will play the violin solo. It'll be a very heavy, big concert—Mahler's Fourth is on the program, too."

"When I heard you practice before, it wasn't Brahms, but it sounded familiar. What was it?" he asked hesitantly, afraid of sounding ignorant.

"Rossini, the solo from the *William Tell* Overture. Do you know the piece?"

"I don't really know anything about music," he was quick to say. "I'm just a music lover."

"Loving it is quite a lot. You can always learn about it if you want to," she said, picking up her cup again.

"The music you played sounded familiar, but I couldn't identify it."

"Are there pieces you can identify immediately?"

"Yes, of course. When you played the Double Concerto and the Bach suite yesterday."

She nodded.

"How wonderful for you that you play the cello. It's such a sad instrument . . ." he heard himself say to his surprise. "I really love it. It seems to me that if you haven't imbibed music with your mother's milk, if you haven't been educated to it from the beginning, or have unusual talent, you can never fully understand it."

"You don't have to understand it," Nita said. "It's enough to love it and need it. Especially to need it."

"With you it's different, you grew up with it. Is the van Gelden music shop your family's, too?"

She nodded.

"I went past there a few days ago and it was closed. Is that permanent?"

"It closed six months ago. There was no one to keep it going. My father's too old and my brothers are busy, of course. And me, too. None of us can drop everything to travel around looking for historical instruments and rare scores and recordings. The shop also needed further investment. There was no alternative. Meanwhile . . . anyhow, my father didn't sell it, even though he had some offers. There was no suitable buyer. . . . No one's good enough for him," she said with a chuckle.

"But you gave up the cello," he ventured.

He had to know more about her. If he had known where this sentence would lead, he would have thought twice. Or maybe not.

She didn't answer at once. And when she did, she said: "I didn't give it up." And immediately she added: "What do you mean, I gave it up?" She stood up and went into the kitchen.

Minutes passed and nothing happened. He looked around, stood up, and then looked at the wall above the sofa and at the kitchen door. He opened the French windows to the balcony, stretched, and breathed in the autumn air. Then he got up the courage to follow her into the kitchen. Nita stood at the sink. It was piled high with plates, pots, and overturned coffee cups. On the gas stove there were circles of burn, as if milk had boiled over a dozen times and never been cleaned up. The floor was sticky, and the faucet dripping.

She was standing with her face in her hands. Her shoulders were shaking. She heard his footsteps and took her hands away from her face. It was dry and very pale. Her eyes narrowed. "Forgive me, please," she whispered. "I'm terribly tired."

"We're leaving," he said quickly. How could he have imposed himself on her?

"No, no, I didn't mean for you to go. On the contrary, please stay, that is, if you want to. I feel as if I haven't spoken to anyone for a long time. Excuse me for saying so, but I like talking to you. I just don't want to dump my troubles on you. Forgive me for being this way, but . . ." She fell silent and seemed to withdraw into herself. There was something so lonely about the way she was standing there at the sink holding back her tears that for a moment he wanted to take her in his arms and put his hand on her brown curls. But he didn't dare cross the distance from the door to her.

"Forgive me," she said again. "I didn't want you to see this mess." She gave him a half-smile and wiped her eyes. "Now that the babies are quiet, I had to start wailing."

Michael looked around. The place hadn't been cleaned for days, or weeks. "Don't you have any help?"

She shook her head.

"Have you had anything to eat today?"

She looked thoughtful, ran her fingers through her hair, and sniffled. "Just a bit," she confessed. "But I drank a lot of fluids."

"And you're breastfeeding!" he rebuked her.

She bowed her head.

"Maybe we should fix ourselves something to eat. We could go down to my place . . ." he suggested after another look around.

"I can't take Ido out of bed now. We could eat here, there are all kinds of—"

"If you like . . ." he hesitated. "We could also try to tidy up a bit here. I could help you, if you like," he said, and he listened with one ear to the sounds from the next room.

"They're asleep," she said.

"Should we get to work?" he asked.

Maybe he would tell her and maybe not. The hardest thing would be to explain it, to himself and to her.

"I don't know if I can eat," she said later, watching him stirring eggs.

"You don't have to," he reassured her. "Just cut up the vegetables we rescued from your refrigerator," he added with a smile. "Then we'll see. While you're cutting and peeling, you can tell me things."

"Tell you things?"

"Why not?"

"Tell you about what?"

"About whatever you like. Maybe even about why you haven't played for a year."

From a bottom drawer in the kitchen cabinet she fished out a vegetable peeler and rapidly peeled a cucumber. "There isn't much to tell. It's a very banal story. I loved someone, I thought he loved me, too. It turned out that he didn't. I got pregnant. He was married. Everything took place in secret. After I got pregnant," she choked, swallowed, coughed, "after I got pregnant, he left me. And I just can't get over it. I can't pull myself together. I told you, nothing special, a banal little story. Cheap melodrama. An Egyptian movie. A soap opera."

"Anything can be described in those terms. You can forgive yourself a little for being so cut up. A lot of people can't allow themselves to give way to their feelings." He scrubbed the frying pan he had fished from the bottom of the sink.

"I didn't want to terminate the pregnancy. I don't know why I'm telling you all this. I'm sorry."

He raised his head from the sink. "I'm glad you can talk to me so openly."

"For a couple of years I lived inside a bubble, even with my music I didn't do as much as I could have. And then the baby came. When that man told me I had to choose between the baby and him, I couldn't get rid of it. I simply couldn't. . . . Maybe I even wanted to bring him up by myself. I'd always done what others considered right. I was the spoiled child of elderly parents with two brothers. You know all that pop psychology." She diced a cucumber.

"It sounds like a happy childhood," said Michael from his place at the gas stove. "You'll find someone else."

"Or I won't," she said, looking at him expectantly.

He looked at her and smiled. There was a certain sweetness in her pouting lips and in the serious determination of her voice, as opposed to the appeal for confirmation in her eyes. "Or you won't," he agreed.

"It's possible to live without love—romantic love, I mean," she announced.

"It's possible." He sighed. "Difficult, but possible."

"Lots of people live like that," she insisted, and she began to slice a tomato.

"Lots."

"And they live and work and so on."

"Definitely. And you're even playing again."

She tossed a diced tomato into a glass dish. "The hardest thing of all," she said reflectively, "is to find a reason to go on living, a meaning." She hesitated, then smiled again. "Sometimes I think I wanted the baby so that it would force me to live responsibly, and then it seems to me that I did something terribly selfish. To bring him up without a father and all that, just so I would have a reason . . ." The dimple appeared, and then disappeared again.

"Maybe you shouldn't be so judgmental and critical. Maybe it's better perhaps simply to accept your own limitations. Why do you think married people have children?"

"Why?" she said coldly. "With them it's the natural, obvious thing to do. But I kept this baby even when I lost all my faith in someone I'd trusted absolutely."

"Trusted absolutely? You should never trust anyone absolutely," said Michael, turning the omelet over and lowering the flame. "Trusting somebody else absolutely is like turning yourself into a baby in a certain sense. There isn't a person in the world without weaknesses. You have to take those weaknesses into account, and deciding to trust someone absolutely means ignoring those weaknesses." He turned off the gas. "What's the situation with the salad?"

She raised her eyes from the bowl. "It's ready, I just have to season it. So what's it all for, what's the point of anything, if you can't trust anyone? What's love without trust?"

"I didn't say 'trust,' I said 'absolute trust.' There's a difference. Do you have any olive oil?"

Nita nodded. "We'll eat over there. It's too dirty here," she said in a brisk, practical tone. She took the plates and cutlery and the salad into the other room. He followed her, waited for her to sit down, and carefully placed half the omelet on her plate. He moved the sliced apples, which were brown by now, to make room for the challah he had sliced. Before he sat down himself he went into the room where the babies were and peeped at the stroller. The baby girl lay motionless on her back. Alarmed, he bent down and put his cheek next to her button nose. Only when he felt the quiet, rhythmic breathing on his skin did he straighten up and return to the living room.

"It doesn't go away," said Nita. "The fear that the baby will die doesn't go away. Even when it's five months old you check to see if it's still breathing when it's too quiet."

"Is it normal for her to sleep so long without waking? I don't remember my son sleeping for more than an hour at a time at that age."

"She's apparently content. She ate enough and nothing's bothering her now. She's a good baby." Nita stared at her plate, and with a slow, lazy movement stuck her fork into the omelet.

"They're the only ones who can give their trust absolutely. But even that's not always sure," said Michael, thinking of the cardboard box. "Only if they're lucky."

"I can't," she said in a choked voice and pushed her plate away. "I can't get it down."

"That too is a matter of decision and choice," said Michael.

"Everything makes me anxious or offends me or hurts me," she said with revulsion. A tear made its way from the corner of her eye to her nose. "I'm sorry. I'm apparently not fit for human company. People in my condition should retire to a convent."

"Not if they have a five-month-old baby who trusts them absolutely."

She smiled, wiped her eyes, and slowly put the plate back on her knees. He looked at her, and it was already clear to him that he would tell her. But not this evening.

"How much time has it been?"

"Since we separated? Since the beginning of the pregnancy. Make the calculation yourself!" Nita said, her voice breaking. "It's disgusting the way I talk. I'm full of self-pity, incapable of accepting my mistake and my stupidity." She fell silent. He ate a piece of cheese.

"I lived in an illusion. I deceived myself. I believed him. I was completely wrong about him," she said. "He said that he couldn't live without me, and I believed him. Maybe I was brought up wrong," she said reflectively.

"What is he, a politician? Who says a thing like that seriously except for salesmen and insurance agents? And politicians. Is he a politician?"

"He's in the insurance business," said Nita, and she burst out laughing.

"I'm not talking about the people who believe such declarations, who take them seriously." Michael gave her a cautious look and put some salad on her plate.

She stuck her fork into a bit of cucumber. "I believed him. Maybe my parents did spoil me." Again her eyes filled with tears.

"It usually works the opposite way," murmured Michael. If they were to let him keep the baby, he could prove that, too, he suddenly thought, he could really give her . . . "Maybe things aren't exactly the way you describe them," he reflected aloud. "Anyone who plays the way you do shouldn't hate herself so much, or, if you'll forgive me, feel so sorry for herself. Don't you think you're very lucky, to have such a gift?"

Nita opened her mouth, closed it, nodded, and said: "When you live with it you forget that it's something special. It becomes a part of you, you forget that it's—"

"And you have a concert. When exactly?"

"The first one right after Yom Kippur, and the second during the week of Succoth."

"In two weeks? So you've got your work cut out for you, and then there's the baby. The world is full of all kinds of things, you only have to be aware of them."

She nodded resolutely and the trace of a smile parted her lips.

"How long have you been mourning him? More than a year? Isn't that enough? You've done your mourning, and now you can begin to live again. After you start living you'll be able to see things in proportion and not be so critical of yourself." He paused. "I want to tell you, too . . ." She looked at him expectantly. "But never mind."

"Go on, tell me!"

"I don't know all the details, but I can tell you that I've experienced this kind of thing before."

She stiffened. "What kind of thing?"

"People—that is, mainly women, because men don't talk about it so openly—have cried over disappointed love. They all thought their lives were over, that nothing would ever happen to them again. And after a relatively short time the whole thing was no longer relevant. I seem to have remembered their broken hearts longer than they did. That's made me very ironic about broken hearts. Besides, you need a bit of fatalism: What happened is a sign that he wasn't the right man for you. He doesn't sound as if he deserved you, if you'll forgive my for saying so."

"Really? Is that how it always is?" she said bitterly. "And what about Callas?"

"What Callas? Maria Callas? What's she got to do with it?"

"Don't you know about Callas?" She sounded disappointed. "Don't you know that she was madly in love with that nothing, Onassis? A multimillionaire, but a total nothing? He'd fall asleep at the opera when she was singing. Can you imagine?" And she added skeptically: "Have you ever heard her sing?"

He nodded.

"So I ask you, is it possible to sleep when she's singing?!"

He shook his head firmly. She went on looking at him demandingly. "It's impossible," he said finally, overcoming his resistance to the way in which she was dictating his answer. Even if he meant what he said, his words were thereby robbed of his intention. "I can't, anyway."

"What have you heard her in?"

He overcame his resistance to being tested in this way. "A few things. *Norma*, *Traviata*. But what makes you think of her in this connection at all?"

"Because she became pregnant by him when she was no longer young. She wanted the child very much, but he insisted that she get rid of it. And she did what he asked in order to keep him. And then he left her anyway, for Jacqueline Kennedy. Callas was left alone, a completely broken woman, and then she died of a broken heart. You can die of a broken heart, you know."

"I didn't say you couldn't," he said defensively.

"Not only in books and movies."

"But Callas didn't have a child. She had an abortion. That was her choice. That's not an insignificant decision, it's a tragic step. It isn't what you did. Maybe you're not Callas after all, if you'll forgive me for saying so."

"But how many times can a thing like that happen in a person's life?"

"A thing like what? Falling in love? Trusting someone absolutely? Meeting someone who looks into your eyes and tells you that he can't live without you? It depends."

"That's not what I meant."

"I don't know you," he said carefully. "I've only heard you play, and seen you with your baby. You play so beautifully, I mean it, so . . . How can you doubt that you'll be able to love again? And if you choose to fall in love with the wrong person again? Is that what you're asking? It's possible." He stretched out his legs and rested his chin on his hand.

"What are you talking about?" She was offended. "I'll never . . . under any circumstances . . ."

He smiled. "So that's what it's all about," he said, and he dipped a piece of bread in the salad dressing. "Maybe it's the thought of getting over it too quickly that offends you, the fact that you can live without him. And maybe even live better without him. After all, he's a married man, it was a clandestine affair—that's no picnic, more like one long humiliation. Maybe you're better off without him. It's certainly a relief. But maybe the fact that it seems like such a good, sensible idea frightens you."

She swallowed the last piece of her omelet. "What do you know about it?" she said at last. "You can just laugh at me."

"God forbid. I'm not laughing at you. I know exactly what I'm talking about. In the first place, I'm divorced myself, and besides, I've been in love, too, and I've heard a thing or two in my life."

"There you are!" she said triumphantly. "You live alone. That's a fact. Do you know how old I am?"

He shook his head.

"Thirty-eight!" she cried. "How many more times will I be able to trust someone?"

He threw his head back and burst out laughing. There was something so sweet about her, like a little girl. He would have hugged her if he could have let himself touch her now. Her face fell, she looked hurt. He stopped smiling. "A wonderful age, thirty-eight, fantastic. And now, as long as the babies are asleep, why don't I help you tidy up the kitchen? And maybe you can put on some music."

And so it was. In the living room Alfred Brendel played Haydn's *Andante and Variations*. From time to time Nita stopped and listened. Once she said: "That's so beautiful!" She hummed with the music, and she said: "What a wonder that Haydn was! Not a stupid bone in his body!"

Michael was silent. This music, which he had never heard before, with its delicacy and its surprising melody, gave rise in him to longing and sadness. He listened to the slow, stately sound of the piano, and he knew that he would always be able to recognize this piece, from the very first note. Again he felt ashamed of his drive to keep the baby, and also a sharp feeling overcame him that the impulse reflected a hidden side of his character and was grossly contrary to his image. Maybe he was simply using the baby as a way, as Nita had said, of giving a new meaning to his life. Suddenly the music—surprising, delicate, and sad, and so different from everything he knew of Haydn—gave rise in him to a strong desire to cry. The sink was already empty. Nita poured water from the kettle into the two bottles and mixed in the yellow powder. Their eyes met, and she smiled. The music came to an end.

"Again, please," said Michael.

"Yes, it really is beautiful," she said as she returned to the kitchen and the music began again. "I wish I could play with Brendel sometime. I've played with good pianists," she said shyly. He really is magnificent."

The chairs were piled on the kitchen table. The floor was almost dry. Everything shone with cleanliness. From Ido's room not a sound was heard. It seemed to Michael that years had passed since he had last experienced friendship, had a normal connection with someone. The pleasant feeling that flooded him was so strong as to alarm him. "Should I wake her to feed her?" he asked.

"Certainly not," she pronounced. "How old is your son?"

"Almost twenty-three."

"And when he was a baby did they still let them cry and only feed them every four hours?"

"I don't think so. I don't remember." He smiled. "It seems to me I remember he was fed all the time. His business was feeding and crying. His grandparents thought I spoiled him, picked him up too much instead of letting him cry. I didn't have the heart to do that."

"When did you get divorced?"

"A long time ago."

"Why?"

"We should never have married in the first place. We weren't suited. We didn't love each other."

"And since then? You never remarried?"

"No."

"Why?"

He shrugged his shoulders. "It never came up."

"It never came up?"

He said nothing and went into the living room, returned to the kitchen, took down the chairs, pulled one out and sat on it, pulled out another and stood it next to his. Then he put the blue ashtray on the table in front of him, lit a cigarette, and pointed at the empty chair. He was about to tell her at that very moment, but a loud wail burst from Ido's room. The baby girl had awakened and her wails silenced the music and also woke Ido.

"What do you do for a living?" she asked him as they sat side by side with the babies in their arms.

"I'm in the police force," he said without taking his eyes off the pink mouth stuck to the nipple. Suddenly he imagined that he felt a tingling in his own nipples as she sucked. The sensation cast him into confusion, and he turned his attention to his body, trying to find out if some frightening sex transformation was happening, that alarming intensification of female characteristics he had heard took place in middle-aged men. Or were these only old wives' tales?

As he had expected, Nita was astonished by his laconic reply. She had never met anyone in the police. She had thought they were all . . . Searching for the right word, she remained silent.

"Prejudices," he muttered. She put Ido back in his crib and he put the baby girl into the stroller. He could tell her tomorrow, he said to himself when he saw that it was almost midnight.

"What do you do in the police?" she asked him as he stood hesitating by the stroller.

"I've just come back from a two-year leave, I was studying."

"What did you study?"

"Law."

"And did you graduate? In two years?"

"No. I'll finish in another year or two, while I'm working."

"And what are you going back to? Something connected with your studies?"

"To the investigation of major crimes. I'm usually in charge of a team investigating murder cases," he said, anticipating her next question.

"That's an important job. It's scary," she said with childish awe, her eyes wide.

"Very important," he replied. She looked at him so seriously that he couldn't help smiling. "Don't you have a sense of humor, you Dutch?"

She thought for a moment. "No. I don't know about the Dutch in general, but there was no humor in our family. There was a lot of irony, if you regard that as humor."

"You need a sense of the ridiculous, at least a creative intelligence, for irony," he said after some thought, "but in fact . . . ?"

"Yes?"

"Irony and humor are opposites. Irony's always aggressive. It has to be, because it's actually a defense."

"In that case, my father is a very aggressive man."

Michael was silent. The moment didn't seem appropriate to him. He moved the stroller. The baby lay with her light blue eyes open and gurgled. It seemed to him that she was looking into his eyes.

"Look how good she is," Nita marveled, "and so beautiful."

"Don't say that," he said, reaching out to knock on the wooden frame of the sofa.

"Are you superstitious? With all the logic you were lecturing me with just now, you're superstitious?"

"I am," he confessed, and in the tone he remembered from the village women in his Moroccan birthplace, he added: "What can I do?" He stood up to go.

"Don't go yet," she said. "Stay a little longer. We'll have a brandy or something." He didn't sit down again, but he didn't make a move, either. "As long as you're here bad thoughts don't come back to torment me," she explained with downcast eyes. "But only if you want to, if you're tired or anything . . ." she muttered.

The baby seemed contented. Now the apartment gave off a clean smell. There was no reason to hurry. Over a glass of brandy he could tell her. When he told her he'd feel better. Maybe. It would be a relief. Now he was completely sure of it, at least until the moment he sat down again and lit a cigarette. With his eyes fixed on the brandy in his glass he weighed the pros and cons again. He imagined how she would go pale, blush, how she would be appalled, how she would demand that they do something immediately, inform the authorities, find the baby's mother. She would ask him why he wanted what he wanted. Again he was filled with a mixture of shame and distress at the wish itself and at the fact that he himself didn't understand it. She was sitting quietly, her legs tucked under her. After they cleaned up she had changed her clothes. The blue blouse she was now wearing was creased, but it was unstained. Now her thinness was very apparent. She rolled the glass between the palms of her large hands and looked at him kindly.

"What kind of a name is Nita? Is it short for something?" he asked to gain time.

"No. That's my full name. I'm named for Nita Bentwich, Thelma Yellin's sister. They wanted to call me Thelma, but my mother knew a Thelma she hated, someone she'd gone to school with, so they decided to named me after Thelma Yellin's sister, who died before her."

"Thelma Yellin? The one with the school named after her?" She nodded.

"Wasn't she a cellist, too?"

"An exceptional cellist. She played with Schnabel, Feuermann gave her his cello, and Casals was her teacher."

"The Bentwich family are from Zichron Yaakov. Didn't Nita Bentwich commit suicide?"

"I don't know exactly. I only know that she was ill," she said evasively.

"So your parents decided in advance that you'd be a cellist?"

"They always claimed that they didn't," she said with a laugh. "They said that it was their small tribute to Thelma Yellin's memory. She was a great figure. My mother always used the word 'great' when she spoke of her. She knew her well. She often told me how Thelma had established an orchestra, about the chamber music she played, about her influence on musical life, how vital she was, things like that. They imagined that I'd play the piano, like my mother. But I chose the cello. Family legend has it that when I was four years old I heard a cello and I demanded that they get me one. My connection with Thelma Yellin was a later addition."

Was it possible to trust with his story someone who had been born with a silver spoon in her mouth? This was the question that nagged at him now. There was no conceit about her, he reminded himself, but to be on the safe side he waited. "And your mother?"

"What?"

"What did she play?"

"I told you—the piano. But her career was cut off. First there was the war and then emigrating here, and then she was busy running the shop with my father. They did everything together." The corners of her lips pursed in a wry expression. "It was because of the shop that she stopped playing. She's a classic example of a woman who sacrificed her career. The war was part of it too, of course. When she was asked, she always said that she was happy. She played only at home."

"Was she ironic, too?"

"No." Nita laughed and took a sip of brandy. "She was anxious. She worried about me all the time. I could never let her know that I was having difficulties with anything. When I was studying in America she was more tense about my exams than I was. And when I had a concert she was a nervous wreck. She was always afraid that I would be mugged in New York. You know," she said thoughtfully, "it's awfully hard to grow up like that. You're not allowed to be unhappy because it destroys your mother. When you're the spoiled darling of elderly parents, and everyone adores you, why should you be unhappy?"

"Why, indeed?"

"I . . . I always had a hard time taking things lightly. Maybe some people are born like that, oversensitive. I'm not bragging about it, it's simply a fact."

"Maybe it's connected to your being an artist."

"Maybe, but then I should be a really serious artist."

He could have postponed the moment of truth, but he couldn't stand any longer the suspense of not knowing how she would react. And precisely at the moment when a pleasant silence filled the room, he heard himself say: "About the baby . . ."

She looked at her glass. "Do you mean Noa?"

"It may as well be Noa."

"What do you mean, it may as well be Noa? That's her name, isn't it?"

"It's not clear," he said carefully. His heart pounded, and he felt short of breath.

She unfolded her legs, sat up straight in the blue armchair, put the glass down on the copper serving table, frowned, and finally said: "I don't understand."

He explained.

"I don't believe it!"

He nodded.

"In a cardboard box? In the bomb shelter? Who could leave a baby, a nursing baby, in a bomb shelter? Are you telling me the truth now? Is this the true story?"

He nodded.

"But she's so beautiful . . . and fair . . . and so good and . . ."

"What's that got to do with it?"

"Who would want to abandon a baby like that? Do you know how many people would be willing . . . would be happy . . . would jump at the chance . . . Who would want to abandon her?"

"Someone who had no choice."

"They could have given her up for adoption," she protested. "If they had to."

"Not if they didn't want anyone to know she existed," he said.

She was silent. He lit another cigarette.

"What are you going to do?"

For a long moment he didn't answer. She waited. Her eyes were fixed on him in tense, cautious anticipation. There were words ready in his mouth, but he couldn't bring himself to say them out loud: *I want her to stay with me.* Even when he said them to himself, they had an irrational, crazy sound. They made him feel disgusted with himself. He coughed. At last he only said: "We'll talk about it tomorrow. I have to sleep on it. Meanwhile she's here, and it has to remain a secret."

"I don't talk to anyone anyway," she reassured him.

"Even if you do," he warned.

"Even if I do, I won't say a word," she promised.

2

Rossini, Vivaldi, and Nurse Nehama

How solemn and beautiful the solo cello sounded in Rossini's *William Tell* Overture, the first piece performed that evening, and how much sorrow there was in the response of the five orchestral cellos. Deep and dark was the opening note. And after it, like a waterfall, came the lament of the others. By now Michael already knew every pause, every breath, every note. And every touch of the bow on the strings, every sweep of the arm in its black sleeve, echoed the words spoken by Nita late this afternoon, as she stood by the French windows looking out at the hills beyond. She had held the cello in one hand and the bow in the other, and she gestured toward the view. "Sometimes I . . ." her voice broke. She swallowed hard. "They come suddenly, with no warning, I feel such longings, undefined longings . . ." She had touched her chest with the tip of the bow. "And then," her eyes glittered with tears, "I ask myself why things turned out like this, and what I did wrong. And what I could have done differently, if anything, why it has to be this way, and . . . My mother's dead . . ." She sobbed.

Michael sat in the corner of the little sofa with the baby girl in his arms while Ido banged a red block against the bars of the playpen. He grumbled when it slipped out of his hand, and he took hold of his foot, trying to get his toe into his mouth. Nita glanced at him, choked back a sob, and said in a broken voice: "And then what I want is to go back to trusting," she said, smiling, or, more precisely, stretching her lips. The dimple did not appear. "And then I hate myself. I know I can't afford to be so full of longings and desires, that I have to channel everything into music and that I'm lucky, as you said. Most people don't have my talent. But I can't help it, I'm addicted, consumed by those banal romantic wishes." You could see the disgust in her eyes. She lowered them. "You certainly must despise me," she blurted out.

"No, I don't," he said quietly, in order not to wake the baby. "How could I despise you? It hurts so much, and I see you suffering and struggling against the pain as if you could avoid it. You can't. Whatever you do, it hurts. That's what happens to people who dive into love. Into the idea of love. Into the fantasy of love, which has no connection to its object—he might as well be a scarecrow, as you said yesterday."

She wept soundlessly. With the back of the hand holding the bow she wiped away big tears, and then she sniffled and wiped her nose. Its turned-up tip turned red, the freckles on the bridge faded.

"I'm always astonished at how people, especially women, can love or long for someone for whom they have no respect at all." Again she wiped her eyes. "Actually," she said soberly, "it's as you said yesterday. I miss being a little girl, close to someone, dependent." Suddenly she shivered and looked at him: "Why are your eyes so sad?"

Now, in the concert hall, Michael smiled, remembering the frightened, guilty tone of the question. "Do I make you sad? Are you giving up on me?" she had probed.

"No, I'm not giving up on you. How could I give up on someone who plays the Double Concerto like you do? I was thinking of my son."

"Why exactly were you thinking of him? Do you miss him?" He answered with a faint "Yes." But it wasn't his longings that were bothering him at that moment, but the sharp memory suddenly gnawing at his chest. First the memory of Maya flashed, then it faded. How little he had thought of her during the past year! Then he thought of this scene: With absolute clarity he saw Yuval, aged fourteen, sitting on the edge of his narrow bed, his face buried in his hands, and himself standing in the half-open doorway. Alarmed, he had asked: "What happened?" and hurried to sit down beside him, repeating his question, putting his arms around him, listening horrified to the adolescent boy's sobs and his suddenly squeaky voice. He had listened to the broken sentences, the gist of which was that his girlfriend, Ronit, didn't want to be with him anymore, not even to talk to him. He didn't know what to say to his son. He could only hold him and hug him in silence. He never saw him cry again.

Nita was right. Where Rossini's music wasn't funny, it was profoundly sad. Of the four parts of the overture, she had explained to him, the first had to suggest an idyllic landscape in the Swiss Alps. But there was also the unavoidable tension between the idyll and the tragic threat hanging over it. The thunder of the timpani now interrupted the sweet melancholy of the cellos. It should have been only a faint echo, but here, under Theo van Gelden's direction, the echo of the timpani was too loud and conspicuous. He was waving the small silver baton that, Nita had told him proudly, her brother had received as a token of esteem from Leonard Bernstein himself after Theo had conducted the New York Philharmonic for the first time, more than twenty years ago. The echo threw the restrained elegy of the cello into all the greater relief. Only now, when Michael's breathing quieted, did he realize how tense he had been. Only now, when he felt the familiar pain in his lower jaw caused by the clenching of his teeth, did he admit to himself how much he had identified with her stage fright.

Nita argued that the cello had to sound both elegiac and pastoral. Again and again she would listen to herself playing. At such moments he was awed by her concentration. Her whole body seemed transformed into one big, stern, critical ear. There were two vertical lines between her eyebrows, and an expression of pain twisted her mouth. She would shake her head angrily and in disgust at herself shout: "Kitsch!" To him the sounds were wonderful. They pierced his heart, touching him to the quick. Sometimes he was ashamed of how much her playing moved him. Especially when he saw her body bend over the cello, the cool power in the arm moving with such confidence, a fleeting expression of pleasure or determination crossing her face, with its closed eyes.

He had loved, these days just past, being in the room when she played. At such moments she seemed to him strong and withdrawn into herself, inaccessible and beautiful. He had a great wish to be near her, to feel again and again the childlike softness that was so evident when she looked at her son or at the baby girl. All the weakness she had exposed on the evening of their first meeting, the vulnerability she sometimes signaled when going about her daily tasks, disappeared when she was playing. When she played he had the feeling that great strength was pouring out of her, like a torrent of underground water. That this strength swept everything else aside, and that everything else seemed to be an obstacle that tested her.

It was remarkable how quickly this intimacy had grown up between them. It allowed her to talk to herself in his presence while she practiced, and prevented him from knowing whether what was melting him now, was penetrating him so strongly, was her actual playing, or a whole world of expectations and wishes he had come to know. Again her words rang in his ears: "What you feel is the truth." But how could he really tell? How was it possible to isolate the impact of the music from every other feeling? And what if he was hearing in her playing now the intentions that were known to him, rather than the pure expression of the music itself? Was there such a thing at all as the pure expression of the music? Did it have any meaning when there was no one listening? And what, in general, was the meaning of talk about music and feelings when you thought about the physical process that caused a tone to reach the brain? You had to remember that the reception of a sound was the result of a physical apparatus, and it was only in the brain that sound waves were interpreted as music. He glanced sideways at the bearded man sitting on his right. As Nita's guest, Michael had been seated with the elite. He had never before sat so close to the stage. He could see the rectangular block of wood with the little hole into which a double-bass player stuck the metal spike of his instrument to steady it, and the shiny black stripe down his trouser leg. And even the scuffed heels of a viola player, who crossed her feet under her chair as she put her instrument to her shoulder, inclined her left ear toward it, and leaned forward. The man on his right wrote something rapidly on the margin of his program. What, for instance, were the thoughts of this important man, no doubt a music critic, whose legs were stretched out in front of him, whose lips were turned down at the corners now in an expression of "Let's see if they can still surprise me." Did he, too, hear the sorrow produced by the cello strings? Was he capable at all of being so moved?

The seat on Michael's left was empty. Nita's father should have been sitting there. Before the concert Nita had introduced Michael to her older brother. Theo van Gelden gave him a swift, curious glance, buttoned his tuxedo jacket,, and firmly shook Michael's hand. It was strange to see the dark masculine echo of Nita's features in his face. Theo's face too was long and narrow, and his eyes were light and very deep-set behind the narrow-rimmed eyeglasses. Thirteen years older than Nita, he had short deep lines on either side of his lips, which were full and pouting like hers, and his pointed chin stuck out. Gabriel, ten years older than she, had a round, plump face, with a short beard that touched his short, thick neck. His pink-white skin was scattered with freckles that climbed from his cheeks to his high forehead, and on his neck there was a dark mark, like a love bite. Curls of his chestnut brown hair, which was strewn with gray, stuck out at his temples, and he kept on smoothing them down. His eyes, too, although small and brown, were set deep in their sockets. They blinked several times as he put his hands together and smiled a kind of crooked smile with one side of his mouth, as Nita said: "And this is my little big brother, who agreed to take part tonight so that we could all play together, even though he doesn't agree with Theo about anything, and even though he'll soon have an important ensemble of his own." She laughed and pinched Gabriel's arm, and he gently patted her hand, showing for a moment a glittering gold ring with a green stone. Only a little taller than she, he had glanced over her shoulder and asked: "But where's Father? Wasn't he coming with you? Didn't we agree that you were going to pick him up on your way?"

"No," said Nita, brushing his shoulder with her hand. "He phoned this morning. He'd forgotten he'd made a dental appointment, and he said he'd take a taxi directly from there. You've got plaster all over your back again. I've told you a thousand times not to lean against this pillar." She pulled him lightly away from the narrow concrete pillar, stepped around him, and patted his back vigorously. "He'll be here soon. Stop being so nervous. It's enough that I'm in a panic, after nearly a year—"

"You'll be fine," said Gabriel absent-mindedly. He glanced at his brother, who was talking enthusiastically to a woman in black, blowing into the mouthpiece of her oboe while holding the body of the instrument in her free hand. Gabriel again turned his head toward the artists' entrance.

"Stop worrying," Nita reproved him. "You know how he hates

hanging around backstage. He'll go straight into the hall. We still have fifteen minutes to go."

Now Gabriel van Gelden was stroking his rounded little beard and gazing from the front of the stage at the empty seat, the only red patch in a hall where all the other seats were occupied. He turned his head a couple of times toward the side entrance, and with narrowed eyes also scanned the stairs, which were full of people sitting and standing. When the cellos finished playing the first theme, he cocked his head at Nita, and it seemed to Michael that he could see her dark eyebrows rising and her face turning pale as she leaned forward in her place at the center, very close to the conductor's podium, among the violins and violas, and strained her eyes to see the empty seat. Then the violins began to play anew, and one after the other the flute, oboe, clarinet, and bassoon entered and answered them. Now a storm broke out, the dramatic second part of the overture. Not only chaos reigned here but also a suspenseful darkness, a hint of the tragedy about to take place. A rapid crescendo mounted and mounted until all the instruments of the orchestra had joined in while Theo van Gelden waved his arms and tried to embrace in the air the echoes of the terrible storm, which continued to swell and then almost subsided, and swelled again with the flute prominent.

When the third part of the overture began with the flute now singing the beautiful familiar tune, which the English horn took over, and the low string instruments joined in the dialogue, Michael listened to it all as if to a story. At a certain moment he even sensed that his mouth was open and, embarrassed, he quickly closed it again. The triangle and the oboe debated with the strings the mysterious nature of the world, but they also depicted sun and meadows, forests and groves. Then the trumpet fanfare announced the entrance of the rebels. Bells and string instruments depicted the galloping horses, and in the hall there arose a world of revolt, heroism, and catastrophe. But you could also hear echoes of another Rossini in it, the much more cheerful one who made Michael laugh.

And yet the trumpet fanfare now overwhelmed hunting horn and bird song. This was the hackneyed tune that was a staple of the police band's repertoire at official functions and festive occasions. Michael now lost his concentration, and looked around the hall. He saw a broad smile on the face of the old man sitting in front of him and drumming with his fingers on the arm of his seat. The young woman next to him rested her head on his shoulder. Her very long dark hair fell over the back of her seat and touched the music critic's knee. Michael had no doubt now that was what he was: he nodded his head and never stopped taking notes. Behind Michael, close to his ear, someone was slowly and steadily unwrapping candies. The rustle of the wrappers got on his nerves, and when he turned his head to glare at two elderly women to make them stop, he encountered a familiar pair of small eyes. Where the woman's chin joined her big bosom, green beads glittered. They were the very beads that had rested on the bosom of the nurse sent by the Child Welfare Bureau to pay him a house call the day before yesterday. She smiled at him knowingly from the seat behind him, popped a yellow piece of candy into her mouth, and then leaned over and whispered into her neighbor's ear.

He turned his head to look at the stage. But he couldn't rid himself of the image of the woman's earlobes lengthening toward her non-neck as if pulled down by the weight of the copper earrings set with blue stones. Nurse Nehama, who had been sent to assess his suitability as a temporary foster family, was now sitting right behind him, and seeing with her own eyes that he wasn't suitable. Here he was, and who was with the baby? He almost turned around to tell her about the babysitter, to explain that he had to be at the concert because of Nita. Instead he stared at Theo van Gelden's back as he stamped his foot on the conductor's podium. Then Michael leaned his elbows against the arms of the seat and buried his burning face in his cold hands. He admonished himself to be logical, forced himself to breathe quietly. He reminded himself that this nurse, like the director of the Child Welfare Bureau herself and the social workers there, were all certain that he and Nita were living together, and bringing up their child together. That they could have no objections to his accompanying her to a concert of hers, as long as they didn't leave the babies alone. But he was not reassured. He exhorted himself to return to the music. Just then the overture came to an end, the audience applauded enthusiastically. He heard cries of "Bravo!" The bearded man on his right sat motionless.

A shudder ran through him because of the little eyes fixed, he knew, on his back, and also because he saw that Nita was standing up on the stage in order to get a better view of the seat next to him, which had remained empty. He noticed that Gabriel van Gelden, who had stood up to shake the conductor's hand, had turned his head to the side entrance of the hall. And Theo van Gelden, too, who then took a deep bow, and motioned to the solo cellist—Nita bowed clumsily—and toward the orchestra, froze for a moment as he looked at the row where Michael was sitting. He turned his head right and left to glance at the side entrances, wiping his brow, in a gesture characteristic of conductors, with a handkerchief he took from his jacket pocket. Then he motioned again to the orchestra. The audience clapped rhythmically. Michael pulled at his white cuffs so they would stick out of the gray sleeves of his suit jacket, and he smiled at the care with which he still dressed and shaved when he went to a concert. It was something that had not changed since the first concerts he had attended thirty years ago. (Thirty? he wondered, shocked. Was it already thirty years? What had happened in the course of those years? Where had they gone to?) When Becky Pomeranz, the mother of his close school friend Uzi Rimon, had taken him with her to the subscription concerts, and dexterously woven Michael's musical education together with their sexual passion. It was strange that his relation to music, the emotions that it gave rise to in him, the compositions that agitated his soul, were connected to women he was drawn to. It was Becky Pomeranz who had infected him with her excitement, who had caused his heart to beat violently on mornings when a concert awaited him in the evening. It was because of Becky Pomeranz that he had embarked on the rituals of shaving and dressing up—in those days it was a long-sleeved white shirt and a dark-blue sweater with pale-blue squares knitted by his mother. The affair had only lasted one winter and spring, until the day Uzi opened a door and stood there looking at them. Because of her his breath still came in gasps before he entered a concert hall. Even now he could hear her whispering into his ear: "Remember this moment, remember that you were here this evening, that you heard Oistrakh himself playing Sibelius live." Her breath was so sweet, and she had been dead over a year now.

Theo van Gelden was an impressive-looking man, and he certainly wasn't the man Michael had seen on the stairs of his apartment building. From the auditorium he looked taller than he really was. His surprisingly dark skin and his silver hair, his tuxedo, which gave him an air of dignity, his rapid steps as he left the stage for the second time, the vigor and authority he radiated—all these went some way to explain his success with women. Or his failure, depending on how you looked at the three divorces and the children all over the place. *"Mille e tre,"* Nita had said of him with a forgiving smile. It was some time before he realized that she was quoting from Leporello's Catalogue Aria in *Don Giovanni*.

The stage began to empty. The drums and cymbals were pushed back. The wind and brass players disappeared, and a number of string players left the stage. Then music began again. A Korean flutist in a blue sequined dress was playing Vivaldi's *La notte*, the "Night" concerto. The seat on his left was still empty. Again Michael contemplated Nita. She looked attractive in her black evening gown, with her shining red-brown hair and very white shoulders. He was as proud of her as if she were his sister or daughter. The dark semicircles under her light eyes, which stained the pale olive of her face, were invisible at this distance. Michael had talked her into putting makeup on them on their way here, after she had kept talking about how everyone would be there—everyone meaning her brothers and her father. With great clarity he saw that he longed to be part of her "everyone." What had started out as a practical measure, an act for the benefit of the Child Welfare Bureau, had become for him the beginning of seeing Nita as a person with whom he could share his daily life. It was a combination, he said to himself now, of her childishly desperate need for love and the absolute conviction with which she applied herself to everything she did, of the different voices that spoke from within her, and also, even though there was no explanation for it, of the way in which she played, the sternness with which she sometimes held her body upright, as opposed to the softness with which she bent over the instrument, the way she would pick Ido up from the carpet to swing him while lecturing her baby on music. There was one moment when she held the baby girl in her arms and rocked her, humming, and at that moment—he had observed them from the kitchen—everything looked so perfect and right that he had to stop himself from hugging them both. Sometimes he doubted himself and thought he only wanted to give the baby a proper upbringing. He wanted to give her everything that was needed, and for that a wife was necessary. But he also wanted the baby to be his alone. As Nita herself had said about her baby.

How much joy there could have been for him in the clean trills of the flute the slender girl held so easily. Her body arched forward at the beginning of every phrase, and straightened like a flower stem when it ended. How much joy there could have been in listening to what you know for certain is beautiful, but for the distress that withered everything and set a barrier between Michael's consciousness of beauty and his ability to feel it in his heart. He saw the sweet face of the baby before his eyes. He still thought of her as "the baby," even though he had grown used to the name he had hastily given her. He thought of the long nights when she awoke every two hours as if she had still not overcome her bottomless hunger, and of the serenity with which he woke up immediately and fed her, pacing the apartment with her on his shoulder after the feeding, alone and yet not in the least alone. How much sweetness, the promise of something for which he yearned, there was in the small face of a human creature whose needs and desires he could truly satisfy, could make happy.

But behind all this arose the suspicious expression on the face of the nurse they had sent from the Social Services Department. She had come two days before Yom Kippur, toward the end of her day's work. He had been waiting for her since morning. At first he had thought of going to work. Nita had even taken her cello to the bedroom, so that the nurse wouldn't see her busy with anything but the babies. He had rehearsed Nita in what to say, preparing her for the eventuality that he wouldn't be at home when the nurse arrived. Of course it would be preferable to be there, so that they could act the couple living together.

"You're cunning," said Nita without a hint of condemnation after listening to him talking to the chief Child Welfare officer on the phone. "I'm naive and quite stupid." The moment she said the word "stupid" her face fell, and he knew immediately what she was thinking. But he agreed with her that he was far more cunning than she, and that it would be better if he were to stay home. "I feel as if anyone can see through me. Everyone seems to know everything there is to know about me, so I give up in advance. The urge to be frank is so great!" she lamented.

The nurse's visit was supposed to come as a surprise. They didn't even know the day for sure. This was also what gave it the air of an ambush, a trap. And it was also what gave rise to his anger now, as he felt the presence of the nurse behind his back. Even though Tzilla, who had connections both with people at the Child Welfare Bureau and with the nurses at the Social Services Department, had told him that he shouldn't take any of it personally, that he and Nita would easily pass muster as a foster family. Especially since they had one baby already, and the baby girl was so robust. Tzilla had been present at the pediatrician's examination. The doctor had bent over the baby and said with satisfaction: "A real little minx!" Michael looked offended, but the pediatrician laughed and explained that this was his affectionate term for girl babies who were one hundred percent healthy. Michael looked over his shoulder as the doctor pulled her legs and let them drop, testing the resistance of her leg muscles. She had screamed as she lay naked on Ido's chest of drawers. The doctor wrote a report for the Child Welfare Bureau. Tzilla had managed to organize things so that a close friend of hers, a Sergeant Malka, was placed in charge of the search for the missing mother. She promised not to say a word to anyone, and she had kept her promise.

Sergeant Malka talked mainly with Nita. Since she had moved to Jerusalem from Kiryat Gat only the year before, she didn't know Michael. This was the situation at the moment (from time to time the words "at the moment" cut through him like a knife). None of his colleagues on the police force, not even Shorer, knew what his frequent disappearances and his sudden rushing off home were about. His absences were received without comment, since everyone knew that although he was back at work he had not yet been given anything serious to do. Shorer kept saying, "after the holidays," smiling at the cliché but repeating it nonetheless.

All kinds of things Michael feared had worked out in a reassuring way. Tzilla, who had worked with him for years as the secretary of his Special Investigation Team, had come to an understanding with Nita at their very first meeting, the kind that arises between women when they know that there are truly important matters at stake, with no time to waste on irrelevancies. Not by so much as a hint did Tzilla betray the faintest suspicion that there might be anything more between Michael and Nita than the connection he had described to her. "It's a close friendship," he said. A new one, but close. There's nothing more to it than that. Don't make anything more of it. Tzilla looked offended at this, and she opened her mouth to say something, but he gave her no chance to. "I just want to make it clear in advance," he had told her, so you don't get any wrong ideas, what we have is a temporary business arrangement based on a common interest. Tzilla expressed no surprise at his desire to keep the baby, nor did she rebuke him for his absences from work. She covered for him in the days after the holiday, when he slipped away early to go to Nita's apartment. And she found a babysitter who made it possible for Nita to practice and go to rehearsals.

Precisely because of the babies the relation between them was practical, free of any romantic innuendoes. We're a baby nursery, Nita had said. He never touched her, aside from pats on the arm, kisses on the cheek. Innocent gestures of affection. And sometimes, when they stood close to each another, when they were bathing the babies, for example, he was careful to avoid touching her by accident, as if he felt that any contact would be almost dangerous for her now. Apart from this, he had a strong sense that he was exploiting her. By chance, she had been there at the right moment and suited his needs. And although she repeatedly told him how much being with him helped her, even though he knew that she meant it, and although he was very fond of her and was never bored in her company, nothing dispelled the feeling that he was exploiting her. Besides, there was something in her thinness, in the brittleness of her tall, austere figure, that kept thoughts of sex at bay. If he felt an urge to touch her, it was to put his arm around her shoulder, to stroke her face, to protect her from the moments of dread and self-hatred, from her compulsive tendency to relive scenes from the past, from things that people had said to her and she had believed implicitly and that she resurrected now in order to verify them in the light of the present. She would suddenly tremble with rage and hurt. He learned to identify and guess what was behind these moments even when they manifested themselves in vague, general statements, baffling to the untutored ear, such as: "All that matters is what people do. Words are bullshit." Or: "Promises of eternal commitment between people aren't worth a damn. Nothing lasts." Or: "There's no such thing as love. It's all sex or lust, and it's soon over. Friendship without passion is much better; at least it isn't doomed in advance to be empty."

At times like these he tried to distract her and turn her attention to simple everyday questions. Such as the exact dates for the babies' vaccinations or how early Ido was with his teething, and how many hours she could expect to sleep that night. Privately he wondered at the forces that impelled her constantly to return to thoughts of past humiliation and pain. Once he even said as much to her. He meant to do so tactfully, but it burst out with a bluntness he had not intended: "I don't know, but if I had been humiliated, if I had felt so betrayed, I would try to put it behind me, and not keep reliving it all the time. Anyhow, you're not in love now, so why keep harping on it? It's plain masochism."

"I'm the first to believe anything bad anyone says about me, never mind who," she had replied, pursing her lips. But the moment Ido fell asleep she resumed work on the solo cello part of the Double Concerto, and played better than ever. And there was the evening when he stood in the doorway between the kitchen and the living room, on his way to his own apartment, and listened to her play the first movement straight through. It seemed to him that he had never heard it played with such depth and perfection before. Moved to the core, he went down to his apartment with the baby girl in his arms. In the last analysis, he said to himself, standing at his French windows and listening to the sounds coming from above, this chance to be in close contact with an artist is a blessing in itself, though his happiest hours were those he spent alone with his baby, looking at her and imagining the life he could give her.

The nurse from the Social Services Department had a double chin. When he saw her face he knew exactly how he should talk to her. Even before this he had some idea, but when he saw the heavy, exhausted face, he was sure. For this was a face totally lacking in charm or grace. It was the face of a middle-aged woman whom life had not treated too badly, but not particularly well either. A woman with hair set in yellow-red curls and a stomach sticking out in front of her. Her legs looked too thin to support the upper half of her body. She was wearing orthopedic sandals, and her toenails were painted a saccharine pink underneath a wide, long skirt. She seemed unsteady on her feet, maybe because of the thinness of her legs. When he saw her weary and suspicious little eyes, he was glad that he had stayed home. She would have had Nita for breakfast, he thought then. She might even have dragged a confession out of her.

"Do you know the sign on your mailbox is unclear?" she admonished him while she was still standing at the door, panting as if she had climbed four flights of stairs. He apologized and promised to remedy this right away. But she wasn't satisfied. "It can lead to misunderstandings. If I weren't so determined I wouldn't be here now," she said in the hoarse voice of a chronic smoker. But she looked as if she had never smoked a cigarette in her life. He repeated that he would take care of it that very day. She fell silent and looked around with a weary, sullen expression, as if she were searching for something else to vent her resentment on. But then her eyes fell on his face. She looked at him and suddenly smiled. A small, would-be flirtatious smile. His facial muscles immediately went into action to return her smile. Filled with goodwill and trying to appear calm, he asked if she wanted to see the baby. Nurse Nehama narrowed her eyes until they were almost closed, then sat down, spread her legs, patted her thighs as if to encourage herself, smoothed out her skirt, took a sheaf of forms and some carbon paper out of her bag, and said: "Could I have a glass of water before we begin and before I see the baby? It's so hot out. A little girl, right?"

He went into the kitchen and hurried back with a pitcher of water and a spotless glass. She studied the glass intently before pouring water into it. He had known in advance that all she would really care about would be cleanliness, even though she might pretend otherwise. She drank the water, looking at him with interest.

"Yes," she said at last, pulling her chair up to the round dining table, "so what have we here?" She licked her finger, leafed through the forms, rummaged in a big black bag with shabby handles, and raised her head: "Have you got a ballpoint? I can't find mine."

"Here you are," Michael said, quickly offering her the pen in his shirt pocket.

She examined it carefully, but it was just an ordinary ballpoint. Then she put on the small eyeglasses that hung on a thick gold chain above a longer necklace of green beads, which wobbled between her double chin and the expanse of her bosom with every move she made. "What have we here?" she said again and sighed. And then—with her head tilted to one side and her eyes open wide as if to give a semblance of life to the dull, vacant gaze—she asked him to tell her the facts again, even though she had already been informed of them by the Child Welfare Bureau. He recited the version he had agreed upon with Nita: They had found the little girl in a cardboard box on the second morning of Rosh Hashanah, and because of the holiday they had waited until that evening before having her examined by a doctor, and had only reported the incident to the police the day after, since he himself knew that on a holiday personnel would be lacking to begin looking for the baby's mother.

Even now, while the flutist—North Korean and French-educated, according to the program—swayed her body to and fro and produced tender sounds filled with feeling and the harpsichordist struck repeated notes in the fourth movement of the concerto *La notte*, he could still hear the suspicious, ugly tone with which the nurse said: "But you didn't take her to the hospital to make sure that she was all right."

Very patiently he explained to her that the pediatrician had said there was no need to take her to the hospital, that she would only pick up an infection there, and that for the time being they could leave things as they were.

"But there are procedures!" the nurse protested and energetically wrote something in the margin of the first page of the form. She moistened her lips as she bent over the paper. Although the visit had gone well, and she had even smiled at the sight of the babies and remarked: "They seem happy here," and although she had looked at him kindly and said as she left: "It'll be all right, I'm not supposed to say anything to you, but I can tell you that it'll be all right," it had been clear to him then, as it was clear to him now, that it wouldn't be all right. A wave of coughing broke out in the audience between movements. Four of the concerto's six movements, two *largo* and two *presto*, had already gone by, and he hadn't even noticed. After the first entrance of the flute, which the North Korean had played with such virtuosity, he had stopped listening, as if he weren't there at all.

It was clear to him that nothing would be all right, because in the end either they would find the mother, or the baby would be given to some childless couple who had been waiting for years. Nurse Nehama had mentioned such couples several times during her visit. Or else they wouldn't find the mother, and the court would declare her eligible for adoption, and he would lose her anyway. It would have been better if he hadn't grown so attached to her. The whole idea was insane. If only he could understand what had dictated his movements at that moment, when he had decided to keep the baby. If it had been a conscious decision at all. Most of the time it seemed to him that some strange force had decided it for him. If only he could understand, he would be able to exert more control over his situation. But he didn't understand. The one time he had followed his instincts without thinking, he had been shown how dangerous it was. And how right he had always been not to act with utter spontaneity. But then he immediately said to himself: Let's say you had taken her to the hospital and she was there now. In the infants' ward nobody would have picked her up and held her, especially not you. So why can't you just enjoy what you have now and not worry about the future? Nothing lasts forever. Look at Yuval, he was once just like this baby, and now he's not yours anymore in anything like the way he was. He sighed. From the glare directed at him by the bearded man on his right, he realized that he had sighed too loud.

Three times the audience called her back to the stage, and then she played an encore. She had apparently played beautifully, but he hadn't been able to be there fully, and none of the beauty had touched him. The lights in the hall went on, the bearded man hurried out before anyone else had a chance to get up, and the stage emptied. He wondered if he should go and see Nita during the intermission, and he wondered how upset she was by her father's absence. Instead he found himself standing next to a pay phone, his breath coming fast. Only after he had spoken to the babysitter, who reassured him, did he light a cigarette and look in the direction of the line at the coffee counter. Without thinking he joined the people crowding in front of the counter. As if in a trance he felt them touching and pushing him.

Women in high heels and elegant clothes elbowed their way past him. Finally someone asked him what he wanted. After that he stood with his lighted cigarette and his cup of coffee, nibbling at the edge of the Styrofoam cup.

He should have felt excited in anticipation of Berlioz's *Symphonie Fantastique*, which Becky Pomeranz had loved so much. It had been years had since he had last heard it. At that time with Becky, he had heard it over and over again, and he knew every note by heart. He knew that Theo van Gelden's interpretation of it was famous. People said he had brilliantly taken over the best of Bernstein's approach to the piece, and when he had an orchestra worthy of him, Nita had read aloud to him from an interview, he was particularly renowned for his ability to produce the tumult of contradictory, stormy feelings in it and to stress the dramatic elements in Berlioz's autobiographical story of a lovesick musician.

Nita quoted this common opinion and then remarked dryly that Theo should be the last one capable of it, since he had never been lovesick in his life, only the cause of it in others. "Maybe that's precisely why he can," Michael had replied, and she had looked at him thoughtfully and said: "Sometimes you can be really banal." She had immediately apologized. But none of this interested him now. He was so restless, in part a result of sitting in front of the Social Services nurse, in part from accumulated sleeplessness—the baby still woke up every two hours at night—and also from the constant anxiety he felt, with differing degrees of intensity, a readiness of his whole body for impending and certain catastrophe. This restlessness made him think, almost with revulsion, of the sounds he knew so well and had once loved so much.

On his way back into the hall, after dismissing the possibility of going home right away, Michael imagined the bells of the symphony's "March to the Scaffold" and the shrill discords of the "Witches' Sabbath" ringing in his ears. He stifled a great sigh as he sat down next to the bearded man, who tensely and rhythmically, but also with infinite boredom, jiggled his crossed leg. Michael opened his program booklet so as to look again at the headings of the "Episodes of an Artist's Life." The grandiloquent words themselves—

Rêveries, Un bal, Scène aux champs, Marche au supplice, Songe d'une nuit de Sabbat—wearied him. And the thought of the despairing lover and the fateful beloved, the jealous quarrels, the hero's wish for death, the execution scene, the witches and rattling skeletons—all this now seemed to him ridiculous and childish. Like a strange and exotic scrap of something he had once heard about but he himself had never tasted.

I'd rather have Rossini, he said to himself as the oboist stood up to play the A from which the musicians tuned their instruments. Again the stage filled up; again they were many. He tried to count them. There were about thirty violins, twenty violas, and eight cellos. On the elevated seats at stage right, behind six double basses, there were six trombones, and on the left, near the second violins, the kettle-drums, cymbals, and bass drum, fluttered the hands of two harpists. In the rows behind the cellos, the woodwind players were crowded, and behind them the trumpets. Over the conductor's podium hung the microphones for the live radio broadcast of the entire concert, now joined by blinding TV lights and two cameramen running around on the stage dragging cables, changing angles, moving a woman oboe player closer to a clarinetist. The second half of the concert was going to be televised. A stir went through the audience as light flooded the first rows and dazzled their occupants. Michael lowered his head as the light hit his face, and he dismissed the thought that if he hadn't wanted to accompany Nita here, he could have stayed home and watched and listened from his armchair. And then he reminded himself of the unique pleasure of experiencing with his own eyes and ears what was impossible to broadcast, music being made here and now.

Gabriel van Gelden, as concertmaster, again stood with his back to the audience and drew his bow over his violin. He listened to the tuning of the violas, the cellos, and finally the violins. On his elevated seat the first clarinetist again and again repeated the recurring main theme—the *idée fixe*—of the entire symphony. The stage rang with loud cacophony as the hall filled with the noise of instruments being tuned. Gabriel van Gelden kept his head turned toward the side entrance.

Theo van Gelden bowed briefly to the audience, and the old man in front of Michael fell silent and again took hold of the young woman's long-nailed hand. Again Michael noticed Nita's dark eyebrows arching as her eyes focused on the empty chair next to him. Their father had not arrived, and this was apparently a concert he would not hear, thought Michael as the music began. How could he have forgotten the soft woodwind opening and the gradual entrance of the strings? The audience's coughing almost drowned out the pairs of flutes, oboes, clarinets. The coughing continued the whole time the music remained *pianissimo*. Michael thought of Becky Pomeranz's full, smooth, brown arms, and of the day when she had played the recording of the *Fantastique* for him, and the seductive tone in which she had told him that its hero imagines murdering his beloved and his consequent ascent to the scaffold, with bells ringing in the distance. He clearly remembered her explaining to him that the trombones suggest the ugliness of the execution with low, sustained notes, and that the *idée fixe*, the theme of the beloved, only returns, from the distance, at the moment the head rolls. And that the witches then appear, with the beloved among them, ugly as they are, dangerous as they are. Her theme, which had been so celestial, so gentle, reappears in a grotesque form, shrilly played by piccolo and clarinet.

Suddenly the beloved's theme now sounded in the hall for the first time. It aroused in him a strong mixture of joy at this encounter with the familiar and great sorrow at the passage of time. At what was no more and could never again be. Becky Pomeranz's brown eyes, shining with intelligence and seductiveness, the frank innocence with which he desired her, and his fear of himself and his lust.

The audience again was spellbound. Stealing a sidelong glance at the music critic, Michael saw him holding his pen up over his program, as if he was waiting to assess the entrance of the strings. But after they entered he wrote nothing, and he put his arm down again. Throughout the first movement nobody around Michael stirred. The air in the hall was still. There was no more coughing. The dark-haired young woman in front of him sat upright, and in the soft passages he thought that he could hear the old man's heavy breathing. Theo van Gelden raised and lowered his hands and the orchestra played as if bewitched. Sound pursued sound, and when he heard the phrases that soared in extended crescendos, Michael allowed himself to be carried away and follow them in the futile hope that they were leading somewhere.

When it was over there was thunderous rhythmic applause, calling Theo van Gelden back to the stage several times. He signaled the orchestra to their feet, and he received flowers from a little girl whom he kissed on the cheeks. Only after the audience was persuaded that there would be no more, and the young woman in front of him said to the old man with surprise, "I actually liked it!" did the lights go on and the audience, many of them smiling, slowly leave the hall. Nita came up to the edge of the stage and motioned Michael to approach. He made his way to her. She looked down on him with her head bowed and her knees slightly bent. He began to tell her how beautifully she had played the solo in the Rossini, but she interrupted him: "My father isn't here. I don't understand it, there's no answer at his house. I phoned during intermission. Theo tried, too."

After repeating several times that her father wasn't here, she quickly added that they would have to go to his apartment to see if anything had happened to him. "But first," she said despairingly, "there's this gala reception, and all three of us have to be there. Only after that . . ."

Hesitantly she asked him if he would like to come to the reception, and he immediately said that he thought he should hurry back to the babies, which brought a certain relief to her face. But it soon clouded over again, and again she said: "I don't understand it. He's always so punctual. I don't know what to think. We even phoned the dentist. There's no answer at his office or at his home. Only the answering machines. He must have been here himself, he's crazy about music and has a subscription."

Michael tried to find something reassuring to say, speculating about aftereffects on her father of the dentistry. But Nita repeated that there was no answer at his house, and then she said: "Gabriel's completely hysterical. We have to keep him here almost by force, because if he suddenly disappears it'll give rise to gossip. All kinds of people will have something to say about why he wasn't at the reception. It would really be best, if you agree, that is, whatever you prefer. . . ."

Michael nodded, patted her shoulder reassuringly, and walked quickly out into the fresh air and to his car, which by now stood nearly alone in the parking lot.

The simple, routine actions—talking to the babysitter and paying her, tucking in Ido, who had thrown off his blanket, feeding the baby girl, who woke up the moment the babysitter shut the door behind her—soon dispelled the emotions aroused by the concert. Unwilling to return her to her cradle, he left the baby lying on his chest for a long time after feeding her. He breathed in her delicate smell and gently touched her cheek with his finger. At moments like these he felt engulfed by a wave of warmth and compassion, feelings he thought he had lost long ago. There was no struggle here, only her simple need of him, which needed no defenses. When he looked at her he could believe that in her life everything was still possible. He put her back into the little cradle, and since he was so exhausted, he fell asleep on Nita's small sofa in the living room, which was far too short for him. Yet he slept soundly and deeply, secure in the knowledge that both babies were asleep in the next room. And it was from this sleep that he was startled by the ringing of the phone.

Theo van Gelden was on the other end of the line. It was he who told him about the break-in, and that they had found the old man bound and gagged and dead. Speaking in a monotonous whisper, he explained that Nita was talking to the police now, and that she was "in a terrible state. The doctor here has given her a pill. There's nothing to be done." He suddenly groaned. "Our father is dead. He's dead and that's it." Sniffling, he said that Nita had asked if Michael would stay in her apartment until she returned. Without ever talking about it, they had agreed to spend their nights apart, and every evening, after the babies' last feeding of the day, he would wrap the little one in the pink blanket Tzilla had brought her, take her downstairs, and put her to bed in the wicker cradle he carried from room to room.

And since he understood at once that he was in the midst of a catastrophe that would disrupt everything, and because of Theo's alienated tone, Michael asked if he could have a few words with Nita. There was a brief pause. Then Theo van Gelden said: "It's not a good idea right now. We've got the police here and an ambulance and so on."

"Precisely because of that . . ." Michael was about to say, and then thought better of it. He had intended to ask her if she wanted him to come to her father's house, if she needed him there, but he realized that he couldn't leave the babies alone and, what was more, he suddenly also realized that if the person responsible for the investigation was someone he knew, everything about the baby would be revealed. And so, curbing his panic, he only asked when the break-in and the death had taken place.

"They don't know yet for sure," replied Theo van Gelden. "They're talking about this evening or late this afternoon. They haven't yet worked out . . ." he mumbled, and then swallowed and sighed. "They haven't worked out the connection between the room temperature and the . . . the rigor mortis."

"Can you talk freely?" asked Michael.

"I'm in the kitchen," said Theo, showing no surprise at the question.

"Do you know the names of the policemen there?"

"There are two of them—no, three. And also a woman from . . . from the forensics laboratory. And a doctor and some other people. I don't know exactly."

"But is there someone in charge? The one who's giving the orders?"

"Yes," said Theo van Gelden impatiently. "One of them talks all the time. A man with a big belly. But I don't remember his name."

For a moment Michael wondered whether to ask him to go and find out, but this would already give rise to suspicion. If the son who had just seen his dead father returned to the scene of the crime to ask the name of the policeman in charge, they would ask him why he wanted to know. Michael couldn't tell him not to mention his name. Something in Michael protested at being left out of the picture. For a moment he wondered if he should try to find a babysitter, or even take the babies with him. How could he possibly be left out of this situation?

"Why do you want to know that? Do you know someone there?" asked Theo van Gelden with some irritation. Michael remembered that the conductor didn't know anything about him. Certainly nothing about his being on the police force. It would be better, he decided, not to say anything about it to him now. Suddenly he heard a smoker's cough in the background, and then a loud and very familiar voice said: "Mister van Gelden . . . we need you over here for a minute."

The phone picked up Theo van Gelden's reply: "I'll be through in a moment, it's about my sister's baby—"

"Okay, no problem, as soon as you're through," grunted the familiar voice.

There was no doubt about it, and yet Michael whispered into the phone: "Danny Balilty? Is that his name?"

"I think so," said Theo, "but now I have to . . . You heard for yourself. Can I tell her that everything's all right? You'll stay there with the baby?"

"Tell her I won't move until she gets here," promised Michael. "And tell her to phone me here when she can talk, and not to mention my name," he added uncomfortably. "But tell her that quietly." He was astonished by his own words. It's Balilty I'm dealing with here, he reflected. From my own world.

Theo van Gelden muttered something noncommittal and unreassuring.

Michael sat listening to his heartbeat. It was stupid of him to think that he could keep the baby a secret. That he had managed it up to now was a miracle. But now that Danny Balilty was in the game, pervasively present in Nita's life for the immediate future, there wasn't a hope in hell of keeping any secrets. And that being the case, what on earth was keeping him here, among babies and dirty dishes? Something in him refused to believe that he was standing here at the kitchen sink instead of rushing to the place where he was needed.

He washed and dried the dishes. Then he prepared bottles for Ido and for his baby. By the time the telephone rang again he could count five cigarette stubs in the ashtray. Nita spoke in a hollow voice: "My father's dead. He died today. Now I don't have a father or a mother."

He didn't know what to say.

"Your parents are both dead, too."

"For a long time now."

"We're orphans," she said, weeping into the phone. "We're all orphans."

He couldn't find any words.

"Now they're concentrating on the painting again. They've already determined that jewelry was taken, but we can't find the photograph of the painting. They took it right out of the frame. I don't know if Father died before . . ." She fell silent and steadied her breath. "He had a rag stuffed into his mouth, and tape stuck over it. He suffocated. I don't know how long . . . "

Michael said nothing. He couldn't find a way to say that her father hadn't suffered, that he must have died instantly. It's not murder, he said to himself, just armed robbery. I don't have to be there.

As if she had heard his thoughts she said, in the same hollow tone as before: "They wouldn't let me see him. Gabriel found him. He was in the bedroom. He was dragged there. Theo saw him, too. But they wouldn't let me in. So I don't know if he was terrified, and for how long he was terrified. It's horrible. Horrible!"

Michael murmured something. Then he roused himself and asked: "Isn't it enough for your two brothers to be there? Can't they let you go home?" He couldn't believe what he was saying. He was talking like an ignoramus. Like someone who had no idea of police procedures. As if he were two separate people.

"I've only just finished describing the jewelry. None of us remembers exactly what there was. All three of us also had to tell them about the painting."

"What painting?"

"I told you," she replied in the hollow voice, without her customary impatience. "It all happened because of the painting. They must have known it was here. And it's worth . . . I don't know, maybe half a million dollars."

"What painting is it, exactly?"

Suddenly a trace of emotion invaded her voice: "Didn't I tell you? I told you. I told you that my father had a painting called *Vanitas* in his house. By a seventeenth-century Dutch painter named Hendrik van Steenwijk. Anyway, they removed it from the frame. It's not here anymore. They turned the whole house upside down. And we . . ." she said in a choked voice, "were angry with him for not coming to the concert! When I think of the hours he spent here while we—"

"It definitely wasn't hours. It's a matter of minutes, if not seconds," he said authoritatively.

"Is that true? Or are you just saying it?"

"It's true. I know."

"It's horrible anyway. I don't know . . . how I'll . . . Well, is Ido all right?"

"He's fine. Sleeping soundly. You don't have to worry about him now."

"They've taken him away. Away from here. Now it's only us here with the policeman who's waiting for us to go so he can . . . can seal the apartment, he says."

"I'm sorry I can't be with you there."

She ignored his appeal. Her hollow voice trembled now: "Because they haven't finished their examination. We're not allowed to touch anything except in the kitchen until they've finished."

"What do you mean they haven't finished?!" He was astounded. "They left before completing their examination?"

"He's still here, the one who doesn't stop talking."

"Balilty?"

"Yes," she whispered. "Listen," she said tremulously, "I know that you don't want me to say I know you. And I didn't say anything, but wouldn't it be better . . . if—"

"No," he said firmly. "I'll explain it to you, trust me. He's a first-class man, believe me, he'll do everything that has to be done even without your mentioning my name."

She was silent.

"Ask him when you can go home."

"I've already asked. He didn't answer. He talks a lot but he never answers a single question."

"It won't be much longer," he promised.

"As if it makes any difference now," she mumbled. "Now everything, everything's absolutely . . ." Her voice took on the hollow tone again. In the background he heard men's voices. "They want me to go look at the list of jewelry," she said. "As if it makes any difference now."

He didn't go back to sleep. Ido woke up only once, the baby girl twice. But he couldn't fall asleep in between. He lay on his back and put her on his chest. Her feet reached his waist, her face was buried in his neck. From time to time she took a deep breath, shuddered, and changed the position of her head. Finally he returned her to her cradle. He couldn't read, either. He lay in the dark and smoked, staring at the red glow at the tip of the cigarette and listening attentively to the sounds coming from the street, even though he knew very well that he would not hear the engine of the car bringing Nita home. They would stop on the other side of the building, the side overlooked not by the French windows but by the kitchen balcony. At last he went and stood on the kitchen balcony and smoked next to the balustrade, tapping his ash into an empty flowerpot standing in the corner. And thus in the first pale, milky light of morning, he saw Gabriel van Gelden holding Nita's arm as he helped her out of a big car and led her into the building.

3

Vanitas

"Who could have imagined it!" cried Theo van Gelden, stopping at the bedroom door in Nita's apartment. He stared at the closed door and went on pacing slowly up and down the narrow corridor. His hands were in his pockets. From time to time, at regular intervals, he stamped on the floor, as if in obedience to some rhythm dictated to him from outside. "After everything he went through in his life," he said when he approached the living room, where Nita and Gabriel were sitting. "A man reaches the age of eighty-two, having lived through the Nazi occupation of Holland, having been rescued time and again, and ends up robbed and killed in his own home here in the State of Israel!"

By now, at six o'clock in the morning, the avocado had already begun to turn dark on the sandwiches Gabriel had prepared. Gabriel was the only one to eat a slice and drink two cups of coffee. Theo only pinched off a piece of the soft part of the white bread and nibbled it abstractedly, and Nita didn't even look at the copper serving table upon which the plate of food reposed. From the moment Michael put the phone down after the first conversation with Theo, he knew that his sense of oppression would not lift. He dismissed from his mind any explicit thoughts about the question of what would happen to the baby from the moment he found out that Danny Balilty was the head of the Special Investigation Team on the Felix van Gelden case. At that moment, brief and clear as lightning, he knew that the matter of the baby could no longer be kept secret. When Danny Balilty was involved in a case, he was sure—in his own unique, sloppy way, as if with a kind of casual nonchalance—to uncover any scrap of information his sense of smell led him to. When

Michael saw Nita in the doorway, in her stocking feet, high-heeled shoes in hand, and still in her black evening gown, with her face hollow and staring, he was filled with guilt at his preoccupation with secrecy, with his own concerns, with the question of how he was going to keep the baby. What was supposed to be the framework in which they would both be protected had in one moment been destroyed. What had seemed a safe place had collapsed like a house of cards. And as had been happening to him lately, in fact ever since he found the baby, came the thought of losing her. And the feeling of the threat of something irretrievable, a loss for which there could be no consolation, overwhelmed him. He would abandon the thought and let the anxiety float like a twig on the current of a general unease, and try to think of Nita.

After Nita had fed Ido, who woke up as soon as the van Geldens arrived, she buried her face in her son's neck. She smiled at him as she changed his diaper. Michael had offered to do it for her, but she only shook her head stubbornly. She had laid her face on Ido's chubby chest and murmured to him. At last she put him in his crib, and she down on the sofa, where she remained quietly, hugging her knees to her body. For Michael, staying here now with her and her brothers was the most natural thing in the world. He had spent many hours of his life with people mourning murder victims, had listened to their conversations, asked them questions. But this time it was different. Not only because he couldn't ask about anything, but also because Nita was so very close and yet so far away.

"It's not certain that it was an ordinary robbery," Gabriel corrected his brother. "It could have been somebody only after the painting. You heard what that policeman said."

Michael wanted to ask what the policeman had said, but there was no need to, because Theo, who couldn't stop talking, just as he couldn't stop pacing from wall to wall, stopped at the French windows and looked outside at the mist-covered hills and muttered: "I heard what he said. But that's only speculation. They stole all the money, all the dollars and the guilder that are missing from where he kept them. And they turned the whole house upside down and took all the papers and jewelry. How does he know, that policeman, that man who asked us, *us* where we were before the concert."

"Do me a favor, Theo," said Gabriel, "put those keys away. I can't stand the noise anymore."

Theo took his hand out of his pocket and threw down the small bunch of keys he had been incessantly rattling. The conductor was still wearing his tuxedo trousers, but he had taken off the jacket. His gold-rimmed mother-of-pearl cuff links gleamed as he stood under the lamp and waved his hand. He resumed his pacing in the corridor, glanced into Ido's room, and said something about how lucky babies were to sleep through everything. Then he continued to pace in the living room. .

"It's not just speculation. The woman from the forensics laboratory said that whoever removed the canvas from the frame was an experienced professional," said Gabriel. He put his hand on his right eyelid, which was twitching uncontrollably. The green stone set in the last coil of his gold ring glittered. Only now, looking closely, did Michael recognize the shape of a snake.

"So it was all because of that painting. I've always hated it," declared Theo, and again stared out though the French windows. "At least you've got a good view here in this stupid place!" he said to Nita, who sat curled up in the corner of the sofa and didn't say a word. "I've always hated it because, in the first place, I don't like all that *Vanitas* business with those skulls. They're always making a fuss about that *memento mori* of theirs, as if anyone can forget that we're going to die. I hate that symbolism, even though the picture itself is a fine one." He took off his glasses and put them down on the copper serving table. Nita leaned her face on her raised knees. "Remember how we all flew to Amsterdam for Gabi's bar mitzvah," Theo said, "and saw the big version in the Rijksmuseum?"

Gabriel rubbed his eyes, tugged at his beard, buried his face in his hands, and was silent. Nita raised her head and stared as if nothing had been said. "You don't remember any of it, you were only three," Gabi now said gently to her.

Again Michael wondered why he remained standing here at the kitchen door. If he wasn't superfluous here now, with all of them here together? Having seen Nita taking care of Ido, he knew he could safely leave. In a few hours the babysitter would come, and then he would leave the baby here and routinely go to work at police headquarters in the Russian Compound. Once he was there he would be able to find out from Tzilla how much Balilty already knew. He quickly put a stop to this train of thought, reminding himself that it was Nita he had to worry about now, if only because he was obliged to her. As for the baby, he'd have to wait and see. Twice he had asked her quietly—as they were standing side by side at the changing table in Ido's room and he was watching her hands stroking Ido's body and her fingers fluttering over his face—if she wanted him to stay or if she preferred that he leave. In that dead, hollow voice, she twice said that she would like him to stay. "If you can," she added in a panic in case she had demanded too much. It was this panic that, if only for a moment, had brought her voice to life. Michael again saw that her regard for the convenience of others, the need to take it into consideration, which was the main sign of life in her as well as the only way to take her out of herself, was exhausting. It was too soon to insist on anything now.

It was clear to him that her father's death, and especially the manner of it, would sabotage what had seemed the beginning of a healing process. He felt he had brought it about by his presence, to his great satisfaction. A great fear threatened to engulf him again when he thought about her collapsing in the next few days. The shadow of Nurse Nehama's all-knowing smile hovered over them as they stood at the changing table. But Michael pushed the threatening shadows roughly aside. He told himself firmly to take things as they came. He couldn't do otherwise. It was said that a baby sensed its mother's emotions in the womb. Did this baby girl already understand that Michael was the main figure in her life now? Could she sense how tenuous his world was? He held the baby tightly in his arms. She squirmed. He looked into the smooth face, pink with sleep. For a moment she looked to him utterly secure in his arms. He almost said to her, I won't let anything happen to you. But the next moment, while she was still in his arms, he found himself engulfed by doubts.

"That trip for your bar mitzvah was quite ghastly," said Theo with a dreamy expression. "They dragged us from one museum to another, in Vienna and Amsterdam and Paris. Father did it for himself and for you. I wasn't interested in such stuff then . . . and Nita was only a toddler." He glanced at her, and she again buried her face in her knees.

When she entered the apartment, over an hour ago, she had run straight to the babies' room, stood next to Ido's bed—Michael followed her and stood in the doorway—and then hurried to the bedroom, threw off her high-heeled shoes, shut the door behind her, and emerged in a wide, floral skirt and a black sweatshirt. Now the skirt was spread out around her, hiding the contours of her body. Only when she hugged her knees to her chest and buried her face in them did her thinness become apparent again. Suddenly he longed to sit down next to her and put his arms around her. Only yesterday there had been a dimple in her cheek and a mischievous gleam in her eyes, and he had succeeded easily in making her laugh wholeheartedly. It seemed to him that he had made her really happy, and this thought had given him profound satisfaction in the past few days. Not many hours had passed since, on their way to the concert, he had said to her: "I've decided that I want you to be happy. I want you very much to be happy, and I know that you will be." And she had given him an innocent, serious, trusting look.

Jerusalem's early-morning cold wind suddenly blew in through the French windows, giving rise to the illusion that autumn had already begun, although Michael could feel in his bones the heat still to come. "Oh, how miserable I was then!" Theo sighed. "And all because of Dora Zackheim, who wasn't at all pleased with me, only with you, Gabi, remember? But it was because of her that we went on that trip. She said that we needed not only music but also more general knowledge and a bit of normal life. It was part of her philosophy, as if there was any chance of our having a normal life . . ." He stopped talking and took a deep, noisy breath. "And when we came back I didn't go back to my violin lessons with her. It was only much later, years later, that I suspected that this had been her elegant way of getting me to quit. But even then I suspected, without knowing it, that she had given up on me. I don't know myself why I left her. But you, Gabi, didn't understand it. She really loved you." Gabriel shifted in his wicker chair, as if he couldn't find the right position, and he rubbed his eyes. "But I saw that painting in the Rijksmuseum," continued Theo, "and I still remember it well, presumably because of the picture we had hanging at home."

Michael cleared his throat, which required it after his prolonged silence, and asked apologetically: "Was your painting a copy? I don't understand, if it was in Amsterdam, how did your father come to have it?"

"The painting in our father's house," said Gabriel, taking his hands away from his face, "was one of three preparatory studies van Steenwijk did for the big one in the Rijksmuseum. They're also oils."

Theo, who had taken hardly any notice of Michael up to now, leaned against the bookshelf and looked out the French windows as he said: "I don't know if you're familiar with this genre of *Vanitas* still lifes. It was a popular subject with seventeenth-century Dutch and Flemish painters. Van Steenwijk was a contemporary of Vermeer's. Not great like Vermeer, but great enough. The art experts rate him in the second or third rank below Vermeer. His paintings have something like the Vermeer light, that soft, yellowish light. Only Vermeer never painted a *Vanitas*."

"You didn't answer his question," Gabriel remarked. "He asked about the painting we had at home."

"The big painting, the one in the Rijksmuseum, is a still life, like all 'Vanitas' paintings. As far as I can remember, there's a flute, books, fruit, a medallion, and—"

"And a skull. There's a skull on the pile of books," continued Gabriel. "A skull instead of a fly or a worm."

"What fly?" said Theo, alarmed.

"Well, in *Vanitas* paintings there's often, let's say, a bowl of perfect fruit, or a vase of flowers in all the colors of the rainbow, but there's always a fly or two hovering, or a worm emerging from some perfect piece of fruit, so that you won't forget that everything is about to rot, to die."

"I hate it," said Theo with a shudder. "I hate it!" He shuddered again and hugged himself. "In any event," he said, turning to Michael, his left arm still holding his right shoulder, "there are three paintings he did before the big one. Studies of details of the big painting. They're smaller but also oils. It's known that there are only these three, and that they form a series. Ours has been in the family for generations, since Father's grandfather, I think. Father liked to tell us that it's thanks to the sales logs they kept in those days that we know so much about Rembrandt's and other painters' financial situations.

Thanks to that, too, we know that there were these three studies. And that all of them contained various details from the big painting, from different angles," he explained, waving his arm in a sweeping gesture. "Two of them were bought by a Scottish nobleman on a buying trip in Europe at the beginning of the nineteenth century. In those days people would travel to Italy and Holland to buy up paintings from impoverished aristocratic families, all kinds of counts and dukes who didn't have enough to eat. Our picture contains the bit with the flute on one side and the skull on the pile of books on the other. It's quite a small painting." Theo held his hands about twenty centimeters apart. "The other two are owned by a collector in Scotland," he added. "Gabi loved that painting, didn't you, Gabi? You felt the closest to it." A gleam of intimacy appeared in Theo's eyes as he looked at his brother.

"They removed the picture from the frame," said Gabriel dully, looking down at the carpet. To Michael it seemed that he was talking to him. "It was someone who knows about paintings, who knows how much it's worth, who knew everything in advance. I just don't understand why the break-in didn't occur when he was out. Why did they have to do it precisely when he was at home? It could have been done while he was at the dentist."

"That character, that policeman, what's his name, Bality?" said Theo, making a face.

"Balilty," Michael corrected him and, until he thought better of it, was about to explain the gap between Danny Balilty's appearance and behavior and his talents. Why should he care what Theo thought about Danny?

"I don't want us to sit *shiva*," said Theo suddenly. "I hate it, with all those condolence visitors, and I don't think it would be a good idea for us to stop working now. They're not going to force me to cancel engagements. What do you say?"

Nita didn't react. She didn't even turn to look at him. But Gabriel raised his face, looked at Theo, and shrugged his shoulders. "I don't care," he said finally. "What difference does it make?"

"Father hated religion and the religious. He wouldn't have wanted it. He was an atheist and he couldn't stand all those rituals," argued Theo.

"But we sat *shiva* for Mother," said Gabriel in a muffled voice through his hands, which again covered his face. He sniffled.

Theo looked at him: "We sat *shiva* for Mother because she wasn't so anti-religious. And in order to be together with Father, so he wouldn't be alone." There was a silence. Theo, who couldn't tolerate it, looked at Nita, who continued to sit completely frozen in the corner of the sofa. "You should go and lie down for a bit, you're completely exhausted," he said. She shivered but shook her head. "You tell her, Gabi," said Theo, "you've got more influence over her than I have."

Gabriel looked at Nita, and Michael followed his look. Her face was very white and she was trembling incessantly in her folded legs and in the arms that hugged them tightly to her. The semicircles under her eyes were darker than usual. And her eyes were blurred-looking, as they had been the first time he met her. Her hair was mussed, as if she had stuck her fingers into her curls and pulled them sideways. How strange it was, the urge that never left him to sit down close to her and put his arms around her. But for the presence of her brothers, he would probably have done so. It wasn't even two weeks since they had met, and he was already so enmeshed in her life. It was strange to be so close to a woman and yet so far from her.

"She'll collapse, and we've still got a long way to go," Theo warned Gabi. "Aside from the concerts we're not going to cancel, we'll have to be talking to that policeman who keeps on remembering new things to ask about—"

From Ido's room there came a loud scream. The baby girl had awakened, and Michael got up to feed her. Ido stirred in his crib. Michael calculated how much longer he would go on sleeping. He wondered whether Nita would be able to take care of him. Soon the babysitter would arrive, and he would ask her to take the baby boy outside. But Nita wouldn't be able to practice today in the fog of paralysis that had descended on her. He returned to the living room.

"This wouldn't have happened if he'd sold it to that crazy Scotsman five years ago. No one would have given him more for it," Theo van Gelden was saying.

"He didn't need the money. It was property, an investment," said Gabriel.

Michael wanted to hear more about the Scotsman and about the offer for the painting, but he didn't dare ask. He was trying to stay in the background, wanted, as much as possible, to erase the fact that he himself was a policeman. As if erasing that would also conceal the story of the baby. But suddenly Theo looked at him and, as if he had read his thoughts, said: "Nita says that you're a big shot in the police. Maybe you can do something."

"Like what?" asked Michael carefully. "What would you like me to do?"

"Do I know? Hurry up the investigation, get them off our backs, tell that guy to leave us alone. He wants me not to leave the country for the immediate future. I have three concerts with the Tokyo Philharmonic two weeks from now. Do you think he'll let me go before then? How can I cancel something like that? Do you think the Japanese would understand? The engagement was scheduled two years ago. It'll be my second appearance in Japan."

"Danny Balilty's a good man," said Michael. "You're mistaken about him. He's a serious person. Even if he talks a little too much," he added quickly.

"Who could have imagined it?" lamented Theo. "How many times did I tell him to sell to the Scotsman. And every time he said no way. That pitiful Scotsman never stopped phoning, and he came to see Father twice." He turned to Michael, as if he saw him as his only potential audience. "The Scotsman is a likable fellow. His great-great-grandfather bought the other two van Steenwijk studies in 1820, which is apparently when our own great-great-grandfather bought Father's painting. So it's been in our family for generations. The Scotsman has two of the three, and he wants to complete the series. He offered Father over half a million dollars, more than he was offered by the Stedelijk Museum in Leiden. But Father refused to sell."

"Why are we only talking about the painting?" asked Gabriel. "The money and the jewelry are also missing. Why are you so sure it was because of the painting?"

"But you yourself said only a minute ago—"

"So what?" Gabriel responded angrily. "I've had second thoughts. Not that it makes any difference."

"That guy—Balilty?" said Theo to Michael. "He said that the other stolen things seemed less important to him. But he doesn't know how much money there was there, and neither do we know exactly. We only know where it was." Again he looked at Michael and said: "Father didn't believe in banks. Because of the Feuchtwanger bank's failure. You remember that, don't you?" Michael nodded faintly, and out of the corner of his eye glanced at Nita. She looked as if she hadn't heard a word. He wouldn't be able to count on her any longer. That was becoming increasingly clear, but he mustn't panic. He would have to wait and see what happened. In the meantime he had better listen to what Theo was saying: "Because he lost all the money he had at Feuchtwanger, he began keeping foreign currency at home. He had a hiding place, more than one. It was a lot of money, and I knew where it was—he showed me. And Nita, too." He turned to Gabriel. "What about you? Did he show you, too?"

Gabriel nodded.

Theo stood up from the wicker chair and began pacing up and down again. "I thought that he didn't show you. You weren't here in Israel at the time, and I thought—"

"He showed me when I came back. In case something happened to him and you weren't in the country. He was very worried about Nita." Nita tightened her arms around her knees.

"He did so we'd know if something suddenly happened to him," Theo continued. "He had a lot of money. The last time he showed me tens of thousands of dollars in guilder. I asked him why in guilder, of all things. But he didn't answer. That's how he was, when he didn't want to he simply didn't answer." Theo snorted and wiped his face. "Did he ever explain it to you, Gabi?"

"No, I have no idea," said Gabriel dully. He stared at the carpet again.

"What I don't understand," said Theo, "is what they're going to do with the painting now that they've got it. They can't sell it. What did they steal it for?" He looked at Michael as if he expected an answer.

Against his will, Michael, who was trying to keep as low a profile as possible, found himself impelled to say something. He started by pointing out that it wasn't his field, that he didn't know much about such things. But he knew that in cases of this kind the local police usually collaborated with Interpol. Usually—so he understood—thefts like this are commissioned by a collector. "That apparently happened with the clock collection that was stolen from the Islamic Museum here in Jerusalem." That's why the stolen goods are so difficult to locate, he was tempted to but didn't say.

"The Scotsman!" Theo burst out. "Maybe it was the Scotsman who sent the thieves because Father didn't want to sell him the painting!"

"Don't be crazy," said Gabriel, sitting up. "I've met him, too. We met him together, don't you remember? He's a nice man, you said so yourself. His wish to buy the third painting is perfectly natural. He already has the other two. That Scotsman wouldn't hurt a fly."

"What do we know about what people are capable of doing?" asked Theo.

"It wasn't the Scotsman!" Gabriel insisted.

"In the first place," said Theo, "Father's death was an accident. They didn't intend to kill him, he died because . . ." He threw a glance at Nita, who showed few signs of life. "He suffocated. There was the gag and there was his emphysema." Theo looked at Michael and looked away again. "Father was in an advanced stage of emphysema. There were days when he had to be hooked up to an oxygen cylinder." He looked at Nita again and then at Gabriel. "And that's why he died. There's a medical term for it. The doctor said it last night," he said, looking at his brother again.

"Asphyxia," said Gabriel without raising his head.

Theo turned to Michael. "Your pal, the policeman," he said, "couldn't understand why they broke into the house while Father was there. They could have broken in when he was at the dentist, as I said, or at the concert, or at his weekly Masonic meeting."

"If he went to the dentist at all," remarked Gabriel. Theo froze. Nita raised her head from her knees and looked at Gabriel. "Maybe he canceled his appointment. Maybe he didn't have one at all," whispered Gabriel. His voice grew stronger as he said: "Father hated going to the dentist. He wanted to be at the concert. The last thing he would have done was go to the dentist just before a concert where all three of us were performing."

"That's easy enough to check," said Michael.

"He had to go through all he went through in his life to finally end up like this," declaimed Theo, as if it no longer was he himself standing behind the words but rather a compulsive need to hear his own voice. "After everything he'd been through," he said again, and again he stood up and began pacing with his hands in his pockets. "And I thought that he just didn't have the strength for the concert," he said suddenly, standing over Gabriel. "We have to call the dentist," he affirmed.

"Leave that to the police," said Gabriel sharply. "What do we have to go running to the dentist for? Father's dead. None of it matters now. I don't want to talk about it anymore." His cheeks were sagging, the skin under his sunken eyes was lumpy, his breathing sounded heavy in the room. Theo bent over the pack of cigarettes Michael had left on the copper serving table. "May I?" he asked. Without waiting for a reply, he lit a cigarette. A cloud of whitish smoke enveloped Gabriel, who waved his hands to dispel it.

"Gabi," said Theo suddenly, "there's something I don't understand. Maybe . . . maybe I should wait until we're alone. I want to ask you . . . never mind, it's not important." He glanced at Michael and fell silent. Nita looked at both of them. Her eyes opened wide, the dark semicircles underneath making them look even lighter. Around the blue-green gray of the irises were thin, dark rings, like lines drawn around their borders. Michael had never noticed them before.

"What did you want to say, Theo?" she asked anxiously. "Stop treating me as if I were a baby. There's no need to hide anything from me anymore. I've already proved that I can cope with . . ."

"It's not because of you, Nita," said Theo, and he looked at her pleadingly. "Really it's not. Even though for me you'll always be my baby sister. What can I do? I just thought . . ." He turned his head toward Michael and then looked again at Gabriel. "It's got nothing to do with anything, because . . ."

"You can speak freely in front of him," said Nita. "As far as I'm concerned, he's family. I trust him absolu— I trust him." She fell silent and lowered her eyes.

"But he's not close to me," Theo argued. "I have no reason to trust him." He gestured with his arm and muttered: "Pardon me, it's nothing personal."

"Even after what I've said?" asked Nita, her eyes filling with tears.

"What did you want to say, Theo? Go on, say it. I don't care," said Gabriel in a muffled voice that seemed to be coming from the carpet.

Michael went into the kitchen to make fresh coffee. From there he heard Theo whisper something. He couldn't make out the words, until he heard him call out, almost in a shout: "I don't understand why. You can explain it to me at least!" Again there were murmurs—Michael couldn't identify the speaker. Michael returned to the living room and put the coffee down on the copper serving table. He was aware that because of him the conversation had stopped. He put a cup of tea down in front of Nita, but she only shook her head and pointed to her throat in a gesture indicating that it was blocked. "Don't go!" she said as Michael began to retreat to the bedroom.

Theo picked up his glasses from the copper serving table and put them back on. He circled around the wicker chair on which his brother was sitting, stood at the French windows, and then sat down on the other wicker chair. When Gabriel maintained his silence, Theo he went on talking: "Nita's okay. She's got nothing to hide. Every move she makes is known because of the baby. But I, for example, do have something I'd rather have kept to myself. I don't like people poking their noses into my business, and still I told the policeman, even though you saw that it was embarrassing to me. So why did you keep quiet? It's all routine for him. Nobody thinks that any of us really . . ." He interrupted himself with a snort of ridicule.

Gabriel didn't move.

"What are you looking for in the carpet?" Theo burst out. "Why don't you answer me?"

"Theo," pleaded Nita. "Stop it, both of you. I can't stand your bickering now."

"I'm only asking," Theo said defensively. "It's not an argument, nobody's bickering. . . . I just want to know why you didn't want to tell him. Why didn't you tell him where you were?"

Gabriel raised his eyes from the carpet. His face, surrounded by the red-brown beard that shone from the light behind him, looked like a mask of rage. His mouth twisted in a lopsided grimace. "What do you care?" he said. "All you care about is your concerts in Japan and for us not to stop working and for none of your plans to be disturbed,

God forbid. And since we're talking about your plans, you can go ahead now with your Bayreuth, and there's no one to stop you anymore. I want you to know that I'll never forgive you for Father's last attack, when you told him about the Wagner Festival. He had that attack, and you walked out and slammed the door behind you! I stayed behind and took care of the oxygen cylinder and everything. Couldn't you wait until he . . . until he died in peace? No, you had to have your say, to tell him about your Wagner, and then you walked out. So why the hell should I tell you anything?" Gabriel buried his face in his hands, and his shoulders shook. Something between a sob and a groan came from behind his hands.

Theo ground his cigarette out in the blue ashtray. His face was now a shade of pale olive. He folded his arms. Michael glanced at Nita. She took her arms off her knees and looked at Theo with alarm.

"What's this? Theo? What's he talking about?"

"Nothing, it doesn't matter. Leave it alone," said Theo. "Really, it isn't important."

"I want to know!" she demanded, and something vital suddenly shone in her eyes as she said: "I'm sick and tired of the way you hide things from me. I'm thirty-eight years old, I have a child of my own. It's time I stopped being the baby here!"

"It's not my fault," said Theo, addressing his brother's bowed head. "Father didn't hear about it from me, and afterward, when he asked me, what was I supposed to do, lie? Say I knew nothing about it?" Theo lit another one of Michael's cigarettes. Michael too wanted one, but he didn't dare move from his place, in order not to draw attention to his presence. So they would go on ignoring him, he stood still and breathed carefully.

"Heard about what? How did he hear about it? What are you talking about? Why don't you ever tell me anything?" The end of Nita's sentence came out in a kind of squeal. There was a note of hysteria in her voice, which had become high and thin. Her eyes filled with tears again, and again she wiped them with the back of her hand. She stretched out her long legs and gathered her skirt around them.

"It's nothing," said Gabriel remorsefully. "Really, Nita, it's nothing."

"If it's connected with Father and Wagner and the emphysema it can't be nothing!" Nita shouted. It was the first time Michael had ever heard her raise her voice. It had a sharp sound, without a trace of hoarseness. "I'm sick of playing this role. I want to know! Theo, what's he talking about? What are you both talking about? Answer me! Now!"

"He's talking about an interview with me in the *New York Times*," said Theo in a businesslike tone. "What I said, what I was quoted as saying, was that my dream was to have a Wagner Festival in Jerusalem, and for Israel to stop ignoring this great composer at last, and that this dream was going to be fulfilled in the coming year. It was part of a long interview in a foreign newspaper. I didn't think Father would see it."

"And *then*," said Gabriel, "Father *did* see it, of course, as he saw everything, and he asked Theo about it. Can you imagine it? Father hears about a Wagner festival in Jerusalem, after all these years when in the most musical home in Jerusalem not a note of Wagner was ever heard! Father, who hated violence so, defended the guy who broke Jascha Heifetz's hand back in the fifties over Wagner!"

"It wasn't his hand," Theo whispered, "and it wasn't broken, and I'm not even sure that it was over Wagner. I think it was over Richard Strauss, and it was Menuhin and not Heifetz."

"He didn't want to lie, he told Father the truth, all of a sudden he can't tell a lie," said Gabriel bitterly.

"Someone, I don't know who, told Father about it," said Theo. "Well, you can imagine how he reacted. But it wasn't that which shortened his life. I can't spend my life not doing what I believe in just because it didn't suit Father. If it was up to him, I'd be running the music shop now. He never accepted my opinions."

"Theo had to have it in Jerusalem," said Gabriel, staring at the same spot on the carpet. "Conducting his Wagner at Bayreuth and Glyndebourne wasn't enough for him. He had to do it in Jerusalem."

"Abroad I wasn't running the whole show," Theo defended himself. "I only conducted when I did *Parsifal* at Bayreuth. I don't expect you to understand why I need to do it. You don't have the imagination for it. You have no idea what it means to conduct a *Ring* cycle or even just a performance of *The Flying Dutchman*. That music doesn't interest you because it has more to it than a couple of period Baroque violins. You simply can't stand—"

"Perverted music," Gabriel shouted. "Perverted music, that's what I say about *Tristan*!"

"Stop it!" cried Nita, putting her hands over her ears. "Stop it! Not even a day has passed, it was only last evening . . ." She fell silent.

Theo bowed his head. "The hypocrisy of it," he muttered. "Do you know how many people are left here who still care about all that? They're all dead! Fifty years have passed! Who cares?"

"Father cared."

"Do you know that in recent months they've been playing Wagner on the national radio here in Israel? On the *Voice of Music*? Two or three times a week, without anyone making a fuss about it?"

"Really?" said Gabriel. "Nobody made a fuss? The first time they played something from *Tannhäuser*, afterward the announcer had to apologize for the technical hitch. There was more than a minute of silence on the air, as if someone had sabotaged the broadcast. They also had to ask people to stop phoning the station. That's how much nobody cared." A dark flush spread over his face as he spoke, and he looked at Theo but avoided meeting his eyes.

Theo drew on his cigarette. "It wasn't because of me that he died," he said weakly.

"You shouldn't have told him," insisted Gabriel, but he sounded calmer, and he buried his face in his hands again.

"I couldn't lie to him," pleaded Theo. "I'm not a child anymore, and I'm entitled to have opinions of my own. There's no reason on earth . . . Wagner is too great to be ignored."

"From there to a Bayreuth in Jerusalem is a long way," said Gabriel angrily.

"That was only a figure of speech," said Theo. "It'll take time for —"

"Then you should be more careful about what you say," demanded Gabriel, and he raised his face, which was still flushed. "We have to decide about the *shiva*. Anyway, there won't be a funeral."

Michael sensed his leg muscles tensing. Nita said: "There certainly will be. I'm not prepared to go along with donating Father's body for medical research. He was murdered. As it is, the police will have an autopsy. I refuse to agree to donating the body."

"It won't help you if he made his intention known. If he declared it officially, they have the legal right to honor his bequest of his own body," said Gabriel.

"He never declared it," said Theo.

"How do you know?" demanded Gabriel, looking him in the eyes.

"Did *you* know about it?" asked Theo.

"Yes, I did," said Gabriel. "He spoke to me about his will."

"And to me, too," said Theo. "That's how I know that he wanted to amend the will to that effect. The question is if Spiegel knows, too. If Father consulted him at all. It's a matter for lawyers. It has nothing to do with the family."

"I want him to have a proper funeral!" insisted Nita. "And not in a year's time, either. I'm sick of all that Dutch scientific open-mindedness. I want . . . I want to bury my father," she said defiantly. "At least let's do that properly," she muttered, bowing her head. "He didn't know that he would die with his hands tied. He didn't die decently, at least let's bury him decently. And where's Herzl? We have to inform Herzl!"

The brothers looked at her and then at each other in silence. Michael felt his heart beat. If there was no funeral, if there was no obituary, if Balilty didn't hear about the death, then maybe Nurse Nehama wouldn't know about it, either. But that, of course, was too much to hope for. Who is Herzl, he wondered, but he didn't dare open his mouth.

"And another thing," said Nita in a determined and not in the least hollow voice, "there's something else I want to say and want you to understand, once and for all! The business of not taking me into account is finished. I want to know what's going on! Without exception! Everything you know I want to know, too. For your information, I'm thirty-eight years old."

"During the past year," said Theo carefully, "it was impossible to talk to you about anything."

"You never tried!" she retorted. "You never came to tell me that you had a dream about a Wagner Festival in Jerusalem. Are you mad?" she suddenly asked as if she had only just understood the meaning of her words. "You talked about something like that to Father? After the Yehudi Menuhin and all that?"

"Menuhin again!" protested Theo. "Nobody broke his hand," he said wearily. "It's one of those myths fostered by ideologues."

"I asked you: Why doesn't anyone inform Herzl?"

"You heard what we said to that policeman during the night," said Gabriel. "Herzl's disappeared. I've been trying to find him for two months now, in order to—"

"What do you mean, he's disappeared?" she pounced. "Has the earth swallowed him up? He can't be abroad. He hates to travel out of the country. And he's not dead, because we would have heard about it. How is it possible that after all these years, he won't know about Father and won't be at the funeral? Because I'm telling you that there's going to be a funeral!"

"If you like, I'll phone Spiegel," said Gabriel, "and find out what the legal position is as far as . . ." Suddenly the doorbell rang. Gabriel fell silent.

"Is it the press?" asked Theo, alarmed. "Are the reporters descending on us now?"

"Why are you talking about reporters?" said Gabriel dismissively. "Nobody knows we're here. That's the reason we came here. Nita isn't a media personality like you, or even like me." Again the doorbell rang.

"Do you think they know already?" asked Theo, with the same alarm.

"What do I care? They won't come here. And if they do, we won't talk to them. They can't force us. They wouldn't expect even you to cooperate and be nice to them at a time like this," Gabriel added bitterly.

Michael looked at Nita. She looked back at him imploringly. He went and opened the door to the babysitter and saw her wide face under the babushka as she looked around in confusion at the scene that greeted her eyes: Nita on the corner of the little sofa, Gabriel in the wicker armchair, and Theo, who had stopped pacing in the middle of the room, a sunbeam catching the black satin stripe on his trousers. Michael accompanied the babysitter to the babies' room and told her what had happened. He looked at the stunned confusion on the woman's face, and at her roughened fingers fumbling with her babushka. He waited for her to sigh and say: "Poor things. Poor things. Poor things." Completely detached, he looked at her as she wiped her eyes, which were often inflamed. She was a simple woman whose face always lit up with joy when she held a baby in her arms. Now, too, as she bent over the cradle and peeped at the baby girl, her lips murmured unintelligible sounds that reminded him of his grandmother's blessings and oaths, and a faint flush covered her cheeks. She rested her arms on the railing of Ido's crib, her gold bangles tinkling. Ido opened his eyes. She held out her arms, and a moment later she was holding him fast against her broad bosom, her cheek against his and her face beaming. Michael asked her to stay overtime and to take Ido out for a longer time than usual. She nodded willingly, murmured "Poor things. Poor little things," and laid Ido on the table to change his diaper. "Of course we won't leave them alone. And the little one?" she asked as she stood over Ido, her reddened hand on his stomach as he kicked and tried to turn over. "What should I do with the little one?"

The phone rang a few times. Nita called to him. "Is it true?" asked Tzilla at the other end. "I heard it on the news. Nita says it's so. Is it true?" Michael said it was. "How are you coping? What now?" she asked with reserve.

"We're coping," said Michael quietly, sensing three pairs of eyes fixed on his back. "I have to talk to you," he added in a warning tone, and he looked at his watch. "I'll be on my way in ten minutes."

"Say something," said Theo to Nita after Michael put the phone down. She shrugged her shoulders.

"It's too soon, Theo," said Gabriel.

"I feel responsible. Up to now Father's supported her. The whole of this last year she hasn't been teaching. And that schmuck isn't going to suddenly start supporting her now, when the child's . . . How old is he now, Nita?"

"Nearly six months," said Gabriel. "You've got so many children of your own, you don't know the first thing about your sister's child."

"That's not true," Theo flared up. "You have no right to say anything about my relationship with Nita and the child."

"Gabi," pleaded Nita, "stop it. He just hasn't been in the country a lot in the past year, but he phoned often. I know that if I'd needed anything he would immediately have given me whatever I asked for. There are worse people than him, believe me." Her lips tightened.

Theo's eyes softened. "That goes for you, too," said Nita to Gabriel, who now stood up. "Without the two of you and . . . without him," she said, looking at Michael, "I wouldn't have—"

"She doesn't have many friends," said Gabriel apologetically, looking into Michael's eyes. "Nita didn't grow up here in the normal way.

She studied in New York, and her best friend lives in Paris. That's how it goes with successful, gifted musicians. A lot of acquaintances, but not many close friends. It's the same with my brother and me. We're not really rooted here. We only look like local heroes," he said with a chuckle. "We're actually complete cosmopolitans. Ask Nita. When she was small, maybe about five, she already had a little cello. She longed to be like all the other children, but she never felt like one of them. And she was born here!"

"Nita's told us about your baby," said Theo. "It's a strange story." He looked at him curiously. "It's like a fairy tale . . . Strange, a baby. My children are grown."

Gabriel gave him a skeptical look.

"It's true that their mothers brought them up," he said apologetically. "But it's a nice story. Nita's told us about the way the two of you have arranged things," he said, coughing with embarrassment. "Gabi doesn't have any children," he suddenly announced, as if this explained something. "He's more attached to Nita's baby than I am," he admitted with effort. Nita stood close to the door that opened into the living room. "Nita is the common denominator," added Theo with a half smile. "Our father, too, he loved Nita more than the rest of us, except maybe for our mother. And Gabi, too." He kept pacing as he talked. Now he was standing close to Nita, and he looked at her affectionately and rumpled her hair. "Are you going to work now?" he asked Michael.

Michael nodded and seized the door handle. "Do you want the little one to stay here with Aliza?" Michael asked Nita. "I could take Aliza and the babies to her house, if that would suit you better."

"Whatever you say. You decide."

"Maybe you could talk to that—what's his name, Balilty?" asked Theo.

"Leave him alone, Theo. It's better if they don't know about my connection with him," said Nita warningly.

"Whatever you say," said Theo, raising his arms and spreading them. "What will be, will be."

4

The Way of the World Makes Sense

"What, you've never been on a case like this?" said Balilty, surprised. "I was sure you were on the case of the clocks that were stolen from the Islamic Museum. Never mind, look at this." He picked up a padded yellow envelope and took out some photographs, shuffled through them rapidly as if they were a deck of cards, and put two before Michael Ohayon, who examined the façade of a large, imposing apartment building with bronze handles on its great doors and a broad sidewalk in front of it. "That's somewhere abroad, in Europe," he guessed. "Switzerland?"

"Zurich," said Balilty. The other photograph was of an interior, showing mailboxes, and a row of doorbells with the names of the tenants visible. One name was circled in red.

Balilty breathed heavily as he leaned over the photograph from the other side of the desk, pushing his paunch against the metal frame. They were in the small office that until recently had been used by the secretary of Emanuel Shorer, chief of the Department of Investigations and Crime Fighting, an office that had once been Michael's. A plastered wall separated this room, now Balilty's, from the one allocated to Michael on his return from his study leave. Michael wondered how he would ever be able to keep anything from Intelligence Office Balilty's sharp senses at such close quarters. Although the wall provided good insulation against noise, and Michael couldn't even hear Balilty's telephone ringing, the physical proximity increased his sense of being besieged, that his life would now be an open book and that Balilty, and after him everyone else, would be able to rummage in it whenever he felt like it.

"Here, a place like this for instance, what do you think is in there?"

asked Balilty, leaning back in his chair. "On the face of it, what do we have here? An art gallery. Solid, respectable, legal, a corporation representing artists and agents. Do you want to look at paintings you might buy? All you have to do is phone and make an appointment. Nobody gets in here without an appointment. They seat you in a big, empty room. Maybe it has a chair and an armchair and a large easel to hold the painting on view. You sit down in comfort, maybe they even give you a cup of tea or coffee, or a drink, and, just like that, you're a client." He took a toothpick out of his shirt pocket, stuck it between his teeth, and took it out again as he went on talking: "But there are clients and clients, and paintings and paintings. Over the counter and under the counter."

Michael looked at the other photographs lying outside the envelope, and put them down one after the other in front of him. He arranged them in a semicircle, from right to left. First an enlargement of a house door, with a red circle around the broken lock, and next to it a photograph of a room turned upside down. Then a photo of an empty armchair. He looked at the chalk outline drawn by the forensics people around this chair, in which the body of Felix van Gelden had been found. A piece of rope, with which they had apparently tied his hands, was still dangling from the slender wooden arm of the chair. He looked at photographs of a rumpled double bed and of a wardrobe before whose open doors lay piles of clothes, shoes, an old camera, and photograph albums. Next was a close-up of overturned drawers, and then a photograph of a heavy, ornate gilt frame. Emptied of its painting, it had been thrown into a corner of the room.

"A place like this is ideal for paintings that aren't Rembrandts," said Balilty knowledgeably as he waved the photo of the Zurich building. "There are people who come there with special requests. Let's say, someone who wants a certain seventeenth-century Dutch painting owned by a certain van Gelden in Jerusalem who doesn't want to sell. They can do something for him. He doesn't have to go into detail, all he has to do is pay, a lot, to get what he wants. They get it for him and deliver it to him, and afterward he can keep it in some secret room, some cellar—what do I know? Until things cool off."

"But no museum would buy it even after things cool off. The word must circulate among all the experts that the picture has been stolen," said Michael.

"Don't be so sure! The curator of the Tel Aviv Museum told me yesterday that even in museums they're not all that fussy. They can buy a painting in pretended or in genuine innocence, and keep it in their basements. Museum curators are only human." Balilty snickered. "They don't want to miss the opportunity of a coup. They're compulsive collectors, too, don't forget. And with the legitimization of the public good on top of it. And the private collectors! That's a world in itself. It's not even as if they want to show the painting to anyone. They're a breed apart. People who have to have something for it to be theirs. We're talking about people who have castles in Switzerland or someplace like that, summer houses in the country, palaces. They're a breed apart. They relate to these things like . . . I don't know. . . . It's not about money, or making an impression. . . . I don't entirely understand it," he confessed.

"It really is a strange business," Michael murmured. "You have to think about it to understand it."

"What's there to understand?" protested Balilty. "Actually it's quite simple. Covetousness, greed, lust for power—everything that holds for money or ordinary property applies here too," he said contemptuously. "The fact that it's about paintings, about art, makes you think that more noble impulses are involved, but that's not so. It only seems that the motivation is more exalted. But it's just plain covetousness and greed, in an area that we're in awe of. All you have to do is substitute the word 'painting'—and seventeenth-century besides—for the word, say, 'diamonds,' and you'll know what's what."

"I don't see it that way," said Michael. "You yourself said that they don't make a profit on it. It's something more complex. It's connected with a love of beauty, with a private communion with beauty, with the wish to be close to beauty, in immediate contact with it, almost to incorporate it. Precisely the secrecy is what makes ownership perfect. It's really very complicated. I imagine the psychologists have a lot to say about it," he said, his voice dying down.

Balilty looked skeptical. Michael lit a cigarette and sensed that the conversation was turning into a cautious dance around the subject they weren't talking about, were avoiding talking about. Tzilla had met him at the entrance to the building. For the past two days they had been wondering what to do about Balilty. "We're not going to be able to keep the secret," she said. "I've already had calls. They want to know how Nita's taking it. 'At the Child Welfare Bureau we attach great importance to the foster mother's mental health,'" she quoted sarcastically, making a face. "You'd better be prepared for more visits from them," she warned. "They're 'at a loss,' the whole thing is 'unprecedented.' That's what they said."

"Any news about the mother? Is there any progress?" he asked anxiously.

"Not a thing," said Tzilla. "They don't have any leads on the mother because the baby isn't a newborn, and they don't know where and when she was born. Trying to track her down through the past two months' birth registrations all over the country is like trying to find a needle in a haystack. But that's what they're doing now. Don't underestimate Malka, she isn't as backward as she looks. She's very thorough."

"She could have given birth at home. It doesn't have to be at a hospital," said Michael.

"Maybe," said Tzilla doubtfully. "And maybe the mother has left Israel," she added. "Maybe she's a Bedouin or Arab woman who gave birth in her village. Sometimes their babies are very light-skinned. Maybe the father's a Jew. Anyway, I wouldn't try to keep it a secret from Balilty."

"What does Eli say about it? Have you told him?" He presumed that she had told her husband. During the years the three of them had worked together, Michael had been a witness to the vicissitudes of their relationship, from Tzilla's discreet and persistent courting of Eli to their marriage and the births of their two children. He wasn't afraid of any disloyalty on Eli's part. Only embarrassment, a kind of shame at the very wish to keep the baby, prevented him from speaking of it directly.

"He thinks so too," said Tzilla, lowering her eyes.

"What?"

"That you should trust Balilty."

"With his mouth," Michael reflected aloud.

"I've seen him behave discreetly. Besides, you have no choice," said

Tzilla. "It'll only complicate things for you. He'll find out anyway. He always does in the end."

Again he felt the knot in his stomach, a quivering knot for which there was no objective justification. Even if Balilty did find out about the baby and his setup with Nita, he would never go to the Child Welfare Bureau and tell them that the two of them weren't really living together. What, then, was he afraid of? The mere fact of his knowing, he said to himself as he looked out the window and took a drag on the cigarette. Of a heavy boot intruding on his private vulnerabilities. Balilty would mock him for his sentimentality. Of being ridiculed, being thought a fool—that's what you're afraid of, he said to himself.

Suddenly he was overwhelmed with dread at the thought of the external world impinging on his privacy: the baby's face, her cheeks that were filling out, her big eyes watching him as he fed her, held her up in the air. In the past couple of days he had even recognized something, a kind of spasm of the lips, which but for the fact that Nita insisted it was too early, he would have been sure was a smile. If it weren't for the connection with Nita, he wouldn't have had to expose himself like this. But without the connection with Nita, he wouldn't have passed the foster family test. He would talk to Balilty, he decided as Tzilla patted his arm, looked over her shoulder, and said: "I have to run. They'll kill me if I'm late." She began striding rapidly, the rubber soles of her running shoes squeaking with every step. She was hurrying to an SIT meeting on a case that had been making headlines for the past six weeks. A couple found strangled in their car.

And now, tipping his ash into the dregs of his coffee, Michael decided yet again to speak to Balilty, and maybe he would even enlist his help. In the end the mother would be found. It was impossible to hide the disappearance of a baby. Unless you left the country, died, or changed your name.

"Yes," Balilty mused. "But it's not a question of money, and they don't even collect paintings as investments." He suddenly roused himself. "So what are we talking about? The psychology of collectors? Is that what you wanted to talk to me about?"

Balilty's face was expressionless, as if he were defending himself in advance against manipulation. There was no point in evading the issue any longer. Suddenly it was quite clear that he knew. Like the heads of two Bedouin clans putting off a decisive discussion with the help of traditional rituals, they sat on either side of the desk, the cups of coffee in front of them.

"You're working with Interpol," said Michael, trying to drag the moment out.

Balilty shrugged his shoulders. "There isn't much we can do at this end. I need information from Europe, that's quite obvious."

"I haven't seen you so pessimistic about a case in a long time," remarked Michael. Their tone was relaxed, as if there was nothing urgent on the agenda.

"What can I do from here?" said Danny Balilty dismissively, turning the coffee cup in his big hand and examining its contents like a fortune teller intent on reading the dregs. "Obviously there are things that don't make sense. Mainly the fact that they didn't break in when van Gelden wasn't home. That's what sticks out most. He was a man with regular habits, they could have done it without killing him. It's very rare for professionals of this kind to get involved with murder. And it's not as if it was for a Picasso."

"But there was no intention to murder him. It was an accident. A work accident."

"I'm not so sure. They would have avoided the accident if they'd broken in when he wasn't home. Forensics said that whoever removed the picture from the frame was a professional, someone who knew exactly what he was doing. Not even a thread of the canvas was left on the frame. It wasn't the original frame, otherwise they would have taken that, too. Van Gelden hid it through the whole war. That picture was his fortune. He and his wife and the elder son, who was born during the war, were hiding in some village in Holland. They had the painting with them. It had been in the family for three or four generations. For him it was like . . . like the Torah curtain that an old fleeing Jew would have rescued from the synagogue in his town in Poland. The thieves were very careful when they removed it from the frame. They removed the lock from the door only when they were already inside. Although they took cash and jewelry, and turned the house upside down—pulled out all the papers, emptied out the drawers, threw the books off the shelves—

it's quite clear that all that was a diversion. The only fingerprints we have belong to people with a legitimate reason to be there. The sons, the daughter, the cleaning woman. I've already alerted all the art dealers and experts in the country, and there isn't even the hint of a lead. Nothing. *Nada*. Every one of them's got an alibi, the same alibi. Gozlan's grandson had a bar mitzvah," he said, snickering gloomily, "and all of them were there, every last one of them. None of them has heard anything. They're making inquiries for me, but one dealer who owes me something has already assured me that it was an outside, a foreign job. And if that's so, there's not much I can do about it except talk to our contact in Europe who works with the Swiss and with Interpol."

Michael was silent.

"Why are you looking at me like that with those eyes of yours, as if I was some suspect?" said Balilty indignantly. "What's the matter? Is there something wrong with what I've just said?"

Michael was silent.

"Is there something you want to ask me?" Balilty demanded.

Michael wanted to speak, but he cupped his chin in his hand and waited. His mouth was dry. He wanted to speak, but he couldn't. He wanted to speak simply, to tell Balilty about the baby, but suddenly the place seemed wrong. The air in the room was heavy. On the desk between them stood the two coffee cups. A fly made its way from one to the other buzzing loudly, and outside the window, open to the fresh autumn air, birds chirped. Everything seemed ready for him to speak, but the words wouldn't come.

Balilty folded his arms and looked at him. The two of them sat there as if playing out a scenario Michael himself had written. Years ago, Michael had taught Balilty the power of silence. He himself had honed and perfected Shorer's theory about the rhythm of silences and the fruits of patience. Victory would come to whomever was able to stand the silence. He could see the wheels turning in Danny Balilty's head and hear the inner voice whispering to him to keep quiet. "People," Michael used to tell him when they worked together, "can't stand long silences. On the whole, they want to be liked. Even psychopaths, or most of them. If you keep quiet long enough they finally say something, to make you talk to them again." Balilty looked into his eyes and kept quiet. If it hadn't been for the fear paralyzing him, Michael would have smiled.

Balilty broke first. "I thought we were friends," he said, offended. "But I see you don't trust me."

"It's not a question of trust," said Michael, quickly finding his voice, "and you know that I'm here in order to tell you something. But your speed simply takes my breath away . . ." he added admiringly. "You've been on the case for only two days, and you already know."

"Oh, please," said Balilty dismissively, "I've already known about that business of yours for ages." He looked embarrassed, and not in the least mocking.

"Even before the van Gelden murder?" exclaimed Michael, astonished.

"Naturally."

"What, have you been following me?"

"Come on! I found out purely by chance."

"What do you mean, by chance?" Michael was alarmed. "Have people here been talking about it? Does everybody know? If it gets to the Child Welfare, if they find out that we, that Nita and I aren't really . . ."

"Aren't really?" repeated Balilty, surprised. "What do you mean, aren't really?"

"Nita and I . . . We . . . there's nothing between us." Michael squirmed and felt himself blushing. "That's to say, not what you might think." With every word he felt more awkward. He rebuked himself silently: Where's your cunning? Who asked you if there was anything between you and her? Since when have you been in the habit of volunteering information about your love life? What do you care what they think? In any event, you can't explain to him about the baby. What can you say to him about it? Do you want to tell him about the second chance? About your fantasy of this time doing everything differently?

An amused smile appeared at the corners of Balilty's lips, and he said: "I don't remember dropping any hints. I don't know what there is between you, I just know that you're living with her—"

"That's not quite right," said Michael, with every word feeling himself sinking deeper into the trap he had set for himself.

"And that you've got her baby, and nobody knows who its father is," said Balilty nonchalantly. "As well as the baby you found, which you're fostering, I understand."

"Are people talking about it? Does everybody know?" How he hated himself for this question.

"Nobody knows except me," Balilty assured him. "And I haven't told anybody."

"And how do you know?"

"Completely by chance. I told you, this time it was purely by chance."

Michael raised his eyebrows.

"What does it matter?" said Balilty, evidently enjoying Michael's bewilderment.

"Balilty," warned Michael.

"The pediatrician? Who came to see you after the holiday?"

Michael nodded.

"His wife?"

"Well?"

"She's my sister-in-law's cousin."

"So?"

"He met you once at our place. Or she did, one of them, I don't remember which one. Anyway, he knows that we work together. He made me promise not to mention it to you or to anyone else, but he was curious about what was happening with the baby. He thought that I knew all about it because he thought we were friends. And after he found out that it wasn't so, that I didn't know, he was sorry he told me!"

"I could kill him," whispered Michael.

"You're lucky it's me. That I'm the only one who knows," said Balilty with a pious look. "No one will ever find out from me."

"Her baby," said Michael, "isn't mine. I'm not his father." The words made him feel like a traitor.

Balilty was silent.

"I tell you, somebody else is his father," he pleaded against his will. "Why should I lie?"

"Okay, okay. Just tell me what it's all about."

Michael told him about finding the cardboard box, about the Child Welfare Bureau, about the Social Services Department, about Nita.

Balilty listened attentively. "That's it? That's the whole story?" he asked in the end, as Michael took another cigarette from the pack. Michael nodded. "Now you know everything," he said, and he examined himself to see if he felt relieved. But the sense of oppression was still there, and maybe it was even stronger than before.

"Why does everything always have to be so complicated with you?" complained Balilty. "Here's a woman. It's so simple. I've seen her. She's young, successful, pretty, nice, healthy—everything you could wish for. You want a baby, you have a baby. Why does she have to have a child by someone else and you have to bring a baby in from the street? How do you manage to complicate things to such an extent? You could have . . . any woman you want. Women are crazy about you. Why does it have to be like this?"

Michael lowered his eyes. "Good question," he said finally.

"I won't tell anyone," said Balilty, and he put his hand on his heart. "No one will hear about it from me," he declared solemnly, "but it's impossible to keep things like this secret for long. And you know as well as I do that you can't bring up a baby by yourself. Forgive me for saying so."

"Why not?" demanded Michael, and he pressed his hand against the knot in his stomach.

Balilty's light little eyes opened wide in surprise mingled with pity. "Because the moment you're put on a case," he said simply, "never mind what case, you won't have a minute to spare, you'll be on call twenty-four hours a day. A baby, as you certainly know, is a full-time job. Don't we both know it? Didn't you bring up Yuval? Don't we remember how he used to wait and wait for you?"

"Maybe now it'll be different," mumbled Michael.

Balilty sighed. "The opposite. It's the opposite of what it should be."

Michael felt like a scolded child. The conversation frightened him because of things he hadn't been prepared for. He could find no sign that Balilty was mocking him, and he would have preferred his mockery to this.

"At our age," said Balilty, musing aloud and crushing the toothpick with his fingers, "we've learned that not everything everybody else does is nonsense. That's to say, sometimes the simple, conventional things are the logical way to go. It's the opposite: In other words, first you love a woman—you find a suitable woman—and then you have and bring up a baby. That's the proper order of things. It's logical. It's the way of the world, and it makes sense, and you know it."

Michael bit his lips and nodded. "Okay, we'll see, we'll see what happens," he said to the air, and he looked out the open window, heard the chirping of the birds, the buzzing of the flies, smelled the smell of autumn.

"How did she take it? The woman? The news of her father?" Balilty asked, businesslike.

Michael spread his hands. "Hard, but you can't really tell."

"They're quite close, she and her brothers," said Balilty, and he pulled a big color photograph out of his desk drawer. "Here's the painting. Have you ever seen it? Look. This is a photograph van Gelden received from a museum in Holland that sent an expert to photograph it. It took us hours to find this, it was with a lot of other photographs in the mess they made of the house."

The skull on the pile of books gleamed in the golden light. At the bottom right corner was a small, reddish wooden flute. The books were piled untidily on top of one another, and on the binding of the bottom one there were Gothic letters. The faded gold edges of the two books above it were meticulously painted. The top book was open, and it looked as if it was about to fall and topple the whole stack. Between the flute and the pink-gray skull floated the narrow face of a woman whose copper-colored hair fell to her shoulders. One of her shoulders was exposed and a radiant white light shone from it. This face, Michael thought, intensified the effect of the skull as something dry and inanimate. "*Vanitas*," he said aloud. "A still life."

"Half a million dollars and uninsured," remarked Balilty.

"Uninsured?"

"Yes. Old van Gelden refused to take the necessary precautions—a steel security door, bars on the windows. So no one would insure the painting. He lived there in that old house in Rehavia with an ordinary wooden door, two simple locks, one above the other, two turns each. No burglar alarm. He didn't believe in banks, his son said, he kept his money at home, foreign currency, and he didn't believe in steel doors, either. He was a character, the old man. Didn't you know him?"

Michael shook his head.

Balilty glanced at his watch. "I'm waiting for a call from Switzerland," he explained. "But it's still too early, only two days have passed. If the thieves have left Israel they may not even have arrived anywhere yet. It wouldn't be hard to get the painting out of the country in a suitcase or a shoulder bag."

"I may have seen him once, years ago, in his music shop. Yuval needed music for his guitar. Later he stopped playing it, just as he stopped playing the recorder. I barely remember what van Gelden looked like. Only that he was tall."

"I knew him well," announced Balilty, blinking with the effort to sound matter-of-fact and conceal his pride. "I met him years ago, at the lodge."

"What lodge?"

"You know, the lodge," said Balilty, coughing. "The Masonic lodge. He was a Master Mason. I joined twenty years ago, because of my father. I first went to make my father happy, and after he died I just stayed on. I saw van Gelden there regularly."

"I didn't know the Masons exist here at all, and that you were a member." Michael was astonished.

"No, you didn't know," agreed Balilty. "Not that it's such a big secret. I don't go around talking about it. But I don't keep it a secret."

"Twenty years?"

"Nineteen, nearly twenty."

"I . . . for me, the Masons, even though I know they're still active in England and America, they seem to me like something legendary. Something that came to an end after Alexandre Dumas, or after Mozart."

"What does Mozart have to do with it?" asked Balilty.

"He was a Mason two hundred years ago in Vienna. Do you know *The Magic Flute*?"

"I've heard of it," said Balilty, embarrassed, "but the organization has changed a lot in two hundred years."

"Since when has it existed in Israel?"

"Oh, since the British Mandate. The British brought it here. There are a number of lodges in Jerusalem."

"And it still exists? Actively? And do young people still join?"

"Of *course* it's alive," said Balilty. "And there are quite a few of my age. We meet once a month, like clockwork."

"And is there still a guard and all that stuff? Masks? And robes and aprons and medals?"

"There's a guard," said Balilty seriously, with a certain reserve, "and he doesn't let just anyone in from the street. He looks through the peephole, and if he can't identify you have to say the password. There aren't any masks, of course not, or robes either, but there's a special garment, a kind of apron worn by the officers, by the president of the lodge. Van Gelden was president two years ago. And we have a skull, too," he said, suddenly chuckling. "On a pedestal. To remind us always of who we are and where we're going. Look, if you're interested, if you're thinking of coming to see, of joining, I can bring you to a meeting as a guest. The last Police Commissioner himself belonged. A lot of members are professors, highly educated people, people with important public positions, we have a judge in our lodge, scientists. Anyway, that's how I met van Gelden. I sometimes went into his shop, too, to consult him about Sigi. You know what a beautiful voice she had. I wanted her to do something with it. She had a voice like my mother's. I used to ask his advice. We got her singing lessons, to learn to read music, all that, but nothing came of it. His shop was something special."

"All I remember is piles of stuff and strange musical instruments."

"He knew exactly where everything was," said Balilty. "He never forgot a thing. He looked like an oddball, but he had his feet firmly on the ground. And if there was anything he didn't know, his assistant, that scarecrow Herzl Cohen, knew."

"What assistant?"

"He had an assistant, in the shop. His right hand. He knew everything. Ask your girlfriend."

Michael thought of Nita's insistence about finding Herzl, but something prevented him from mentioning it now. "And why isn't he in the picture, this assistant?"

"Now? Do you mean where is he? Actually, we're looking for him."

"And did you meet socially, too? Outside the lodge? With van Gelden? Did you ever go to his house?"

Balilty chuckled. "That's not the way things work in the Masons.

In this case there are a couple of things that don't make sense," he said thoughtfully. "For example, the fact that he never had an appointment with the dentist at all." Balilty stared at the dregs sticking to the sides of his cup. "Van Gelden didn't have an appointment, but he told his children that he had one. So where was he? Who did he meet instead of going to the dentist? I asked the children where he could have gone. They didn't know so much about him. Not even Gabriel, the younger son, who was the closest to him."

"Where do you think he was?" asked Michael. His fingertips tingled as if his hand had gone to sleep.

Balilty shrugged. "I have no idea," he said with a smile. "And I have no idea what it's all about. I would have thought that a man his age, a man like him, whose children are public figures, they would have more known about him. But he was the one who knew everything about everyone else. Like in the shop. He was the only one who knew exactly where everything was. You always had to wait for him, to ask him, because that was the way he wanted it, to keep control. He may have been a Dutchman, but he had the soul of a German Jew. You know the kind, they were always so rational and unprejudiced. But they wouldn't do business with the Germans, he and his Herzl, who looks like a scarecrow, with his hair standing up like this." Balilty rolled up a sheet of paper and put it on his head for a moment. "He disappeared some time ago. I don't know what they quarreled about after forty years. None of the children knows, either. I told you, we're looking for him now. Maybe he knows something."

"What could he know? The shop's been closed for the past six months."

"Ask the daughter. He was very thick with the family. He even had a key to house."

"So he's a possible suspect. He could easily have been in on it, the painting and everything," said Michael, surprised.

"I told you, nobody knows where he is!" protested Balilty. "And the van Geldens say that it's out of the question. You could rely on him completely. And besides, he's half crazy. Money and paintings mean nothing to him. They dismiss it out of hand. And don't tell me that wonders will never cease. As I've told you, I'm looking for him anyway."

"What time exactly did van Gelden die? What does the pathologist say?"

"The pathologist puts it in the afternoon—four o'clock, half past four, five, six, no later than seven."

Michael hesitated. In a certain sense, the very question would be a betrayal. "Where were they at that time, his children?"

"You know where she was," said Balilty, puffing out his lips. "At the hairdresser."

"And the others?"

Balilty narrowed his eyes, and he pressed the cigarette lighter and examined the flame. "Why get into it?" he asked reluctantly, raising his eyes and looking at Michael. "You don't have to. Do you really want to?"

Michael shrugged.

"Theo van Gelden is the number-one fucker in town, if you'll excuse the expression. That afternoon he had a date with a woman of fifty and a girl of nineteen. Both of them he . . ." The gesture of his hand and elbow left no doubt as to the nature of Theo van Gelden's activities with the women in question. "And his brother, his brother is something else again." Balilty's face clouded over.

"He didn't want to say anything," said Michael indiscreetly.

"He didn't want to say anything because he didn't want his brother and sister to know that he had a meeting with his father's lawyer. Neither of them, neither he nor the lawyer, is willing to say what it was about. For the time being I don't have a way to force them."

"There's a certain Scotsman . . ." said Michael.

Balilty tapped the desk. "I've heard of him. McBrady is his name," he said. "I heard about him on the first night, but it turns out that he's in a hospital in Edinburgh. He's diabetic and has had a leg amputated. He's not interested in paintings at the moment. What can I tell you? It's better to be young and healthy than old and sick. Even if you've got money."

"So what do you think the chances are of solving the case?"

"Not good," admitted Balilty. "However much I'd like to, what with the lodge and everything. But if it's a foreign job, there isn't much chance. Unless something unforeseen happens. As you often used to say, 'Wonders will never cease.' Something might happen."

Michael looked at his watch. "I have to go," he said uncomfortably. "I promised to take —"

"Look at you," said Balilty with a laugh. "You've become a family man overnight."

"I have to relieve the babysitter early today." He felt himself blushing as he walked to the door. Balilty stood up and hurried to open it. He looked up and down the corridor, took Michael by the arm, and conspiratorially asked him: "Haven't you told Shorer anything?"

"Not a word," said Michael, appalled. "And don't you say anything to him!"

"Me?" exclaimed the offended Balilty. "I only wanted to know if you'd told him. I thought he knew everything about you." The gratification in his smile was unmistakable.

The babysitter closed the front door behind her as he was changing Ido's diaper. Ido was kicking his legs and cooing happily. The doorbell rang. Michael quickly pressed the adhesive strips together and, holding Ido in his arms, opened the door to Nurse Nehama, who was panting as she looked at him in surprise. "I spoke to the babysitter on the phone only half an hour ago. Didn't she tell you?" He almost choked with panic. With difficulty he stopped himself from asking her if she had come to take Noa away. He opened the door wider and with an effort smiled at her. "You look pale," she said, concerned, as she sank into the same armchair in which she had sat on the previous visit. "It must be hard for you," she added with evident sympathy. "It's a terrible thing that happened to you."

Michael sat down on the chair next to hers and seated Ido on his lap. Fascinated by the nurse's long necklace, Ido tried to reach it. Nehama held out her arms. "Do you want Nehama?" she cooed. "Come to Nehama," she said, removing the necklace and the chain from which her glasses dangled. Ido's eyes followed the necklace, which she put on the table. He squirmed in her arms as he tried to grab hold of the green beads. Nehama returned him to Michael's lap.

"Noa's just fallen asleep," he said, finally finding his voice.

"How is she?" asked the nurse, wriggling her shoulders and rubbing the back of her neck as if to relieve tension. Then she again put on her necklace and chain.

"I think she's all right," said Michael, and he rebuked himself for the paralysis that had overtaken him. "I don't think what's happened has affected her any," he ventured.

"We have no way of knowing how they feel," stated Nurse Nehama. "They don't tell us anything," she said, winking and chuckling. "The question is only if her behavior has changed. Is she eating well? Sleeping? Is she calm?" Michael nodded, but he immediately realized that this would not be enough.

"Come and see," he said, and he stood up with Ido in his arms. "She looks wonderful to me," he said persuasively from the doorway. He tried to see the tiny room, in which there wasn't even space for two cribs, through Nurse Nehama's eyes.

"Sleeping, my eye!" Nehama's laughter rang out. "She's wide awake! Look at her." The baby was lying on her back, cooing at the musical rabbit dangling from the roof of the stroller. The nurse pulled the string. At the sound of the first notes of Brahms's *Lullaby*, the baby waved her arms. Nurse Nehama exclaimed admiringly: "How she's developed in the two weeks I haven't seen her! She's grown so much and she's calm and alert. Really, it's as if nothing had happened to her. It's a pity I can't see the mother. Aren't they sitting *shiva* here?" she inquired sharply.

Michael muttered unintelligibly. Finally he said: "We're doing our best. We didn't want all that commotion here. You know her brothers are very—"

"Yes, I can imagine," said the nurse respectfully. There you are, he reassured himself, she's impressed by important people. But his body refused to quiet down, and his knees shook.

"I'll tell you the truth," she said, and he stopped breathing. "This isn't an official visit. We just thought, in the office, that you might need help." She looked around. "Advice, or something like that. In another couple of days the Child Welfare Bureau inspector will come, and she's the one who'll make the decision. And how is Miss van Gelden feeling? We can send her a psychologist if the police don't —"

"She's fine," Michael assured her. "She's even playing the cello again. Everything's as usual," he said, and he felt he had gone too far. "Relatively speaking, that is," he quickly added. "Of course it's very hard for her. The police will probably send her a psychologist.

They've already spoken to her about it." He stared at the lamp. How hard exactly should Nita be taking her father's murder both in order to appear normal and in order not to give them a reason to take the baby away? He put Ido down on the carpet and picked Noa up.

"We thought that if it was difficult for you, maybe you would prefer to give her up—"

"Certainly not!" cried Michael, alarmed at the force of his cry. "Look," he said, and he gripped Nurse Nehama by the arm. "For us she's a consolation, a great joy, a real help. It would shatter us if they took her away from us now." He looked into her eyes, which narrowed to two slits. "It would really shatter us. Especially Nita. I know you understand me, I can sense that you feel for us," he said. He made his tone as desperate as he could and again looked deeply into the dull pale green of her eyes.

Nurse Nehama opened her eyes wide. "I'm glad you feel like that," she said, and she turned to leave the room, drawing herself up to her full height with a dignified air. "It's true, I do feel a lot of sympathy for you and your case. I promised you that everything would be all right, didn't I? I'm still promising you that, except that it doesn't only depend on me. The inspector will be here in a day or two. The baby is really adorable. There shouldn't be any problems."

"We're really attached to her, we want to take care of her," pleaded Michael, and he felt his face burning.

"All we can do is hope for the best, as they say," said Nurse Nehama. "I believe that things usually work out for the best for all concerned," she concluded, and she made for the door. "We'll be in touch," she promised reassuringly. She set the straps of her bag firmly on her shoulder and stretched her lips into a bright, professional smile.

Serves you right, he said to himself as he dressed Ido and put him in his carrier. Serves you right, he repeated as he got Noa ready to go out. When you want something, anything, so much, you become easy prey to anyone. Anyone can intrude on you now. Balilty and Nurse Nehama are only the beginning. What do I actually want? "What do I actually want?" he said aloud to Noa as he fastened the snaps of her blue corduroy outfit. She looked at him gravely with eyes that seemed to have grown bigger and darker during the past few days. They were now blue-brown. Suddenly she smiled. This wasn't the automatic spasm of parted lips he had seen the week before, but a real, gum-showing smile that also involved the eyes, which never left his face.

A second passed before he said: "You're smiling at me, you already know me." His eyes were moist as he smiled back at her. "I have to write it down," he announced as he laid her in the carrier that he removed from the stroller. "I have to write down that today, on the twentieth? The twenty-first? Of September nineteen ninety-four, at the age of, let's say, six weeks, you smiled a real smile for the first time." He carried both babies to the door. "Come on," he said solemnly, "let's go tell Nita that you smiled at me. Maybe you'll smile at her, too."

He went into the concert hall through the artists' entrance, pushing the heavy wooden door with his shoulder, since he was holding Ido's baby seat in one hand and, in the other, Noa's carrier, at the foot of which was stuffed a bag holding diapers, bottles, and other baby equipment. He sat down in the second row, at the end closest to the doors of the half-dark hall, and set the portable baby seat and the carrier down on either side of him. Then he looked at the stage. The rehearsal should have been over a few minutes ago, but it seemed to be in full swing. On the seats around him various instrument cases were scattered, on the seat in front of him a gaping violin case, with photographs pasted on the inside of the lid and a semitransparent envelope of spare strings in a corner of the space intended for the instrument. A light jacket had been casually thrown over the seat behind him, with an instrument case visible beneath it. The orchestra was on the stage at full strength. Some of the musicians had placed their instrument cases under their chairs, and others had left them at the foot of the stage.

Facing the orchestra and seated on the edge of a tall, narrow stool sat Theo van Gelden, who now stamped his foot and clapped his hands. "Ladies and gentlemen," he cried out. "We're not leaving until the syncopations are right." A murmur of protest arose from the back of the stage. The regular concertmaster, a gray-haired man with his glasses pushed up to the top of his high forehead, tapped his bow on the belly of his violin. "Ladies and gentlemen," he echoed, "we can't finish until the radio people are finished with their tests. But we'll start late tomorrow." The grumbling did not die down, and one very young man holding a clarinet came up to Theo, turned to the orchestra, and shouted: "Why are you behaving like timid bureaucrats?" A violinist in the back row said something and everyone around him laughed. "Listen to the greenhorn!" cried a trumpet player from the rear. "We were like that, too, once." Again laughter broke out.

Nita shaded her eyes, looked into the hall, and waved to Michael. She and Gabriel were sitting at the front of the stage, very close to Theo. From the distance the bottom half of her body in the full skirt pushed in by the cello looked like a kind of blue hill. Now, as he looked at her, she seemed very beautiful, absolutely radiant. For a moment he felt a breath of the scent of the nape of her neck. Two days before, when they had met in the doorway to her kitchen, he had suddenly kissed her. Her lips were soft, and her total submission had taken him by surprise. Nita had the habit of touching those nearby. From that moment on she touched him all the time, small, gentle touches. When she looked at him the next morning her face was illuminated by a tender, yielding light, and the joyful signals of her body—especially coming after Avigail's reserve—held great promise. She could be a home for him, he thought now in happy surprise, and the knowledge that they were so close to each other filled him with pride.

Gabriel held his violin with his shoulder and cheek as he rubbed his bow with rosin. Someone bumped into the cello case lying between Gabriel and Nita. "May I take this away from here?" he asked loudly. When Nita nodded he picked it up and carried it off the stage. Theo looked impatiently at his brother. Gabriel put the rosin away in the case under his chair. The concertmaster stood next to Theo, looking at him expectantly. Theo said: "Just a minute, Avigdor."

"From the beginning?" asked the concertmaster, and though Michael tried hard, he could make out only a mumble from Theo, who took off the jacket draped over his shoulders and laid it at his feet.

"Bar one," called the concertmaster. "What, from the beginning?"

protested the woman standing behind the timpani. "Number one," said Theo, raising his hands. "Four bars *tutti,* and then the cello solo. We'll do the whole first movement, and then we'll see."

Two technicians dragged cables down the hall and stopped at the foot of the stage. Michael turned his head. At the end of the hall, above the last row of seats in the balcony, there was a light on behind a big glass window. Looking as if they were creatures in an aquarium, three figures moved silently in the broadcast booth, signaling at the technicians down below. The latter went down on their knees and pulled cables under the stage. Theo van Gelden brought his arms down and the entire orchestra played the opening notes. With the first loud sound Ido's head jerked in the baby seat, his eyes opening and his lips parting. Michael quickly put one hand on his cheek, while with the other he searched the seat for the pacifier, fished it out, and pushed it into the child's mouth. Ido's body relaxed, but his eyes remained wide open. He seemed to be listening intently to the entrance of the cello, which now began to play its opening solo.

Theo stopped Nita after a few bars. "What does Brahms write here?" he asked rhetorically. 'In the style of a recitative, but always in tempo.' Not so freely, Nita, please. From the beginning!" He clapped his hands and the orchestra played the first bars again. Nita, her lips tight, repeated the notes she had been playing night and day for the past couple of weeks, twenty-two bars in all, at the end of which—Michael knew, she never stopped talking about it—there was a sustained *f* that descended to *e.* And then the four horns and a clarinet entered, and Theo stopped them after two bars. Noa moved in her carrier. Michael put his hand on her stomach. Theo called out: "Once again, cello solo just from the *f,* from the *f* to the *e,* come in again."

This time he let them play the complete phrase without interruption. Gabriel held his bow above the violin, let it glide over the strings, and hinted at the theme with a warm, clear tone. This was the first time Michael had heard him play. Nita had told him that Gabi could have had a big career as a solo violinist if he hadn't been overcome by what she called a "mania for historical performance on period instruments." He also remembered her saying: "He can't stand Brahms anymore. Only Baroque music exists for him. The nineteenth century makes him sick, but maybe on our behalf he'll come back to it now. After all, he agreed to play the Double Concerto with us."

Gabriel's violin sounded very beautiful to Michael, but it didn't tug at his heart the way Oistrakh did in the recording of the piece he had known for years. He rebuked himself for his inflexibility. Then the orchestra entered to present the theme in full. A few seconds later, Theo slapped his thigh and shouted: "No! No! No!"

The orchestra stopped playing. A technician climbed onto the stage, adjusted the microphones, and signaled the men in the booth.

"What do we have here?" asked Theo. He got off his high stool. "We have triplets in the violins and flutes. Instead of two quarter notes, you must squeeze in three! Please! I beg your pardon," he said, leaning toward the violas, "forgive me for sending you back to elementary school. Leave emotions and Brahms aside for a minute. I'm simply asking you to learn to count! Oboes, clarinets, trumpets, violas!" He paused for a moment and pointed at the wind instruments. "You're being drawn into playing the two quarters with the triplets instead of against them! It's two against three! Let me remind you again: Don't listen to the triplets in the flutes and violins. Don't listen! Avram," he said, bending toward the principal violist, "do you hear what I say? Don't listen to their triplets!" The principal violist nodded and turned to the group of musicians behind him to repeat the instruction. Theo went on: "Just count! Please count! Once more from fifty-seven, from the end of the violin and cello solos. And Gabriel, I want strong violin, not historical violin."

Gabriel said something. Theo got off his chair and stood before his brother. "Gabriel," said Theo, very loud and threatening. "What do you want me to do? What Leonard Bernstein did before his performance with Glenn Gould? Should I stand up in front of the audience and explain that I'm playing in your tempo against my own better judgment and the way I understand the music? Is that what you want?" There was something artificial about Theo's behavior, as if he had staged the scene in order to create an opportunity to tell the anecdote about Bernstein and Gould.

Again Gabriel said something.

"At the next rehearsal," pronounced Theo. Gabriel filled his cheeks with air, tugged at his beard, and let the air out noisily.

"Again!" cried Theo. They played a few bars, and then suddenly the big wooden doors were flung open, the lights went on in the hall, and everybody froze. With a stunned expression on his face, Theo turned his head toward the entrance and stared at the large group of people bursting in with television lights and cameras in the wake of a young woman leading by the arm the mayor of Jerusalem, Teddy Kollek. He entered the hall with a slow, heavy tread, dragging his feet and with his head down as if to make sure of his footing on the marble floor. Looking neither left nor right, his creased blue cotton jacket flapping, he carefully mounted the steps to a row of seats in the center of the hall. His arm was gripped by the young woman, who was talking loudly. He let himself down into a seat. After him came two cameramen and two men in gray overalls dragging huge television lights.

"Excuse me, what is this?" demanded Theo, taking off his glasses and jumping off the stage. The baby girl stirred in her carrier, and Ido sucked noisily on his pacifier and rubbed his eyes with his fists. "What is this?!" said Theo again. He stood at the end of the row where the mayor was seated. Teddy Kollek greeted him genially and waved toward the stage. "Hello, everybody!" he said with absent-minded patronage. He dropped his arm with a heavy thud on the arm of the chair.

"But we're having a rehearsal!" cried Theo, outraged.

"Didn't anyone tell you?" asked the young woman as she straightened the hem of her cream-colored jacket. "German television is here for an interview with Mr. Kollek. It was arranged weeks ago," she added indignantly. "

"Nobody told me!" announced Theo in a tone combining indignation with disbelief.

"It won't take long," said the woman, "half an hour at the most," she promised.

Theo spread out his hands. Teddy Kollek folded his arms and stared in front of him with open indifference.

"Where's the manager? Where's Zisowitz? Why didn't he coordinate with me?" said Theo. His face was pale. He went down to the foot of the stage, looked at the orchestra, and then turned to look at Kollek, who planted an elbow on the arm of his chair and supported his heavy face with a big hand. His eyes were half closed. The sentences in German spoken by the young woman echoed in the hall as the camera focused on her face. Theo flung his arms up and let them fall to his sides in a gesture of helplessness. "Break!" he announced, and he put on his glasses.

The concertmaster stood up quickly, leaned toward Theo, and whispered something.

"Ladies and gentlemen!" said Theo, "I know we're running late, but I want another hour today, so we'll finish an hour late. We have to complete the first movement today."

There was no mistaking the disgruntled expressions on the faces of some of the musicians. The timpani player tugged at her big T-shirt and rummaged noisily and demonstratively in the plastic bag she had hidden behind her drums. Gradually the musicians rose from their places. Michael took hold of the handles of the carrier in one hand and the handle of the baby seat in the other and hurried out of the hall.

Nita followed him. She undid the buckle of the strap around Ido's stomach and picked him up. He laid his face on her shoulder and nestled against her for a second, then threw his head back and began to wriggle. After a brief consultation they decided that Michael would wait until the end of the rehearsal. She returned to the hall to feed Ido backstage, in the hope that he would fall asleep. Michael remained seated in a red velvet armchair in the lobby. Noa was sleeping. A few of the musicians came out into the lobby and sat down in chairs near him.

"He's a terrorist," muttered the timpanist as she took a big sandwich out of a plastic bag.

"It's against the rules," grumbled the clarinet player who had yelled out on stage. He poured himself a cup of coffee from a blue plastic thermos bottle.

"Don't complain," said a big, fat man with a heavy Russian accent. "It'll be harder work with his brother."

"Are you going over to him?" asked the timpanist with her mouth full. "Are you going to switch to his ensemble?"

"*Nu*," said the Russian, "conditions will be better. He's paying better. But there will be more work. He will pay by the rehearsal." He burped. "Capitalism!" he explained with a smile. "No tenure," he added.

"I wouldn't take the risk," said the timpanist, folding her plastic bag neatly. "He can fire you from one day to the next, and you'll be left with nothing."

"*Nu*, he already fired Sonia two weeks ago. And Itzik, too."

"Which Itzik?" asked the clarinetist, screwing the empty cup, which was still dripping, back onto his thermos.

"*Nu*, Itzik!"

"There are two Itziks," said the timpanist. "The trumpeter or the violinist?"

"The violinist, the violinist," said the Russian.

"He fired Itzik?" said the woman, aghast. "How could he fire Itzik?"

"What I can't understand is why anyone setting up a Baroque orchestra should take Itzik on in the first place," said the clarinetist with a laugh.

"*Nu*, it's going to be a very good ensemble," said the Russian, looking at Michael. "There has never been a historical performance Baroque ensemble like it here."

"How good can it be if it's just a second job for the top players?" asked the clarinetist.

"*Nu*, it will not be a second job for long," promised the Russian. "He's holding auditions all the time."

Someone came into the lobby and clapped his hands. "They've finished. We're starting," he called out from the entrance. The musicians began returning to the hall. The Russian held the big wooden doors open as Teddy Kollek, accompanied by the young German woman holding his elbow, shuffled out, followed by the cameramen and the people with the television lights. As the musicians emerged from backstage, Theo van Gelden was already sitting on his high stool. Nita beckoned to Michael from the entrance to the hall. She put Ido into his arms. "He'll sleep now," she promised, stroking Michael's arm. "But if he doesn't fall asleep, if there are problems, just take them both home and I'll make my own way back when the rehearsal's over."

Again he returned to the end of the row and placed Ido at his right and Noa at his left. Everyone sat down and Theo called out: "From twenty-six on." That was from before the entrance of the violin until the full presentation of the main theme of the first movement. After a few bars Theo interrupted: "Are you the police band or what?" he called to the wind instruments and the timpani. "Can't you see what's written? Can't you see that everyone has *fortissimo*—except for who? Except for the horns, trumpets, and timpani. They have only *forte*! *Forte*, not *fortissimo*!" In a softer voice he added: "Brahms wanted the orchestration to be balanced, for the violins and the clarinets to be heard. If the trumpets and timpani are too loud, it sounds like a police band."

At that moment, without any warning, Noa started screaming at the top of her voice. There was laughter from the orchestra, and Theo turned around with a grim face, but he said nothing. Michael hurried out with both babies. He looked at his watch and decided to wait in the lobby until the rehearsal was over. From behind the closed doors he could hear the first movement from the beginning, interrupted by occasional roars from Theo. Again and again they repeated passages while he fed Noa. He listened to the music and to the baby's loud sucking noises and her sighs in the brief intervals between sucks. Ido fell asleep, enabling Michael to stand with Noa in his arms next to the wooden doors and pace up and down beside them until he heard her burp, and at the same time listen to the music. He had never imagined that he would ever be present at the actual work of preparing a piece of music for performance, with its prosaic moments of rustling plastic bags, grumbling, and complaints. It was work that later, in the evening, under the bright lights, would bring tears to the eyes of such as Becky Pomeranz.

He heard Theo call out: "Okay! That's enough for today!" and moved away from the door. He sat down in a corner armchair and waited, with the two babies, until Nita came out of the hall, holding her cello in her hands. "Don't wait for me any longer!" she said. "It was probably a mistake to drag you here with them. We have to stay on to clear up a few more things, and when Theo says 'a few more things' you never know how long it's going to take. If Gabriel or Theo doesn't take me home, I'll get a cab," she added at the sight of his hesitation. "Don't worry, I'm fine. I'm fine as long as I'm working."

A few hours later, as Michael kneeled down next to Gabriel's body, he thought for the first time of what was to haunt him for many days to come. Less than three hours separated his persistent whistling of the main theme of the Double Concerto's first movement from a tormenting question: How different could things have been if he hadn't done as she asked? How much, if anything, could he have prevented if he had continued to wait for her in the place where Gabriel van Gelden was murdered?

5

Morendo Cantabile—Dying Away, Singing

The body was sprawled in the corridor behind the stage, at the foot of a narrow concrete pillar. The upper half of the body was lying in a pool of blood flowing from the severed throat. Michael, who had witnessed many horrible sights, looked only for a moment at the almost decapitated head. Only a narrow piece of skin at the nape of the neck connected it to the shoulders. It seemed to Michael literally to be hanging by a thread, about to fall away at any moment and roll along the corridor onto the stage and down the steps one by one into the hall.

As he stood there averting his face from the body and suppressing the wave of nausea that threatened to overwhelm him, it occurred to him that this was the first time he had seen a murder victim a short time before his death, totally alive, not to speak of playing the violin. For the first time in his life he was standing over the corpse of a man in whose company he had spent hours. The thought in itself gave rise in him to a great unease, and to the muffled recognition that this time everything would be different, that he was involved in this case in an improper way, and that perhaps he should summon someone else right now—someone other than Tzilla, someone who would be able to take over the case if he were to collapse. But why should he collapse? he thought angrily. When did he ever collapse, and what did words like "collapse" and "break down" mean anyway? Did they mean that he would lose his ability to think logically? That he would faint? Anyone would think that he was the injured party here, not Theo or Nita.

With the thought of Nita—it wasn't even a thought, just a sharp, momentary sting in his darting mind—and her relation to this man whose throat had been cut and who was lying in a pool of blood, he began to recover. He forced himself to look at the corpse. For the second time. After the first look, which had been vague and unfocused because of the horror, and then became too personal, the second was something else. This time he looked at the dead Gabriel as if he were only an ordinary corpse, only a case, because he knew in advance what he was going to see. The moment he looked for the second time he said to himself that he could do it, that Gabriel was only a case. But he didn't dare think of Nita yet. For a moment her face flickered before his eyes, and he closed them, as if to drive her away, as if he were saying to her, Not now. As if he were forcibly pushing aside—and he really did need force to do it—the memory of her existence.

The doctor from the Magen David Adom ambulance, which had been summoned even before the police, behaved as if she had been waiting for Michael's arrival only in order to repeat a familiar gesture—raising her arms helplessly and letting them fall with a thud onto her heavy thighs. "That's how he was when we arrived. There was nothing I could do, and I didn't move him, I barely touched him," she said, and she turned immediately to Nita's reaction, which she described as an attack of "clinical hysteria. She screamed and screamed and screamed. We couldn't stop her." There was no mistaking the note of alarm and also the hint of condemnation in the description, in which the phrase "I've never seen anything like it" was repeated several times before she said: "I finally gave her a shot. These two had to help me hold her down." The young doctor pointed to the two adolescent boys standing in the narrow corridor next to the metal cabinets blocking the way to the more spacious part of the building that housed the orchestra's and the conductor's offices. "They're volunteers. They've never seen anything like this before," she said reproachfully. "Sixteen is really a little early for this." One of the youths had a fixed smile on his pale face and the other was leaning against a cabinet with his back to them.

The concertmaster emerged at the bend in the corridor, squeezed past the metal cabinets, and approached them, swaying on his feet. He too averted his face when he passed the corpse. He was the one who had called the ambulance and then the police. "I didn't know . . . I didn't know if he was really dead, and I thought that the first thing was to see if it was possible to save him," he said apologetically.

Heavy footsteps sounded on the other side of the thin wall separating the stage from backstage. Puffing and panting, the forensic pathologist appeared. Even his breathing sounds like humming, thought Michael as he reluctantly recognized Eliyahu Solomon as the pathologist on duty. Hurrying behind him came two forensic investigators. Michael wondered if two would be enough. He marveled silently at the speed with which they had arrived.

The traffic jam had barred his way through King David Street and obliged him to turn on his siren at the Mamilla traffic lights. As he had pushed on toward the concert hall, he had stared, as he always did now, with astonishment at the frameworks of the luxury buildings that were replacing the razed old neighborhood, and then pushed on toward the concert hall. His astonishment—sometimes accompanied by revulsion—at the changes in the view emerging beyond the traffic lights returned whenever he stopped at this intersection. After glancing, with a sense of relief at their survival, at the Muslim cemetery on his left and the "Palace"—the imposing round edifice that housed the Ministry of Commerce and Industry—on his right, he looked straight ahead. For months he had been contemplating the systematic destruction of old buildings. They had left a building once visited by Theodor Herzl untouched, like a single tooth in an old person's mouth, while, like a set of gleaming white false teeth, the new buildings now stood behind a big sign announcing "David's Village."

They had called him on the police radio when he was already on his way to the Russian Compound, after depositing the babies with the afternoon babysitter. At that moment he was at the Mamilla intersection, staring at stickers proclaiming THE PEOPLE ARE WITH THE GOLAN and JUDEA AND SAMARIA ARE HERE on the back window of the car in front of him. The driver was hastily shutting his window in the face of the barrage of curses let loose by a woman in rags, the beggar woman known as the Madwoman of Mamilla, who plied her trade among the cars stuck at the traffic lights, thrusting a filthy hand at the drivers, grinning or growling with her toothless mouth. The address given him by the dispatcher on Shorer's orders filled him with terrible panic. "He tried you first at home," she said, and her voice—a familiar froggy croak—sent a shiver down his spine, as if she had scratched with a stone on a pane of glass.

"I was on the way," he said into the two-way radio, mainly for the sake of saying something, and he turned into the right lane. The chill that had flooded in him, that had filled the pit of his stomach at the sound of the address, had not been dispelled even by the words "the body of a man" the dispatcher had added, as if urgency justified her lack of caution about reporters listening in to the police frequency. The chill increased the closer he got—speeding past the long row of cars drawn up at the seemingly unchanging traffic lights—to the concert hall.

He was chilled, his knees felt weak, and his teeth chattered. How could Shorer find him if he spent his days waiting for babysitters? he castigated himself. He speeded up. The afternoon babysitter, the one they had taken on specially for Nita's rehearsals, had been half an hour late. "Because of the traffic," she had said angrily. The bus route had been changed for the visit of the American secretary of state. "And the day before yesterday it was because of some rabbi's funeral," she panted. "Three hundred thousand Hasidim for a rabbi nobody's ever heard of! It's impossible to live in this city anymore—it's either terrorist attacks or Hasidic funerals or state visits with limousines and motorcycles. Even if they're only going from the King David Hotel to the prime minister's house on Balfour Street, they shut the whole damned city down because of them. What do they care? They're not in a hurry to get anywhere."

Between waves of the shivers he heard himself asking the dispatcher about whether Forensics had already been informed and sent to the scene. He heard his calm, matter-of-fact voice, the familiar voice routinely and automatically on tap for such occasions. Nevertheless it sounded strange to him now as he asked whether the pathologist had already been sent to the scene. When he had parked, at the rear entrance of the concert hall, he turned to the radio again and asked that Tzilla be sent to the scene.

The young Magen David Adom doctor stood next to the skinny pathologist, whose checked shirt emphasized his concave chest and his thin, hairy, white arms. Polishing the lenses of his round spectacles punctiliously, he questioned the doctor briefly in his singsong voice, the silences punctuated by constant humming. He sounded as though he were practicing an endless recitative. She responded to his questions curtly and with evident irritation. When she received the call, it was already "too late," the doctor said, and now Michael heard the echo of a faint Russian accent in the phrase. "The body was in the same position as it is now, sprawled out like a rag, with all the blood, and the legs folded," at the foot of the concrete pillar. She hadn't let anyone touch it, she asserted, no one but she had approached it. She described once more, this time without the note of complaint and condemnation, Nita's hysterical fit, and that she had sent Nita to lie down in "Mr. van Gelden's office."

"Which van Gelden?" asked Michael.

"The other one, the one that's alive," she answered unthinkingly. She then looked embarrassed and horrified.

"Where's the office?" Michael asked the concertmaster, who pointed to the bend in the corridor. He began walking in that direction, turning his head to make sure that Michael was following him. The concertmaster stopped at a door and said in a voice that turned quickly from confusion to open fear: "Weren't you here today at our rehearsal?" Michael nodded vaguely, knocked at the door, and opened it without waiting for a reply.

Nita lay huddled, curled up on her side on a pale couch in a corner of the room. Under the wool blanket it was possible to discern her knees drawn up close to her stomach. Her eyes were closed and her white face looked like a waxen mask. He hurried to her side, bent down, and took her wrist in his hand. The pulse was weak and faint. Everything's lost, he thought as soon as he saw her face. She'll never recover from this. She would never again with a shining face lay her curly head on his shoulder or rub her cheek against his arm. For a brief moment he wanted to gather her up in his arms and escape. Then he roused himself, feeling disgusted. She's alive, he reminded himself.

Theo was sitting on a small chair very close to the couch. When Michael opened the door he removed his hands from his face and turned his head.

"It's you," he said, seeming startled. "They sent you?" Theo asked in a tone of alarm. Then he immediately recovered and wiped his face with a few rapid movements of his hands. "Maybe it's better this way," he mumbled. "Precisely because you know . . . I don't know what's going to happen to her, she . . . She's really in a state," he said in a tremulous voice. "I don't know what we're going to do when she wakes up. I dread it."

"She won't wake up for a few hours."

"Who could have imagined it?" whispered Theo. "Within a week, it isn't even a week yet, both of them at once. I just don't know what to say."

"Who found him?" asked Michael.

"Nita," said Theo in a shocked voice, as if he had only just become aware of the scene that his sister had come upon. "Nita went to look for him, people were waiting for him. I was still working with the timpanist on the stage. Nita went to look for him." He took a deep breath and expelled it. "And she found him."

Michael was silent. He let go of Nita's hand and sat down on the edge of the couch.

"It was an hour . . . about an hour ago that she found him. Have you seen him?" Michael nodded, but Theo had covered his face with his hands again and did not see the nod. He repeated his question. This time he raised his head and exposed his face, which was the gray-yellow of old wax, with green-black semicircles under his eyes, like the ones under Nita's when Michael had first met her.

"I saw him," said Michael. "But I don't know much yet."

"Who could want to do such a thing?" whispered Theo passionately. "And in such a way . . . with all that blood and all."

Michael said nothing.

"I simply don't understand it. Were they trying to decapitate him, or what? Who could have wanted to cut off Gabi's head?"

"In the meantime, stay here and think about that question. It's quite crucial."

"It's unbelievable," mumbled Theo between his hands, in which he had buried his face again.

Michael got up and again stood next to Nita. She didn't move. Her breathing was so quiet that he had to bend down close to her to feel it on his face. He straightened up. "I'll be back soon," he said, and he closed the door behind him.

The forensics people were moving carefully through the crime scene, the pathologist was pacing up and down the corridor, and the concertmaster was standing with his back pressed against a metal cabinet. He asked if he was needed here, and when nobody answered him he remained standing in his corner. Michael turned to him. "Where is everybody? Where are the musicians?" he asked.

"Some of them have already gone home, they went before we found . . . before we knew . . ."

"And the rest?"

"They're in the lobby," said the concertmaster, massaging his neck. "I told them not to leave, but they couldn't have gone anyway. Those who didn't see . . . see Gabriel," he said, swallowing hard, "heard Nita's screams. It was terrifying, they're all in shock, nobody dared leave," he said.

Michael asked him to tell them again to stay where they were. The concertmaster shifted his weight from foot to foot and muttered that he would prefer not to take the responsibility on himself. "I don't know how they'll react, it would be better if you told them yourself."

Michael nodded to Yaffa, one of the forensics team. She looked at the scene and then at Michael, and at last said to the concertmaster: "Come with me, I'll tell them." The two of them left via the stage.

Again heavy footsteps were heard from the direction of the exit, overwhelming the light steps of Tzilla, who came in jingling her car keys and short of breath. "I asked Eli to come, too," she whispered to Michael when she reached his side. "We'll be together at least." He nodded and then she confessed: "I got a terrible fright. I thought at first that it was her," she said, lowering her voice even more. "I calmed down when I heard it was a man." As if she grasped the absurdity of her words, she added with embarrassment: "I mean that if it had been a woman . . . Never mind, it doesn't matter. What's going on here?" She shook herself and looked for the first time at Gabriel's body lying at the foot of the concrete pillar. The keys stopped rattling. She clenched her fist around them. After a few seconds she opened her hand and they dropped to the ground. Michael bent down to pick them up. She turned her face away. "Who is it?" she asked, her hand at her throat, and she looked at Michael.

"Gabriel van Gelden," he replied. The forensics investigator kneeled down not far from the body, picked something up from the floor with tweezers, and dropped it into one of the plastic bags he had in his case. "The younger of Nita's brothers," added Michael.

"And I'm Doctor Solomon," said the pathologist. He hummed, straightened his shoulders, puffed out his concave chest with a noisy breath. He went on humming as he rummaged in his bag and took out, one after the other, a thermometer, a camera, a magnifying glass, and a pair of gloves, laying them in a straight row at his feet. "Don't you go and faint on us now," he said to Tzilla as he went down on his knees next to some drops of blood outside the pool, not far from Gabriel's nearly severed neck. He pulled the gloves on, took up the magnifying glass, drew very close to one of the drops of blood, shone a flashlight onto it, hummed and crooned to himself, and said in a hollow voice: "Can I have a bit more light here?" The forensics investigator lit a mobile spotlight, stood it close to the wall, and directed it onto the corpse.

Yaffa returned to the corridor from the side entrance, followed by the concertmaster, who walked with his head bowed. "Avigdor," said Yaffa to the concertmaster, "please stay over there for a minute." She pointed to the corner by the metal cabinet. "We told them," she said to Michael. "They'll be waiting for you in the lobby." The other forensics investigator stood next to the pathologist with the camera in his hands. He photographed the body and the drops of blood from close up. Then he photographed small areas around the body, sometimes focusing on a single tile, until he put the camera down, took a thick marker out of his shirt pocket, stood close to the corpse, and waited.

"What have we here?" said the pathologist in his singsong. He examined the droplets outside the blood pool with the magnifying glass. "We have an irregularly shaped drop, come and look," he said waving at Michael, who went down on his knees and peered through the magnifying glass. "Do you see these drops?" asked Solomon. "Do you see that they're not round, that their contours are blurred, jagged?" Michael nodded and Yaffa silently photographed the drops of blood. "So we can already say," Dr. Solomon summarized, "that they fell to the floor from above. In other words, that the initial position of the victim was upright. This blood was spilled while he standing."

Tzilla's face, as she kneeled beside Michael and looked at Gabriel's neck, was very pale, and her lower lip had disappeared completely between her teeth.

"Do you see that the wound goes almost completely around the neck?" asked the pathologist, and he examined it though his magnifying glass. "Okay, we'll talk about that in a minute," he said, and he hummed. "Now the temperature, but before I move him, let's do some photographing," he announced, focusing his own camera on the corpse. For a while all that could be heard was the clicking of cameras. After that the pathologist made room for the forensics investigator to squat and draw a white line all the way around the body. Yaffa resumed taking pictures. It looked as if she was doing it with her eyes shut in order to avoid the sight of the gaping throat.

The pathologist touched both sides of the body, holding the thermometer in his left hand. "First the surface temperature," he singsonged. "And now here," he said after a while, turning the dead man over onto his side. With sharp, rapid movements he undid some of the body's clothes. "Aha! That's it!" he said after examining the thermometer and raising his eyes to the concrete pillar at the foot of which Gabriel was lying. He wiped his hand on the pillar and studied his glove with interest. "You see," he said to Michael. "Look, the plaster comes off the pillar. That's what he has on his shirt, you see these marks?" Michael followed the pathologist's finger. "We would only have seen them in the laboratory if he had a light-colored shirt on, but since it's a dark one, we can see them now. This white on his shirt must come from the pillar. Excuse me for going into matters within the province of my forensics colleagues, but this white on the shirt interests me because of the position."

"What does it mean?" asked Tzilla.

"It means," sang the pathologist, "that we know not only that he was standing but that he was leaning with his head against this pillar, like this." He tilted his head back as if resting it against a pillar. "Maybe, I don't say definitely, but maybe, someone came from behind and pssst."

Dr. Solomon drew his hand over his throat in a cutting gesture and resumed his kneeling position next to the corpse, the thermometer in his hand. After a few moments of absolute silence, during which the forensics investigators prowled the long corridor, fingering, photographing, marking, and kneeling, Dr. Solomon announced: "Between one to two hours."

"Where's Nita?" asked Tzilla, and the concertmaster emerged from his corner to tell her.

Tzilla was horrified. "She's the one who found him? Like this?"

"Yes," replied the concertmaster, and he approached them, bowing his head apologetically, so that the bald pate shone between the two rows of curls on either side of his head.

"When?"

"At about . . . three, say a quarter past three. I'm not sure, but it was after we'd already finished, and the only people left were the ones who had to talk to Gabriel, about his Baroque ensemble. He was making a revolution . . . changes," he tried to explain and fell silent. "We couldn't find him." Then he added, almost with surprise: "Suddenly he wasn't there, all of a sudden he was gone, he'd disappeared, and now . . ." He choked and buried his face in his hands for a moment, then took them away again and shook his head. "It's unbelievable," he muttered in a broken voice. "It's so . . . so . . . absurd." Then he straightened his shoulders, took off his glasses, and in a spurt of demonstrative matter-of-factness began to discuss the timetable: "We finished the rehearsal at half past, a quarter past two. He was still there then, that's to say, a minute before he was there, and now . . ." He hesitated and looked at his watch.

"Now it's four forty-seven," singsonged the pathologist, "so we also have the time coordinate and a drop of one degree in the temperature, and calculating a one-degree loss per hour . . . approximately, I can't be definite here," he warned the investigator kneeling next to him, "I'm only reminding you that the temperature drops one degree an hour. So we could be talking about two hours or an hour and a half. Which means that death occurred between half-past two and three," he explained to Michael. "But let me check the rigor so that we have as much data as possible."

He examined Gabriel's face, palpated the jaws, and poked his yellow rubber-gloved fingers into the mouth "The tongue isn't swollen, as I thought," he remarked with satisfaction. "Remind me to make a note of that later, and photograph it, too. It could be important. The jaw still opens, not easily, but it opens. You know the drill," he said, looking expectantly at Tzilla with his pale eyes.

Tzilla nodded like a diligent pupil and declaimed: "If the jaw muscles are stiff, three hours have passed since death. If you can't move the hands, six hours. Stiffness in the legs, dead eight hours."

"In weather like today's," amended the pathologist. "Only in autumnal weather like today's."

"So there's actually no rigor mortis at all yet," said Michael.

"It's about to begin," promised the pathologist. "It's on the way. Now let's check the livor mortis. "He turned the corpse onto its side again and lifted the shirt. "You see: the spots were on the back, and when I turn him, they slide over there. If you press a place where there's a discoloration," he said as he pressed a bluish-purple spot, "the pressure moves the blood to the sides."

"Already? After only an hour?" exclaimed Michael.

"You have to take age into account. How old was he?"

"Forty-seven, about, if I remember correctly."

"Well, at that age, there's already venous insufficiency," the pathologist murmured. "There's already discoloration after an hour, you can see the spots."

"What a color!" Tzilla murmured. Under the dazzling white light the spots blossomed blue and purple.

"That's what happens when the blood is deoxygenated," the pathologist said with a brief hum. "You must have seen these things before."

"You never get used to it," she said, sighing, and she raked her fingers through her short hair.

"Ah," said the pathologist dismissively, "when you have to, you can get used to anything. Human beings are incredibly adaptable creatures." He hummed and pressed a big spot, causing it to flow to the side. "Look, I press, and the color turns white, you see, and that shows us again," he sang, "that death took place less than eight hours ago, because . . ." He waved a gloved finger at Tzilla, and she obediently said: "After eight hours the blood vessels close and the spots don't move."

"Very good," he pronounced and returned to viewing the neck through the magnifying glass. "I don't want to touch this with the tape measure," he said with a hum. "A clean circular cut like this you don't want to spoil." He put down the magnifying glass and picked up the camera, brought it very close to the cut, and clicked several times, humming. "We'll take a few decent close-ups." Then he returned to the magnifying glass. Michael kneeled next to him while Tzilla stood back and averted her face. "You have to look at it from the scientific point of view," admonished the pathologist, "it's not a person anymore, it's a case. Say that to yourself until you're convinced." Tzilla remained where she was, with her face averted.

"Look at this mark!" said Solomon, placing his finger on the corpse's neck. "Do you see it? Like a bite? It's got nothing to do with the case, but you might as well learn something."

"What is it?" asked Michael, and he turned away from the sight of the finger on the brown mark.

"Call that man over. What's his name, Avigdor?"

Avigdor stood before Solomon with a frightened expression. "He has one of them, too," said the pathologist, gratified. "Do you play the violin?" Avigdor nodded. "He's the concertmaster," said Michael. "There you are!" said Solomon with satisfaction. "It's an inflammation a lot of violinists and violists have. A piece of plastic—I think it's plastic, I'll have to check—on the violin does it under their chins, just like the mark on our gentleman here. Was he a violinist?" he asked, pointing at the corpse. Michael nodded. "I'm sure we'll find another one under here," said the pathologist, lifting the dead man's beard. Then he bent over the mark, magnifying glass in hand, to examine it. Slowly his hand moved down from the chin to the neck.

"You see," said Solomon, handing Michael the magnifying glass, "the cut goes around most of the circumference of the neck. Do you see that there's no major difference between the right side and the left?" In the seconds that his eyes strayed away from the magnifying glass, unprotected, Michael got a glimpse of Gabriel van Gelden's eyes, which had remained open. The expression of horror frozen on them and the memory of the dead man's shy smile paralyzed him. Although he was looking through the magnifying glass, he could neither see nor think, and he grunted vaguely and returned it to the pathologist, who said with satisfaction: "From this we can conclude a number of things. Number one, the cut was not made by a knife."

"Not by a knife?" repeated Michael. When he looked at the corpse without seeing the face, from the neck down, it was easier.

"Definitely not. A knife isn't even in its action. With a knife we wouldn't have obtained a circumferential cut like this one, either. But I can also tell you something else, which is number two: There are no hesitation wounds here. Not that I can see anyway."

"What are hesitation wounds?" asked Tzilla faintly.

"It means that it wasn't a suicide," said Michael.

"Look over here," said the pathologist to Tzilla, not noticing that she took care to look away as he continued: "You see, there are no little wounds on the skin here, as if there was an attempt to estimate how deep to go. When someone is about to commit suicide he first tries out the weapon, the knife or rope or whatever it might be. And so we have little wounds in addition to the big wound. There's no such thing here. There are no hesitation wounds, only one clean cut," he pronounced, shining a flashlight onto the neck. He hummed.

"With what?" demanded Michael.

"A thin wire. Or maybe a plastic cord. Fishing tackle, let's say. If it's really thin it can cut the head right off, slicing between two vertebrae."

"A wire?"

"If it's sharp enough. If enough force is exerted. If it's tightened from behind, let's say, wrapped around the killer's hands, or something. If there's a counterforce from behind, then it can pass precisely between two vertebrae and cut through the neck just like this. Theoretically, death here might have been the result of anoxia, a lack of oxygen to the brain. If a sudden strong pressure is exerted on the neck the whole thing doesn't take more than a minute. Because of their small diameter, arteries close off before the larger, less compressible trachea. Something thicker, like a cable, could cause either strangulation or stoppage of the blood to the brain. But I'm not sure that in this instance there was enough time for that. The neck is a sensitive area," he explained, putting the flashlight down next to the corpse. "I'm sure that there wasn't time for him to be strangled, but we'll have a look anyway."

The flashlight shone directly onto the gaping neck. Michael averted his eyes.

"If he'd been strangled we would have seen bulging eyes, burst blood vessels in the eyes, edema, blueness in the face, a swollen tongue, and so on," Solomon argued with an invisible opponent. "But this deep cut in the neck proves that there was no pressure at all. In strangulation the cause of death is the closing off of the large blood vessels leading to the brain, which is not what we have here," he added in an argumentative tone, as if someone had demanded proof. "Here we have a circumferential cut. Someone cut through the front part of the neck and penetrated deeply through the cartilage. The resistances, that is, the front of the neck and the back of the head pressing against the pillar, made for the speed and depth of that cut."

"Maybe the plaster on his shirt has nothing to do with his death. Maybe it got there earlier. In the morning, let's say," said Michael. He heard his voice tremble. Every second he stood here might be the moment Nita woke up. How could he have left her alone? She's with Theo, he tried to reassure himself. She's not alone. She won't wake up so soon, he thought. His legs felt heavy. But he had to listen to everything the pathologist had to say.

"Maybe," said Solomon doubtfully. "They'll find out more at Forensics. But it isn't so important. It's clear that he was standing, because of the drops of blood I showed you before."

"I remember," said Michael, his voice still trembling uncontrollably, "someone once telling me about death by vagal reflex, where pressure on the neck leads to a sudden drop in blood pressure and instant death, even before the loss of blood."

Dr. Solomon let out a whinny of laughter. "All these speculations are really superfluous," he said condescendingly. "If you sever someone's arteries and trachea he's dead—with or without a plunge in his blood pressure."

"So, what are you saying? He was leaning against the pillar, and someone from behind with a thin wire . . ."

"Or a plastic cord, if it was very thin and strong," Solomon interjected.

"Slipped the cord around his neck from behind, and pulled? Like this?" Michael stood behind the pillar, put his arms around it, and pulled the two ends of an imaginary cord.

"Yes, more or less," agreed Solomon. "Remember that I haven't examined everything yet and that this isn't a lab. But that's how I see it. The victim was standing, leaning against the pillar, his throat was exposed, and after . . . Just a minute!" he cried with sudden animation, looking intently at the palm of Gabriel's right hand. "Look at this!" he cried triumphantly, and he hurried to look through the magnifying glass: "Look, do you see this cut?" Michael kneeled down next to the body. He looked through the magnifying glass at the cuts on the inside of the dead man's right thumb and index finger joints. The thought pierced Michael that only a short time ago this hand had been holding a violin bow. Then the pathologist examined the left hand. "Here it's fainter," he murmured.

"Did he resist?" asked Tzilla.

"He didn't have much of a chance to. But you see how thin the cord was. He grabbed it with both hands, instinctively, to free himself, but of course to no avail. It's important for us because it confirms our theory of the method."

"A wire? A nylon cord?" Michael speculated, thrusting aside the mental picture of the distorted face, the struggling hands. "I suppose it didn't leave any traces on the neck?"

"How could it?" said the forensics investigator dismissively from behind him. "A uniform cut, a smooth cord," he said. "But if we find the cord it'll show traces of the neck. Only we haven't found it yet." And he looked at Yaffa, who was moving from tile to tile on her knees.

"We need more people!" instructed Michael. "At least two more." Yaffa looked at the investigator, who nodded his head and left in the direction of the stage.

"Even if we find it," remarked Tzilla, "it'll be clean, no? Whoever murdered him will have cleaned it."

"They can clean it all day!" said the investigator. "There are things you can't wipe off. And maybe we'll get lucky and find the gloves somewhere, because he had to have worn gloves, otherwise he would have cut himself. You'd better check for cuts on people's hands. Where could he have hidden the gloves if he's still here?"

The investigator wasn't much older than Yuval, Michael reflected as he repeated the words, "if he's still here." But he already has a degree in chemistry and solid achievements in his field.

"You know our pathologist Kestenbaum, don't you?" intervened Solomon. Michael smiled and nodded his head. "You know what he likes to say? 'Every contact leaves a trace.' He always says it in English," said Solomon, snickering. "Hungarian English. So we'll keep samples of skin from the neck and examine the weapon under a microscope later for a match. If you find it for me, I'll find something on it. Or they will," he said and looked toward the forensic investigator. He picked up the thermometer again and added glumly: "I don't think we'll find particles of metal on the neck. It seems to have been a very smooth wire."

Michael left the pathologist and the forensic investigators at the scene, crossed the stage, and walked through the hall toward the big wooden doors leading into the lobby. He pushed the heavy doors open and saw a large group of people waiting for him in the distance. Tzilla followed him, beckoning to the concertmaster, who trailed slowly behind them. Only when Michael was already outside the hall, as he was letting go of the wooden doors closing slowly behind him, and staring at the people waiting for him, did the significance of what he had seen hit him. In a flash, he thought of Nita bending over her open cello case, kneeling down and removing from a narrow compartment a thin, semitransparent envelope, like the one he had seen earlier in the open violin case.

He pulled the wooden doors open and ran back into the hall, stopping next to the open violin case on the seat in the front row. Tzilla stood holding the door as if she were unsure which side of it she should be on. Avigdor, the concertmaster, was still standing in the hall, at the end of the first row of seats, as if crossing the distance to the doors was too much for him. At the sight of Michael running back down the aisle and stopping at the violin case, he recoiled in alarm, and then he hesitantly approached the seat in the middle of the row. "That's my violin," he said with obvious apprehension. "I shouldn't have left it here like that. It's a very valuable instrument, but in the . . ." His voice died away, but his hand gesturing toward the back of the stage completed the sentence.

Michael sat down on the seat next to the violin case, picked it up, and laid it on his knees. First he looked at the photographs of the young couple and baby attached to the red felt lining inside the lid. Then he carefully passed his finger delicately over each string of the violin, touched the cloth folded under the gleaming reddish instrument, and fingered the block of wrapped rosin in the little compartment. Only then did he extract the thin, semitransparent envelope and carefully remove the strings rolled up inside it. "Four," he murmured as he felt each of them with his fingertips. Avigdor stood over him wringing his hands. "I always have four," he said tremulously, "because they snap. You can never know . . . I'm always prepared. . . ."

"And this is the thinnest," said Michael, holding one of the four between his fingers and stretching it out to its full length.

"That's the E string," said Avigdor, as if apologizing in the name of all the strings. "It's the highest, that's why it's the thinnest."

"Dr. Solomon!" Michael shouted at the top of his voice, and Solomon quickly emerged from backstage and hurried to the edge of the stage, where he remained standing under the weak light. "Could it . . . ?" asked Michael loudly and suddenly stopped. He looked at Avigdor, looked at the string, and then mounted the stage. "Could it have been a violin string?" he asked in a whisper as he stood very close to Solomon and stretched the E string between his hands.

Solomon felt the string with his gloved fingers, then peeled off the right-hand glove, threw it aside, and felt again. He nodded and hummed. "It could, why not?" And after a pause he added: "If it's long enough. We'll have to check the length—you'd need seventy, eighty centimeters at least to wrap around the hands," he added loudly.

"Shhh, keep your voice down," warned Michael.

Solomon looked at him uncomprehendingly.

"I want it to remain under wraps. Like that time with the bra strap. Do you remember? When we didn't reveal what the woman had been strangled with?"

Solomon nodded. "You said it was effective during the lie-detector test," he recalled.

"The less they know, the more we'll know," pronounced Michael, adding less authoritatively: "Maybe." He peered into the half-lit hall, where Avigdor had dropped limply into the seat next to the violin case. Tzilla was still standing at the end of the row.

"Shimshon!" Michael called out. "Come here quickly!" The young forensics investigator bounded over the stage as if he'd been waiting for the call.

"It could be," singsonged Dr. Solomon as he fingered the string. "It definitely could, but maybe it's a little on the short side."

"Does it have to be from a violin?" asked Michael.

Dr. Solomon frowned judiciously. "No, I'll have to look at viola strings, too," he said without humming at all. "They used to make strings out of catgut," he said with a chuckle. "Is there a viola here? We also need a cello, and maybe a double bass. We have to check the length and thickness of the strings."

"The musicians are sitting outside with their instruments," Shimshon reminded him.

"I'll go and get someone with a viola," volunteered Tzilla, who had also mounted the stage in the meantime.

"I don't want them to know what we're looking for," said Michael. "From now on keep it to yourselves."

"So how will we check?" asked Shimshon. "How'll we find out?"

"We'll have to invent something. Slip it into other questions. And we have to check their hands."

"There's no reason why we shouldn't start with the violists," said Tzilla. "Most of the string players are still here. Some of them were going to work with him." She turned her head toward backstage and shuddered. "I'll go get one of them, and you think about how we can put it to them."

"Bring a cellist, too," Dr. Solomon called after her as she pushed the heavy wooden doors.

"I'm going to faint," Avigdor said weakly from the dimly lit hall. "I feel sick."

"We'll get you some water in a minute," promised Michael, and climbed down from the stage. "Sit still and breathe deeply," he said as he sat down next to him. "Stretch your legs out in front of you and take a deep breath." Then he casually asked: "Where were you while Gabriel van Gelden was backstage?" Avigdor choked and coughed at length before managing to say: "I . . . I . . ." Michael waited. "After the rehearsal, when he left the stage, I thought that we were taking a break. At least until he would come back to talk to us. So I went outside, into the fresh air. I had something to eat. There's a kiosk that sells sandwiches. I didn't have time to eat in the morning."

Michael fingered the violin case. "Are all your strings in here?" he asked.

Avigdor nodded. His breathing was shallow and rapid, and his hand trembled. "I always have four spares," he said. "To be on the safe side."

Dr. Solomon came down from the stage. "Allow me," he said, and, taking the four spare strings, he ran his fingers carefully over them, one by one. After a moment he nodded at Michael and walked over to the stairs at the side of the hall. "It would be possible," he said to Michael when the latter approached him, "with these thicker violin strings, too." He glanced at Avigdor, who raised his eyes, his head trembling on his neck. "I have to ask him a couple of questions," he said, excusing himself, and he went over to him. Michael didn't hear the questions, but he heard Avigdor's answer: "This is the A string and this is the D," he muttered. "And this?" asked Dr. Solomon, holding the thickest of the strings. "That's the G," said Avigdor weakly, as if reluctantly. "The viola is tuned a fifth lower," he added, his voice trembling. "Why . . . why, do you think . . . ?" he asked anxiously. "But that's impossible!" he cried out, and Michael saw in his frantically blinking eyes the image of Gabriel van Gelden's severed neck.

"Don't say anything to anyone for the time being, please," he warned. Avigdor choked, swallowed, shook his head, and clasped his hands together.

"Are there four strings on the viola, too?" asked Solomon.

Avigdor nodded and said: "Yes, but they're a fifth—five notes—lower."

"So they're thicker than the violin strings," Solomon clarified.

Once more the wooden doors opened slowly and Tzilla came into the hall. Behind her was Yaffa from Forensics and two other women. The thin one with the cropped hair was holding a viola case, and the younger one—still almost a girl, with a long braid hanging down the side of her neck and dangling over her chest—was holding a cello.

Tzilla took Michael by the arm and drew him aside: "These two didn't leave the building either during the break or after the rehearsal," she said. "The one with the short hair says that she waited with the cellist in order to persuade Gabriel van Gelden at least to take her on as an extra player. She's a pupil of her mother's or something like that. Anyway, I don't think there's any connection . . . I told them we were conducting a search. Neither of them saw the body, not really. They think we're looking for a knife."

At his request the violist opened her case and took out her instrument. Michael put it next to Avigdor's violin, and in comparison to the gleaming red-brown of the violin, the viola paled to a faded yellow-brown. Pretending to be looking for something, he took the cloth out of the case and spread it out, unwrapped the rosin, and fingered a semitransparent envelope. "What's this?" he asked.

"Spare strings," replied the violist, and she watched his hands opening the envelope.

"There's only one here," he said.

The violist took out the coiled string and peered into the envelope as if to make sure there wasn't another one inside. "Only one," she said apologetically. "Only the G."

"Is this the thickest?" asked Solomon, feeling the spare string with his fingers.

"No, this is the G," she said, surprised at the question. "The thickest is the C."

"And how many did you have this morning?" inquired Michael.

"One," she admitted guiltily. "I intended . . . but I forgot . . . I have some at home," she promised.

"Did you have the C or the G in your case this morning?" asked Michael.

"It's the G," she replied uncomprehendingly. "Actually, I should have had an A, because it was my A string that snapped at the last rehearsal, but . . . "

Michael touched the spare G string, and then he turned to the instrument and felt the A tautly strung on it. He handed the viola to Solomon, who examined it and whispered: "Of course, without a doubt." As Solomon unrolled the spare G string to its full length, he pursed his lips doubtfully and added: "But the length . . . I don't know, you'd need almost a meter to go around the pillar and hold it tightly at both ends." Then they spoke to the cellist, who opened her cello case and, kneeling beside it, took out the instrument and put it down carefully. She removed the cloth and music from the case, and took the spare strings from their envelope without any questions. Michael kneeled next to her. Solomon sat on the seat near them and rubbed his knees.

The cellist had three spare strings. She chewed the tip of her braid as she nodded to confirm that there had been three strings there all along.

They asked the two women to wait outside. "You can leave your instruments here. We'll call you in a minute," said Tzilla, and shepherded Avigdor away toward the big wooden doors. "You wait here, too. Here, sit down in this armchair," they heard her say gently to him.

"It's less than half a millimeter thick," said Shimshon, holding the spare cello D string.

"Quite definitely less than half," said Solomon. "It's really thin—there wouldn't be any problem with this one, it's also . . . Just a minute, let me measure it." He took a tape measure out of his pocket, laid the string out at his feet, pulled out the tape, and announced: "Exactly one meter long."

"In other words," reflected Michael aloud, "the cut could have been made with a string from any of these instruments?"

"With any of the thin strings, definitely," said Solomon, and he hummed. "That includes the A strings of the violins, violas, and cellos. But I'm not sure that the length of the violin strings is right. You never know when things you once learned might come in handy. All of a sudden those violin lessons that made my life hell when I was a boy are paying off."

Michael nodded and was about to speak when the wooden doors opened and two men and a woman came in. Yaffa waved and beckoned to them. The only one Michael really knew was the short, bald man, but he recognized them as people from Forensics.

"You sent for us," said the bald man to Shimshon, "and here we are."

"Start with all the string players," Michael said to Tzilla, and then he explained to the forensics investigators, who were standing in a group behind Shimshon: "Why should we look for fishing tackle backstage in a concert hall? Does anyone come here to fish? We can assume that we're looking for a string from a fiddle of one size or another."

"Do you really think," said Shimshon sourly, "that things are so neat? That if we're next to a river it's a fishing line and if we're in an orchestra hall it has to be a fiddle string?"

Michael shrugged his shoulders. "Sometimes it's as simple as that. Solomon says it's a thin wire or plastic cord, and here we have a very thin cord."

"Strings tear," protested Shimshon.

"I don't know," interrupted the bald man. "They used to make violin strings from twisted lambs' intestines, but now they're plastic with metal cores."

"They don't tear, they snap, from material fatigue," said Michael, thinking once more of the string snapping in the living room, remembering his surprise at the absolute suddenness of the sound of the snap and the broken string dangling over the cello's bridge. He had wondered at the practiced, efficient movements with which Nita had quickly and calmly replaced the string with a spare. He was holding the baby in his arms, and he came closer to see her loosen the wooden peg with her right hand, pull out the end of the broken string, and observe the care with which she held the end of the new string and threaded it through the bottom end and brought it over the bridge and along the fingerboard to the neck of the instrument. He had watched her hand as she wrapped the string around the peg and tightened it, as she plucked the string and listened attentively, plucked the other strings, and suddenly, catching him staring intently at her hands, she had raised her eyes and smiled in amusement, as if he were a child gazing in wonder at the hands of a magician.

"What is it?" she had asked, laughing.

He had shrugged his shoulders and said: "Nothing, I've just never seen anyone doing that before. What I'd like to know is why. . . . How does it snap?"

"It just does," she had said, amused. "Like the kitchen shelf that suddenly fell down the other day. I asked you why it fell without anyone touching it, without anyone even being in the kitchen, and I hadn't put anything new or heavy on it either, and you said 'material fatigue!' Which apparently also applies to cello strings."

"It's got nothing to do with the way you played?" he had cautiously asked. "You pulled the string very hard with your finger."

Her face had clouded. "It's a difficult passage," she defended herself. "You try to play a loud *pizzicato*. Look, it says *fortissimo* there," she said, nodding at the music stand. "Try it and see for yourself.

"Nita," he had said then. "Stop it, I know you're working, I just want to understand. Why are you acting as if I'm some kind of music critic? You know I'm a total ignoramus in these matters."

"It's been such a long time since I've played . . . And even before, I never thought I was so great . . . It's natural for me to lack self-confidence . . ." she had said, embarrassed. Then she had taken a deep breath and continued in a clear, reasonable tone: "It's got nothing to do with the way you play. If you ask me why a string snaps, then there's only one real answer. They say that differences in temperature can sometimes cause it, but in my opinion the only answer is material fatigue."

"Does everybody know how to thread it in like that?" he asked.

She laughed. "Of course, and fast, the way they change a racing car's tires. Do you think it doesn't sometimes happen in the middle of a concert?"

"Paganini . . ." Michael said, remembering, and he almost mentioned Becky Pomeranz by name, but at the last moment he only said: "Someone once told me, when I was a boy, about how all of Paganini's strings during a concert . . ."

"Not all of them," Nita corrected him, "just three. According to the legend, he had one string left, on which he played the rest of the concert, and the legend also says that he made them snap on purpose in order to demonstrate his virtuosity . . ." She had inclined her head, put it very close to the cello, plucked the strings one after the other, and said: "Okay, is that a fifth? What do you say? Not quite, eh?" Again she had loosened the peg and then tightened the new string, plucked, listened, nodded, and, finally satisfied, said: "Now it is."

"Begin in the lobby, and go through the cases of all the string players," said Michael to the forensics investigators. "You don't have to say what you're looking for, just ask about everything, find out if they're missing any of their spare strings. Soon more forensics people will be here, and they'll join you, but at this stage you're the only ones who know what we're looking for. Later on, if we don't come up with anything there, come back here and turn the place upside down until we find an unattached string lying around somewhere. Meanwhile, Shimshon, you can stay here backstage and start searching. The killer wouldn't have put it in his pocket with all that blood on it," Michael muttered. And then he added, firmly: "It has to be lying around here somewhere."

"Sure," said Shimshon, "together with the gloves."

"Quite possibly," said Michael briskly, ignoring the sarcastic tone.

"You wish," Shimshon whispered, and Michael wondered whether to pretend he hadn't heard.

But then he heard himself saying in a puzzled tone: "What's your problem? What's annoying you?"

"I don't believe in such neat, symmetrical solutions," mumbled Shimshon. "There's a ton of electric wiring here, why shouldn't it be an electrical wire?"

"A cable would have strangled him, a single strand would have snapped," said Solomon, sticking a slender brown cigar into the corner of his mouth. "I'm not going to light it," he reassured them. "I only want to hold it in my mouth. There's no doubt that the best thing for the job is a thin string from a string instrument."

"What difference does it make what you're looking for?" said Michael. "Call it a wire or a plastic cord, if you like, as long as you find it, and quickly. Believe me, if you show me a fishing line with blood on it I'll be delighted. But meanwhile let's start looking through their instrument cases. We won't have another opportunity to search the musicians before they have a chance to . . ."

"If one of them did it," said Shimshon, "do you think he's going to tell you that one of his spare strings is missing? And besides, can you identify a certain string as belonging to a certain instrument? Is there a difference between the A of one cello and the A of another cello?" He looked at Solomon, who shrugged his shoulders and pulled down the corners of his mouth to express his inability to answer the question.

"We've got nothing to lose," Michael summed up, and he turned to the newcomers. "Shimshon will explain to you what we're looking for and why, and then you'll go talk to the people sitting in the lobby," he said as the heavy wooden doors opened with Tzilla standing there holding them apart with her arms.

"Do you want them in here?" she asked loudly, against a background of murmurs. "Eli's arrived, he's here with Sergeant Zippo," she said, making a face.

"Zippo?" said Michael, astonished. "I didn't know he was still with us. I thought he'd retired."

"Where do you want them?"

"Here first of all, all the string players, one by one, in the corner of the hall," said Michael impatiently. "And come here. Divide them into groups, and over there, in that corner, take one group yourself and find out how many spare strings each one of them had. And check to see if any are missing."

"There are eighteen string players here."

"Then go and get the rest of them," he said impatiently. "All of them, *now*."

Tzilla looked at him. "How am I supposed to do all that at once?"

"Zippo can help you," said Michael. "And I also want . . . Does this orchestra have a manager?"

"It does, and he's already outside in the lobby. I told him to wait a minute, and Eli also brought . . ." She hesitated and looked at him uncertainly.

"Well?" demanded Michael.

"That girl, Dalit, the one you asked me last week if they're sending us recruits straight from kindergarten now. . . . The thin, blonde one, with short hair, you know, Dalit."

"I want to talk to him, to the manager, now, after I talk to Eli," said Michael, trying to suppress the thought that too many fronts had been opened at once, that he was acting nervously and chaotically instead of systematically, and that he should go back to the room behind the bend in the corridor instead of obeying impulses that didn't even calm him. His agitation was different from what it usually was, but then it was different every time, he tried to tell himself. Anything but to think about the significance of Tzilla's sudden seriousness.

For Tzilla had now turned to him with a grave expression on her face: "Eli wants to talk to you outside," she said, before we begin. "I've already filled him in on the main points." His heart sank even before she said: "And I have something to say to you, too." She frowned as she gave him a stern, rebuking look and followed him out of the hall.

Eli wasted no time on preliminaries. "Look," he said after making sure that there was nobody within hearing distance, "you know that Shorer put you on the case because of your knowledge of music, because it's . . . well, your kind of case. . . . You know what I mean," he said, squirming with embarrassment. "Who should he have put on the case if not you? But if he knew, it should be clear to you that you wouldn't be here even as an adviser!"

Michael said nothing. He stood there quietly, but the thought that Nita might suddenly wake up and not find him there made him clench his teeth and tighten his muscles.

Eli Bahar cracked his knuckles. "I've worked with you on so many cases," he said in a soft, pleading tone, "it's the ABC that you taught me yourself, always talking about our blind spots," his tone grew heated and embittered, "and all of a sudden, all of a sudden you're closing your eyes. I'm thinking of you, believe me," he urged. "Of you, too," he added, and he waited. When Michael didn't react he went on: "You yourself would never agree to such a thing with anyone else. You're too personally involved, it could ruin everything. You yourself taught me that! You would never have allowed it with anyone else!"

"I think I can keep things separate," said Michael. He hesitated and silenced the chorus of contradictory thoughts clamoring inside his head. "And since it's already happened, maybe it's better that it's me and not—"

"Thank God I'm not the one who has to decide," said Eli. "But you know yourself that it's not right, and Tzilla, too . . . Tzilla, why don't you say something? We can talk to him, we're friends, no? We've been together long enough. . . ."

Michael wiped his forehead with the folded handkerchief he took out of his jeans pocket. His hands were cold, and he rubbed them against his burning cheeks. He should have stayed sitting at Nita's side until she woke up. If she hadn't awakened already. She mustn't wake up and not find him there. If only he could be having this conversation while holding the baby in his arms, or warming the bottle, his hands would not be trembling so idiotically that he had to rest them on the wooden railing next to them.

"He's a grown man and responsible for his actions," said Tzilla. It was impossible not to hear the note of criticism in her voice. "If he says he can keep things separate, then maybe he can. I," she stressed, "wouldn't be able to, but maybe he can. How long can you hide something like this?"

"Hide what?" said Michael in a panic, tightening his grip on the railing, which felt sticky under his palms.

"Your connections with them, hide them from Shorer, hide them from everybody. It's impossible to work like that! If Shorer's daughter weren't about to give birth any minute, he would have found out long ago."

"I don't have any connections with 'them.' What 'them' are you talking about? There's no 'them' here, only Nita."

Tzilla shrugged. "I don't want to tell you what you yourself would have said to me if I'd given you an answer like that," she said, averting her green eyes from his face. Her long silver earrings swayed gently. "And what about the baby? What's going to happen with the baby? Are you just going to go on as if nothing's happened?"

"I haven't thought about it yet," he admitted, suppressing a twinge of regret for having told her about the baby in the first place.

"I don't believe it!" said Tzilla in despair. "How can you not think about it? That's the first thing you should think about. She needs you now to help her with her baby, too—and not as a detective! Are you going to just leave her on her own now? Are you capable of interrogating her? What are you going to do? What are you going to do with the baby?"

Michael said nothing. He should never have involved Tzilla in the business with the baby—that was a big mistake. Facing the couple's disapproval and condemnation, the thought suddenly crossed his mind that they had almost turned into his enemies, into one of the forces trying to take something away from him, either the baby or the case. Like a big stain the knowledge began to spread through his consciousness that the baby would be taken from him anyway, even if he were now to give up the case.

"There's no need to decide everything at this moment," said Eli, sighing. "Let's leave it alone for now. It's between you and Shorer," he added. "Why do you have to get so emotional about it? It's his business, after all," he said to Tzilla and then looked at Michael, waiting.

"I don't know yet what I'm going to do," Michael admitted, "not at this stage anyway. If it doesn't work out I'll give up the case. . . . I'll talk to Shorer." Suddenly a calm indifference came over him, with one part of him saying it'll be all right and another saying whatever happens happens. His hands felt warmer.

"But what do you intend to do right now? You're both still sharing the same babysitters! You're over there at her place all day long!" cried Tzilla. "And how can you take a case like this and take care of a baby? When will you see her?"

"When indeed," murmured Michael. He glanced at his watch, dismissing thoughts of a warm, smooth cheek and a toothless smile. "But first I have to see how Nita is, and then I'll speak to Shorer, and maybe I'll phone my sister and—"

"Phone your sister? What for? To ask her to come?"

Michael nodded.

"Your sister Yvette?"

"My sister Yvette. Why not? I've never asked her before, not when Yuval was small. . . . Why not?"

"Actually, it's a good idea," said Tzilla, and the expression of tension and distress on her face began to fade. "She'll talk some sense into you. There are moments in life . . . I can hardly believe that I have to say this to you now; it's only what you've always said yourself. There are moments in life when you have to choose. Either you want a baby or —"

"Yes? Or what? If you've got a baby you can't work?" He looked at her intently, and she blushed.

"It's not the same thing!" she protested indignantly. "First of all, I didn't work for six months when Eyal was born, and with Yosefa I didn't work for three months. But here it isn't just a matter of a baby! It's a matter of a woman that you . . ." She blushed. "That you're kind of living with."

"That's not true!" protested Michael. "It's a practical arrangement, friendship, there's no . . . There's no reason why I shouldn't . . . I'll decide for myself!" he said finally in a tone which made it clear to all three of them that the discussion was over. "And now please get hold of Balilty for me and another two people from Forensics. And what's this about Zippo? What made you bring Zippo, of all people? And what's that girl doing here, the thin one with the hungry eyes, with her tight jeans, what's her name—Dalit?" Eli opened his mouth to say something, but shut it again at the sight of Solomon approaching them.

"I've been looking for you," Solomon complained. "I've already gone over everything with a fine-tooth comb."

"Here I am," said Michael calmly, amazed at the feeling of relief that overcame him at this justified, legitimate interruption of his conversation with Eli and Tzilla. "What can I do for you?"

"I'll be off in a minute," hummed Solomon. "They're taking the body away, it's packed and ready. And tomorrow I'll give you a final answer. We'll begin work on the body tonight, but in the meantime you can forget about the violinists. Shimshon agrees with me," he said, waving the three strings he held in his hand. "Too short for our purposes, hardly half a meter long, and the viola strings aren't long enough either."

"What's left?" asked Michael, and he finally lit the cigarette he had been holding for the last few minutes.

"Cello and double bass, but the bass strings are too thick for cutting. The only suitable ones in length and thickness are cello strings, if at all."

"If at all what?"

"If it was really an instrument string. We won't know until we find it."

"A cello string?" asked Tzilla meaningfully.

"If a string instrument string at all—then a cello," said Solomon. He hummed.

"There you are," said Tzilla grimly. "What have I been trying to tell you? Did you hear that?" she said, confronting Michael with her arms outspread. "A cello! What do you intend to do about that?"

He gave her a hard stare. "Are you working with me or not?" he gambled.

Tzilla blushed. After a moment of silence she said: "What kind of a question is that? Of course I—"

"Then please get to work." Her face fell. "Let's all get to work and stop wasting time," he said in a more conciliatory tone. "Let me worry about the rest. After all these years you can give me a bit of credit. And I promise you I'll talk to Shorer. I'm not trying to deceive anyone. But meanwhile get hold of Balilty for me—and send her away," he said, nodding in the direction of the skinny girl with the eager look in the tight jeans and long T-shirt. "Now I'm going to Theo Van Gelden's office."

6

His Majesty Sent for Me

Theo van Gelden stood over Nita, who was still lying huddled in the same position. When Michael knocked once briefly and immediately walked in, Theo started back with an expression of alarm on his face. "There's no change," he said, touching her arm. "It's like a coma, she hasn't moved at all, I don't know—"

"There's no point in trying to wake her," said Michael after holding her wrist and feeling her pulse, which was still weak and slow. "The doctor said it would take a few hours, so why don't you just let her sleep?"

"I thought we could go home," said Theo, and he bit his lower lip. His gray hair emphasized the yellowish tinge of his face. He took off his glasses and parted his handsome lips: "I . . . I can't stand being cooped up here for hours, I've got a terrible headache, and the thought . . . I wanted . . . And I can't leave her here alone." He looked at Michael as if asking for permission to leave her, but Michael only shook his head. "We'll take her home soon, but meanwhile you stay here with her," he said.

Theo nodded. His face took on a look of ostentatious resignation. He looked at Michael and nodded again, staring at him as if expecting praise for his obedience. Finally he put on his glasses again, pushed his hands into his pockets, and began to pace from the door to the window and back again, with the measured steps Michael remembered from the time in Nita's living room after Felix van Gelden's death. He paced to and fro, stopped at the couch, rubbed his cheek as if scraping his hand against the several-days-old bristles, and rubbed his forehead. His fingers lingered on the small dimple on his chin as he said: "I have to notify . . . cancel . . . I don't know what . . . Japan . . . the concert the day after tomorrow where Gabi was supposed to play in the Brahms Double Concerto . . ." again he looked at Michael expectantly. "You must think I'm a terrible person," he said, "but I can't help thinking about these things. I don't know how I can think about them now," he apologized, "but I'm not responsible for my thoughts," he announced, raising his hands defensively. "I'm not used to it, so much death at once, someone should tell me how. . . . What can I do? I feel like a person watching a horror movie . . . as if I'm not here at all."

As Michael removed the pack of cigarettes from his shirt pocket, took one out, and went over to the big window, Theo sat down at the desk, clasped his hands, and looked at the portrait of Leonard Bernstein, his face contorted in pain and pleasure, his head thrown back, and his crossed hands holding a baton against his chest. The photograph hung on the wall next to the window, opposite a photo of a sizable orchestra during a concert; only the back of the conductor, who was sitting in a wheelchair on the podium and waving his skinny arms, was visible. It looked as if the trembling of the arms had been caught by the camera.

The window at which Michael stood overlooked the Old City walls and one end of the King David Hotel. He gazed at the view and at the smoke escaping from his mouth, and for a moment he felt completely at a loss. He knew that he, too, should be in the lobby, beginning to conduct the interrogations, examining with his own eyes the string players' knuckles for cuts.

Two police cars were already parked at the end of the street, and in the one closest to the building he could make out the blurred figures of two uniformed policemen waiting in postures of bored anticipation. He thought about the body, wrapped in a shiny black plastic bag, strapped to a stretcher, being carried to the ambulance where no doubt Solomon would sit in the front seat, humming insights on life and the world into the ears of the driver. But Michael went on lingering by the window, next to Theo, waiting, to tell the truth, for Danny Balilty, as if his arrival would signal the beginning of the real action. Why he should be waiting so expectantly for Balilty, as if his coming would solve his problems, he had no idea.

He turned his back to the window, stood opposite the big photograph of the orchestra with the conductor in the wheelchair, and looked at his stooped, hunched back. "Who's the conductor?" he asked, and Theo looked up absently: "Stravinsky, here in Jerusalem, more than thirty years ago, in sixty-one," he said, and he looked at the photograph as if it were an old acquaintance he hadn't seen for years.

"I didn't know he'd been in Israel," said Michael, surprised.

"Once, near the end of his life. He conducted the *Firebird*. I was eighteen then, almost nineteen." Theo smiled and looked at his hands. "They carried him up to the stage like a sack—until he began to conduct. Then he was . . . well, not a sack," he said with a giggle. "He was amazing—everyone was stunned. Because of that concert—okay, not only because of it, but it was definitely a turning point—I finally made up my mind to become a conductor." He shook his head, as if trying to banish the memory, and looked at Michael, who now gave him a short summary of the facts, taking care not to describe Gabriel's position before he was murdered, and not to mention the word "string." Among other questions, he slipped in one about Nita's cello. "I understand that it's a very valuable instrument," he said, and he stole a glance at Theo, who said: "Of course, there are very few like it in the world."

"I didn't see it in the hall," said Michael. "Did she leave it somewhere?"

"It's here, in the cabinet behind the door," said Theo with dreamy indifference. "She put it there after the rehearsal, before . . ." and Michael, who was afraid that any question about the strings could expose what he was trying to suppress, ground out his cigarette stub in a rusty lid on the windowsill and went over to the cabinet. He opened the brown sliding door and looked at the piles of scores threatening to spill out. On the floor of the cabinet, which covered the wall behind the door, under the hem of a big coat, lay the familiar case. He pulled it out and removed the instrument, ignoring Theo's stare as he silently and attentively followed his movements. Michael kneeled down next to the case, which he laid on the soft carpet, close to the chair on which Theo was sitting, and rummaged inside it, touching the cube of rosin, fingering the green felt lining of the case, and removing the semitransparent envelope. There were two strings coiled up inside it. Before his eyes he saw her fingers threading and pulling, and with all his might he tried to remember how many spare strings she had then in the living room, but all he could see were her busy, competent hands and the expression of concentration on her face. Only she would be able to tell him how many there were to begin with. He spoke in a dry, indifferent tone as he asked Theo about the instrument.

"No, it's not a Stradivarius," Theo confirmed, and he bent over the cello lying between them. "But a 1737 Amati from Cremona is something, too. Amati specialized in cellos." Theo turned to look at Nita, who did not move, and he sighed. "A Jewish millionaire who was very moved by her concert with the Chicago Symphony gave it to her. I remember it as vividly as if it was yesterday." A spasm of a smile crossed his face, and once more he launched on a compulsive monologue: "She really did play it well, the Elgar Cello Concerto. Do you know it?" Not waiting for an answer, he continued: "The piece Jacqueline du Pré made so famous. Maybe you saw her play it on television, a brilliant performance, no doubt about it. In my opinion," he said, scratching his head, "the concerto itself is an irritating piece of no special significance, but Jackie really made it. When Nita performed it, Jackie was no longer able to play. And the truth is that I thought that our father should have given her a cello like this long before that concert in Chicago, and I told him so, but—well, it doesn't matter anymore. You've heard Nita play, you know what she's capable of, when she actually gets down to playing, that is, because for the past year she hasn't been playing, she canceled engagements—never mind, yes, she deserves this cello."

"It's beautiful," said Michael, stroking the reddish surface. "I understand it's a special wood."

"It sure is," Theo murmured. "Years of drying, with special processes. It's a big deal."

"Are the strings special, too?" asked Michael, carefully plucking the strings one after the other, pinching the thinnest string twice.

Theo narrowed his eyes and gave him a penetrating look. "In the old days they used to be gut and the thinner strings were sometimes made of silk. You could tell which string belonged to which instrument. Every cello, every violin had its own strings. You could even tell who had made them. But in this century they began to make them of metal and plastic. For years now we've had standard strings of two types, concert and normal, and there are only a few factories that produce them." He rose from his seat, shook his legs, pushed his hands into his pockets, and resumed his tiring walk from one end of the room to the other.

"Does Nita have concert or normal strings?"

"Concert, of course," said Theo.

"There are only two spare strings here," said Michael.

Theo did not stop. His head was bowed, as if he were measuring his steps, and he muttered something unclear.

"How many spare strings does she usually have?" asked Michael, keeping his voice was casual as possible.

Theo shrugged his shoulders. "I don't have a clue," he said absently. "I haven't been privy to Nita's habits for years. I suppose she must have a few more at home."

A loud sigh and a single sob rising from the couch froze them both. But Nita's eyes did not open after the sob, although she straightened out her legs under the blanket and then clasped them to her stomach again. There was a suspenseful silence for a few seconds, and after it became clear that she had gone back to sleep, Michael asked, in a low voice, the question that always grated on him: "Did your brother have any enemies? Anyone special that you know about?"

"I've been thinking about it for the last hour—who could have done . . . who could have wanted . . . I haven't any idea," said Theo, and he sat down on the padded chair behind his desk. He spread his hands out and looked at them in turn, feeling his knuckles, which were big and broad like Nita's. Michael stole a glance at them, automatically checking for signs of scratches. But Theo van Gelden's hands, like Nita's and those of the concertmaster and the other two string players, were smooth and unmarked. "You saw him yourself," said Theo, shrugging his shoulders. "You couldn't say he had any real enemies. I, for example, have a lot more," he said, snickering. "The wonder is that nobody did it to me, that I'm not the one lying there," he said, nodded toward the door. Then his face grew grave again. He rubbed it with both hands, and then once more he spread out his hands and looked at them. "There've been all kinds of pressures lately, because of changes he wanted to make in his ensemble. You know that he's started a period instrument Baroque ensemble. He was a great perfectionist, and there was great competition for places in it. You can't imagine the fuss and commotion. And he was full of plans about it, about who would play and who wouldn't. How they'd be paid and how much. He picked up and considered all kinds of payment methods, one from a London ensemble, which pays its members in reverse: the fewer rehearsals needed, the more they're paid. It's an incentive for them to practice hard at home, which is something that never happens here. Nobody here does any work at home, because the more rehearsals, the more overtime. There were hard feelings, definitely, all kinds of grievances—but real enemies? To account for something like this?" His hands went up to his throat.

"The Double Concerto you were working on—wouldn't Avigdor, the concertmaster, normally have played the violin solo?"

"The concertmaster doesn't necessarily play the solo violin part. It's actually quite rare, especially in Romantic music, for the concertmaster to play solo, even when he's one of two soloists. Anyway, I see the solo parts in this Brahms concerto as so individual, so soloistic, that I would never give them to an orchestra's concertmaster and principal cellist, however good they may be."

"But in your previous concert, the one with the *William Tell* Overture, Gabriel acted as concertmaster."

"So what?" said Theo indignantly.

"Don't you think something like that could give rise to bitterness in the regular concertmaster? Avigdor is your regular concertmaster, no?"

"Yes, yes," said Theo impatiently, "but several other of the best violinists sometimes act as concertmaster, and in any event Avigdor is always paid the same. In fact, he was delighted when Gabi was concertmaster. He saw it as an honor to give way to him."

"Sometimes I wonder how people in an orchestra feel when the notes they play are swallowed up again and again by the sound of the other instruments or when they have to play the same two notes over and over. How much frustration must there be in waiting for their turn to play, and to play whatever everyone else is playing."

Theo interrupted him: "You have a very romantic idea of how these things work. I'm not saying that people don't burn out after twenty, thirty years, but on the whole things go well. When there's an atmosphere of excitement and enthusiasm, people forget things like that. You can see it in the Chicago Symphony, no one feels superfluous there. That's how it is in a really good orchestra. In Berlin, well, there the members get paid by the concert, and they share in the orchestra's profits. And they pick their conductors themselves. That's unusual. But sometimes, especially here, orchestras behave like government bureaus, and naturally there's a lot of routine, and it's a job like any other. There are grievances, complaints, and demands for change, and backbiting and scores to settle. But not in this orchestra, and in general a lot depends on the conductor. A good conductor can raise an orchestra up, sweep it along. Anyway, have you seen Avigdor? Could he kill anybody? And certainly not like that."

"I don't know anything about Gabriel's private life," said Michael. "Nita hasn't told me much about him. I don't even know if there's anyone who has to be notified. All I remember is that he was married once, a long time ago, and that he doesn't have any children. But maybe he lives with someone, maybe there's a woman he's close to. In any case, family has to be notified."

"What family?" said Theo dismissively. "We're all the family he has."

"Perhaps his ex-wife then?"

"She's been living in Germany for the past seven years," said Theo, "and there's no contact between them. And certainly not with us. She's a terrible woman. Vulgar, greedy, all she ever gave him was trouble. None of my wives was anything like her, thank God. And you should know," he said, raising his voice and waving a finger, "I've had a lot of wives. I'm an expert on wives," he announced without a smile. "He never had any children, and there are no relatives worth mentioning, either." Then he lowered his voice to a hesitant whisper and dropped his eyes. "But there is . . . someone . . . maybe we should tell Izzy."

"Izzy," Michael repeated. "Who's Izzy?"

"He . . . he lives with Gabi, in his apartment," said Theo, rising to his feet and pushing his hands into his pockets.

There was no room for delicacy now. "Your brother lives with a man? In the sense of living together, of having a homosexual relationship with him?"

"I think so," said Theo, and he resumed his pacing. But this time, instead of keeping his eyes on the ground, he stared at the window and cleared his throat before saying: "I've never asked him directly, but they weren't just apartment mates. I have no problem with it. No problem at all. Live and let live, it doesn't bother me, and a lot of artists . . . musicians . . . you wouldn't believe how many. . . . When I first came to New York I couldn't believe it. Copland, Mitropoulos, and of course . . ." He looked at the photograph of Bernstein. "In short, it's quite natural in our profession, maybe it's even somehow connected with it in essence."

So natural and obvious that no one had ever mentioned it, not even Nita, thought Michael as he asked: "Is that the man I saw after your father . . . when you were sitting . . . who came to Nita's with Gabriel. The fair-haired, short one?"

"That's right," said Theo, nodding with an expression of relief. "So you've already met him. They've been living together for over two years now," he explained, "but we've never spoken about it, we never made a thing of it, even though I'm sure that it wasn't easy for my father." He sighed. "Now the whole thing seems silly," he whispered, and he chuckled hoarsely. "Death always puts things in the right proportion."

"So your father knew."

"I'm sure he knew," said Theo. "But he never talked about it."

"Nita's never said a word."

Theo shrugged his shoulders. "Maybe because he hasn't been around recently. And anyway, do you two talk about everything?"

"Who? Who hasn't been around recently?"

"Izzy. But maybe she just didn't think about it," he said, and it was obvious that he didn't believe it himself. "Izzy was away at a conference, I think, of mathematicians or computer people. I don't understand that stuff. After that he went on a trip, and he came back . . . he came back the day that our father . . . or the day before that. He was in Holland, actually. And Nita's so shy anyway, she's not a big talker at the best of times."

"If they lived together he has to be notified," said Michael. "And I'll have to talk to him, of course."

"I'll tell him myself, in a minute, or do you want to? We can do it from here, right now," he said, rousing himself and pointing to the telephone.

Michael raised his hand. "Later, and not by phone. Were you and Gabriel close?"

Theo cleared his throat, dropped his eyes, rubbed his hands, and raised his head. "It depends on what you call close. When we were small we were together a lot, we studied with the same violin teacher, Dora Zackheim. Have you heard of her?"

Michael nodded faintly.

"We both studied with her, but we're very different, we were always different in everything, and in the last few years we haven't really talked, and we had all kinds of disagreements."

"You were in competition with each other," Michael ventured. "Sibling rivalry."

"Sibling rivalry is an exaggeration," said Theo, making a face. "Too dramatic. I don't know if there even really was any competition. It would be more correct to speak of differences, differences of temperament, of distance. Gabi was an introvert, closed off, and I, well, I . . ." He smiled. "You already know something about what I'm like."

"So he never spoke to you about his relationship with his companion, with Izzy? You don't know if they were on good terms? If they'd quarreled recently?"

"Not as far as I know," said Theo, embarrassed. "I never heard of any problems between them. It makes me a little uncomfortable to realize how little I know about my brother's private life," he admitted. "Everyone in my family, except for me, is so secretive, I'm the only one everyone knows everything about," he added in a plaintive, even pampered tone, which suddenly betrayed a kind of affectation that made Michael wonder if this was how he got his way with others, especially women. "As far as Izzy's concerned, I hardly know him . . . I didn't see them together often, I didn't see Gabi often, for that matter. Especially not recently. I've been abroad, and he's been traveling a lot. Before my father's death, the last times we were all together, I think, were at our father's birthday and on the anniversary of our mother's death." He suddenly fell silent and looked at Michael with a startled expression on his face. "You're not thinking of Izzy!" he exclaimed, evidently shocked. "That he came here and . . ." He gave a brief laugh. "Nonsense. What nonsense! Like some stupid movie!"

"You didn't see him around here today?"

"No."

"What exactly happened backstage? Where were you when Gabriel was there?" asked Michael casually, as he returned the cello to its case.

"Me? Where was I?" Theo said in confusion and frowned as if he were trying to remember. "I . . . I think I was with the timpanist. I hadn't succeeded in getting what I wanted from her during the rehearsal, and I was still working with her. . . . The rehearsal had ended at about half past one. Some of the people started to disperse, some stayed behind. Gabi had a meeting scheduled with all kinds of possible additional candidates for his ensemble, and he left the stage. I didn't notice exactly when, and afterward, I think, they began looking for him because he'd disappeared, and then Nita went backstage and . . . the rest you know."

"But nobody was wandering around backstage? Nobody saw anything?"

"I don't know, really," Theo said apologetically. "I was busy . . . we were supposed to have a dress rehearsal tomorrow morning, and the timpani . . . I wasn't paying any attention."

"You, at any rate, never left the stage during all this time?"

"What time? After the end of the rehearsal?"

Michael nodded.

"Not that I remember. I don't think so." Theo hesitated. "Maybe just . . . but I don't remember if that was after the rehearsal or during the break. I think it was during the break. I had to make a phone call, but my memory's terrible, you can't rely on it. Yes, now I realize that people were wandering around, it would have been very risky for . . . for whoever did it. At any moment someone could have . . . But in the end it was poor Nita who found him." Suddenly his face took on an expression of alarm. "Are you asking about *me*? Do you want to know what *I* was doing? Are you trying to suggest . . . ?" The expression of alarm had given way to one of indignation. His handsome lips twisted. "*Me*?" he asked heatedly.

Michael was silent.

"Are these questions supposed to be about what you people call an alibi? Are you asking me about an alibi?"

"Were you on the stage all the time?"

Theo nodded. The indignant expression did not leave his face.

"So who was close to Gabi, aside from Izzy?" asked Michael as he looked through the window at the cars drawing up outside the building. He saw returning orchestra members he recognized, their faces showing confusion, and newspaper and television reporters from the two channels with photographers and cameramen in tow. Even if he left through the artists' entrance, he thought with a feeling of dread, their cameras would flash in his face. He had always hated that, but this time it was out of the question, he decided, absolutely out of the question. Let them talk to Balilty, he said to himself. Only the front entrance was visible from the window, and he was sure that Balilty would be arriving through the side entrance.

"Really close? Maybe Nita," said Theo hesitantly, and he swallowed, his Adam's apple rising and falling. "Closer than me, at any rate." He threw his head back and massaged the back of his neck. "Look," he said, "I . . . please don't think . . . I loved Gabi, but it's complicated. We're very . . . we were very different, two different people. I was closer to our mother, Gabi was his father's son." The corners of his lips twisted. "We're completely different. Nita, too. In our approach to music we were very different; even though we both played the violin. Other musical families," he said bitterly, "see to it that each child plays a different instrument, but when Gabi wanted a violin too, nobody objected. They let him have what he wanted. And Dora Zackheim, too."

"She preferred him," Michael guessed.

Theo shrugged his shoulders. His lips pouted. You could imagine him as a child. Sulky, but pretending to be indifferent, with the charm of someone aware of his own good looks, but full of suppressed resentment. He lowered his head and remained silent.

"Did he ever talk to you about intimate subjects? Personal things?"

Theo blinked and looked at the tips of his shoes. "No," he admitted with an effort. "I didn't know much about him, and ever since I realized what his relationship was with Izzy . . . I was completely confused, the possibility had never even occurred to me, and my father . . . poor man." He chuckled. "Me with all my divorces, Gabi with his boyfriend, Nita with her illegitimate child—none of us the way we were supposed to be."

"Did it bother him? Your father?"

"I don't know," Theo admitted. "How much can you know about your father if he chooses not to talk? He never reacted when he heard things about us. When Nita got pregnant and that character of hers—not that we ever met him, but I made inquiries—when he left her in the lurch like that, and she was so broken up, my father didn't even take an interest in how she was. I tried to talk to him, both about her and about Gabi—tactfully, of course, about Gabi—but he never said a word. In serious discussions—you have to remember that I wasn't here much either—he would sit in that armchair of his, where . . . where he was . . . where they found him, and say nothing. Not a word. Nita did speak to him once about Gabi after I tried. I think that with her he was more communicative. To me, at any rate, he said nothing."

"What's your brother's friend like?"

"I hardly know him. I only met him a few times, and Gabi didn't say: This is my lover—only, this is Izzy. All I know about him is that he's a mathematician. He's polite, with a gentle manner. He knows something about music, too, he's studied it and even plays the harpsichord. He's very big on original instruments, on historical performance—authentic music," he added with a curl of his lip. "Gabi once told me that he'd learned a lot from him, and he talked about him as if he were a real musician, but I've never heard him play. To me he spoke very little . . . and I know that he never liked . . ."

A knock on the door interrupted him. "They told me you were here," said Yaffa from Forensics, looking around the room. "I thought you'd want to know . . ." she added and glanced at Theo, who stopped pacing, drew himself up, measured her with a practiced appraising look, letting his eyes dwell on the region of her groin, which was emphasized by her tight jeans, and then looked straight into her eyes with a quizzical stare.

Michael gestured toward Nita in order to hush Yaffa, and went over to the door. "What didn't he like?" he asked Theo with his hand on the door handle.

"What?" Theo replied in confusion.

"Izzy," Michael insisted. "You said that he didn't like something. What didn't he like?"

"Oh," said Theo, remembering, and he waved his hand dismissively. "It's not important. He didn't like my interpretation . . . the way I conducted all kinds of things, especially classical works, Mozart and Haydn, but he was critical of my Brahms, too. He told me once that he disagreed with me about the trumpets and drums I was using. He said that I should use the kind that were used in Brahms's time. He said this in connection with the *German Requiem*—but that's got nothing to do with . . ."

Michael looked at Nita, who lay still, and then went out and shut the door behind him. "I thought you'd want to know that we've combed the scene," Yaffa whispered. "We haven't found anything, and we've begun searching the hall. Maybe we should search the offices, too. We're combing every inch of the stage and the hall now, but it's a big area, it'll take time. And Balilty's waiting for you in the hall."

"Tell him I'll be with him in a minute," said Michael, and he felt his pulse racing, as if something decisive was about to take place. He went back into Theo's office and asked Theo to wait for him there. "We'll take Nita home soon," he promised, and he set out for the hall, via the stage.

From the floodlit stage—where the Forensics crew was crawling on their knees, collecting crumbs with tweezers and dropping them into small plastic bags—the hall looked dark, even though it too was also fully lit, and there, too, two men were crawling between the rows to comb the carpet for clues. Michael stood at the edge of the stage and shaded his eyes, and only then did he see Balilty, sitting in the last row before the gallery, on the row's next to last seat before the aisle, his legs stretched over the seat in front of him, rolling a scrap of paper between his fingers. When Michael reached him he saw that it was a bubble gum wrapper. The popping of the gum had been audible from a distance. Balilty put the wrapper down on the seat to his left, sat up straight, and patted the empty seat on his right. "I hear it was a real horror movie," he said as he folded his hands on his paunch. "Slit throat, pool of blood, the works."

Michael nodded.

"The whole press corps is waiting outside. It's the van Gelden family, after all. The papers will be filled with it by this evening. Eli's put people at all the entrances, no one's being allowed in. The whole building's the crime scene, no?"

Michael sighed.

"Your majesty sent for me," Balilty reminded him as he turned his face toward him. The expression of satisfaction, almost gratification, twinkling in Balilty's eyes for some reason failed to arouse Michael's indignation. "Van Gelden, Gabriel, throat slashed," he remarked to the air. "You surely want to tell me that the two murders are connected. Do you want to get your hands on the stolen painting case, too? The first van Gelden case? Is that what it's about? Did you see the piece of ass they put on your team? I've had my eye on her for a month already. What a body!"

Michael nodded. He lit a cigarette and held the match in his hand. Balilty stood up, went over to the corner of the hall and came back with a rusty lid, and laid it on the back of the seat in front of them. He sat down noisily and folded his hands ceremoniously. "Is that all you want from me?" he asked provocatively. "You didn't have to drag me here for that. You could have sent for the file. Believe me, you'd be no further along than we are. We don't have a single lead."

"Maybe Gabriel van Gelden was the legal heir to the painting," remarked Michael.

"I would have told you that. Actually, van Gelden's will divides up the property pretty fairly between them. I checked it out. The shop's divided between the three of them, the cash too, the house and the painting go to your girlfriend. You've made a good deal there," he said, winking audaciously. "And he even gives her permission to sell them."

"To sell the painting?" Michael was astonished.

"That's what it says: 'And she may do as she pleases with them.' Which I take to mean that she's entitled to sell the painting."

"So why didn't he sell it?"

"Do I know? He preferred to wait. Maybe the market was weak, what do I know? He didn't lack funds. It was a family heirloom, don't forget, and then there's the Holocaust. You know what it's like with them."

"It'll have to be looked into further," said Michael, sighing.

"What did you think, that I didn't check out the will? That I didn't check with Zurich and Paris if anyone ordered the break-in? Is that what you wanted me for?" Balilty repeated.

"No, not only for that," Michael admitted.

"What then?" Balilty said sharply, turning his body with a sudden movement, like a sleepy tiger momentarily awakening. "You don't need any more manpower. The whole police force will be here soon. They even took Tzilla off her case for you. If Shorer weren't preoccupied now with other things, if the Commissioner weren't busy with the state controller, they would have shown up here themselves hours ago. We're involved with very important people here, very, very important—so what do you need me for?" The provocative question expressed deeply felt humiliation as well as triumph at soon being invited into areas to which he had previously been denied entry. "And you?" he added in a softer voice. "You shouldn't be here at all, you're part of . . . never mind, it doesn't matter. What can I do for you?"

"I want . . ." Michael restrained himself. He had to tread carefully, to choose his words so that Balilty would trust him and not go on the defensive and put obstacles in his path. "I want you to be part of the Special Investigation Team. I want to ask you to be in charge of the case officially, or at least to work with me on it."

Balilty nodded noncommittally, leaned back in his seat, again stretched his legs over the back of the seat in front of him, and said nothing.

"First of all, it's logical because of the connection with old van Gelden's case," said Michael hopefully, but Balilty didn't react. "You understand," continued Michael, "I have a problem here. I know the people involved, especially the sister, but I want this case. By chance, by luck, I've been at loose ends, between things, so they put me on it, and I want in. Eli and Tzilla have already talked to me," he added quickly. "I don't have to be told all over again how unhealthy it is, and how impossible it is to be objective when you're an interested party. Not that I am an interested party, but I am involved, and that's exactly why I'm asking you, because I trust you to clue me in if I miss anything because of my involvement. You'll see things where I can't see them, or don't want to see them. And of course I won't be able to interrogate Nita. And anyway," he added briskly, "the two cases now have to be connected."

Balilty took a deep breath, puffed out his cheeks, and blew the air out noisily. "I'll have to think about it," he said after a long pause. "I'll have to think about it a lot. It isn't simple. First of all, I may be in the midst of something, and second, it's going to be a difficult case. From what Eli and Tzilla tell me, I understand that any one of these klezmers could have . . . That's almost a hundred people—look at what's going on here—and you're living with this woman!"

"I don't live with her. I've got an arrangement with her about . . . about the babies."

"Do you remember what I told you a few days ago? When you came to my office, and I told you that there was a logic behind doing things in the normal way, like everyone else? And by the way, how's the search for the mother going? They'll never find her, I tell you, never. But whether they find her or not, don't you think you've gone a little crazy about all that? The last thing you need in your life is a baby. Since when have you been so crazy about babies?"

Michael sighed. "How much time do you need?"

"To think about it? Let's say an hour or two," said Balilty. He winked and smiled. "Do you think I don't know that I'm a total idiot? We both know what will happen in the end. But I've got my principles. I have to think about it and I am thinking about it. I may be an idiot, but I wasn't born yesterday. I know when I'm being an idiot. At least I'm not like all those women who run after you with their tongues hanging out. I think, and they don't." Michael waved his arm dismissively and was about to say something like, "Which women?" But Balilty put a hand on his arm and stopped him. "Like everyone else, I've got a soft spot for you, Mr. Ohayon. I'm like putty in your hands. What is this, anyway? You whistle and I come? Without a second thought? I have to think of myself too, no?"

"What risks are you taking? What's so terrible about what I asked for?"

"Are you kidding?" said Balilty, and he stretched his legs out again, folded his hands on his paunch, and stared at the stage and the people crawling around on it. "I'll be given the title of head of the SIT, and my role will be to cover your ass? You'll do exactly what you like, and I'll be your puppy dog, and we both know it. And even so, I'm not saying 'no' on the spot, please note," he said, pausing and waving his finger. Then his body relaxed and he added, with resignation: "You're simply used to getting everything you ask for. You think no one can resist your charms. Well, it takes more than a pair of brown eyes to melt me," he said, staring at the stage. "Even if they're yours. And don't frown like that," he warned as he turned back to Michael. "That won't get you anywhere."

"How can you say I'm used to getting everything I want?" Michael protested.

"Okay, maybe not everything," said Balilty, softening after giving him a hard stare. "Maybe there's something you wanted that didn't fall into your lap, even though I'm damned if I know what it is," he grumbled, and he softened again. "I don't mean *everything*, but there are areas where you're used to getting whatever you want. This time it may not be so easy, because I, for example, may not be able to come running when you call, because I may be working on another case. In other words, I may be too busy. Did you ever think of that?"

"What are you working on?" asked Michael suspiciously.

"Tell me, are you no longer with us at all? Don't you read the newspapers? Has this business with the baby—I haven't even see her yet—fried your brains completely? Haven't you even heard of our latest coup?" Balilty looked at him curiously. "You're not the same man I knew, I don't know. . . . You make me feel disoriented, you're completely out of it."

"Recently," Michael admitted with embarrassment, "I haven't really been in touch. I've had all kinds of things—"

"So you don't know that we've found pictures worth millions? Picassos? Van Goghs?"

"I haven't heard about it," confessed Michael.

"How would you hear? You're too busy warming bottles day and night, changing diapers, running home like some . . . Your mind's not here." Balilty shook his head and looked reflectively at the seat in front of him.

"How many times do you intend to tell me that?"

"You sound exactly like a woman," said Balilty disapprovingly, and

Michael made a face. "Why are you so sensitive? I like babies, too," Balilty said quietly, and he chewed energetically. "Here's the story," he said, and he took his feet off the seat in front of him. "Are you with me? A few days ago we caught this woman, Clara Amojal, the owner of an art gallery in Tel Aviv, with a French tourist, Claude Raphaël. Very respectable people, she has to be about forty-five but she's a looker, a real looker." He paused as if conjuring her up before his eyes. "Caught them with six paintings, including a Picasso and a Van Gogh."

"How did you get onto them?"

"We were tipped off," admitted Balilty. "We would never have caught them otherwise. But we got an anonymous phone call, someone called the police three days ago with a license plate number, the fraud division got onto it, and I . . . they brought me in because I'd brought them in on the van Gelden painting. We stopped them on the Tel Aviv–Jerusalem highway. Thanks to the anonymous phone call. All the caller said was do yourselves a favor, search the car. Motti—do you know him? the baby face with the pink cheeks?—Motti took the tip seriously and decided to go for it. They stopped the car and searched it and found six paintings. Don't ask!" he said chuckling. "It's a museum. I'm telling you, you sit in that apartment in Yefe-Nof—a really fancy place, not far from where Begin lived—with the six paintings from the car and the eight we found in the apartment, and you're in Paris. Van Gelden's painting's nothing compared to those."

"Do you think there's a connection with the van Gelden case?"

"I don't know, I don't know much yet," said Balilty. "We arrested the pair, the art dealer and the Frenchman, but they don't know anything about van Gelden. They hadn't been in business long. There's apparently a Jerusalem man involved, but we haven't found him yet. I interrogated them myself for two days, a polygraph test and so on. Their lawyer," he grumbled, "got me to agree to let them go when the test turned out okay."

"You agreed? How could you agree to such a thing? You already had them locked up and you agreed? We never—"

"I figured that it's worth trying," Balilty interrupted impatiently. "I've got my eye on them. They can't take a piss without us knowing about it. Everything's covered. The apartment, the car, the business in Tel Aviv. While they're outside they may lead us further. Anyway, they didn't seem to be lying about van Gelden. They don't know anything about it. Interpol is very interested in the case."

"If the paintings aren't forgeries," said Michael.

"Even if they are, they're at a very high level. The experts have been examining them for two days already and they haven't found any proof yet that they're fakes. I tell you, the forensic lab is a joke compared to them, even with all their microscopes and their computer scanners. Do you know how to determine if an old or important picture is a forgery or not?"

Michael shook his head.

"Didn't you also study that at the university?"

Michael shook his head again. "I have no idea," he assured him.

"Good," said Balilty with a satisfied sigh, "because I can give you an expert lecture on it. You'll surprised by what I know now about colors!"

Michael murmured something admiring.

"No, don't say, 'Very interesting.' It's a whole world, I tell you, a whole world! For example, if a painter in the seventeenth century wanted a particular blue, let's say ultramarine, do you know that shade of blue?"

Michael looked at the Forensics people, who had left the stage and were scattering through the hall, and at the two who were bearing down on the row where they themselves were sitting. "Okay, it's a very deep blue," Balilty continued didactically. "In the seventeenth century they used a semiprecious stone, I happen to know it because Matty likes it, and I once had a girlfriend who called herself a goldsmith . . . anyway, there's a stone called lapis lazuli, which the ancient Egyptians liked. Do you know it?"

"I think so," said Michael. "I'm not sure."

Balilty looked gratified. "Well, in the seventeenth century they used to grind it into powder to produce ultramarine. You're a historian, aren't you?"

Michael smiled.

"This is historical knowledge," promised Balilty. "It was only in the nineteenth century that they began to obtain this color artificially.

That way you can tell the age of the painting. And if this method doesn't work, do you know what the ultimate method is?"

"No, what?"

"The ultimate method," said Balilty rolling the words pleasurably around his tongue, "is to bombard the picture with radiation, and then put photographic film on the painting to measure the radiation emitted by the chemical substances in it. Did you know that?"

"Certainly not. It sounds incredible," said Michael, who was truly astonished. "Are you sure? Is that information reliable?"

"What do you mean?" said Balilty, offended. "I'm *telling* you!" He laid his hand on his heart. "I got it from the finest experts! I've been sitting with a Frenchwoman from Interpol for the last two days. It's her specialty. She's got a pair of other specialties, too," he added with a wink. "And afterward you can compare the results of that test with a chemical analysis. And there's something else, too: If the picture is painted on wood, like they did in Italy until the middle of the sixteenth century and in Holland until the beginning of the seventeenth—did you know that it's possible to count the age rings on the edge of a wooden board?"

Michael shook his head. The people from Forensics were already very close to them.

"And what I've learned about the age of the wood they painted on!"

"Van Gelden's painting was on canvas," Michael reminded him.

"I know," said Balilty. "I was only telling you."

"Do we have to move?" Michael asked Shimshon, who was standing at the end of their row with another man from Forensics.

"You can go on sitting here for a minute," said Shimshon, and he went on talking to the man next to him.

"Do you want me to put you into the picture here?" Michael asked Balilty, who put his head to one side, smiled, and said: "Why not? I may as well hear the facts. It's hot as hell in here. What are they looking for now?"

Michael explained.

Balilty pursed his lips in a skeptical expression: "How would the weapon get down into the hall? If one of them did it, it would make more sense for it to be near the body, the string or whatever it was. I'd concentrate on the backstage area. On unexpected places, too—kitchens, filing cabinets. And it wouldn't necessarily be here at all. Only if the murderer's still here."

"I'd like you to speak to Nita when she wakes up," said Michael hesitantly as they rose to leave the hall. "For you to be the one who interro—who asks her the necessary questions. About her spare strings, too." Balilty stopped between the end of the row and the wooden doors.

"Please," said Michael. "You know I can't do that myself."

Balilty cocked his head and grinned. "What are you going to tell Shorer?" he asked.

"We'll cross that bridge when we come to it," Michael muttered.

"He'd never have sent you if he knew—"

"Shimshon!" someone shouted from the back of the stage. "Shimshon!" Shimshon abandoned the last row before the gallery and bounded lightly toward the stage. Michael looked at Balilty, and they turned back and climbed onto the stage. One of the Forensics people was standing in the wings, his face shining with sweat. "Over there, just lying there," he marveled, pointing to an old baby grand piano that stood where the corridor curved toward the stairs leading to the back entrance. On top of the piano was a big pile of music scores, old newspapers, and a large roll of the yellow packaging tape that had been used to seal doors and windows during the Gulf War. There was a thick layer of dust on everything, and more piled papers on the floor at the foot of the instrument. "I opened the lid completely by chance," the investigator said to Shimshon, "not thinking I'd find anything. There's so much stuff on the lid, it's as if it hasn't been touched in years," he said, a proud smile already spreading over his face as he handed something to Shimshon, who carefully took the thin metal wire, one end of which was still coiled around a small wooden peg, and held it in his open palms as if he were a priest holding the consecrated host. He breathed over it carefully. Michael went over to them, and Balilty leaned against the corridor wall close by.

"What do you say?" Michael asked Shimshon.

"It could be. Definitely, but we have to examine it. Of course it must have been wiped clean," he grumbled as he looked through the magnifying glass Yaffa was now holding over the wire stretched between his hands. "It's from a string instrument, no doubt about it," he said with satisfaction.

"Here, in a plastic bag, just lying inside!" said someone triumphantly.

"Now we'll find the gloves, too," said Shimshon. "If there's a string, there'll be gloves, because it's impossible to do what he did without gloves and not cut your fingers. Have you looked at the musicians' hands?"

"We're looking," said Michael, "at everybody's hands. We haven't found a single cut yet."

"I suppose musicians have to be careful of their hands," said Shimshon absently as he put the string into a transparent bag. "You must be on good terms with God," he said to Michael. "I have to hand it to you, you were right and I was wrong. *Touché*," he announced, making a deep bow and doffing an imaginary hat.

"Before we celebrate, we have to send it to Solomon," said Michael. "To see if it's the murder weapon."

"We've changed places," said Shimshon, smiling. "Now you have to check it out, be the skeptic. . . . Anyway, the main thing is we've found something."

"Gloves? You want gloves?" The cry came from near the piano, and Yaffa, both hands outstretched, was waving a pair of fine, light-brown, thick leather gloves at them, a wide smile on her face. Shimshon ran up to her and snatched them from her hands. "Where were they?" he demanded. "Lying here innocently," said Yaffa, pointing at the piano, "just underneath beyond the pedals."

"These are no ordinary gloves," said Balilty. "That's soft, special leather. They don't belong to just anyone."

"We'll have to question the musicians about that, too," said Michael as he looked at the fine fur lining of the soft leather gloves.

"They could belong either to a man or a woman," said Shimshon. "Someone with quite big hands."

"Lots of musicians have big hands," said Yaffa. "I noticed that today. And they've got long arms, too."

"As if the body adapts itself to their needs?" mocked Shimshon. He put the gloves carefully into a little bag. "The best thing would be," he reflected aloud, "if we could take all the musicians to the lab and test for traces of fur on their hands."

"Too late," said Balilty. "They all washed their hands after the fingerprinting, especially the one we're looking for."

"No such thing," said Shimshon heatedly. "You could find it under their fingernails. It takes days for all the traces to disappear."

"Aren't there any prints inside? Isn't it possible to find prints inside the glove?"

"We'll test, we'll see," muttered Shimshon. "But we have to look at their hands."

"We'll look," promised Michael. "But you have to remember that precisely the person we're looking for may no longer be in the building."

Shimshon handed the sealed bag to Yaffa. They were still standing in the corridor next to the piano. One of the Forensics crew was emptying the contents of a trash bin into a big plastic bag, and Michael looked unseeingly at the hands in thin plastic gloves as they rummaged through rotting apple cores and candy wrappers. The moment he heard the sounds—the others went on talking as if they hadn't heard anything—he froze. His heart pounded. In the distance, from the direction of Theo's office, he could clearly hear the warm tones of a cello, and as he hurried toward the other wing, where Theo's office was, he realized that the notes were very familiar, and at the door he no longer had any doubt that someone was playing, wonderfully, something he knew well, maybe Bach. But then he heard the scratchy, muffled sound, and he knew that it was not Nita playing, but a recording, an old one at that.

Inside the room Theo stood at the radio, his hands at the knobs. The radio had been playing at full volume, which Theo had just turned down. His face was very pale and his expression one of horror. "I didn't intend to play music here now, I just wanted to hear the news, to see if they already were . . ." he said tremulously. "I switched it on without looking, and there was the *Voice of Music*."

Michael stood on the threshold and looked at Nita lying on her back. Her open eyes, pupils dilated, were staring at the ceiling. The hoarse sounds of the old recording filled the room. Now, as he stepped inside, he suddenly noticed the sound of the accompanying organ.

"I couldn't switch it off, because of Thelma Yellin," Theo said, as if in self-defense, as the sounds came to a stop. He looked at Nita, who kept her eyes fixed on the ceiling.

"You have been listening to the *Adagio* from Bach's piano *Toccata, Adagio, and Fugue in C major*, arranged for cello and organ by Arnold Holdheim," the announcer solemnly said, adding that the recording, from the early fifties, was from the Voice of Israel radio archives and was played in honor of the cellist Thelma Yellin, whose hundredth birthday it was today. In the time remaining before the news, the announcer said that Yellin, who had been a student of Casals's and had done much for music in Israel, died in 1959 at the age of sixty-four.

Theo's hands trembled as he turned off the radio. Michael leaned against the wall. Nita did not turn her head. Her eyes, very dark because of the dilation of her pupils, stared straight ahead, and her voice was hollow and hoarse as she said: "Maybe it's my turn now—and that'll be it."

Michael sat down next to her on the sofa. "What are you talking about?" he asked, alarmed, laying his hand on her arm.

"Thelma Yellin. It's no coincidence," she mumbled and closed her eyes. "It's a sign that—"

"A sign that what?"

"A sign that it's my turn now. First Father, then Gabi, and now me."

Michael held her cool, dry hand. He wanted to shake her, or suddenly embrace her, but he suppressed these urges.

"And then Theo. After me, or before me," she said as if she were vomiting the words one after the other. But her face abruptly went white, and she sat up straight and said: "And Ido? What will happen to Ido? Where's Ido?" She trembled violently and lowered her feet to the floor.

"He's fine, I promise you. I spoke to the babysitter just now, only a minute ago, and he's fine."

"But after me, what will happen after me, who'll bring him up?"

"There'll be no after you!" said Michael. "You're staying alive."

"Forever," said Nita, "like everyone else."

"In the meantime forever," said Michael, and he couldn't resist putting his arm around her.

Theo sank into a chair and buried his face in his hands. Michael turned his head, sensing that they were not alone in the room. Balilty was standing in the doorway and silently surveying the scene.

Michael looked at him questioningly, and Balilty shrugged his shoulders and stepped back. Michael stood up and joined him outside the room.

"She's awake," he said to Balilty. "She should go home now. Somebody has to talk to her as soon as possible, and it shouldn't be me. Will you go with them? And take their statements? At home?"

"Do I have a choice?" asked Balilty, rummaging in his pockets. He took out a piece of paper and held it at arm's length. "What's written here?" he asked finally. "What time is written here? My glasses. . . . "

"Half past five."

"Does it say the Israel Museum?" he asked loudly, keeping his expression carefully nonchalant.

"Yes, and there's a phone number, too."

"All right, I can go right now, but I've got a meeting later at the museum, with a big expert, in connection with the paintings. Okay, maybe I'll send someone else to the museum. We'll see. I need a woman when I go with the two of them," he said. "I'll take whatshername, with the body, the young one. What's her name? Dalia?"

"Dalit."

"I'll take her. And what about you?"

"I'll come too, but only for a short time. I still have to talk to the orchestra manager, and afterward I have to see the guy who lived with the victim. Tzilla will get hold of him for me," Michael thought aloud.

"What guy is that?"

"Not now," said Michael absently.

"Who'll get rid of the reporters outside?" complained Balilty. "And what about the ones waiting outside her house? How long can we keep it secret that we're all there?"

"Don't let her see the news," warned Michael. "Or listen to the radio. Not a word."

"Well, you've got me where you wanted me, right in the middle of it," said Balilty to Michael when they were standing in Nita's living room, after Balilty had brutally cleaved his way through the many media people, repulsed a woman reporter standing at the door ("You won't get anything here today, my friend," Michael heard him say to her, "and that's a promise"), and pushed Nita, whose face he had covered, inside, where she sank trembling onto the sofa.

Michael picked up the baby and held her cheek to his. She drew her head back, as if she wanted to examine his face from a distance. The color of her eyes, which had wavered between blue and brown, was now a coppery brown. He stretched out his arms so that she would be able to see his face from the right distance and wrinkled his nose. She looked at him very seriously and suddenly smiled a happy, trustful smile.

"She's cute," remarked Balilty, standing behind Michael's shoulder. "She looks happy," he added, surprised.

"Of course she's happy," said Michael indignantly, laying his cheek on hers.

"What do you call her?" asked Balilty.

"Her name's Noa," replied Michael, feeling a twinge of embarrassment as he saw himself reflected in the baffled expression on Balilty's face. "Do you think I'm an idiot?" he asked.

"Of course not," protested Balilty. "It's just a little strange, that's all . . . And what are we going to do with her now? You have to go to the victim's apartment. Forensics are already on their way there."

"She'll be with me," said Nita in her normal voice from her place on the sofa. "She and Ido will stay with me and Theo. And with you," she said, looking hesitantly at Dalit, who was sitting on one of the chairs in the dining nook.

Michael didn't turn a hair, he didn't even ask, Are you sure? His experience had taught him that different people dealt with tragedy in different, and often surprising, ways. There was no reason not to let Nita look after the children, and in any event she wouldn't be alone. She looked at him as if she read his thoughts: "Life goes on," she said to him. "At least for now, I can't afford to die. Single parents can't die."

Ido was sitting on Nita's lap, gurgling and tugging at her curls. Both babies looked completely calm, for nothing had happened in their world. The phone rang. Nita didn't move, and Michael picked up the receiver. At the other end of the line there was a prolonged silence until a deep male voice asked hesitantly how Nita was. Michael offered her the phone. "Who is it?" she asked, and Michael shrugged his shoulders. She didn't move. "She'd like to know who this is," he said. The voice at the other end mumbled something unintelligible, followed by a silence and then by the sound of the dial tone. "He hung up," said Michael.

Again the phone rang. It was Tzilla, saying, "I found him. I didn't tell him anything. He doesn't know yet what's happened. You'd better get over there right away, because it'll be on the seven o'clock news." He wrote the address down on the back of an envelope. "It's near Palmach Street," said Tzilla. "Do you know where it is? You can't enter it from . . ."

"I'll find it," said Michael, and he looked at Balilty, who was placing a tape recorder on the dining table. When he was at the door he saw Theo standing up from the wicker armchair, pushing his hands into his pockets, and starting to pace toward the French windows.

7

The Three Faces of Evil

From the sour expression on the faces of the two men in the mobile forensic lab parked one building down from the one in which Gabriel van Gelden had lived, it was obvious that they had been waiting for a long time. Michael parked next to them and got out. "Are you Chief Superintendent Ohayon?" asked the older of the two, who was sitting next to the driver. Michael nodded.

"We've been waiting for you," said the driver, a young man with thick eyebrows and pitted skin who was scratching his ear. "Should we come up with you?"

"No. You'll have to wait a little longer," Michael replied.

"Call us when you're ready," said the young man. The older one wiped his flushed face with the back of his hand. "Will you be long?" he called after him.

Michael turned his head and shrugged his shoulders. "I hope not, but you never know," he said. He wondered whether he had sent for them too early. On the other hand, he decided, it was better for them to wait for him than the reverse.

"You could have called us for later," complained the perspiring man with the flushed face. Michael didn't reply as he advanced toward the three-story building with the rounded façade. At the entrance he stopped and looked up. There was a yellow light burning in a window on the third floor. Some weeks before, they had changed the clocks, and he still wasn't used to it. At half past six it was already dark.

Whenever he felt a wave of shock at the sight of someone weeping unrestrainedly at the loss of a loved one, whenever he stood before the expressions of stunned shock and disbelief that preceded the absorption of the fact, he wondered at his failure to acquire the armor that is the gift of habit. And not only was he not immune, he realized again, but he seemed to be more and more vulnerable and open to the grief of others. In other words, weak, he denounced himself as he sat tensely facing the quietly sobbing man. A glass-topped table on a single metal leg separated them. Izzy Mashiah sat in the middle of a black leather sofa, Michael in a deep, wide armchair, it too covered in soft black leather. Tensing his arms on the broad armrests in order not to sink even farther into its depths, he scrutinized this Izzy's reactions, suppressing his own emotions and quickly classifying the man facing him as belonging to the category of the emotionally restrained: those who do not burden their surroundings with screams and shrieks, those whose weeping is held back and civilized. And yet—they weep instead of turning to stone, instead of their expressions congealing into a frozen mask, which tells you that they are no longer with you in the room, that their souls have escaped to another place because they cannot bear the burden of the facts. Therefore they enter a state of what the police psychologist, Elroi, had once described as "total absence as protection against being overwhelmed by emotion." The impact of this pain on himself, the pang of pity Michael felt because of it, he had to blur or push aside, he warned himself as he slowly activated the tape recorder and placed it on the glass table while Izzy left the room.

He went into the other half of the apartment, from which came the clear sounds of running water, hoarse sobs, sniffles, running water again, and then a long and disturbing silence. When he reappeared, his body bowed, he sat down again in the middle of the black sofa, without a word about the whirring tape recorder breaking their mutual silence.

Even though he was crying now like someone for whom tears were not exceptional, there was nothing effeminate about this man, whom Michael had disturbed at his work when he rang the bell. When he opened the door, before Michael told him the news, it was obvious that he had risen hastily from the desk with a long printout piled up at the side of a computer whose screen was filled with tables and columns of figures. Izzy Mashiah had opened the door as if he had been waiting tensely for the bell to ring. He opened his mouth to say something, froze, and then stared at Michael with surprise that changed into open disappointment. He had been waiting, it turned out, for the plumber, who was coming to fix a leak in the central heating system. A plastic bowl stood under the white pipe to receive a thin trickle of rusty brown water. He'd been waiting for him since lunchtime, he explained even before he asked Michael what he wanted. With a smile of recognition, he then remembered Michael from the condolence call he had paid during the *shiva* for Felix van Gelden. Izzy made a broad gesture with his arm to invite him in, remarking with a sigh on plumbers' well-known unreliability. He looked at his watch, saying that Gabi should be back any minute now. He had no idea where he could be, he added with a puzzled expression, and pointing to the black leather chair, he suggested that Michael sit down there to wait for him.

From the first moment Michael realized that Izzy Mashiah was not in the least surprised by his visit, taking it for granted that he had come to see Gabi either about Felix van Gelden's death or about Nita. In view of this assumption, Michael was afraid that questions about Izzy's movements during the day would seem absurd. Nevertheless he twice asked Izzy whether he had seen Gabi during the morning, whether he had been to the rehearsal, whether he and Gabi had spoken during the day. And Izzy readily told him that he had spoken to Gabriel on the phone at about one o'clock in the afternoon, during a break in the rehearsal. Gabi had told him about the Teddy Kollek interruption, and that because of it the rehearsal would take longer than expected. Gabi was very tense, he said in a worried tone of voice, as if he enjoyed displaying intimate knowledge of the other man's moods.

"He had a hard day ahead of him," he explained with a wry pursing of his thin lips and a cluck of his tongue that did nothing to hide his pride. In an expression of indignant complaint at the burdens imposed on his friend by the world, he went on to explain, without having been asked, that Gabi was tense because of the meetings he had scheduled for after the rehearsal with potential members of the ensemble he was creating, and especially because of the confrontation he was expecting with a certain woman violinist, a second violinist in the big orchestra. By this he meant the orchestra that Theo led.

The violinist insisted on obtaining a place in Gabi's ensemble orchestra on the grounds of her seniority and the fact that she needed the extra money ("It's incredible what some people think they've got coming to them," Izzy muttered). "It must be because of her that he hasn't come home yet," Izzy said with a giggle. "This fury is probably detaining him." He shuddered. Theo had trouble with her, too—she wanted him to promote her to the first violin section. He himself had once heard her standing in the lobby and holding forth to a big group of musicians about the frustration and mental anguish of the players who sat in the back rows of the stage, where no one in the audience could see them. She was demanding rotation, at least, in the seating arrangements. "Theo really does sometimes rotate them. Once every few months, he told me so himself, he changes the places, mostly of the strings. He'll move a violinist with seniority forward to increase motivation. I'm telling you this because Nita says that you're almost part of the family . . ." he explained. "That's why I'm going into these details with you . . ." Izzy's voice died out in embarrassment. "He'll be here in a minute," he resumed, and he offered Michael something hot or cold to drink.

Michael looked around uncomfortably, and feeling acutely aware of the invidious irony of his position, he examined the room, which was exquisitely neat and tidy and gave off a warm family atmosphere, with a mass of blooming little red flowers on the windowsill.

He had heard the sound of the choral music while he was still in the entrance lobby. To his frustration he was unable to identify it, though it sounded familiar. The music ended as he stood in the living room, which also served as a study. Out of the corner of his eye he took in the stereo system. Izzy breathed carefully on the LP record, put it in its sleeve, and covered the player with its transparent plastic lid while Michael looked with admiration and awe at the harpsichord standing in the corner near the desk. It was a small walnut piece of furniture that looked like a brother of the cabinet in Nita's living room, except that here there were no floating cherubs but a row of gilt lions decorating the façade. The lid was open, and there was music on the rack above the keyboard. "What was that chorus singing?" Michael ventured. In this field he was always afraid of exposing his ignorance.

Izzy smiled. "It's only four voices," he said, waving the record sleeve. "Pergolesi's *Stabat Mater*. Don't you know it?" he asked, surprised. Michael shook his head and looked at the sleeve to gain time. "Only four voices?" he marveled. "It sounded like . . ."

Izzy looked at him forgivingly. "It's a fine performance," he commented dryly, in his low, pleasant voice, which featured a rolling Slavic "*r*." Izzy Mashiah was on the short side, broad-shouldered, with a sturdy body. His face had the red-brown tan of a fair-skinned person who has spent much time in the sun. His graying, wavy hair was combed back, exposing a high, smooth forehead. His chin, round and slack, gave his face an expression of rather querulous weakness, and also a kind of eagerness to appease.

His first reaction to the news of Gabi's death was a convulsive smilelike grimace, then his narrow little mouth pursed before emitting a strange sound, almost a laugh, which burst out in a groan at the sound of the word "murdered." He removed his horn-rimmed glasses as he listened to the dry account Michael gave him only after he had answered all his questions. Before that, Izzy had explained that he had not left the house because the next day he was to present a research proposal, on which he was going to have to work all night long, adding that he had to stay home anyway because of the plumber. Only after all this did Izzy express surprise at the question.

Michael had not discerned any uneasiness behind the surprise. It sounded innocent of any knowledge. Izzy's high forehead arched in a question that he restrained out of politeness, and he explained without protest that there was nobody who could testify to the fact that he had not left the house, except, perhaps, for the departmental secretary at the Institute, to whom he had spoken twice during the day: "Once she phoned me, and the second time I phoned her," he said, and he looked at Michael in growing perplexity at his pedantry. Uneasiness began to appear in his voice, and he twisted his gold ring—three coils ending in a snake's head with a tiny green stone for an eye; a similar ring, Michael recalled, had adorned the third finger of Gabriel van Gelden's left hand—when he was asked to state exactly when the secretary had called him.

He took the ring off and put it on the glass table top, arched his brow again, and asked in surprise: "Do you have to know exactly?" He looked at Michael, who nodded, and finally admitted that he couldn't remember. "Although," he suddenly added, "I could reconstruct it because of the radio," he said, putting the ring back on his finger. "It was when the *Voice of Music* was playing the Mozart Quintet for Piano and Winds," he said happily, and he quickly picked up the newspaper lying neatly folded next to the sofa and began paging through it. "Here you are," he announced with relief, as if he had regained control over chaos. "Since they played the Bruckner symphony first, that's about forty-five minutes, and because the Mozart ended at noon, it was the last piece in the morning concert, then she phoned during the second movement—I'd never have phoned anyone during that piece—then we can put her phone call at about twenty to twelve, something like that. But why do you have to know?" he finally dared to ask, and there was already a faint tremor of anxiety in his voice and a frown between his eyebrows, above the brown frame of the thick-lensed glasses he again put on. No, he hardly ever went to dress rehearsals, especially not if Theo was conducting. With an ingratiating smile he remarked: "I have a hard time with Theo, particularly when he's conducting. And Gabi doesn't like me coming to them either, and anyway, I'd never have gone today, what with everything I had to do."

"Are you a mathematician?" Michael inquired.

"Not at all," Izzy said, surprised. "I'm an epidemiologist. What made you think I was a mathematician?" And then he hastened to add that he was connected with the Weizmann Institute and also with the university hospital.

"I thought that because of something Theo said," Michael explained.

"Ah, Theo," Izzy said. "He barely knows me. He isn't interested in other people. Even if someone had told him what I do, he wouldn't have remembered. Gabi doesn't like us to meet, Theo and I, because in my presence Theo suffers what Gabi calls 'affability attacks.' That drives Gabi crazy, Theo's forced attempts to be nice to me. You know him. I don't know if Theo's friendly to you. I do know that Gabi is very appreciative of what you're doing for Nita. But I don't know what Theo thinks about it." He waited for a reply.

Michael observed that he had spent very little time in Theo's company, and that he didn't know him well enough to say.

"Yes, but with me he made a special effort, that's what Gabi said, because he wanted to seem open-minded, about me and Gabi, that is. People who aren't really open-minded often go out of their way to demonstrate open-mindedness," he added with a smile, "if you know what I mean. But the main reason he tried to be friendly to me was because I attacked him, and here too it was important to him to appear open-minded, open to criticism. I said things to him about his performance. . . . Are you interested in music?"

Michael shook his head. "I'm interested," he said uneasily, "but I don't understand anything about it."

"Well, I don't know why I said what I said. I didn't mean to, it just came up during a discussion of Wagner," he said with a smile that revealed two rows of very big white teeth and a little gap on the left side where a tooth was missing, marring the radiance of his smile. He said all this in his deep, pleasant voice, and the more he spoke the more pronounced the vertical line between his thick eyebrows became, and now, as Izzy stroked his right ear with a delicate finger, Michael noticed the big scar next to it. His face was smoothly shaved, and his eyes, light and small, glittered and blinked, reminding Michael of the way he had seen Gabi blink, and the thought of Gabi's face and of his open staring eyes as he lay at the foot of the pillar brought the image of his nearly severed neck to the forefront of his consciousness. He suddenly felt weak in the knees, and precisely because of this weakness he forced himself to ask Izzy once more if he was sure that he hadn't been out of the house all day.

"Not even to the grocery store," Izzy Mashiah assured him, and he spread a big, narrow hand on his chest. His long, delicate brown fingers stood out against the black sweatshirt he was wearing, and the ring on his finger glittered greenly. And only then, as if waking from a dream, he removed his glasses, rubbed his eyes, which immediately turned faintly pink, and asked carefully and pleasantly why Michael had to know, what actually had happened today. His shoulders tensed, and he sat up and moved away from the back of the soft sofa.

Michael told Izzy the facts. He was careful not to mention the string, the gloves, the position of Gabi's body. "A cut on the throat" was the phrase he used to describe the cause of death. He made an effort to mobilize the detachment necessary in order to examine Izzy closely, to identify any trace of falsity in the outburst of emotion, in the breakdown he was now witnessing. One day he would have to collect all his impressions of the first moment at which people heard of the death of loved ones.

They could be classified into categories. First, the restrained as opposed to the unrestrained. In this classification, there was perhaps a hint of the origins of the mourner—the silent and restrained, but so manipulative, grief of those of Polish extraction, as opposed to the vociferousness of those from Morocco, for example, where it sometimes seems that the exact moment when a scream is required is dictated by the etiquette of the rites. There should be a subgroup of the restrained weepers, and a subgroup of the frozen, those who not only don't shed a tear, but it seems that at the moment they hear the news their souls detach themselves and fly off to some distant place, their faces looking like masks. If you ask them what they feel, they don't know what to reply. These were the ones the psychologist Elroi meant when he talked about absence. There was also a distinction between those who cried without tears and those who shed them. There were those who talked—ceaselessly, compulsively, like Theo—and those who were completely silent. And there were those who cried soundlessly, the ones whose tears got to you despite the force of habit and despite your efforts to remain detached. They tore at your heartstrings, like Izzy Mashiah now.

Izzy's shoulders shook, his face was buried in his hands. Twice he asked if it was really true, and how exactly had it happened, and when and if Gabi had suffered.

Michael refrained from going into details. He replied briefly and vaguely. He again reminded himself, in the light of Izzy's determination to know the details, that every alibi could be refuted, that everyone was a potential suspect. You couldn't allow your likes and dislikes to dictate who was a murderer and who wasn't. His sympathy for Izzy in his grief was a weakness. It was like a warning he himself could have formulated, and that he also could have heard from Tzilla, and Eli, and of course from Balilty.

"We had so many plans!" sobbed Izzy, and he buried his face in his hands again. His voice was muffled: "I was sure that of the two of us I would die first, and now I have to bury him, and go on living."

Suddenly he took his hands away and said in a hard voice: "I don't know who or what did this, but I swear to you on my life that Gabi didn't kill himself. Of that you can be sure!" He shook his head and tried to catch his breath.

"Let's say that he didn't commit suicide," said Michael slowly, "and we have no grounds for assuming that he did. Do you have any idea who could have murdered him?"

Izzy let out a hoarse snort of laughter and shook his head. "No one, no one could have wanted to kill Gabi," he said in a tone of profound conviction, and he fell silent.

"It wasn't an accident," said Michael. "It was planned, deliberate murder, and the person who did it was taking a very big risk. We have no alternative but to assume that someone wanted very much to kill him."

Izzy again buried his face in his hands, removed them after a few seconds, sniffled, wiped his face, raked his hand through his hair, and nodded. "We have no alternative," Izzy repeated Michael's words. "But I have no idea!" he said with sudden vehemence. "I can't even imagine it! Could it be connected with his father?" He shuddered.

"In what sense?" Michael asked, leaning forward attentively.

"I have no idea!" said Izzy. "It just seems logical, but I don't know how."

"I'll put the question differently, and ask you directly: Who could have gained from Gabi's murder?"

"I don't know, I really don't. I can't believe it."

"Could you have benefited from it?"

"Me? Benefited?" Again Izzy let out a hoarse snort of laughter. "You don't understand anything," he whispered in a husky voice, bowing his head.

"Who owns this apartment?"

"What do you mean? Officially?"

Michael nodded.

"Gabi, but we intended . . ." He looked at Michael with alarm, and then he smiled bitterly. His voice changed as he said softly and disbelievingly: "Are you interrogating me now?"

Michael said nothing.

"You're here on duty!" he exclaimed, astonished. "Is that possible when you're living with Nita? Is that allowed? Pardon me for asking, is this an official interrogation?"

"An interrogation, but not official."

"What's that supposed to mean?"

"An official interrogation takes place after a cautioning, in my office. This is more of a talk, but I can't honestly tell you that this talk is unrelated to the investigation."

"In that case," said Izzy as he sat up, "there are a few things I have to tell you. Even though the apartment is registered in his name, he treated it as our common home. As for insurance, for instance, Gabi bought life insurance, a large amount, about a year ago. And I'm the beneficiary. I got a policy too, at his wish, but he's not the beneficiary, that too at his express wish. He himself filled out the forms for me, all I did was sign them. He'd been given the opportunity of a good deal, his insurance agent . . . Anyway, I pointed out that I was only forty-three, but he insisted. And he insisted that my daughter, not he, be the beneficiary . . ."

"You have a daughter?"

"Yes. I was married . . . I was married for ten years before. . . . before I knew, before I understood that—"

"And have you had relations with other men besides Gabi?"

Izzy nodded slowly, as if in dawning comprehension. "I think I understand what you're getting at, but our story wasn't the ordinary kind."

"There are no ordinary stories," said Michael, and he hated himself for the patronizing tone. "When you approach an intimate story, it's always special," he said, trying to soften his words.

"No," said Izzy, "you're not understanding me. You probably . . . I don't know your preferences. I imagine you prefer women. What with Nita . . ." Michael restrained a spontaneous impulse to put the record straight with regard to Nita. "Anyway, I assume you harbor the usual stereotypes about homosexual love, and you probably think that I hung around parks and had all kinds of . . . But it wasn't like that. First I met Gabi, and only then did I grasp . . ."

"Really?" said Michael, surprised. "Until then you thought you loved women?"

Izzy squirmed in his seat. "It's not so easy to explain. I don't even know if I love men. Sometimes I think that I just love Gabi, but apparently that isn't the whole story, because I always had difficulties with women, I was always problematic . . . but not in the stereotypical sense. I never had relations with men before Gabi. But I don't suppose you believe me, because of your prejudices about gays," he concluded on a note of indignation.

"We're speaking frankly," said Michael, "and I can tell you in all seriousness that I don't even know what prejudices I possess. I've hardly ever had any contact with homosexuality, that is, in my life outside work."

"But in your line of work you come up against the most sordid side of it, I imagine."

"Everything becomes sordid in my line of work," said Michael. "When you're talking about murder there isn't much room for beauty or elegance. But I have to tell you that I've never before gotten to know a couple of men living together. I simply haven't come across that kind of relationship. Not personally, that is. And to tell the truth, I can't see any difference in principle between your reaction and the reaction of a woman . . ." embarrassed, he immediately corrected himself, "or a man. I mean a spouse," he concluded uneasily. He himself was surprised by his frankness and the simple directness with which he spoke.

"You see, the way you're searching for words exposes your prejudices."

"It's a matter of habit, too," said Michael. "I'm simply not used to speaking frankly to . . . about this subject with someone who's involved in . . . I'm not used to talking to a man who loves another man about his relationship."

"What I'd like you to understand," said Izzy with the same passion that had erupted previously, "is that we lived as a couple in every respect, a full partnership, love and friendship and concern and . . ." Again he sniffled, wiped his eyes with one finger inserted behind the thick lenses of his glasses, and took a deep breath before he went on. "And there's a good relationship, not just correct but good, between me and my ex-wife, and my daughter, she's sixteen now, she comes to visit us, and everything's open and aboveboard. That's what we decided. And this apartment is registered in Gabi's name because it was his before I turned up, before we met and I came here to live with him. I don't even know if he has a will, and I loved him, I would never . . . never . . . What are you talking about—gain?" He suddenly flared up. "I have nothing to gain from Gabi's death! Only to lose. It's . . . it's utter ruin for me. Gabi's death for me is . . ."

He looked at Michael and his eyes grew damp again, his expression softened. "You can't help it, it's your job. I understand. I'm trying to understand. But you mustn't . . . I'd like you to rid yourself of stereotypes and prejudices and not think that every homosexual is a . . ." He looked at Michael expectantly. "And anyway," he remembered, "I haven't been out of the apartment all day, and . . . What time did Gabi? . . . What time did you find him?" he asked, groaning.

"In the afternoon," Michael said, avoiding an exact reply. "And we'll have to go into things here—his papers, and so on, and get more details from you, and I'd like you to take a polygraph test, with your permission, of course."

Izzy shrugged his shoulders. "Is this the moment when I should ask for a lawyer?" he muttered. "But I don't need a lawyer," he said, and he raised his head high. "I tell you: I loved him. He loved me. We were close. Really close. You wouldn't understand. I'll take your polygraph and do whatever you want. I have no problem with *that*," he said, "only with the fact that Gabi . . . I don't know how I'm going to . . ." He removed his glasses again and buried his face in his hands.

"There hasn't been any crisis in your relationship recently? Differences of opinion?"

"No," said Izzy, after removing his hands from his face and sitting up. "I'd like . . . What I'd like now is to be left alone," he said softly. "I can't—"

"I'm afraid that's impossible."

"Can't you wait for a day? A few hours? To give me . . . I've already told you all I know."

"We're investigating a murder. The murder of the man you lived with. Whom you loved. He was murdered."

"I loved him . . . love him. That's all I know now."

"And you have no idea who didn't love him?"

"To such an extent?" Izzy shook his head. Then he took a deep, noisy breath. Finally he looked right at Michael with an expression of resignation and said: "There weren't a lot of people who loved him, but neither were there a lot who hated him. Gabi lived in a way that didn't . . . that didn't arouse extreme or powerful emotions. Except in my case, meeting him wasn't something that . . . Theo didn't . . . that is to say . . . it's complicated, but not to such an extent, because Theo also loved him, I imagine. The concertmaster, Avigdor, didn't like Gabi, and some of the musicians didn't like him in the way that people don't like perfectionists. And there was the business of the personal contracts with each of the musicians he was planning, that is, instead of a collective bargaining agreement. Some of the musicians were angry about this, and Theo didn't like it either. Some people said about him that he was a hard man, demanding, uncompromising. Gabi was a very serious musician. And a lot of people interpreted his shyness—he wasn't an exhibitionist like Theo—as arrogance. They called him a snob. And there's that character Even-Tov, the choral conductor, who also wanted to set up a Baroque ensemble, but people preferred Gabi. Maybe he really hated him, but if you saw him you'd realize that murder isn't an option, it's the last thing you would imagine in connection with someone like Even-Tov, he's . . . it doesn't matter."

"And aside from the orchestra and music?"

Izzy looked at him with surprise. "There wasn't anything apart from music in his life," he explained. "Music was his whole world, it was thanks to music . . . because of my playing . . . well, not my playing exactly. I'm not much of a harpsichord player, but he heard me playing once at the YMCA and that's how we met. Gabi couldn't talk to people who weren't interested in music, even his ex-wife—who's a terrible person, apparently, I've never met her, only talked to her on the phone, about money. Even she's a musician first of all, an excellent harpist. Gabi didn't have any other world. And we had very few friends, people from my work, and he traveled a lot, so it's hard to keep up steady relationships. He only returned a few weeks ago from a long trip, a concert tour."

"What's so complicated between him and Theo?"

Izzy smiled almost dismissively. "What's there to explain? It's a classic case of sibling rivalry. But that's got nothing to do with . . . Theo was jealous of Gabi, because Felix loved Gabi more. He was closer to him, always. Theo was his mother's favorite, but that wasn't enough for him. He always wants everything, Theo, and he wanted his father, too. But it's impossible to explain briefly, or to describe Theo in a few sentences. He's a complicated creature. Theo is also a considerable musician. You can't ignore him, especially when it comes to Bruckner or Mahler or Wagner, if you care about them. He sometimes has demonic power. No one can dismiss Theo's charisma. You can hate what he does, but you can't dismiss him. In any event, Theo's not a murderer. You can't be considering that seriously. But their relationship was complicated."

"And did Gabi love Theo?"

"Love?" Izzy seemed taken aback. "For me love is a word with pleasant associations, and there wasn't anything pleasant about their relationship, but he was . . . Yes, maybe you could use the word love here. Maybe he did love him. They were very different, but close, too. And their childhood, in that house . . . Yes, you could say he loved him. And also repudiated him. At least you could say that he had mixed feelings about him. And Theo, Theo loved Gabi too, in the final analysis, in his own complicated way. With a lot of anger. And also jealousy, fear, admiration. Theo also tried to ingratiate himself with Gabi, and also . . . all kinds of things, but he certainly didn't murder him."

"Why not?"

Izzy looked at him, astonished. "Why should he have murdered him?" he argued. "The question should be why should he, not why not. I can't imagine any motive he could possibly have had, financial or otherwise. There had been no change in their relationship recently. Nothing had happened to change anything, so why now? Theo had problems with Gabi for years!" He stopped and gasped for breath. "Since the days when they were both studying with Dora Zackheim. Maybe even before then. But she's the one you should talk to if you want to understand them. I've got asthma," he warned. "I hope I'm not going to have an attack now."

Michael opened the window. The tape recorder went on running.

"I don't have any idea!" cried Izzy in despair. "Not the slightest. Maybe it was someone I don't know. Aside from Even-Tov, who wanted to be in his position, I don't know of an enemy. Not even that violinist I mentioned before. Don't take me seriously, but couldn't it have been some psychopath? A random attack? Out of the blue?" he asked naively, his round chin wobbling. "I suppose not," he said, sighing.

"And Gabi's ex-wife?"

"Her? Never! What would she get out of it? Who's going to send her alimony now? And besides, she's in Munich."

"And your wife?"

"My wife?" said Izzy, astonished. "What's she got to do with it?"

"Well," said Michael, fingering an unlit cigarette. "You left her for him."

"Five years ago!" cried Izzy, holding up five fingers. "All of a sudden? After we've been living together five years?"

"Five? Not two years?"

"Two years properly, here in this apartment. And before that three years. . . . Who told you it was two years?"

Michael said nothing.

"You don't know her," said Izzy more softly. "When you meet her you'll understand why it's out of the question. My wife is wonderful. An unusual person. I simply . . . it just turned out that way. I had no choice . . . It wasn't because of her . . . I wanted to . . ." Again he buried his face in his hands. His shoulders shook.

He agreed to Michael's request to show him the apartment. In Gabi's study there were piles of music, a violin lying on the piano, a big desk, red and pink geraniums on the windowsill, and a huge lithograph in black, brown, and red of three women in seventeenth-century dress. One of them, sitting in the picture's foreground, playing a flute, another, standing behind her, plucking a lute, and the third singing from a leather-bound book of music in her hands. On a narrow bed, covered in black fabric, lay musical scores. Some of them were open, showing written annotations. Michael picked up one with a yellow cover that said Vivaldi.

"Did Gabi like Vivaldi?" he asked. Izzy, sitting on the piano bench, nodded. "Vivaldi, Corelli, Baroque music in general. Bach, of course. If he'd had the choice he would have preferred to live at the end of the seventeenth century and the beginning of the eighteenth. I said to him sometimes that for him music ended before the Classical period began. Or maybe he was ready to include the High Classical period, above all Haydn and Mozart. It was a joke between us that Beethoven and Brahms were too modern for him. But that's nonsense, of course. He could listen to Brahms when it was well played, and to Verdi and even Mahler."

The two men from Forensics stood in the living room and looked around.

"There isn't much here," said the one with the pitted face and the angry scowl. "We'd better begin over there," said the fat one with the flushed face, and they made their way to the study, one of whose walls held a bookcase crammed with music and books.

"Everything in this room is his," confirmed Izzy. "It was his study. My work space was in the living room." The scowler collected the books and music and emptied the desk drawers into brown cardboard boxes. The fat sweating one dusted for prints and without much ado took Izzy's fingerprints, after briefly explaining to him that it was necessary in order to distinguish him from others, as someone with legitimate access to the apartment. To Michael's question about spare strings, Izzy responded by taking a rectangular box out of one of the drawers and holding it out.

"It's a completely new box," he explained to Michael, who was struggling to undo the box's tape. "There should be four strings in every one of the little envelopes inside."

Michael stood in the doorway to the bedroom and looked at the bed, feeling slightly embarrassed. It looked like any other couple's bedroom. Two night tables on either side of the bed; on the one closest to the window, at the far end of the room, were a few books next to a reading lamp, among them a thick Mozart biography in English. Next to it, open and facedown, a thick book with a black binding. Michael picked it up. It was a history, with photographs, of musical instrument making.

"Was this his side of the bed?" he asked Izzy as he leafed through the book.

"No," replied Izzy. Then he pointed to the other side of the bed. "That was his side," he said in a choked voice.

On Gabriel van Gelden's night table was a pile of thrillers, all in

English, among them a hardcover copy of Anthony Price's *A New Kind of War*. On the floor was a paperback. Izzy approached the bed and picked up the book. "This is what he was reading last night," he said, stroking the cover. "He loved detective novels. Especially those by this Dutch writer, Robert Hans van Gulik, whose books are set in sixth-century China."

Michael refrained from preventing Izzy from touching the book and the surface of the night table, from which he now removed a half-full glass of water. Izzy's fingerprints would be all over the room anyway. The forensic men were already standing in the bedroom doorway, and Izzy pointed out Gabriel's night table, whose drawers they now emptied into black plastic bags that they carefully placed in a cardboard box.

Michael followed Izzy into the living room. Izzy switched off the computer and sat down at his desk, leaning his elbows on the narrow space in front of the screen and burying his face in his hands. Michael cleared his throat and said: "You'll have to come with me now to the Russian Compound to give evidence."

"Give evidence about what? What do I have to give evidence about?"

"That's what it's called," explained Michael. "It's the usual procedure. There are all kinds of things we have to ask you."

Izzy shrugged his shoulders. "Everything seems completely fantastic," he said, "and nothing matters now anyway. I'll do whatever you say. Evidence, polygraph, whatever you like."

They had to wait for the forensics people to remove the cardboard boxes from the apartment, and only when the scowler nodded his head did Michael signal Izzy. Izzy locked the door and went downstairs with a heavy tread to Michael's car. They drove in silence. Izzy stared straight ahead with a blank expression. From time to time he shook his head and groaned, sighed, took a deep breath. When Michael parked the car at the gate to the Russian Compound, Izzy said: "I want to see him."

"Who?" asked Michael, trying to buy time.

"Gabi. I want to see him."

"That's impossible at present," said Michael. "He . . . his body is at the Forensic Medicine Institute. They're doing an autopsy." A shiver went down his spine at the thought of Izzy, with his trembling, child-like chin, standing over that gaping throat and nearly decapitated head. In order to distract him he quickly added: "Are you sure you're ready to take a polygraph test? If you're not really willing, the test is worthless."

"What difference does it make to me?" mumbled Izzy. "Do you need active willingness, or is it enough just to agree?"

"It's enough if you agree, if you really do."

Izzy spread out his hands and let his head fall back. "What difference does it make now," he said dully. "It's all the same to me."

"Anyway, it's not admissible in court," said Michael. "If you're thinking about consulting a lawyer and so on."

"So why do you do it at all?" asked Izzy as they walked to Michael's office.

"I'm asking you to take the test in order to establish your credibility," Michael admitted frankly. "Your willingness to take the test is in itself a basis for credibility, because you probably know that even though the test is inadmissible, it's very difficult to deceive the machine."

"Really? What's so difficult about it?"

"There are all kinds of indicators. I'll explain when we get to it."

"What I want, the only thing I really want, is to see him one more time," said Izzy in a broken voice, and he was about to plead for it again but fell silent at the sound of the voices coming from Michael's office.

"We used to call her Four-in-One!" Zippo's voice was rising loudly behind the closed door. "You wouldn't remember that religious madwoman, you're too young, but the woman in this case reminds me of her. Even though she was as skinny as a string bean and this one's not as thin, and Four-in-One looked like a bag lady and this one wears pants . . ." Michael opened the door and Zippo's voice died away. Eli Bahar was sitting behind the desk in Michael's chair, sorting through a pile of papers.

"There's a ton of stuff here from the orchestra already . . ." he said, "and the gloves . . ." He fell silent when he saw Izzy standing behind Michael. On the way here, Michael had already wondered how to introduce Izzy, and now he said: "Izzy Mashiah, Gabriel van Gelden's companion." Zippo dropped his jaw, quickly shut it again, and tugged at his military mustache.

"Start taking his statement," Michael ordered Zippo. And, turning to Eli: "Come outside with me for a minute."

"Do you have the forms?" he asked Zippo as he stood in the doorway waiting for Eli to squeeze his body through the narrow space between the desk and the two chairs, on one of which Izzy was already sitting, his face yellowish. Zippo nodded.

"Is he gay?" asked Eli coldly as they stood outside the office.

"Yes, but not the kind . . . They've been together five years, the last two years living like a married couple. You have to treat him like a spouse."

"Yes, but wife or husband? I've never understood how they themselves see that. By the way, I hear you've given Balilty . . . that he's heading the team or something like that."

"Because of the robbery case."

"They've brought the Felix van Gelden file. You asked for it, remember?" said Eli Bahar.

"Where's Tzilla?"

"Still at the scene, with Raffy and Avram. We don't have a lot of time to waste, and I've been sitting here pushing papers. I've become the team coordinator," he said disconsolately. "I'm the secretary. And that Dalit's with Balilty. But you know that, you said they had to have a woman there. You should see her work. Does she work! On the business of the gloves. I'm telling you, her ambition is something else! She's already phoned here three times. I haven't told you yet that those gloves belong to the woman double bass player."

"What do you mean? They're a woman's gloves?"

"A woman with big hands. Tzilla phoned to tell me. The musicians brought it up. The bass player wears gloves because she has low blood pressure and has a problem with cold hands. Anyway, she has a pair like that."

"It's September!"

"Apparently she has several such pairs. She kept this pair at the concert hall. She wears them there because of the air conditioning. Anyway, the drummer and an oboe player identified them, and others recognized them, too, because of the color—Tzilla calls it mustard—and because she always wears them. They all joke about them. Everybody knows about them."

"And where's the bass player herself? Why isn't she here?"

"That's a problem. We can't find her. She went to the airport right after the rehearsal, to pick up someone or something—it's not clear. She lives with her mother, who's so old and out of it that there's no way of knowing anything definite. Avram's responsible for picking her up. He'll bring her in when he finds her."

"And where did she keep the gloves?"

"They've got lockers there, but she apparently kept them somewhere else. We won't know until we talk to her. The gloves have only been partly examined. They haven't been taken to the lab yet."

"Let's have a look at the file," said Michael.

"You're not giving up the case, are you?"

"Which case?"

"The Gabriel van Gelden case. Haven't you thought about what I told you? You're not giving it up?"

"For the time being, no."

"For the time being," repeated Eli grumpily. "And what about Balilty?" he added sullenly.

"You'll manage," said Michael trying to calm him.

"Of course we'll manage," said Eli Bahar, "but I wonder if *you'll* manage."

"Let it go for now," said Michael with growing irritation. "I don't want to worry about it now. While Zippo is filling out the forms with Mashiah, I want to go through the Felix van Gelden file."

"It's in Balilty's office."

"Here it is," said Eli, pointing to a large envelope. They had seated themselves on either side of the desk in Balilty's office. "Everything's in there, all the findings in the case."

"Is there any progress with the string?"

"No," said Eli. "I got in touch with an expert, who told me that there are a number of outfits that make them. It's impossible to tell what particular instrument a string came from. None of the musicians reports a missing string. Nita van Gelden's the only one we haven't talked to yet. But Balilty will check it out."

"They haven't questioned her about her strings yet?" asked Michael, astonished. "Her of all people?"

"Maybe they have," said Eli, and he averted his face in embarrassment. "I imagine they have. But Balilty doesn't tell me everything. Do you want me to find out?"

"Not at the moment," muttered Michael, and he emptied the envelope out onto the desk. He should really leave the matter of Nita's strings to Balilty and keep his nose out of it, he thought as he went slowly through the contents of the envelope. He peeped into the plastic bags, read the reports, fingered the rope old van Gelden was tied up with. "What's this?" he asked, holding a transparent little plastic bag up to the light.

"It looks like . . ." Eli Bahar picked up the piece of paper that had been attached to the plastic bag. "It's the surgical tape they used to gag him. That's what it says here."

"What else does it say?"

"Nothing."

"What do you mean, nothing? Aren't there any laboratory findings?"

Eli rummaged through the papers and said: "No."

"They didn't examine it at Forensics?"

"What do you want from me? Ask Balilty," said Eli resentfully.

"That's exactly what I intend to do," said Michael. He tapped his ballpoint pen on the desk impatiently until Theo answered the telephone. He asked for Balilty immediately, without inquiring about Nita or the babies. In the background he could hear voices and noises, and a few seconds passed before Danny Balilty said: "Sir!"

"The tape they gagged Felix van Gelden with —"

"What about it?" Balilty's short, rapid breathing was noisy, as if he were holding the receiver right next to his mouth.

"Didn't you send it to Forensics?"

"What for? There was no need to."

"So you didn't send it."

"No, I didn't," said Balilty defiantly. "Why do you think I should have? Is there something unclear there?"

"Until we check it out, we won't know."

"So send it."

"That's exactly what I'm about to do. Is there anything new there?"

"Nothing special," said Balilty gloomily. "I'm recording everything. Can it wait for the team meeting tomorrow? Or do you want to hear it before then?"

"When I finish here, we'll see."

"Do you intend to wait there all night for the reply from the lab? About that surgical tape?"

"In any event, I've got Izzy Mashiah here," said Michael.

"Who's Izzy Mashiah? Oh yes, the boyfriend. . . . Do you want us to bring in the other two this evening as well? For questioning? Do you want us to interrogate them at the station tonight?" asked Balilty.

"You decide," said Michael. And he added nervously: "Did you check Nita's strings?"

"I actually did," said Balilty in a careful, neutral tone. "You could say there's a possibility that the object came from her."

"What does that mean?" asked Michael, and he wiped away the dampness that suddenly filmed his brow. "Is it her string?"

"It might be," mumbled Balilty, "but it's not definite. We're still looking. There's a question of memory."

"She doesn't remember how many strings she had?" demanded Michael.

"More or less," said Balilty with hostility. "Could we talk about it somewhere else? I'm not finished here yet."

"Have you been in touch with your sister?" asked Eli after Michael had finished talking to the duty officer at the forensics laboratory.

"Not yet, it's late and—"

"What do you mean, late? It's only ten o'clock! Does Yvette go to sleep with the chickens?"

Michael looked at him with astonishment. In all their years of working together, Eli had never spoken to him so rudely and aggressively.

"I'm sorry," said Eli, "but this whole business is getting on my nerves. Who's interrogating Nita? You haven't said a word about her. Is Balilty interrogating her? This business is driving me crazy."

"Do you mean the business of the baby?"

"The whole thing. The baby, your girlfriend, the . . . the whole mix-up. I don't know if you . . . if I . . . if it's possible . . . and Shorer, really!" He blinked. Long, dark eyelashes covered the green glint in his eyes. Among the stubble on his head there were patches of silver.

Michael said nothing. When he looked inside himself, at what he really thought and felt, his heart sank. He was afraid of losing the baby. Maybe he would never again experience the delight of seeing the tiny mouth waiting expectantly for a bottle, of its sudden smiles, of the baby's sweet odor. At lunchtime today, when he had brought her home from the concert hall, she had fallen asleep while sucking rhythmically from the bottle. He had sat for a long time watching her sleep. He looked at the thick down of her hair, which had grown a little darker in the past few days, and his finger had brushed the flushed cheek. Before leaving the house on his way to work, when the babysitter rang the bell, she woke up. She lay on her stomach, raised her head, and looked around without focus, until her eyes encountered his face, and the light blue latched onto him. When he had put her in the carrier and hung up the little rabbit to which he thought she was attached, her head turned sideways and she smiled with what seemed to him obvious pride, to the admiring exclamations of the babysitter.

Now he looked at Eli Bahar imploringly. "Stand by me on this. Give me a little. . . . Please?"

Eli Bahar lowered his gaze with embarrassment, pursed his lips, and said nothing.

"It's difficult. Complicated. I'm not saying it isn't." Michael heard his voice echoing. There was a faint note of falsity in what he heard, but he himself didn't know what caused the sense of falseness and what it really was, even though he was prepared to share it with Eli Bahar. Only he himself couldn't define it right now. There were so many contradictory feelings tumbling inside him. "It's like a washing machine," he finally said.

"What's like a washing machine?" asked Eli, alarmed. "What washing machine?"

"My head, my thoughts, they're churning as if they were in a washing machine, without stopping. . . . Everything's in a jumble and I don't know—"

"Okay, let it rest for the time being," acquiesced Eli Bahar. "But you'll talk to Shorer soon?"

Michael nodded.

"And Balilty? If Balilty is running the show," Eli continued, "then I can't bring in Rafi, even if we need to . . . I'm not on such great terms with him either. I don't know what will happen. He's not easy to deal with, you know that yourself."

"We'll see," said Michael. "We'll see tomorrow. Let's go and free Izzy Mashiah from Zippo. And by the way, maybe you can tell me what the hell Zippo's doing here in the first place?"

"I couldn't stand seeing him like that, at loose ends, hanging around with nothing to do, looking for an audience for his stories while he waits for his pension. Now he's telling me about Jerusalem in the old days. Before my time. About all the crazy people there used to be here. When you arrived he was in the midst of telling me about Rabbi Levinger's aunt, the madwoman everyone called Four-in-One, who used to wander around downtown Jerusalem sticking little labels on people. She believed that Buddha and Jesus and Moses and Mohammed were all one person. I remember my uncle's stories, now I get to hear them from Zippo, too. He says he's going to write a book about all those crazy people. Why not send him off with the surgical tape?"

And so Zippo—his real name was Itzhak Halevi, but no one ever called him that; he was Zippo because of a story about his cigarette lighter, one he was only too happy to relate to anyone who did, or didn't, ask—Zippo went with the piece of evidence to the Forensics laboratory at national police headquarters, and Michael went back to his office and sat down opposite Izzy Mashiah. Eli Bahar pulled up the chair near the door.

"Are you sure you're willing?" asked Michael.

"I've already said so," replied Izzy impatiently.

"Then I just have to explain to you what it's about. Have you ever taken a polygraph test before?"

"Me?" said Izzy, horrified. "I've never even been in a police station before."

"There are two methods," Michael explained. "One of them we don't use."

Out of the corner of his eye he saw Eli Bahar's mouth opening and closing, the expression of protest freezing on his face as Michael continued: "That method has been a complete failure. It contains trick questions, questions that . . ." He hesitated, sensing the waves of opposition coming from Eli, who had never liked Michael's frankness with suspects, on more than one occasion having expressed his objections and his fears that one day his chief would go too far.

Izzy waited in silence.

"Okay, let's say you're asked a series of questions whose answers are known in advance. For instance, whether your name is Izzy Mashiah, whether you were born in Jerusalem, whether your father's name is, let's say, Moshe, whether your wife's name is Shula, whether it's true that yesterday you were caught in bed with the upstairs neighbor."

Izzy sat up straight in his chair and folded his hands.

"You're suddenly asked a shocking question. And then conclusions are drawn from your reaction to the effect of the abrupt transition itself. We're against this method, because we think that it doesn't indicate anything. Even any kind of sudden change—the light going off, a lizard running across the floor—influences the reactions of the person taking the test. We're in favor of the second method."

Eli Bahar rested his elbow on the desk and cupped his chin in his hand. "Explain it to him," requested Michael, "and I'll go talk to the polygraph technician."

"I'm already at the door," said Eli, quickly jumping up. "I'll go talk to her."

"The second method, the one we prefer," Michael went on, "is based on the assumption that only a few people are capable of outwitting the machine. Therefore it's better to inform the subject of the questions in advance, before he's connected to the polygraph. I'll tell you what the questions are going to be, and then we'll connect you. The different variables—blood pressure, sweat, adrenalin—will tell us the rest."

"How long will it take?"

"Ten minutes, a quarter of an hour at most."

"Does it hurt? Do they prick you?"

Michael suppressed a smile. He almost murmured: Oh, the sweet anxieties of the survivors! Our world has been destroyed, our beloved is lying on the table in the Forensic Medicine Institute with his body split wide open, and we're still worried about a pinprick.

"It doesn't hurt," he said reassuringly. "You'll be connected to a machine they way you are for an EKG. We're also willing for you to go to a private outfit to have it done, and we'll accept their conclusions. A lot of suspects offer to undergo a polygraph and go to a private institution for it."

"There's no need for that," said Izzy. His breath was rapid and shallow as he asked to hear the questions. Michael listed them one by one. He remembered the quickening of Izzy's eye blinks when he asked about any crisis in the relationship, about any recent changes.

"Who's going to question me? You? The other guy? The technician?"

"I am. The technician never questions people. He doesn't even have to be in the room. Tonight it's a woman, and she'll be there only to check the functioning of the machine, to see if it's inscribing the movements of the needle properly, if any of the wires come unstuck. I'll ask the questions and I'll begin with the ones with known answers and without any problems, as I told you before. Then I'll proceed gradually to the complicated ones."

"So the whole thing's completely mechanical," said Izzy with frank relief. "Like a psychological test of some kind. There's nothing mysterious about it. Any idiot can ask the questions."

"Precisely," said Michael, not batting an eye. He didn't tell Izzy how concerned he was with the rhythm of the questions and their formulation. He didn't tell him that the problem was that the polygraph wasn't at all like a psychological test, that, on the contrary, with the polygraph it was impossible to go at a subject from different angles. And he didn't tell him that the brevity of the time available demanded virtuosity in the composition of the questions and control over their tempo. It was impossible to leave and return to the subject over and over again.

"Okay, no problem," said Eli from the doorway. "She's ready and waiting."

Michael stood up, but Izzy Mashiah didn't move. "So why isn't the test admissible in court? If it's so mechanical and unequivocal?"

"Oh, that," said Michael, again sitting down. He exchanged a quick look with Eli, who pulled up the chair and sat down looking resigned. "Do you want me to explain?" Izzy Mashiah shrugged his shoulders, but he didn't get up.

"The polygraph isn't admissible because there are situations in which people feel that they have a license to lie. When the person being examined isn't conscious that he's lying, in which case the reactions are simply not meaningful."

"What do you mean by license to lie?"

Michael looked at Eli Bahar. "Tell him about the lecture," he said.

"Right now?" protested Eli.

Michael did not reply.

"If you insist," Eli said unwillingly. "Once I was at a lecture where the lecturer asked a policewoman to come forward, and he showed her a series of cards, tacked them to a cork board, and then told her to read the numbers on the cards. Out loud, from one to seven. But he said that when she came to the card with the five on it, she should say 'seven.' And that's what she did. They connected her to a polygraph machine, and when she reached the card with the five on it she said seven. The needle didn't move because she didn't feel she was lying. She felt that she was obeying the lecturer's instructions. That's what's called a license to lie."

"The question is, what authority has authorized the lie," added Michael. "It hasn't been researched, but I'm sure that if you studied the reactions of Orthodox Jews to a polygraph you'd discover that they'd have no trouble lying if their rabbi told them to or if they thought they were doing God's will."

"You didn't warn him about his rights," whispered Eli, fingering the cassette of Michael's conversation with Izzy Mashiah as the technician was attaching him to the machine.

"I didn't think it was necessary," Michael admitted. "Not only is there no motive that I know of, but unless we obtain proof to the contrary, it appears that he didn't leave the house all day. He didn't even ask for a lawyer."

"But there aren't any witnesses saying that he didn't go out," said Eli.

"We'll ask him."

"Twice!" said Eli Bahar excitedly as they stood in the corridor. "He lied twice!"

"Not quite," said Michael, examining the graph again. "The first time it's clear, when I ask him about any crisis or a change in the relationship. But the second time, when I ask him if he left the house, it's inconclusive."

"Twice!" insisted Eli. "Do you want to keep him here?"

"For the time being," said Michael reflectively. He tried to suppress his surprising feelings of disappointment over Izzy's results.

"You can begin with him now, and I'll go talk to Balilty, and then come back later. You begin, and soon the others will be coming back from the scene, and we'll have some more manpower here."

At past one o'clock in the morning, Michael stood in Nita's apartment. All the lights were on. When he bent over the baby, asleep in the stroller, he realized it would soon be too small for her. She had grown so much in the past month that he would have to transfer her to a crib even when she was at Nita's. He suddenly remembered that he hadn't called his sister, Yvette. Maybe it was a good thing he hadn't, because, as it turned out, that policewoman Dalit had succeeded in locating and producing an Ethiopian girl with a bright smile who was ready and willing to step in and take care of the children on a live-in basis. Dalit's eyes gleamed with self-esteem, with a sense of her indispensability, as she made haste to tell how she had found her. By chance the policewoman had heard about the Ethiopian, Sara by name, and found out that she was available while she waited for a college course to begin. By chance, too, Dalit was familiar with Sara's suitability—the woman had worked for a year as an assistant at the Wizo Day Care Center and the children had adored her. And Dalit also knew that Sara was looking for a place to stay and that she had no money.

Balilty, standing next to Ido's crib, nodded. "It's impossible to talk to her, to your girlfriend. All she says is that she's not sure, she doesn't remember. Maybe she's still under the influence of the sedative the doctor gave her. If it goes on like this we'll have to call in another doctor. It seems to me that she's on the verge of flipping out. I thought of getting help from Elroi."

"What about the strings?" asked Michael. "All the rest can wait."

"That's just it." Balilty studied the floor tiles. "She can't remember, and her brother says that he simply doesn't know. She's not communicating. Theo's the opposite. Once you get him started he doesn't shut up. But you try with her first, just the preliminaries, the basics. Afterward we'll talk."

"Are you assuming it was the same perpetrator in both cases?" asked Michael.

"What, two different people, by chance, in such a short space of time, killing off two members of the same family? Give me a break!" said Balilty, and then he asked what had resulted from Izzy's interrogation. At that moment the door to the bedroom opened and Dalit stood there, a slender figure in jeans. She crossed her arms under her little breasts and leaned, posing, against the doorpost.

"Yes?" said Michael.

"I thought that you . . . that you wanted to bring me up to date," she said with a mixture of eagerness and vulnerability, passing a tentative hand over her cropped fair hair.

"In a minute," said Balilty. "Meanwhile you can make another round of coffee."

"Your baby's awake," she announced with a forced smile.

"I have to prepare her bottle," said Michael. And to Balilty: "Come into the kitchen with me. We can go on talking there."

"I've already done it," said Dalit. "Two bottles." Michael asked how she knew, at her age, about preparing bottles for babies. "Nita told me how," she said familiarly.

"I don't know what we'd do without her," said Balilty admiringly. "The girl's a treasure."

"We have an au pair," said Michael encouragingly as he sat on the double bed in the bedroom with Nita and stroked her hand. It was the first time since the discovery of the body that the two of them were alone together. When she spoke at last, Nita's voice was hoarse, as if she had been shouting for hours on end. She kept her eyes fixed on the blue rug at the foot of the bed as she whispered, "It's like waking up in a fright again and again from a nightmare. It's as if that's become a reality."

He didn't understand what she was talking about, and he said nothing. She rubbed the edge of the bedspread with her free hand and didn't take her eyes off the rug. "Do you want to know what was worst for me at the first moment?" she asked. He nodded. She raised her head and studied his face as if to make sure that he meant it. Before fixing her eyes on the rug again, she warned: "It's terrible, what I'm going to tell you." He tightened his grip on her hand. "I haven't told you till now. I couldn't tell you. I didn't have the words. Now I have them. For months, really months, every day, almost every hour, sometimes every minute, especially until Ido was born, but afterward too, it's haunted me. . . . A recurring image, a recurring nightmare, a kind of vision that never left me, not when I was sleeping and not when I was awake. As if I were seeing a film. It haunted me all the time."

She fell silent. Her hand was cold and clammy in his. He didn't move. After a few seconds of silence she said: "The image was of my severed head. I saw myself with a string, holding the string at both ends. I put it on the upper part of my throat and pulled with all my strength. Then I saw my throat cut through. It's as if I was seeing myself double. As the one being beheaded, and as the one doing the beheading. The blood beginning to flow, rivers of blood, streams of blood, and my head falling." She choked back a sob and was silent. Michael bowed his head and closed his eyes. He shuddered. He opened his eyes again and looked at her. She didn't move. Her eyes remained fixed on the blue rug, as if the streams and rivers of blood had collected there. "It's probably connected to my feeling that I was stupid, that I deserved to be punished. As if this stupid head deserved to be cut off for being gullible despite everything it knew."

"That's why you gave up playing all that time." Michael whispered what had become clear to him just at that moment. He had the feeling that he was shouting.

"That's why I didn't play," she agreed. "Everyone thought I was depressed because of my broken heart. But it wasn't that, it was simply fear. I wanted to play so much! It was so . . . But whenever I saw the cello I saw the strings, and whenever I saw the strings I thought of the severed head, and that ruined my joy in the music. This fear ruined music for me."

A mixture of sorrow and horror filled him, and he heard himself asking: "Why didn't you tell me this before?"

"I couldn't. Even before I met you I began to . . . I thought it was beginning to go away. Later, when you turned up, it was better. When Father . . . when my father died, it came back. But I told myself that it would go away by itself. I couldn't," she pleaded, "I couldn't say it in words. It was so vivid and real that . . ."

He loosened his grip on her hand and looked at her: the yellowish tinge of her skin, the eyes that were sunk in their sockets, the dark half-moons under the blue-gray irises ringed with black, the soft light of the lamp surrounding her. Her lips trembled and on either side of her mouth deep lines were etched. A dark shadow filled her hollow cheeks. Only her chin trembled. The rest of her face looked as tightly clenched as a fist.

"And today," she whispered, "when I saw Gabi, it wasn't only that Gabi . . . that Gabi . . . that I wouldn't have Gabi anymore, which is something I can't even begin to grasp—and not just that anyone who saw that sight will ever forget it as long as she lives—in addition to all that, I had the feeling that it was me I was seeing lying there. That someone had copied that image, my vision, which was something I had never said a word about to anyone. And somehow someone knew about it and did it to Gabi instead of to me. By mistake. Gabi is a mistake." She raised her head, leaned toward him, and looked into his eyes: "I should have been lying there with my throat cut! Me and not Gabi!" He held her hand again, and felt his own hands growing cold. From moment to moment his dread grew greater. "Suddenly I saw what it looked like in reality. What it would have looked like if I'd really done it. I think . . . I feel as if I taught someone how to do it. Or . . . or as if I did it myself."

Precisely at this moment his dread began to dissolve. Instead he felt the beginning of a new clarity, of a sober coldness. "What do you mean, you did it yourself?" he asked in a stern, distant tone. "Did you do it yourself?"

"I don't think so," she whispered, and she raised her eyes to him. "I couldn't have, could I? It isn't possible, is it? I couldn't have done it without knowing, could I? Could I?" she asked in horror, gripping his arm with all her strength. Now he was split in two, twins: one brimming over with panic, with terror, with a tumult of contradictory feelings threatening to overwhelm him, and the other, who with a cold, stern, controlled voice asked: "Do you really think you did it?"

"I told you: No. It's not possible. You know that I loved Gabi. But how could anyone else have reconstructed so exactly what I had in my head and only I knew about? How is that possible? Maybe the only answer is that I did it unconsciously."

"Unconsciously," he repeated. "Unconsciously," he said again and fell silent.

"I once heard an interview with a professional hypnotist," whispered Nita, "who said that even under full hypnosis you can't make people do things they're completely opposed to doing."

"That's true," said Michael. "There's no doubt about it. It's one of the things always brought up when hypnosis and its possible dangers are being discussed. A man won't commit a murder under hypnosis unless he's already murderous. But you're not talking about hypnosis now, but about something else. And there are precedents for the kind of thing you're talking about. People have committed murder in a fit of insanity and afterward not remembered it."

The blood drained from her already pale face, and her hands shook. "Then it is possible?" she whispered in a choked voice. "That something like that could happen. In that case, I'm a danger to everyone, and I should be . . . I can't be left alone with Ido, with the children. . . ." She stood up, clutched her throat with both hands, and swayed on her feet. Michael stood up, too, and held her firmly. "You have to arrest me now, to take me away from here because I may have . . . I must have . . ." Her eyes rolled up and she began to jerk convulsively.

He slapped her once and then began talking fast. It seemed to him that everything now depended on what he could recall about memory loss under similar circumstances. "Listen!" he said to her sharply. "Listen to me! Are you listening?" She didn't move. "Listen to me. That's not the way things work. I know one instance of a boy who killed his parents and his brothers and sisters in a moment of madness. He can't remember anything about it. Nothing. Neither the moment when he picked up the Uzi nor the moment when he shot them dead. Twenty-four hours have been wiped out of his memory. Not only that moment, but everything that preceded and followed it. That's not the way it is with you. You remember everything you did during the day. Go on, tell me what you did, and you'll see that you remember all the rest. Everything surrounding the moment when you found Gabi lying there. Talk slowly. You have nothing to worry about regarding the children. I won't leave you alone—with them or without them." He put his hand on her arm. "Until we get to the bottom of this, you won't be alone," he promised. "But now tell me everything you remember up to the moment when you saw Gabi and what happened afterward. Everything, every detail."

"Are you sure it wasn't me?" she whispered with a hint of relief. She breathed more quietly. Her anxiety attack had passed. He himself didn't know where he got his certainty from. If Balilty had heard him now, he would no doubt have raised his eyebrows and said something sarcastic, and Shorer would have said that it might be a very cunning technique, but he had never heard of it. How well do you really know her? he imagined Shorer mockingly asking him. And who knows anyone well enough to be able to predict all his actions? You're again relying on a belief based on intuition. And the minute the first crack appears, the whole thing will come down like a house of cards. In *The Big Sleep* Humphrey Bogart as Philip Marlowe fell in love with a murderess. But he himself wasn't in love, and Nita wasn't a murderess. This wasn't a seedy private eye's office in New York—there were no whiskey bottles at his elbow. This was a normal apartment. In the next room Balilty's cold, sharp logic held sway—and a crying baby. Philip Marlowe had no baby. Nor did the woman he fell in love with. And again, above all, he wasn't in love with Nita.

She spoke slowly, trying with all her strength to concentrate. Someone knocked on the door. "Not now," called Michael, and Nita trembled. Slowly she reconstructed the rehearsal. When she had described the work on the last movement of the Double Concerto, she said, with an effort: "And after that I don't remember." Michael asked about the packing up of the instruments, and about those who had remained onstage. He wondered if she'd noticed Gabi going backstage. She brought her eyebrows up in concentration. In a hollow, almost dead voice, she said she couldn't picture it, and then immediately resumed talking in the halting stammer, as if in a dream. She brought her eyebrows together over the bridge of her small nose.

"Do you remember seeing the concertmaster, Avigdor, on the stage then?" She shook her head weakly. "Or Mrs. Agmon, the violinist who was looking for Gabi?"

"Nothing," mumbled Nita, burying her face in her hands. "Nothing. A complete blackout."

"She wanted to talk to him about her husband," he said, trying to jog her memory. But she shook her head firmly and said that it was all in darkness. She had no sensation of walking on the stage, she wasn't certain she had been on it at all at that point, but she also had no memory of having been anywhere else. "It's like an event from your childhood," she said dully, "that you don't really remember, that you've only been told about, learned about from a photograph album. That's much different from really experiencing it yourself. That's what it's like for me until the moment when I'm standing over . . . seeing Gabi." Only now did a stream of tears begin to flow down her hollow cheeks.

"There's a whole bit," she said through her sobs, "that I don't remember. As if there's an abyss in the middle." Suddenly her body stiffened. She sat up straight.

"What is it?" he asked tensely.

"There was . . . once . . . I remember . . . in a hotel in Columbus, Ohio, where I stayed overnight after a chamber music concert, an old movie on television called *The Three Faces of Eve*. Have you heard of it?"

"*The Three Faces of Eve*?" he asked, astonished. "I know that movie. Joanne Woodward, in a wonderful performance."

"She has two personalities, and one doesn't know about the other. Even then it terrified me. I couldn't sleep all night."

"It has a happy ending, with the third personality that triumphs in the end," he said as if in a dream, remembering that his Uncle Jacques, his mother's younger brother, had seated him on a wooden chair in a middle row, glanced at his watch, announced that he had to make a phone call, promised to be back soon, and only returned for the final scenes. Michael too had been terrified by the movie.

"Eve Black, the one who comes out of Eve White, puts a rope around her little daughter's neck and tries to strangle her," said Nita absently, and she hugged herself. "And luckily her husband appears when the little girl screams, and then the woman loses consciousness and wakes up as Eve White, the housewife who suffers from headaches and doesn't remember anything. I've also suffered from terrible headaches this past year."

Michael kept quiet and stroked her arm.

"She told the doctor that she hadn't done anything. She didn't remember anything. She was convinced that she was innocent," said Nita, agitated.

He remembered Joanne Woodward's meek housewife's face twisting in pain, her hands clutching her lace collar. He also remembered a ridiculous hat.

"It's lucky you saw the movie," mumbled Nita. "At least you don't think I'm crazy. The doctor explains to her that she's not mentally ill, but that she's suffering from a split personality."

He was silent. His memory of watching the movie; worried because Uncle Jacques hadn't returned, that the seat next to him was empty, of encountering fine acting for the first time. "She was fabulous," he heard himself say. "It was totally convincing."

In a hoarse whisper Nita said: "What's important is that it's possible to pass from one personality to the another, and the one doesn't know about the other. There was a rope around the little girl's neck, and the woman pulled it with all her strength, like this." Nita raised her fists and moved her arms apart.

"Nita," said Michael, pleated the bedspread. "Do you remember that one of your strings snapped a few days ago, and you replaced it?"

She nodded.

"Do you remember how many spare strings you had?"

"He's already asked me that," she said in despair. "I don't remember whether it was two or three. It was definitely not one, and certainly not four."

He led her into the children's room and sat her down on the folding bed next to Ido's crib. Sara, who was kneeling in the corner, smiled her soothing, white-toothed smile. She didn't look more than thirteen.

The bedroom had been turned into a conference room. "What is it with her?" asked Balilty, who was sitting next to Michael on the double bed. He then remarked on "Dalit's excellent performance, even though she has no experience." Then he sighed. "Theo van Gelden can't remember when he left the stage and went off to phone, or how long it took," he complained. "It looks as if nobody here has a motive. And we haven't learned anything new about Gabriel, either. Did you talk to that guy?"

"I did. And there's already a polygraph. And a reply from the lab about the surgical tape."

"So," said Balilty mockingly, "have you caught me being sloppy?"

"I sure have," said Michael and looked, not without pleasure, at Balilty's chubby face, which froze.

"Are you serious?" said Balilty finally. His small eyes gleamed with suspicion.

"Absolutely!" said Michael. "There were down feathers on the tape."

"I don't believe it!" said Balilty, but you could see the wheels of his mind rapidly turning. "Down?"

"Down!"

"Like in a pillow? A quilt? That kind of down?"

"Yes."

"On the surgical tape?"

"On the tape that was on van Gelden's mouth."

"From a pillow?"

"Apparently. They're comparing it now with the old man's pillow. We'll know more in the morning."

"Are you trying to tell me that they first suffocated him with a pillow?"

"I'm not trying to tell you anything. The facts speak for themselves."

Balilty peered at him, and then in the direction of the door. "They haven't been told?"

"No, and they won't know it so quickly either," Michael warned.

"No, of course not!" said Balilty. He looked horrified. "What can I say? It was a screw-up."

"You said it."

"Yes, yes. I said it. Would you have done it any differently?"

"How should I know?" said Michael. "I'd like to think so. But to be honest, I don't know."

"It seemed like an ordinary robbery," contended Balilty. "How could I have guessed that they suffocated him first and only tied him up afterward?"

"In our profession there's no such thing as 'it seems like,'" exclaimed Michael, regretting the authoritative, patronizing tone of his banal statement when he saw Balilty's crestfallen face. "Forgive me," he said.

"Okay, I've already said it was sloppy. What do you want me to do now?

"Think about everything from the beginning."

"Okay, I'm thinking. And what I think is that we should talk about it at the meeting tomorrow. Do you realize that it puts them in the clear?" he asked, nodding toward the living room.

"How?"

"They had a concert. And before that each of them was busy. They have alibis."

"So it seems."

"You yourself took her to the hairdresser's before the concert. You told me so."

"Yes, but not her brothers."

"One of them is no longer with us."

"But he was then. And the second one is very much with us. At the moment, anyway."

"Do you think that . . ." Balilty sounded worried. "Then we have to put them under guard. In shifts. Around the clock."

"You're heading the team, right?"

Balilty nodded absently.

"Then do it," said Michael.

Balilty looked at him uncomprehendingly. "Why are you making an issue of it?"

"Because if I give the order to have them put under surveillance, people might say that I'm only worried about Nita and the baby and so on."

"You see," said Balilty. "It's already coming up. And we haven't even begun yet."

8

Anyone Who Wants to Live Outside Life

The thought of Joanne Woodward's face in *The Three Faces of Eve* assailed him again in the midst of the meeting, while Tzilla was standing at the table handing out, in order—first to Balilty and then to Michael, and to Dalit before Eli and Avram—the cups of coffee and omelet rolls Zippo had brought from the Yemenite's stand on the corner of Jaffa Road. Puffing and panting, Zippo had returned from his mission and put the bags down in the middle of the conference table. He removed a small container from one of them, took off the cardboard lid with a flourish, and insisted that they all breathe in the smell of authentic Yemenite *hilbeh*. When Tzilla averted her face in disgust, he reminded her of the medicinal properties of the odoriferous spice, especially as an enhancer of virility. Part of Michael's mind registered Tzilla placing the long roll wrapped in oil-stained white paper in front of him. As he looked at the stain he suddenly saw Joanne Woodward's face filling the whole screen, an image he wasn't at all certain was even in the movie.

The face twisted, altered, contorted, and transformed itself into something completely different. The woman in the movie didn't know what was happening, he said to himself in a panic as the face disappeared and he again stared at the oil stain. Each one of her personalities was separate. They lived in one body, even in one soul, and the "good" one knew nothing about the "evil" one. He barely remembered the details, even though he had seen the movie again on television a few years back. But something about the way the woman spoke when she was in her vicious, evil role, the echo of her hoarse, mocking alto laughter, rang in his ears. He thought he remembered her saying: "She doesn't know anything about me, but I know everything about her." Only then did he notice that he was stirring the sugar around and around in his cup and sprinkling drops of the black liquid onto the notes Eli had prepared for them. Zippo ate noisily and praised the sharp green sauce, offering it around with a generous expression. He smacked his lips, chewed noisily, and wiped the edges of his mustache. Dalit sat between Michael and Balilty, who sat at the head of the table and ran the meeting. It seemed to Michael for a moment that she was sitting too close to him, that the gap between them was closing, that she was edging her elbow over to his, that her knee kept touching his, accidentally on purpose. And maybe it really was by accident, he rebuked himself as he peeked at her profile, which looked completely detached from these contacts. The coffee break had been a good idea, he thought as he unenthusiastically chewed the fresh roll soaked in the frying oil. It had done something to dispel the heavy atmosphere in the conference room after Eli Bahar's outburst against Balilty.

There really was something infuriating about Balilty's indefatigable jocularity. Even after a sleepless night, he kept cracking jokes, interrupting everyone, making ironic remarks about down pillows.

Tzilla had passed around a summary of the lab report, and they all had studied the enlarged photographs of the feather particles in silence. The feathers on the tape that gagged Felix van Gelden were indeed identical to those from his pillow. Balilty's remarks were irritating, too, in that they exposed his embarrassment at his slip-up.

Michael blinked in order to dissipate the oppressive thought of *The Three Faces of Eve*, and he tried to concentrate on what was being said about how Felix van Gelden had apparently been suffocated. "It doesn't take a lot of time or strength, a minute would do it," said Eli Bahar. "With his emphysema, a minute's pressure with the pillow would be enough. A child could do it, a woman easily."

"I wonder why they had to kill him if all they wanted was the painting. It would have been so much easier to steal it when he wasn't home," said Michael, and Balilty nodded, muttered, shifted in his chair, and then observed that Felix van Gelden himself had the painting examined by experts and its authenticity confirmed beyond a doubt, pigments and everything. Then he asked with a worried expression if they could "conclude that it was the same person involved in both murders." His small eyes narrowed as if the light hurt them.

"From the looks of things, it isn't clear what the connection is. Maybe Mashiah has something to do with the painting, maybe he's involved in it," Dalit said hopefully, and she daintily extracted a slice of tomato and a strip of cucumber from her roll. She inclined her head toward the narrow corridor outside where Izzy Mashiah was waiting for his ex-wife to bring his passport.

"And all this time, with all these complications," said Balilty, "we're forgetting the simple questions. Such as: Who stands to gain? I mean dirty things like money. Who stands to gain? We haven't seen Gabriel's will yet, if he had one. We'll soon see. But what's definite is that with Gabriel out of the picture what would have been divided in three parts—the old man's house in Rehavia, the shop, whatever—will now be divided in two. I don't know what she lives on. What does she live on?"

"Savings and an allowance her father gave her. But she intends to go back to teaching and performing and recording," replied Michael matter-of-factly, as if he had been asked about a historical date.

"And her father left her the painting. We mustn't forget that," said Balilty. "And him?"

"Who?"

"The maestro."

"I wouldn't worry about him if I were you. He makes a lot of money, and he's got plenty."

"And he's also got ex-wives and expenses, and so has Izzy Mashiah, who may stand to benefit from Gabriel's will, if he left one."

"Half a million dollars isn't garbage," reflected Zippo aloud. "It has to mean something."

"It's completely clear from the polygraph that Izzy Mashiah knows nothing about the painting. Nothing we don't know, anyway," Eli pointed out dryly.

"But it's also clear, so you said, that something had gone wrong in the relationship, that there was some sort of crisis," Tzilla reminded them. The crease on her upper lip seemed deeper than usual, as if it had made up its mind to remain there forever, giving her mouth a tough, stern expression.

"We'll have to work on that, maybe this morning," Eli muttered, and he looked at Balilty as if he were expecting an outburst. A flare-up before the coffee break had been on that subject.

"What crisis?" Balilty had argued. "It's some little disagreement you're trying to blow up out of all proportion to provide a lead."

Eli had puffed out his cheeks and expelled his breath noisily. This was enough for Balilty to explode and say: "Get used to the idea that I'm in charge of this investigation now, and I do things differently from his majesty." He had jerked his head toward Michael, who said nothing.

"The difficulty here," Michael now reflected aloud, after pushing aside the remains of his roll and—despite all his resolutions to cut down—lighting another cigarette, "is really the size of the sum. It's hard for us to accept the idea that the theft of the painting might be just a diversion. That Felix van Gelden was deliberately murdered for some other reason."

Balilty gave him a long look. "That's how you see it?" he asked with a serious, concentrated expression.

"It's a possibility we have to take into account, even, or especially, if it was someone close, on the inside."

"I don't believe it!" cried Dalit.

"Nobody asked you," muttered Tzilla, looking down at the table.

"I can't see any other explanation for the fact that the break-in, which had to be well planned, professional, with much inside information, took place precisely when he was at home. Not to mention the fact that they suffocated him first."

"But there could be another explanation for that!" Zippo protested. "Maybe he surprised them in the act."

"Maybe," said Michael, making a face.

"You, in any event, insist on seeing a connection between the two cases, meaning that the old man's death was deliberate murder too," said Balilty.

"And you?" retorted Michael. "Can you *really* ignore the connection between the two cases? Do you have a better explanation?" He saw Balilty's eyes narrowing even further, as if he was well aware of what lay behind Michael's emphasis on the word "really," as if he could hear him thinking that if only he, Balilty, hadn't made that stupid mistake, he too would have insisted on the connection.

"If that's so, the two sons are in the clear," mused Balilty aloud. "They seem to have alibis for the time when the old man was murdered." He gave Michael a sharp look. "And as for her," he said, gazing at the window opposite, "she was at the hairdresser's. You can relax."

"I'm not at all sure that they're in the clear. Anyway, that's not the reason I see a connection," Michael said angrily, propping his elbow on the table and resting his cheek on his hand so as to hide the involuntary tightening of his mouth, the painful clenching of his jaws. "And I ask again: What about the strings?"

Balilty sighed. "She doesn't remember if she had two or three strings, as you know, and what I think is—I already thought so yesterday—is that we should simply go after all those who don't have a spare thin string . . . I can't remember the name, what do they call it again?"

"The A string. But we have to wait for a reply from Forensics," said Michael, and suddenly he felt the blood stopping in his veins and his heart beating wildly. He had left her with the baby. But she wasn't alone, he reminded himself. And anyway, he scolded himself, she didn't do it.

"We have the answer from Forensics. I got it at five o'clock this morning. It was the thinnest cello string." Balilty shot out the words. "They're comparing it to her strings now. She uses a special kind on her cello."

Only the sound of Zippo's chewing broke the silence around the table.

"So," said Michael thoughtfully. He felt a great void within him. What if she did it? If she did it, nothing matters anymore.

"The A string from a cello," said Balilty again, staring at Michael, "is the string that was in the piano, and it's the murder weapon. Besides Nita, there were eight cellists there yesterday. And it turns out—it's lucky we had the sense to check the exact kind of string when we questioned them—that only two of them had spare strings of that thin kind." He glanced at the piece of paper in his hand. "A strings. I checked it out in Tzilla's notes at six o'clock this morning. Well done, Tzilla. But they all declared that they had the same number of strings as when they left home. So who knows?"

"The polygraph? How about getting all of them to take a polygraph test?"

Balilty sighed. "Yeah, yeah, later. First of all we had to hear from Forensics that it was really the murder weapon, because, thank God, as your friend Kestenbaum says," he shot a look at Michael, "'Every contact leaves a trace.' Cells, skin, I don't know what. The main thing is that they confirm it."

"And Nita van Gelden? What spare strings does she have in her instrument case?" asked Eli Bahar with suspense.

"That's it, she has neither a D nor an A. She only has . . ." Again he looked down at his piece of paper. "G and C, but she says that she thinks she remembers using her spare A a few days ago, and that you . . ." he waved at Michael, "were there when the string snapped."

"But I don't know," said Michael, shifting in his chair, "if it was an A, D, G, or a C that snapped. I'm trying to remember now if she said anything then, but all I remember is that she asked me, 'Is that a fifth?' That's all she said," he announced, and he wondered if he was only imagining that he could see disbelief on their faces, or if it was really there. "I can't even read music," he said in a choked voice. "All those words don't mean a thing to me. Even 'fifth'—I don't really know what it means."

Balilty finally broke the oppressive silence: "There's no need to jump to conclusions," he said in a fatherly tone. "Even if we assume, for the sake of argument, that it's her string, from her cello case, not that I know how to prove it," he said, swallowing, "but assuming that it really is hers, anyone could have . . ." He paused. "Especially anyone who was at her place, let's say . . ."

"If you're thinking of Theo," said Michael, "he's never alone in the house with her as a rule. I've spent most of my time there recently, and I know more or less who's been in the apartment. Someone could have taken the string in the concert hall. This doesn't mean that Theo's completely in the clear—"

"We have to check the maestro's story again." Since the early morning, when the question of Theo's passport and his unwillingness to hand it over to them had come up, Balilty had been calling him the maestro. ("Do you think," Theo had protested to Balilty in Nita's living room, "that I could even dream of going abroad at a time like this? I wouldn't even go to Japan," he added sullenly, again bringing up his commitments in the Far East.) "As for Gabriel van Gelden, we'll never know."

"What won't we know?" asked Zippo.

"We'll never know where he was when his father was murdered," explained Dalit, her eyes darting alertly from Balilty's face to Michael's.

"We certainly will," said Michael firmly. "We'll know today."

"How? How will we know?" asked Zippo, tugging at his mustache.

"His brother will tell us. Theo will know."

"How the hell do you know?" asked the astounded Balilty.

Michael did not reply. He was trying to reconstruct the situation and the sounds he had heard when he was standing in the kitchen. He remembered clearly Theo imploring, "You can explain it to me, at least." Again there was an oppressive silence. Balilty tapped the point of his yellow pencil on the table top in three-beat time. Then he looked at Michael doubtfully, banged his hand on the table, and said: "Let's move on."

Balilty ran the meeting as if it were a Passover seder. He delegated tasks, called on speakers, did everything by the book, and from time to time nodded to Dalit and said: "Did you take that down? Take it down!" She would return the nod eagerly. She would chew the end of her pen with a look of concentration on her face and then lean over to Balilty and whisper something in his ear. Her assiduous efforts to make herself indispensable seemed to be succeeding. Already at the beginning of the meeting it had become clear to Michael that Balilty was becoming dependent on her. He had seen Balilty's eyes sliding over her backside and down her legs as she raised herself on tiptoe to close the window when an uproar broke out below among the Arab women looking for detainees who had disappeared, while the bells of the Russian Orthodox Church began to peal. She remembered everything, and now, as Avram reported on the gloves, her pale narrow face was expressionless and her light eyes downcast as she diligently took down all the details. Under the prominent cheekbones her cheeks looked hollow, giving her an austere, almost ascetic look. This vanished, or at least became questionable, if you took into account her mouth, if you looked at those beautifully full lips, which lent something surprisingly sensual to her face. The sharp chin almost canceled out the sensuality, or at least gave it a certain coldness, and even cruelty. Michael roused himself and turned his attention to Avram. Dalit opened her eyes wide and took her hand away from her chin.

"Tell them about the place," she reminded Avram like a loving wife reminding her husband of an important point he had forgotten in a joke he was telling. "Tell them about her locker," she reminded him when he was on his third sentence.

"I'm getting to it," said Avram, blushing. As always when he blushed, tiny blue veins caught fire on his face, and one of them began to pulse on his temple, and he began, as usual when he was embarrassed, to stammer. Tzilla gave Dalit a quick, sharp, hostile look, as if she were making a mental note to include this image in the dossier she was compiling against her.

"But there's no reason to think that Margot Fischer had anything to do with it," said Avram, his blush subsiding. "As I said earlier, told you before, and it shows up in the polygraph tests too, everybody knew about the gloves. Somebody must have taken them." At the beginning of the meeting they had talked a lot about this double bass player, Margot Fischer, who had arrived out of breath, confirmed that the gloves were hers, demanded to know why the police had them, and referred briefly to a chronic illness. "Raynaud's disease, it's called," said Avram. "Her hands are always cold." She told of the jokes about those deerskin gloves, which were part of the orchestra's folklore. They were a gift from a colleague in a German radio orchestra, also a woman bass player who suffered from a circulatory problem. Margot Fischer was a short woman, and Michael remembered how she had nearly vanished behind her instrument, even though her arms were unusually long.

Avram spoke of her hands, which were large in proportion to her body. "But not as big as a man's," he observed, adding that the gloves were too big for her. "She kept her gloves in her locker," he said, "and everybody knew it." Then he spoke about the location of the lockers, next to the administration offices. "No," he said, answering a question from Eli, "everyone has a key only to their own locker, but there's a master key. She has no idea how the gloves got out of her locker, but when we pressed her she admitted she might have forgotten to lock it yesterday, because she was distracted," he added.

The way Avram bent over his notes seemed to express a certain affection for Margot Fischer and trust in the story she had told him about the events of the day before. On the day of the murder, he related in her name, she hadn't used the gloves. She had arrived late for the rehearsal and had no time to dawdle at the lockers. Theo van Gelden had no patience with latecomers, always having something harsh and insulting to say to them. So she had rushed onstage gloveless and struggled with her stiff fingers until they warmed up and she no longer needed gloves. "On bad days," he said sympathetically, "she has to keep them on until the very moment she must begin to play."

"There was no blood or fingerprints inside the gloves," complained Balilty. "Forensics thinks that whoever it was wore thin plastic gloves or even a plastic bag inside the gloves. There was a scrap of plastic there, too small for a fingerprint, and it may just have been there by chance. It was only a scrap," he said, staring out the window.

"But you haven't said anything about Fischer's relations with the victim," said Zippo dramatically. He bit his lower lip with his big yellow teeth as he studied the notes in front of him.

"She doesn't have much contact with the other musicians," explained Avram. "She's older than most of them. If you saw her you'd know that she's not interested in having any relations with them. She's . . . not like other people. She's a bit weird. What people used to call an old maid. There's actually something childish about her. She's a kind of loner. Theo van Gelden called her Glenngoulda," he said, embarrassed as if he were betraying a confidence in spite of himself. "She explained to me that it was because of some famous pianist who was always very careful of his hands and wore gloves. Black ones. He's dead. She said that he went mad, but that his hands were insured for millions."

"But we don't know much about her," remarked Tzilla. "The gloves are hers. All kinds of things happen in the world, she could have been somebody's accomplice."

"There's nothing like that, I promise you," said Avram.

"They didn't find any prints inside," Balilty reminded them. "But the string made two cuts in the leather. And there's that scrap of plastic inside."

"I talked to her," said Eli Bahar. "I asked her about her relations with the van Gelden brothers. And I got the feeling that she's not the type. You can see right away that there's nothing complicated about her. She's simple, like a kibbutznik. The kind of woman who lives alone with her sick old mother. That's why she went to the airport, to pick up her mother's brother, who comes from America to see her twice a year."

"Right," said Avram quickly, "we checked that, too. She left as soon as the rehearsal was over, because she was late to meet the plane. That is, she thought she was late. It didn't arrive till the middle of the night. There was an engine malfunction. The time of arrival and the passenger list both check out."

"She even thought of dropping in on her mother after the rehearsal to see how she was, but she gave up on that because she was running late," added Eli Bahar. "You can see that she's not the type to be mixed up in anything. She's a responsible person," he explained.

Balilty's eyes darted from one speaker to the other. "Have you got the hots for her, or what?" he said brusquely. "You're talking like teenagers, both of you. What's going on here? Everyone falls in love with the person he's investigating." He glanced quickly at Michael and turned away. "She didn't come back till late at night, and she left her old mother stuck there and us, too."

"She was stuck herself!" protested Eli Bahar. "What happened with her," he explained in an offended tone, "is that she had to stay at the airport till her uncle's plane landed. She was there for hours, and she didn't know when she would be able to get back. When she finally got back home we were waiting outside the door, in a police car, and she was alarmed that something had happened to her mother, who'd been alone for so many hours. I saw her myself, she doesn't know anything," he promised.

"And then, when we told her," continued Avram, "you could see that she was shocked, you could see that it was the first she had heard about Gabriel van Gelden's murder."

"She liked and admired him very much, and she agreed to a polygraph on the spot," Eli interrupted him. "We're wasting our time on her, believe me. You could see that she didn't know anything about it and that she was upset. She has no motive. She'd even been accepted into that ensemble, that new one, that Baroque you talked about," he explained to Michael. "Here you are, here's her statement, you can see what she says." He bent over the papers in front of him and rummaged through them. "Where is it? It was right here."

"'His early music orientation is very interesting and attractive to me,'" Tzilla read from the copy in front of her. "'And I regarded it as an honor to work under Gabriel van Gelden as director and conductor.'" Tzilla raised her eyes and looked around. "What exactly does she mean by 'early music orientation'?" she asked with her eyes on Michael.

"He can explain it to us later," said Balilty coldly. "It's something in music, some kind of theory. What's important now is that you took her passport."

"We have to see if the gloves fit someone," Tzilla reflected aloud.

"We're not talking about shoes here. They're big gloves, they'd fit anyone," said Avram.

"We don't have the slightest reason to suspect her," said Eli Bahar.

"But you have to take into account that people who look as if they've given up on life and everything suddenly do things," said Dalit, stretching her arms. Her small breasts rose under the tight T-shirt.

"What things?" asked Tzilla, and her hostile expression showed a sign of something close to curiosity.

"There are desires that people bury for years, and insults they swallow, and suddenly they break out," explained Dalit with a dreamy look. "We once had a neighbor . . . Suddenly, one day, out of the blue, after you'd forgotten to even think about her as a human being, when all she did all day was cook and clean and in the evening sit in front of the TV mending clothes, one day she got up and—"

"When are you seeing Shorer?" Balilty asked Michael, who shook his head and with an inaudible sigh said: "Later, if his daughter doesn't give birth today. Or if she's given birth and everything is okay. I have to phone him."

"We have to find that partner in the music shop, the one you told us about," said Tzilla."

Michael nodded. "He wasn't a partner, he was an employee," he said, and he gave Balilty a questioning look.

"What did she do, that neighbor of yours?" Tzilla asked Dalit.

"She ran away from home," said Dalit, quickly swallowing the end of her roll, "with all their savings. Her husband searched for her for years."

"We're looking for him," said Balilty, shrugging his shoulders. "It's not easy to find someone who lives alone and doesn't talk to his neighbors. Everybody in this case is weird, different. Artists!" He swelled his cheeks. "But this old guy isn't even an artist. His apartment is locked, as if nobody's been there for years."

"He disappeared quite a while ago," said Michael, hearing Nita's voice as she demanded that they notify Herzl. "Nobody's known where he is for months."

"He wasn't at the old man's funeral, either," said Balilty. "We looked for him there."

"And he had a key to van Gelden's apartment," put in Eli, "old man van Gelden, that is."

"There's no question about it, we have to find him," summed up Balilty.

"So who's going to do it?" asked Zippo.

"You," said Balilty. "From now on, that's your job. Dalit will give you the details."

"We'll never find the painting." Tzilla's voice echoed despairingly. "Maybe nobody even smuggled it out of the country. It could be anywhere, even in this employee's, this Herzl's closet."

"Nothing's certain," muttered Eli. "We hardly know anything yet. It could be the opposite, too. We haven't spoken to enough people yet. And we haven't even got the official report from Forensics yet."

"What do you mean, the opposite?" said Dalit, sitting up.

Eli Bahar lowered his long eyelashes. "Nothing special," he said, wiping his face. "I just thought that there was another possibility—that someone knew that Gabriel knew something about the painting, about the robbery and the murder, and the culprit got nervous and wanted him out of the way. . . . But we don't know anything like that yet."

"And did the husband find her?" Tzilla asked Dalit across the table.

"In Bogota, of all places," replied Dalit, collecting the crumbs into the paper wrapping. "She had a tailor shop there, with seamstresses and everything. She'd become a lady."

Because of the absentmindedness with which Balilty assigned and detailed the next tasks; because of Dalit's question: "And what about me, what do you want me to do?" and her crestfallen look when Balilty replied: "You have to go back there, right away, we can't leave the van Geldens alone for so long"; because of the flagrant transparency of Balilty's attempts to appease Dalit by his flattering remarks about what a good listener she was and how she would thus be able to make "the maestro and his sister talk"—because of all this, Michael had the feeling that the meeting was disintegrating, petering out with no conclusion. When he heard the knock at the door, he knew that it was over.

"There's a Mrs. Ruth Mashiah here looking for you," said the uniformed policeman in the doorway to Michael. "She says she and her husband were told to come."

Michael glanced at Balilty. "Should we do this together?" asked Balilty.

"Why not?"

"Two are better than one," said Balilty as he stood up slowly from his seat at the head of the table. "Did she bring his passport?" he asked the policeman, who made a face as if to say: I have no idea. Then he said: "The media are waiting outside—TV cameras, reporters, everybody. One of them's been here all night."

"You see what a mess we're in because of the Commissioner's troubles with the state controller. If he were here he would already have had a press conference. Will you talk to them?" Balilty asked Michael.

"Not on your life," said Michael with an expression of horror.

"So it's up to me?" asked Balilty unenthusiastically. "I'm no good at talking to the press, and besides, I don't want my face all over the papers," he muttered. His eyes wandered around the table and came to rest on Dalit. He paused and pressed his lips together reflectively.

"It has to be someone with a lot of experience," said Michael quickly.

"Bahar, will you be the press officer?" asked Balilty.

"That's very irregular," protested Eli Bahar. "It's usually the head of the team."

"Who says so?" flared Balilty. "We'll decide what's regular and what's irregular here. Do you agree or not?"

Eli said nothing and stood up. "Make them wait outside, at the entrance to the building," he said to the uniformed policeman.

But they didn't wait outside. Cameras clicked the moment the door opened, and a flash momentarily blinded Michael, who averted his face as he elbowed his way through the crowd, feeling a burning sensation under his chest as it became more and more certain that everything was going to become known, including the story of the baby. Balilty followed him with a stern expression, both of them deaf to the questions flung at them from every side, and ignoring, too, the cries of "The public has the right to know!" and "He's a world-famous conductor!" as they took the brief walk to the office at the end of the corridor, where Izzy Mashiah was waiting for his ex-wife to arrive with his passport.

She has a key to the apartment, Izzy had said as the interrogation was ending at four o'clock in the morning. From the way he had spoken to her on the telephone, murmuring into the receiver with his head bowed and his back to Michael and pretending to himself that he was alone in the room, Michael sensed that they felt mutual responsibility and concern for each other. "We're close friends," Izzy Mashiah had explained when he insisted on calling her and waking her up as early as an hour later so that she wouldn't hear of Gabriel van Gelden's death from the papers or the 6:00 A.M. news, which she always listened to compulsively. Michael had signaled to him in the middle of the conversation and Izzy raised his head, said "Excuse me for a minute," into the receiver, heard Michael out, and then repeated his request to bring the passport with her.

"I don't know what for," Michael heard him saying loudly and indignantly, for his benefit. "That's what they say, that's what they want. You know that," he stressed, "but they don't know it. Why should they?" There was other talk, too, and someone named Irit was mentioned, and the care they should take when they inform her of Gabi's death.

"Who is Irit?" Michael had asked when Izzy put the phone down and his hand hovered over the phone as if he were about to dial again.

"My daughter," said Izzy, and he folded his arms as if to demonstrate his resignation at the prospect of spending hours waiting idly for his ex-wife and his passport.

Now Michael examined the small, thin woman who looked first into his eyes and then into Balilty's. She had small, slanting brown eyes, framed by crumpled lids she seemed to be straining to keep open, and surrounded by a delicate net of wrinkles. Her cheeks, too, were covered by the same fine wrinkles, and also by freckles, which were generously scattered over her little nose. Everything about her seemed small and wrinkled, except for the smooth area around her mouth. She had short, frizzy, light brown hair sprinkled with gray. Her wrinkled hands, covered with golden-brown spots, lay on the metal top of the office desk, and her short, thin fingers with their flat, pale nails drummed on it as if it were a keyboard.

While he was still standing in the doorway with Balilty, he saw her slowly take her hand from Izzy's and put it down on the desk in front of her. Her fingers—the thumbnail was a bruised blue—had begun to drum as soon as Michael sat down opposite her. She pointed to the brown envelope lying in front of her. "Izzy's passport, as you requested," she said, and she looked at the two of them with open curiosity. For a moment a flash of anger glinted in her slanting eyes, and her hand rubbed her forehead as if to erase some invisible spot.

"Mrs. Mashiah," said Balilty, and she stopped rubbing her forehead. "We have to talk to you, too."

"Well, of course you do," she said in a clear, youthful voice. "I imagined you would," she said again, this time angrily, and she clamped her lips shut. Then she opened them again and added: "But you'll have to excuse me if I'm not focused," she said, looking into Michael's eyes. "Because first of all I slipped in the bath and hurt myself, and I've got a terrible headache that started last night." She pointed to the middle of her forehead. "And then, the news about Gabi . . ." She fell silent and spread her hands out on the desk in front of her, looked at Balilty, and waited.

Izzy heaved a long sigh. For a few seconds this was the only sound in the room. She looked around expectantly. "So, you wanted to talk to me?" she said in an authoritative and impatient voice. It suddenly sounded familiar to Michael, a voice he had recently heard in an entirely different context. The feeling grew more intense as she added an impatient "Yes?" Balilty went first. He pulled some forms out of a file drawer. Michael knew the technique, having used it himself on more than one occasion. Balilty sat down slowly, took a ballpoint pen out of his shirt pocket, and began to ask her questions about her identity. Patiently she gave him her name, address, and occupation. He heard her say "social worker," and the bell began to ring in his head. He had a clear suspicion now as to where he knew her voice from. Balilty asked her with uncharacteristic formality, as was his habit when he felt uncertain, where she worked. She smiled pleasantly as she replied: "I'm director of the Child Welfare Bureau in the Social Services Department."

Balilty's hand, thick and solid, rested on the form. The room began to spin. He didn't give Michael so much as a glance. And precisely this avoidance of eye contact betrayed his thoughts. Michael found it difficult to concentrate and recall what he knew about the Child Welfare director. He had only the policewoman Malka's reports, as conveyed to him by Tzilla, and one very brief phone conversation. It had taken place before Nurse Nehama's first visit, and he remembered the clear, youthful voice and authoritative but reassuring tone with which she had spoken to him. Malka, according to Tzilla, felt respect bordering on awe for the director, and constantly referred to her intelligence. Michael had described the Child Welfare Bureau to Balilty as a threatening, nearly sinister agency. About Nurse Nehama he had not said a word to him.

Just before this morning's meeting Tzilla had responded to Michael's anxious look by saying: "There's nothing new. They haven't found out anything yet." She said this unwillingly and bitterly, as if she wanted once more to convey her objections on principle to the whole business. When he complained despairingly: "It won't help now anyway. Even if they don't find the mother, they'll take the baby away from me," Tzilla shrugged her shoulders as if to say, You brought it on yourself. And then he added: "Even if I weren't on the case. Just because of my connection with Nita. I can't say now that I'm bringing the baby up by myself. I'm in a bind whatever happens."

Tzilla's face softened. "Malka told me that she hasn't heard yet from the Child Welfare Bureau," she said encouragingly, as if to make amends for her earlier critical tone.

"You're not taking it down," remarked Ruth Mashiah to Balilty, and again she rubbed her forehead.

Balilty quickly bent over the form in front of him and wrote something down. Then he raised his head, looked at Michael, and said: "I'll take the gentleman to another room, so that we can have a little chat alone, and you stay here with the lady." He spoke in a conspiratorial whisper, as if he were leaving the field clear for an intimate, even romantic encounter. Michael was about to protest, but Balilty gave him a warning look and jerked his head toward the door.

"Just a minute," said Michael hastily. He leaped for the door with Balilty behind him. In the corridor they conferred in whispers, and after Balilty had turned his head in all directions like a weathervane and raised it toward the stairhead above them as if on the alert for some danger, he said without looking at Michael: "I'm not prepared to get into it. First straighten things out with her, or we can send somebody else entirely, Tzilla, for instance. Otherwise she's going to ask me about you and Nita, and in the end I'll be to blame. She knows your name, she knows which end is up. You saw her yourself—you can't fool her. When are you going to see Shorer?"

"Shorer won't solve this. It's too late for Shorer to solve anything now," said Michael bitterly. "Nothing will make any difference now. Just tell me if you knew."

"What?" said Balilty, confused. "If I knew what? That they'll take the baby away from you now?"

"No, that she's the director of the Child Welfare Bureau."

"Are you crazy?" said Balilty, offended. "How the hell was I supposed to know? Didn't you see how shocked I was? You told me a completely different name, not Mashiah at all. Do you want me to get Tzilla to interrogate her?"

"No," said Michael, a strange, almost dreamlike calm descending on him. A fatalistic feeling. "We'll do what you said. You'll talk to him about the polygraph results, and I'll talk to her. I don't see any problem. I feel quite competent to question her."

And so it was. With his head bowed, Izzy Mashiah followed Balilty out of the room, and at the door he sent a despairing, hopeless look at his ex-wife, who nodded at him as if he were a child she was leaving behind on his first day at school. She rubbed her forehead and turned to look at Michael. For a few seconds they sat in silence, until she interrupted it by saying calmly: "Izzy has told me about you. I know the case from another angle. You're the one who's living with Nita van Gelden and her baby and the baby you found?" She asked the question matter-of-factly, as if it were the most natural of questions. "I'm surprised to see that you're involved in the investigation, in view of your interest in the case. In our profession we're very strict about keeping our private lives separate from our work. Aren't such things significant in the police force?"

Michael said nothing.

"I would have thought that since you know the kind of work I do, you'd have a more serious attitude toward my schedule and not keep me here for hours. It's obvious that Izzy has nothing to do with it, and neither, of course, do I."

"I know of you as Ruth Zellnicker, not as Ruth Mashiah," said Michael defensively.

"My maiden name. I started at the bureau before I married, and that's how I'm known there," she explained and sat up straight in her chair.

"Were you in the vicinity of the concert hall yesterday, the day of the murder, at any time during the course of the day?" Michael asked her as if she hadn't said anything. "Did you see Gabriel van Gelden yesterday?"

She looked at him gravely, tilting her head to one side. She had a long, thin, and very wrinkled neck. Then she took a deep breath, leaned back, and began to talk. Yes, she had been near the concert hall building yesterday morning. Apparently at the time of the rehearsal. "But," she stressed, "I didn't go inside. And the last time I saw Gabriel was . . . a few days, maybe a week ago, when I brought my daughter to the apartment. I brought him some books." Since her car was being repaired, and since she had to leave town, she had walked to the concert hall to get Izzy's car, which Gabi had been using. Because of her daughter, she had keys to Izzy's car, and also to the men's apartment. Her relations with Gabi were very correct, she added, and she even liked him. Irit, her daughter, was very attached to him. She herself had not had very many conversations with him. Theo she hardly knew. She had only met him once, at the celebration of Nita's baby's circumcision. Gabi had often consulted her about Nita, especially during her pregnancy, when Nita had seemed on the verge of a breakdown. "He told me she had stopped playing completely, which had never happened before." She herself had been opposed to an abortion in this case, mainly because of Nita's age. "It's not a good idea to abort a first pregnancy at the age of thirty-seven. Besides, Nita wanted the baby." She had spoken to her and even suggested professional help, therapy and so on.

She hadn't really known Felix van Gelden. She had met him but they had never spoken. "Except at the shop," she added with a faint, mocking shrug. She had been a good girl, who played the recorder and the piano, and had bought her music there. She also remembered the mother, who had made an impression on her because of her height and her fair hair combed back in a bun. "An aristocratic figure," she mused aloud. "Didn't you know the mother?"

Michael shook his head. Determined to keep the conversation within the limits of the facts of the case, he fended off any hint of familiarity, but he was already afraid, as he listened to her with an effort, that the boundary would soon be breached.

Naturally she was shocked, she said with the directness that had characterized her speech, with its guttural *sabra* accent, from the beginning. She didn't have the luxury of giving way to her feelings when Izzy was on the verge of collapse. He had been so attached to Gabi she didn't know how he was going to cope with his death, and especially the manner of it. She herself, she went on, had seen so many terrible things, in her work and outside it, that it had become second nature to her to keep her distance, to show reserve in displaying her feelings. "And sometimes in having them, too," she added with a smile that made her face look younger, tightening the network of wrinkles on her cheeks, bringing a twinkle to her slanting eyes, and suddenly revealing a hint of the youthful charm she must once have possessed. "You can be overwhelmed, if you're not careful," she said, and she switched off the smile. In spite of his relative youth, she went on in a worried voice—she was a few years older than he—Izzy suffered from severe medical problems. "Part of it comes from his asthma and allergies. People don't know how serious asthma can sometimes be. It can be fatal."

"Tell me, please," said Michael, "how you managed to maintain such friendly relations? Didn't it upset you that he left you for a man?"

She looked thoughtful. "You mean as opposed to him leaving me for a woman?" she asked.

He looked at her and saw her brown eyes regarding him with great seriousness.

"I don't know," he admitted, aware of the interest aroused in him by the question. "That too, maybe. But in general, being left. For anyone."

"I don't know if it makes any difference whether the external agent is a man or a woman. I imagine it does. Although to tell the truth, in our case anyway, the main difficulty was in dismantling the framework, in breaking up the home."

"Go on," said Michael.

"As far as relations between a man and a woman are concerned, in other words from the romantic point of view, our marriage was already quite dead before Izzy met Gabi. We were just good friends. As soon as they met, I knew, I knew right from the beginning. But that's something connected with intimate details I have no wish to go into now. I'm prepared to say only that the separation enabled me, or even compelled me, to realize myself and to confront my own truths. And Izzy never deceived me. I had no reason to bear him a grudge." Again she rubbed her forehead, pulled at the corners of her eyes as if she wanted to straighten them, laid her hands in her lap, put her head on one side, and said: "You're divorced."

He nodded. Years ago he had understood that in order to create a sincere atmosphere in an interrogation, especially in a case like this one, he, too, had to open up.

"Do you have children?"

"One son. He's grown up now."

"How old was he when you got divorced?"

"Six."

"You didn't bring him up?"

He shrugged his shoulders. "Partly," he said. "As much as possible."

"A hostile divorce," she said sympathetically. "Not a friendly one."

"Not particularly," he admitted. "But in recent years it's been . . . less of a problem."

"Okay, so it's really hard for you to understand. But our daughter has something to do with it. The realization that for her sake it's worth making an effort. And besides, there's a basic feeling of affection between us." She took a breath and added: "And all those years, until the relationship with Nita, you've lived alone?"

"More or less. There have been a few failed experiments," he found himself replying. For a moment Avigail's face floated unhappily before his eyes. Then it disappeared. Ruth Mashiah looked at him with wide eyes. "You want the baby," she said at last.

He tried to swallow. His mouth was completely dry, and he nodded.

"And you're not Nita's baby's father."

"No, I'm not," he admitted.

"Actually, you've only been with Nita for a short time. Nita told Gabi and Gabi told Izzy. He didn't know that Izzy would tell me."

"Why didn't he know?" Michael sat up straight.

"Who? Gabi?" She smiled. "Don't you know anything about couples? Do you think that Gabi wasn't ambivalent about my relationship with Izzy? He was sometimes jealous. He didn't like Izzy telling me everything, or almost everything."

"I thought that between men there would be more . . . I don't know."

"Couples are couples. There's no difference between heterosexual couples and others in this respect. To tell the truth, it seems to me that with them the jealousy can sometimes be even worse. Perhaps because of the isolation to which they think they're doomed, there's more dependency between them. With Gabi and Izzy it was like that. Anyway, I know that you've only been with Nita for a short time."

"That's not important," he argued.

"All of a sudden you want an instant family? With a ready-made baby?"

"What's wrong with that?" he protested, swallowing with an effort.

"Nothing wrong. In principle. Except that there's a long line of people waiting, and I hate line-jumping. Besides, you're actually a single parent, and if Nita's your partner in this, then she's in no fit state at the moment. And above all—and I wouldn't mention it outside this room, in case people consider me crazy—above all, you're a policeman, a detective, and I understand that you're good at your job."

"What's that got to do with anything?" He was flabbergasted. He had been bracing himself to hear about Nita's disturbed mental state, about her involvement in two murder cases, about her being a suspect even, and mainly he had been expecting a verdict couched in professional jargon about the lack of emotional stability in view of the circumstances.

"It's got a lot to do with it. We always take the professional status of adoptive families into account. You understand that what's important is not your wish for the baby, but the good of the baby."

"But even Nurse Nehama said—"

"I'm not saying that you don't take care of the baby properly. For the moment, at least," said Ruth Mashiah. Her expression became hard, concentrated, and aggressive. Her tone was critical: "The information you gave us was inaccurate."

Michael said nothing.

"But the important thing, as I say, just between us, is that you're an investigative detective."

"Why?" His voice rose indignantly. "I have a steady income, benefits—"

"If Nita could have provided a balance . . . But she's not stable either. When all this is over she'll be concertizing abroad again . . . And it's impossible to predict how long your relationship will last. It's not clear at all if you'll be able to manage it."

"What exactly has to be managed?" He heard the hostile tone in his voice, and gave himself a silent warning.

"Do you think it's a coincidence that you've lived alone all these years? I've learned some things about you, you know."

"Are you talking about the irregular working hours and . . . ?"

"About your working hours, too," she interrupted him. "But that's marginal compared to what I've learned about you in the last few days. I've read your whole history. It's very problematic for a single parent, and officially you're a single parent. Do you want to tell me that you have plans to live with Nita?"

"That wasn't my intention to begin with," he admitted, after deciding that his best bet in the circumstances was to be frank and honest. "But things . . . change."

"That's not enough to rely on," she stated. "We're talking about a baby with her whole life ahead of her, and you can't provide her with any stability."

"You can't know that," he protested angrily.

"Why not? Don't you know anything about people? Can't you come to conclusions from what you know about them and their personalities? I'm telling you that I've read all the material about you in the police files."

"That's confidential, for internal use only!"

"You waived confidentiality when you applied to us," she reminded him calmly. "You waived medical confidentiality, too. I'm sure you'll agree with me that these things have to be checked before abandoning an eight-week-old baby to her fate."

"Abandoning to her fate!"

"Without optimal suitability, it can be abandonment. Again, I know from what I've learned about you that you understand very well what I'm saying. You're perfectly capable of seeing things from my point of view. Your personality—excuse me for being blunt—your personality is not suitable for an adoptive single parent."

"I don't know what gives you the right to come to a decision like that so quickly, without even talking to me," he said, trying to suppress the panic, the hurt, and the anger flooding through him.

"You're obsessively dedicated to your work, to the point of total exhaustion. There are whole days when you don't go home. But I've also learned that your personality, your preference for solitude, your withdrawal, your perfectionism—I've read your reports—are inherent in the nature of a real detective."

"I don't believe it!" he whispered. "I haven't the faintest idea of what you're talking about. I thought you were a rational woman. I can't understand what you're getting at."

"Can't you? Don't you read detective fiction?"

He looked at her to make sure that she was serious, that she expected an answer to her question.

"I don't like detective stories," he finally said. "I have no idea what the connection is—"

"You don't like detective stories? You of all people? What a pity. I'm an addict," she confessed. "And Gabi was, too. It was one of the things I had in common with him. We would exchange books and . . ." She sighed. "Only a few days ago I gave him a detective story by a Dutch writer he liked a lot. His stories are set in seventh-century China. You have no idea how much you can learn about ancient China from his books. In general, you can learn a lot from detective stories."

"Listen," he said wearily, "Dostoevsky didn't think it necessary to teach in this way."

"Anyway," Ruth Mashiah continued stubbornly, "this Dutchman was a diplomat in the Far East and may not be a great writer, but he has a fascinating hero, a prosecutor called Dee, who also lives alone. Why don't you like detective stories?"

He shrugged his shoulders. The conversation sounded surreal to him, but he felt impelled nevertheless to answer her honestly, as if the very effort to answer all of her questions provided a way to change the situation by impressing her with his sincerity. "They seem completely unreal to me. I don't have the patience for them. Everything's known in advance. It's all so contrived. Except for *Crime and Punishment* and Simenon's *The Snow Was Black*. Those I could read again."

"But *Crime and Punishment* isn't a detective story!" she argued.

"My literature teacher at school said that it was a classic of detective fiction," he said with a half-smile, embarrassed by what seemed to him the transparency of his attempts to charm her in an almost childish way.

"It's not a detective story because it focuses on the murderer's consciousness. The question that interests the reader of *Crime and Punishment* isn't who killed the old woman, or even how he's caught, even though that provides an element of suspense. It's how Raskolnikov will live the rest of his life after the murder. How he'll come to terms with what he's done."

"So you do understand what's not interesting about detective fiction. It's the same in *The Snow Was Black*, the same as in Dostoevsky. In ordinary detective stories they never tell you about what's going on in the murderer's mind." Michael hesitated, wondering how much benefit he could derive from a discussion like this. Did he have a chance of impressing her if he spoke seriously? The need to impress her made him feel indignant again. And how could he know what was likely to impress her? She wasn't a simple woman, some Nurse Nehama, for instance. And precisely because of this he felt impelled to express himself superficially, to be almost provocative. "In detective stories there are often suspects who exist only to serve the plot. Those are not real characters. And there's always a murder. And the books always end with a solution. You never know what happens to the characters afterward. Except where the murderer dies at the end, which is very convenient. And the whole question of the difficulty of proving the case in court hardly exists at all in this type of literature, and when it does exist, as in the Perry Masons, it's entirely unreal. Everything is solved so quickly. And, in general, everything is cleared up."

"What's wrong with that?" she asked with surprise. "Can't you accept the rules of the game? Gabi used to say that he found a lot in common between detective novels and opera, the same logic."

"Everything serves the plot, the mystery," Michael persevered. "There's no room to breathe, no beauty. No digressions from the central concern. Everything's functional. A conversation like this, between us now, couldn't take place in a detective story, because it's not functional. I don't have the patience for it. I have enough mysteries in my work. And the conclusion—whatever happens in the middle, the conclusion is always disappointing. Either you know too far in advance who the murderer is, or you feel you've been tricked, that the writer's pulled a rabbit out of a hat."

"But no one likes detective stories only for the mystery!"

"No? Why do they like them then?"

"Because of all kinds of other things. The riddle, the mystery is only part of the contract, the agreement between the detective story writer and his readers, and the truth is . . ." Ruth Mashiah fell silent as he opened his mouth to say something about secret agreements, but changed his mind.

During the seconds of silence he wondered if she could really take the baby away from him. How come, he reflected, she didn't see what he, and only he, would be able to give the child? An opposing thought mocked this complaint. They want somebody conventional, he reminded himself, a regular, warm family. What would he do if they took the baby away from him, he wondered in terror at the sight of Ruth Mashiah's tilted head examining his face. What would he do with all the things he'd bought, with the crib he'd ordered, the baby dresser, the toys? He was surprised by and ashamed of this petty concern. They weren't going to take her, he assured himself, they weren't going to take her away so fast. He would fight.

"More than anything else, people read detective fiction for a sense of innocence," said Ruth Mashiah.

"A sense of innocence? Ah, a sense of innocence!"

"Yes, that's what I think. We all walk around with feelings of guilt," she said, ignoring his mockery.

"About what exactly?"

"I really don't know if you'll accept this," she said, sighing. "But in short I'd say that the feeling of guilt stems from a desire to kill one's father. At least as far as men are concerned."

"Oedipus, oh, Oedipus!" cried Michael, and he was silent for a long moment. "Okay, no wonder I don't need your sense of innocence. My father died when I was a small child." And then, because he read the disappointment in her eyes and saw her tensing her body for the explanation he knew in advance—that there was no connection between the historical date of his father's death and the feeling of guilt in his heart—and also because of his own oversimplification, which suddenly embarrassed him, as well as the anger he felt at this cheap psychologizing, he added: "Are you saying that the reader of detective stories is relieved of guilt feelings because he's not the murderer?"

"He identifies completely with the detective and his sense of justice. For as long as he's absorbed in the novel, he's sure he's one of the good guys. He's also alone and doomed to eternal loneliness like the detective. At least until the truth is revealed."

"I don't know what you're talking about!" he suddenly burst out. To his own surprise, her words gave rise in him to more anxiety than if she had asked the expected practical questions regarding how much time he would be able to spare for the baby, his ability to cope with family crises, Nita.

"About the fact that I've studied you, and that you have the detective mentality. A detective can't really afford to get married, and if he does, he runs into complications. And he certainly can't bring up children. That's what it's been like since Sherlock Holmes, maybe even since Edgar Allan Poe."

"I read detective stories when I was young," he said angrily. "I don't remember any of that being an issue."

"But maybe you do remember the loneliness of the detective in the novels?" she asked without a trace of mockery. "Naturally it's more extreme in fiction, but the idea . . . I've always noticed it. Even Inspector Maigret. I'm sure you like him, Simenon's Maigret."

He nodded. "There's a Madame Maigret, too," he suddenly remembered.

"There is," she agreed, "to bring him his slippers in the evening, and give him his soup. Did you ever hear him talk to her seriously? They live like two strangers."

"Because he's a detective? What's it got to do with being a detective? Madame Maigret is a simple woman, and the inspector is actually—"

"You don't know how simple she is. You don't really know her at all. All you know is that she's presented as a housekeeper, and Maigret hasn't even fallen in love in recent years. At most he's been attracted to someone, mainly out of curiosity and the wish to know the truth. Detectives don't fall seriously in love. They have only passing attractions. Almost always, anyway."

"Assuming you're right," he gave in finally. "What's it got to do with my baby?"

"Don't say 'my baby.' She's not yours!" said Ruth Mashiah sharply. "You're a temporary arrangement. The police are looking for the mother. You have to be ready to see the baby go."

"I can't bear to think of it," he said with his head bowed.

"You have to think of what's best for her. Maybe you were never really meant to be a family man," she explained. Seeing him open his mouth, she added: "Forgive me. Maybe you're ready now, but it's still too early to tell. Detectives hardly ever have intimate relationships. They lack basic trust. I see in your work, too, that you really don't rely on others."

He felt himself going pale with anger. "This is real life," he said in a strangled voice. "Your criteria have to be serious! Even though this is a private conversation! How can you, on the basis of cheap detective novels . . . a person in your professional position . . . talking so irresponsibly—"

"Why cheap?" she protested. "What's cheap about Simenon? What's cheap about Chandler? They show you the essential tragedy of the detective figure. The price he has to pay for knowing the truth."

"I'm not interested in discussing detective stories anymore," Michael said nervously but resolutely. "I'm really astonished by your statement that I'm not cut out to be a family man. It's irresponsible, not to say impertinent," he said, his voice rising.

"You're angry because you know I may be right," she said calmly. Panic filled him at the thought that this was one of the only times in his life that an interrogation was slipping out of his hands. Looking at the little woman, at the lively slanting eyes that never left his face, at her capable little fingers, at the bruise on her thumb, he felt that she wasn't out to get him, that he could trust her to a certain extent, but her words hurt him anyway. The feeling that her statements had nothing to do with his yearnings grew stronger. He wanted to talk about what was behind his words "impertinent" and "irresponsible," he wanted to tell her about Avigail, about the relationship that was doomed from the start. He wanted to tell her that it wasn't his fault and that it wasn't he who had decided on the break-up. But these wishes were weaker and more muffled than the wish to protect himself against her and to return the interrogation to normal channels. Even though at the same time he knew that there was no such thing as normal channels. He suddenly felt that this irrelevant conversation, so threatening to him, might lead to things he knew nothing about.

"Explain to me what you mean, and then we'll leave the subject. Tell me why I'm not—"

"I mean that real detectives are dangerous idealists. They work on the premise that there's a world with laws, a nearly utopian world. They're filled with the certainty that their mission in the world is to discover the truth at all costs. It seems to them that they're capable of restoring the disrupted order of the world. At the same time they're constantly in contact with and exposed to the cruelty and darkest motives of human beings, and in order to protect themselves, in order not to be contaminated, they have to in some sense live outside of life. There's nothing more rare than a happily married detective, with two or three children, who comes home in the—"

"That's in books," he interrupted her angrily. "You don't know what you're talking about! Why, in this very investigation, on this very case, there's a married couple, close friends of mine, and they—"

"I was speaking more about the classic detective mentality. Your friends are apparently not made of the same material that you are. You know very well what I mean. I can see it in your eyes. Even Gabi, who was quite detached, said to Izzy—Izzy told me—that you seemed to him a sad if not tragic man, and quite alone. I was very impressed by this, coming from Gabi. Maybe these originally were Nita's words. Gabi didn't notice people much, and he certainly didn't have any deep insights about them. What he said impressed me so much that I immediately went and read up on your past. A baby needs an adoptive family that is involved and present and alive."

"How dare you assume such things about me without . . . without—"

"I've had a lot of experience. Do you know how many people have passed through my office?" And again, despite the cruelty of the words themselves, and despite his feeling—a kind of certainty as nagging as a toothache—that she was absorbed in a purely narcissistic exercise, as if she had been waiting for an opportunity to say these things simply because they were her idea, the tone of her voice nevertheless was kind, with something soft and compassionate in it. "I'm assuming that you're intelligent and honest with yourself. Somewhere or other you knew that it wasn't going to work even before Gabriel van Gelden was murdered."

"That's not true," he said firmly. "I saw no reason why it shouldn't work. And I still don't. I know that I can give the baby things that . . . And I can definitely live . . . live with Nita. It can be a lasting relationship . . . all our lives."

"All our lives," said Ruth Mashiah dismissively. "It's unlike you to talk in such clichés. What do any of us know about all our lives?"

He looked past her shoulder and said nothing.

"Gabi told Izzy that it wasn't a romantic attachment," she remarked gently. "I'm talking to you privately. I haven't made any use of my inside information. Gabi told Izzy, and he didn't know that Izzy would tell me. Izzy apparently forgot what I do for a living. If you believe in that kind of forgetting." He looked at her in silence. "I intended to ask you to come and see me in my office, but then this happened." She shuddered.

"Gabi didn't know a thing about his sister. Besides, things change," he said like a child.

"It's not really relevant," she said gently. "You don't seem suitable to me, but maybe we'll find the mother. . . . Wanting isn't enough to make you suitable. She's only two months old." Then she added, rebukingly: "You can still have a baby if you decide to. Do you know how many couples who can't have children have been waiting for how many years? Ten years? And here we have a healthy two-month-old baby! How can I give her to a man who lives alone and, what's more, is a detective!"

The time has come to attack, he said to himself. "You said that Izzy told you everything."

"A lot," she corrected him. "Nobody tells anybody everything, as you surely know."

"Okay, a lot. For example, do you know where Gabriel was at the time his father was murdered?"

She frowned and pressed her fingers to a spot in the middle of her forehead. "It was on the day of the concert that opened the season, right? Izzy was at a conference in Europe. No. I don't know anything about that."

"And about the recent crisis in their relationship?"

"Crisis?" She sounded genuinely surprised. "What crisis?"

"We understand from things that came up in the interrogation, in the polygraph, that there was a crisis."

Again the fine, delicate eyebrows met over the slanting brown eyes, which seemed to retreat inward in an effort to concentrate. Michael was suddenly reminded of her ex-husband's eyes. "I don't know. It seems to me, because of the circumstances, his father and everything, that Gabi was in an almost manic mood before his father died. And then, of course, after he died—"

"Okay, a mood, call it that. But maybe you know what it was about?"

"Family affairs, things connected with Gabi's father." She seemed to be making an effort to remember. "You understand," she said, leaning forward, her hands on the desk and her little fingers interlaced, "Izzy's like a child in some ways. He was sometimes afraid of Gabi. Especially when Gabi withdrew into himself, Izzy would think that he didn't love him anymore, that it was coming to an end. In Izzy's eyes, love could be over from one day to the next. He's like a child. Sometimes it drove me wild to see how hard he tried to please him."

"There's no difference between a homosexual couple and . . ." Michael mused aloud.

"What did you think?" said Ruth Mashiah, surprised. "I told you before, the dynamics are those of any couple. Sometimes Izzy would ask me not to tell Gabi that we'd met. Especially not if we'd had a good time. Say we'd eaten a good meal in a restaurant. Once, after I happened to mention to Gabi that I'd been at an Italian restaurant in Tel Aviv with Izzy, Izzy was furious with me because Gabi had accusingly told him that by not telling him about it himself, Izzy had made him, Gabi, look like a monster of jealousy."

"You said it was an idyllic relationship," Michael said reproachfully.

"But it *was* idyllic!" she said, surprised. "What do you expect from an idyll in the real world? In the real world, between two people in an intimate relationship, there's almost always an element of deceit. Because of fear—mainly because of fear. Fear of jealousy, fear of hurting the other person, and especially fear of losing the loved one. You know it yourself. That's why you live alone," she said quietly. "And me, too," she added in a whisper. "It's hard to accept these things. But there was really love there."

"And dependency. And fear. And secrets," added Michael.

She shrugged her shoulders.

"And what happened recently? In their relationship?"

"First of all the new ensemble. Getting it going swallowed Gabi up. He was busy with it all the time. Then there was the ghastly death of Felix van Gelden. Gabi was very, very attached to his father, and the fact that he was dead, and the manner of his death . . . I think he was depressed. He was certainly in mourning. And aside from that, and in addition to everything else, Izzy felt guilty for not being here when it happened. Even though he cut short his trip, left in the middle of the conference, and came back. Besides that . . . A few days ago he told me that Gabi was worried about something, and that he wouldn't tell him what it was. That there was some lawyer or something, someone who called him from Amsterdam." She rubbed her forehead again. "I have a headache," she apologized.

"From Amsterdam?" Michael glanced at the running tape recorder, and wondered how he was going to play the tape back to the team. He decided to erase the first part of the conversation.

"That's what Izzy told me a few days ago. But I don't remember, because I didn't always have the patience to listen to all the details of what was bothering him. Sometimes he really is like a bitchy woman." She smiled. "It's impossible to avoid stereotypes," she said apologetically.

"How will Gabriel's death affect your life?" he asked directly.

She nodded and sighed, as if the question was only to be expected. "From the financial point of view it won't really change anything," she reflected aloud. "From the emotional point of view it will be harder for me now. Izzy will be more dependent than ever and maybe even . . . Maybe he'll even want to come back home and I . . ." Her eyes strayed with a lost look around the room, and for the first time she seemed to have lost her confidence, her omniscient certainty. There was something in the sight of her eyes darting from him to the door that encouraged him with its human weakness. "You'd like him to come back?" he guessed.

"Not really," she said after a long silence. "I've already become accustomed to the freedom of living alone. And I also have relationships with other men. . . . Nothing serious," she admitted. "But at least they have something normal about them, if you know what I mean. There may be some thought of repair, of restoring the structure that was destroyed, things like that. But no, not really," she said firmly. "Gabi's death, for me, and also for Irit, is a disaster."

He looked at her in silence.

"I've only just realized that. I didn't know up to now, I had to think about it," she explained with surprise. "But I really didn't kill him," she said suddenly. "I don't know how sure you can be of that now, but I feel the need to say it. I didn't kill him and I have no idea who could have killed him or why." Her mouth tightened for a moment. Her finger pressed the middle of her forehead. "And neither did Izzy," she added.

After that she agreed immediately to a polygraph test, consented to having her bank accounts examined, signed forms, waived the right to a lawyer, and agreed to sign the statement he would draw up. "Anything I can do to help . . ." she said as she stood up, and she added quickly, "as far as Gabi's murder is concerned." When she was at the door she stopped and turned around: "But if you need help now with Nita, considering her emotional state of mind, I'll be happy to do anything I can. How is she really?" she asked with concern, approaching the desk. He switched off the tape recorder, and on an impulse of despair, in response to a dangerous craving, as part of his mind, shocked by his rashness, was warning him against it, he told her.

9

Better, I Think

The sight of the gleaming gold medallion swaying rhythmically to and fro before Nita's eyes aroused in him a feeling of participation in some ancient rite. This feeling would not have existed, of course, he observed mockingly to himself, if it had been a polygraph test and he himself had been asking the questions. He stood in the corner of the big room, far from the medallion. The psychiatrist had his back to him, hiding Nita's face as she sat before him. There was something about the instruments themselves, he said to himself—the scratching of the polygraph machine's needle and its tracing of the graphs, the objectivity of the measurements—that neutralized the ritual sensation evoked by the gleaming gold medallion swaying from side to side in the steady hand in front of the woman seeking redemption. The calm, monotonous voice, at once authoritative and suggestive, announced: "You are tired. . . . Your eyes are heavy. . . . You want to sleep. . . . Your eyes are closing." These words canceled time and conjured up dank caves, forests, tribal witches. At the same time, he knew that hypnosis was a simple technique. How it worked had been explained to him long ago by Elroi. And only a few minutes earlier Ruth Mashiah had given him a lecture about it. The psychiatrist's broad back hid Nita's face, but not her feet in the pale, narrow shoes whose toes pointed up as she stretched her legs in what appeared to be a state of total relaxation.

"I don't think it's possible," Elroi had said that morning, as Ruth Mashiah and Michael sat in his office. His usually reserved, calm face hid his shock. Only something in the way he shook the bowl of his the pipe over the wastepaper basket, absentmindedly scattering crumbs of blackened tobacco around it on the floor, betrayed something of his agitation. "You know it's not just inadmissible evidence, it's also against the law. Just forget about it," he said almost with disgust as he rose from his chair.

Ruth Mashiah, who had insisted on accompanying Michael to Elroi's office, rested her chin on her palms. "This is a woman in great distress," she said, "and since we have her full cooperation, I don't see how it can be against the law."

"Look, Ruth," said Elroi in the tone of voice that had given him a reputation for patronizing condescension, "we've known each other for a long time, and I know you as a person for whom ethics, professional ethics, are a matter of overriding importance," he said rebukingly. Only when they were standing at Elroi's office door had Ruth Mashiah mentioned the fact that they had been at the university together. "We dated when we were young," she said with a smile before knocking at the closed door, "and now he's the chief police psychologist."

"I tell you the following: First of all—and you know this, too," he said, nodding at Michael—"the use of pentothal, or any other so-called truth serum, is forbidden, not even in order to identify a rapist. And in most instances hypnosis is, too. It's obvious from what you've said that the lady in question is a suspect. At least for the time being," he quickly added at the sight of Michael's face as he opened his mouth to say something. "At the moment she's a suspect," he said. "She's not just a witness you're trying to get an identification out of. No one in our department will do it. No one here will perform hypnosis in this case." He tapped his pipe on the edge of the round glass ashtray and looked at Michael. "You seem very involved in this case," he said carefully. "Do you have you any special interest in the lady? I mean any personal interest?"

There was a momentary silence. Ruth Mashiah rescued Michael from his attempt to formulate a reply by stating firmly and decisively: "It's a matter of distress. She's in severe distress, and we thought we could kill two birds with one stone—"

"It's out of the question!" said Elroi, and he sat down again. "If she's in distress, refer her to a specialist, and then, if he decides that she needs hypnosis as part of her therapy"—he spread out his arms—"go right ahead. I'd be the last to object. You won't have any difficulty finding someone, Ruth. You know enough people in the profession, and it would be better if hypnosis were recommended by a psychiatrist. What does Miss van Gelden herself say about it?"

"She . . . she doesn't—" stammered Michael.

"She's in a terrible state," Ruth Mashiah quickly intervened. "She'll agree to anything that will bring her relief."

Elroi made a skeptical face. He squared his shoulders, which were square enough to begin with. "And you want to use whatever comes up in this hypnosis for purposes of the investigation?" Michael shrugged and Elroi sucked on his empty pipe. "I know you use all kinds of tricks with your suspects," he said, and he averted his face.

"She's not a suspect yet," protested Michael.

"You're not prepared to see her as a suspect," Elroi corrected him coldly, "but that's what you yourself made me think she is. Without intending to. On the contrary." And in a weary tone, as if he knew it was pointless, he repeated: "You know that we only use hypnosis with witnesses, and even then it's not admissible, because it isn't clear what comes from authentic memories, and what's been planted in the suppressed memory. Especially when we're dealing with a suspect. Even if we were talking about retrieving the memory of a human face," he reflected aloud, "for instance that of a rapist," he explained to Ruth Mashiah. "A rape victim is capable of repressing the memory of her attacker's face. Even then truth serum is out. Even if popular legend says that the intelligence services use it. About which I don't care to comment."

"The problem," said Michael, "is that we don't have any time. I have to know today whether we're dealing with a witness or a suspect, and this is the only way."

"Why today? What's so urgent?" demanded Elroi.

Michael floundered. He didn't know how to explain the significance of his coming meeting with Shorer that evening, and so he said only: "I promised Emanuel Shorer to clear it up by this evening."

"Shorer knows that you're talking to me about hypnosis?" Elroi asked, astonished. "He's going along with the idea?"

"He doesn't know about it," Michael reassured him. "We haven't discussed methods, but the conclusions have to—"

"What about his daughter? Has she given birth? She should have had the child by now," Elroi recalled, but he didn't wait for a reply.

"I'd rather you didn't go into the details," he said quickly. "I have a definite feeling that I don't want to know any more than I have to. I have a bad feeling about this whole business," he said, turning to Ruth Mashiah. "But if you want to refer her to someone for help, on your own initiative, there's no problem with names. I can give you a few. Just remember that I don't know anything about it."

Ruth Mashiah shook her head. She had no problem finding someone, she knew the serious people in the field, she said, and for the first time she mentioned Dr. Schumer's name.

"I thought of him, too," admitted Elroi unwillingly. "For the hypnosis. But I'm not sure that he—"

"But he'll be able to tell us, we can rely on his ethics and responsibility, and he's had a lot of experience," said Ruth Mashiah, raising her frizzy little head. "He's the one they called on to wake that girl up, after she'd been in a hypnotic trance for a week and they couldn't bring her out of it. Do you remember the case?"

Elroi nodded quickly, as if to stop her from saying anything else. But she went on, as if determined to have her say: "And he was one of the people mainly responsible for formulating the Hypnosis Law. It was he who was responsible for banning hypnosis for entertainment purposes."

"Yes, yes," said Elroi, and he looked at Michael. "But if you intend to use the material afterward as evidence—"

"I don't know yet what I intend to do. It depends on what comes up," said Michael.

"It can only be done if the right to medical confidentiality is waived," warned Elroi. "Only if the court obliges the therapist, the hypnotist, to give evidence."

"Okay, we'll see," said Michael impatiently. "First we have to talk to this Doctor Schumer."

"And also to Miss van Gelden herself," Elroi reminded him.

"Of course," said Ruth Mashiah. "It would be impossible without her agreement."

Shortly afterward, when he saw the bedroom door in Nita's apartment closing behind Ruth Mashiah, Michael was filled with unfocused dread. He was afraid that Nita would break down. He was afraid of what Ruth Mashiah would discover, and he was afraid that they would even take her child away from her. Only when she came out and firmly shut the door behind her, giving him an encouraging nod, was he slightly reassured. But then, while Ruth Mashiah was setting it up with the doctor, he imagined Shorer saying to him, quietly but filled with disgust: How could you? Breaking every law in the book and not even bringing it up at the meeting! Not only are you involved with Nita, you don't know anything about Ruth Mashiah either. She's a suspect herself! He recalled these unspoken words an hour later, as he turned his face toward Nita, who was standing at the French windows and staring at her son, who gurgled to himself as he made strenuous efforts to remain on all fours in the middle of the carpet. "Nita!" cried Michael. "Did you see? He crawled!"

She turned to the window and nodded. "I saw it, wonderful," she said indifferently, shivered, and looked again at Ido. She muttered, as she had been doing for the past hour: "What's going to happen? What's going to happen?"

The sound of running water came from the kitchen. When he peeped inside he saw Sara's thin, dark arms circling above the sink. In his own arms the baby girl writhed with what had been diagnosed as a stomach ache. He held her with her belly pressed against his shoulder, feeling her spasms, patting her bottom, breathing in the fragrance of her neck. But he was distracted. Ruth Mashiah emerged from the bedroom. "He'll see her at a quarter past one," she said with relief. "He understands the urgency of the situation. Will you take her there?" And without waiting for a reply: "I'll meet you there. I've written down the address." Then she disappeared.

"Where's Dalit?" Michael asked Sara, who smiled the same forced white-toothed smile whenever he addressed her.

"She went with the gentleman," she said.

"Where's your brother?" he asked Nita, who turned slowly toward him, grimaced, and with an effort, as if she'd lost her voice, said: "I suppose I shouldn't say 'Am I my brother's keeper?' Or maybe I should?"

"What gentleman did she leave with? Theo?" he asked Sara, and she nodded fervently. "Where did they go?" he asked Nita, who weakly spread out her arms and then dropped them heavily to her sides.

"I didn't hear anything. I don't know anything," she mumbled.

He pressed the baby girl to his shoulder. For a moment he was acutely aware of the absurdity of this cozy domestic scene with the two babies, as if all were right with the world. Ruth Mashiah's words of warning rang in his ears: Don't say "my baby." She's not yours! Now he stood close to Nita, leaned over her, and touched her shoulder: "I'm sure you heard something. Where did they go?"

"To look for Herzl," said Nita sleepily. "They left me here with Sara."

"Does Balilty know that they're looking for Herzl?" She didn't answer.

In the time left before the appointment with the psychiatrist, he tried to contact Shorer at the hospital.

"Who are you?" demanded the maternity nurse. "What's your relationship to the patient?" He gave up and replaced the receiver.

"I haven't heard anything," said Shorer's secretary, who picked up the phone at the first ring, as if her hand was resting expectantly on the receiver. "Nothing since early this morning. I've been here at the phone all day. Please get off the line now, and leave me your number." Michael looked at the damp spot his hand had left on the receiver. He was suddenly seized by a vague apprehension, bordering on anxiety, about Dalit and her freelance enterprises. He dialed again, trying to locate Balilty. He intended to complain about her disappearance, but nobody knew where to find Balilty. Eli Bahar answered him coolly, almost with hostility, responding vaguely to all his questions. His voice changed only when he asked: "Did you get in touch with Shorer?" Now it was Michael's turn to answer vaguely. "It's all been routine," said Eli Bahar. "The orchestra musicians have been turning up, one after the other. Balilty went to see the pathologist. Then he has to follow up something about the painting. We won't know more till tomorrow. Just Tzilla and me," he replied when Michael asked him who was questioning the members of the orchestra.

Nita's eyes opened and closed as she sat in the deep armchair across from the swinging medallion. Her body was relaxed and quiet. The lines at the sides of her mouth seemed blurred, and her agonized expression had softened. The doctor warned her several times not to move or utter a sound. They had already been there for hours. When they first arrived, all three of them had been together. Then the doctor had taken Nita into the consulting room. Not a sound from there could be heard in the waiting room, where Michael sat next to Ruth Mashiah, chain smoking. He listened intently, with his head bowed, to her explanations. In her dry, clipped voice, she said: "Hypnosis is based on the principle that no one is ever prepared to give up the wonderful cosmic experience undergone by the mind in the fetal state."

"I didn't know that the fetus had a mind," muttered Michael, looking up.

"Of course it has, that's already been proved," said Ruth Mashiah. "Now that we have ultrasound, there's no problem in proving it. We know for certain that at three months the fetus has a mind."

"But the term 'mind' is problematic. It's not clear what it means," said Michael, stubbing out his cigarette, which left a charred black hole in the styrofoam cup.

"At three months," said Ruth Mashiah firmly. "Even the Talmudic sages knew this. That's why they ruled that a dead fetus three months old and older has to be buried. And, for example, when music is played to a woman in the sixth month, the fetus can be seen dancing."

"You can see it?" asked Michael, astonished. Ruth Mashiah nodded and asked for a cigarette.

"What kind of cosmic experience are you talking about?" he asked as he bent to light her cigarette.

"What?" she asked absently as she inhaled, coughed, and looked at him with surprise.

"You said that hypnosis was based on—"

"Ah, yes, you want a detailed explanation. I thought it was obvious."

"Well, it's not," he said with some irritation, straining to hear what was going on in the other room. There wasn't a sound to be heard.

Ruth Mashiah crossed her legs and leaned back in the plastic armchair opposite him. She rubbed her forehead. "I can't get rid of this headache," she muttered. "I've had it all day. And I haven't called to find out how Izzy is, either. Is he still at the Russian Compound? We have to think about the funeral arrangements, too. It's terrible when you think about it. To die like that. For nothing. Do you people take care of the arrangements?" Michael looked at his watch, but she didn't wait for a reply. "Okay, a cosmic experience is one in which a person has no doubt or question that he is utterly protected. All he has to do is adapt his reflexive reactions to the pressures of his surroundings. The mature individual undergoing hypnosis receives a big bonus in exchange for being prepared to surrender his will to another. He obtains a pardon in advance for anything connected with conscience or morality—he does what he's told, and he's not guilty or responsible for anything."

Michael nodded.

"A hypnotic trance is a state of consciousness in which the subject is not responsible for his actions. All the sensory nerve paths, including sensitivity to pain, that lead to the central nervous system in the brain switch off during hypnosis."

"Isn't the connection between the senses and the center in the brain physiological?" asked Michael, interrupting the didactic stream of words and causing Ruth Mashiah to tilt her head sideways, put her little hand on her face, and press her fingers to her forehead again.

"Don't you recognize the unity of mind and body yet?" she asked without mockery. "Don't you know that the unconscious controls biology? It's the mind that governs the biological functions. How do you think Indian fakirs lie down on beds of nails? Why don't they feel pain? The principle is identical with hypnosis. What closes down is the place where the brain receives reports. Hypnosis can enable one to undergo an operation without pain. The nerves respond, but the receiver in the brain is shut off. Do you really not know these things?" she asked with surprise. "I thought that it was obvious to any well-informed person, especially one in your line of work."

"I know something about it, but not so clearly," Michael said, confused. "I didn't connect the fakirs in India with hypnosis."

"That's why it's so powerful," said Ruth Mashiah. "And that's why it's impossible to hypnotize anyone, as you sometimes see in the movies, without his express consent. Otherwise the most that happens is that the subject falls asleep. Haven't you ever tried it?"

"I don't think I could," reflected Michael. "The abandonment . . . the loss of control. I seem to lack the wish for that cosmic experience you talked about," he said with a conciliatory smile. "I can't give up my control over what happens to me, not even for the sake of a fetal experience. I prefer responsibility," he said almost apologetically.

"It's not only the surrender of control," said Ruth Mashiah, looking at him closely. Her slanting eyes narrowed to slits. "Because we're not talking about mere consent. The subject has to agree, but he also has to be able to trust the hypnotist in order to empower him."

Michael was overcome by panic. "She won't place her trust in him," he said, looking at the door. "She can't trust anyone anymore," he said despairingly.

"I'm not so sure. She's got more strength than you think. You shouldn't think in absolute, romantic terms," Ruth Mashiah said reassuringly. "Don't forget that she wants to know, too. We're dealing with a wish, with a need. An adult doesn't lose faith in humanity just because of one person. Even if he wanted never to trust anyone again, he would find it difficult to maintain a decision of that kind." She dragged on her cigarette and emitted a little white puff of smoke, looked at the cigarette, and muttered: "Why am I smoking?" She threw the cigarette into the empty styrofoam cup Michael was holding. Then she took it from his hand, stood up quickly, and filled it with water from the cooler standing in the corner of the waiting room. Her body was youthful and boyish in the loose trouser suit she was wearing, and her movements were light. Suddenly he saw himself holding this body and burying his face in the frizzy little curls. She sat down again opposite him. "The hypnotist must see when the subject's eyes begin to droop. Then he must pounce."

"Pounce," repeated Michael. He imagined a snake swallowing a rabbit.

"To seize the moment, to say at the precise time: 'Your eyes want to close, you want to sleep.' That's how the hypnosis begins! Haven't you ever seen it happen?"

"I've seen it," said Michael. "I've seen it in the movies, and once at the police station. But I never really understood it."

At that moment the door opened and Dr. Schumer beckoned to Michael to enter. Ruth Mashiah stood up quickly.

"Only him," said the psychiatrist.

For what seemed like a long time he sat in front of the desk, next to Nita, who looked less tense, as if she were already reassured by the mere possibility of abandoning herself to sure hands that would protect her against herself. Dr. Schumer reported the essence of their conversation to him. In a reserved tone he repeated the facts Nita had given him—and her wish to know the truth. It seemed to Michael that he added the last phrase unwillingly. But there was no explicit sign of this on his expressionless face. Then he mentioned her request that Michael be present during the process. He spoke of what was customary and what was not, mentioned medical confidentiality, and made a remark about the blurring of the boundaries between Michael's professional involvement and his relationship with Nita.

"This is very irregular," he pronounced, and he pressed his lips together. He looked at Nita, who seemed to shrink in her seat. "Why don't you join Ruth outside for a few minutes, Miss van Gelden?" Michael followed her jerky movements as she stood up and walked toward the door, twisting her fingers around the fabric of her wide, flowered skirt. She slammed the heavy door as if she was not in full control of her movements. Left alone with the doctor, Michael tensed his body as if to repel any attempt to reopen the discussion of ethics, but Dr. Schumer did not press him. Once he said: "I understand that you're also very close." Michael repressed the urge to ask what he meant by the "also." For the most part the psychiatrist spoke about Nita's fixation on the idea of hypnosis as a kind of redemption.

"It's not a solution to real problems," he warned. "I told her this, and I also explained to her what it's important for you to know too, that repression is a defense mechanism, and sometimes desirable and necessary. Very difficult things can sometimes surface. I must tell you, too," he said, clearing his throat, "that I don't get the impression that she's suffering from a split personality. Even though she explained to me things she'd seen in an American film I don't exactly recall. But I do understand very well her fear because of the special, the terrible, circumstances. In any event, it's important for you to take account. . . ." His voice grew stern and authoritative, his strange, narrow face hard and resolute. Dr. Schumer's pale eyes were very close together, and his forehead was unusually low, so that his thick hair seemed to be growing right out of it. "If for a single moment her emotional well-being is in the balance against *your* wish to know, her well-being will come first. The police aspect of the process doesn't interest me at all, and I refuse to cooperate for that purpose. I want this clearly understood. All right?"

Michael nodded.

"You'll see for yourself if anything too problematic comes up. If such material was initially registered by Nita's consciousness as forbidden to remember, she could react with signs of distress, because hypnosis can lead to strong inner conflict. It can lead to severe hysteria or even psychosis. I'm telling you in advance: In that case I'll break off immediately. I'm not prepared to put her at risk. Or myself. It's a very dangerous business, suddenly to bring up repressed material. Do you understand?"

Michael nodded.

"She asked for you to be present while I hypnotize her. It might not be a bad idea, because you can help me with the questions. After all, I know very little about the circumstances or about her."

Michael nodded.

"And most important, at least until she goes into a deep trance, is that you remain absolutely silent," he said when he stood, holding the door handle. "Your presence must not give rise to any stimuli at all. Surely you understand that." Without waiting for an answer, he opened the door and asked Nita to come back in.

Now she sat in the deep armchair, her eyes closed. The room was absolutely quiet. Michael watched the arm in the white sleeve putting the medallion down on the corner of the heavy desk. He saw the expression of relaxation spreading over Nita's face. Her mouth was slightly parted, and the lines of anguish slowly melted from her features. Even though he was taut as a bow, even though he had deliberately avoided following the movement of the gleaming medallion, the thought crossed his mind, and after it the wish, that the doctor's instructions had worked on him, too. Maybe he too was hypnotized, put under a spell without knowing it. Dr. Schumer sat down in the chair in front of Nita and told her to open her eyes. Michael remained standing, leaning against the wall and looking at her open eyes. Now their color was dark gray. They looked like deep lakes. She seemed so completely awake, he found it difficult to believe that she was sleeping. The doctor repeated a few times: "You feel comfortable, safe." Her arms lay limply on the wooden arms of the heavy armchair.

"You're at the rehearsal for the concert," said the hypnotist. "The beginning of the Brahms Double Concerto. You're about to start playing."

Nita smiled. A big, radiant smile, blurring the dark borders around her gray eyes. Suddenly they shone. She parted her legs, and a few seconds passed before Michael realized that she was holding an imaginary cello between them.

"Theo stops you for the first time," said the psychiatrist after glancing at the sheet on which he had noted the course of events, according to Michael's reconstruction.

She removed her hand from the imaginary cello and held it as if she were holding the bow. "How many times does he stop you?" asked Dr. Schumer.

"Lots." She giggled. "He's arguing with everybody. With Gabi too. About the tempo. As always." She smiled.

"Do you like it when they argue?" asked the doctor.

"No." She shuddered. "I hate it!"

"But there's something enjoyable about it, too."

"We're working together. All three of us. As we used to. We're making music," said Nita, and again her face glowed. "We're playing. As we used to. The arguments aren't important. They're part of our work." Suddenly her lips twisted, and tears flooded her eyes. "Father's dead," she said and uttered a tearful sob. She wiped her eyes with her fists and sniffled.

"Do you like it when Theo interrupts you?"

"Sometimes we learn from it. Theo knows a lot," she said in a childish voice.

It seemed to Michael that all these expressions were familiar to him, but now they seemed grotesquely exaggerated.

The doctor glanced at Michael. "Do you want to ask her something?" he asked in his normal voice, and Michael wondered why he wasn't whispering. But he nodded and came closer.

"You're taking a break," said Dr. Schumer.

Nita laid the nonexistent cello at her feet and looked around. "Is the case backstage?" she wondered, and she rose lightfootedly from the armchair. "Ido's here," she said happily. "Michael brought him. And Noa, too. She's wearing orange overalls. They used to be Ido's. And there's a music box on the carrier, Ido's biting Matilda, his rabbit."

"It's after the Teddy Kollek break. What happens after that break?" asked Michael.

"Ido's gone," she said, surprised. "He was here, and now he's gone. Michael took the children away."

"And everyone's returning to the stage," Michael reminded her.

"Everyone's coming back on," she agreed, and she bent down as if to pick up the cello.

"Do you rehearse the whole concerto?"

"The second movement," she said as if in a dream. "There's only time enough for the second movement. Theo doesn't yell much." She smiled again, gently. "He's pleased, but he doesn't say so. That's how he is. He thinks it's good. He says: 'So far, so good.' He doesn't look at Gabi. Gabi plays wonderfully! Really beautifully!" She dropped her eyes and raised them again, looking straight into Michael's eyes. Yet he felt that she wasn't seeing him at all. "And I play well, too. Yes, I play really well," she said clearly and without any affectation, as if she were stating a fact, but a blush spread over her cheeks.

"Theo says that the rehearsal is over. Then what? Do you put away your instrument?"

"Yes, everybody does. There's a lot of noise. Mrs. Agmon is standing in the hall. Near the stage."

"And who is on the stage? Can you see them leaving the stage?"

Michael watched her shaking her head as if with an effort.

"Is Gabi on the stage?"

"Gabi leaves. He has to do something." Her eyes narrowed. A dark shadow invaded the lakes. "He goes offstage."

"Who else leaves the stage now?" asked Michael, and he listened to the heavy breathing of the doctor, whose eyes never left Nita's face.

"I don't remember. . . ." Her face twisted, her eyes closed, her mouth opened, she wrung her hands, her legs writhed, her face was white. "Gabriel leaves," she said, gasping for breath. "He has to . . ." Her head fell back.

"She's losing consciousness," said the doctor, "we have to stop. She's showing clear signs of distress."

"Just one more question," pleaded Michael. "Just one."

The doctor raised his hand in a determined gesture. "Don't answer that!" he said authoritatively. "Forget that question. You're at the end of the rehearsal again," he said soothingly, and Nita's body suddenly relaxed. "Open your eyes and don't remember the question." She raised her head and opened her eyes.

"Is she awake or asleep now?" asked Michael.

"She's back under deep hypnosis," said the doctor after a few seconds of silence. "I'm not prepared to put her through that again."

"But we don't know anything we didn't know before," said Michael in despair. "Nothing! I have to try. . . ."

The doctor looked at him doubtfully.

"For her sake. We have to give her an answer to the question of whether she did it."

"I'm prepared to give it one more try. But not in the same way. We have to ask the question differently," said the doctor, glancing again at the sheet of paper on the desk. "Maybe it would be better if I asked it now."

"But ask her first how many spare strings she had at home before the rehearsal," said Michael, breathing fast.

"How many spare strings did you have at home before the rehearsal?" asked Dr. Schumer mechanically.

She frowned. "Three," she said. "The A snapped and I replaced it."

"Three before you replaced the string or afterward?" whispered Michael.

Schumer repeated the question. "Before," she said hesitantly. "Three before I replaced it."

"Again, which string did she replace?" asked Michael with a pounding heart, and he listened to Schumer repeating the question.

"The A," she said a matter-of-factly.

"Does she have another one at home?" whispered Michael, and Schumer repeated the question.

"I might have," she replied reflectively. "In the wardrobe, at the top, where I keep my old cello. But it's been years since I played it. There are four strings in an unopened envelope up there."

Michael swallowed hard and suppressed an urge to run back to the apartment and check then and there. "Now ask her about after the rehearsal," he said sternly.

The doctor hesitated, and then he said calmly: "The rehearsal is over."

Nita nodded.

"What do you do now?" he asked.

She opened her eyes wider. "I put the cello down. I want to put it away. The case isn't there. I have to look for it. I ask Avigdor. The case . . . they put it in back."

"You go backstage?"

She nodded.

"With the cello in your hand?"

Again she nodded.

"Do you find the case?"

"It's behind the wall. I have to put the cello in Theo's office. I can't just leave it lying around. It's my cello. My Amati."

"Do you go into Theo's office?"

"I go into Theo's office," she said firmly. "The door is open. It isn't locked."

"Is Theo in the room?"

"He's on the phone. He's talking on the phone. He says, 'It's absolutely out of the question.' He sees me and stops talking. He waits for me to leave the room. I put the cello in the big cabinet. As before. As always." Her dark eyebrows frowned with perplexity, with the effort.

"Do you leave the room?"

"Theo says, 'I'll call later,' and he hangs up."

"Do you leave the room together?"

"I have to pee," she said suddenly.

"Right then?"

"Right then. At the door I notice that I have to pee. I want to use Theo's bathroom."

"There's a bathroom in Theo's office?"

"Next door. It's clean."

"And Theo?"

"He locks the office. I tell him to wait for me. But when I come out he isn't there," she says, surprised. "I call out, 'Theo! Theo!' but he doesn't hear me. He doesn't answer. I go to the end of the corridor."

"Back to the stage?"

She shook her head vigorously. "No. To the other end."

"What other end?" asked Michael, astonished, ignoring the doctor's warning look.

"To the far door. Because maybe Theo went in that direction." She suddenly shivered.

The doctor resumed questioning her. "Is he there?"

"No. There's nobody there," she said like a disappointed child.

"Do you see Gabi?"

"No. Gabi isn't there either. And the light isn't working."

"What do you mean, the light isn't working? Is it dark?"

"It's dark. You can't see anything. The curtains are closed. So I go back."

"Do you go back to Theo's office?"

"No. Theo locked it," she said like a child explaining something self-evident. "I went toward the light."

"Are you afraid of the dark?" the doctor asked gently.

"Everything's so strange," she said, beginning to squirm.

"You go back to the stage the usual way," said the doctor. She suddenly relaxed.

"I go back."

"Do you see Gabi?" asked Michael.

"Gabi's leaning against the pillar, as always," she said, smiling. "He's talking to someone. I hear Gabi's voice."

"What's he saying?" asked Michael, and he felt his body tensing and stiffening, the blood pounding in his temples.

"He says: 'Vivaldi is my field. Vivaldi is my field.' He's angry."

"Who is he talking to?" asked the doctor.

Again her face twisted and turned white. Her eyebrows knotted. "I can't see,," she said in a whisper. "I can't see clearly. They're behind the pillar." And suddenly a terrible scream broke out of her.

"Don't answer! You're not to answer!" said the doctor quickly. But she was trembling all over. "You don't remember who you saw. It doesn't matter who was standing there," said Dr. Schumer in a firm, calm voice. Michael saw her legs relaxing and the color coming back to her face. He was overwhelmed by a terrible feeling of frustration. And by a violent wish to shake her. And by guilt about this wish.

"You're standing in the corridor," said the doctor after her breathing had calmed and her eyes were wide open. "Do you have a string in your hand?"

She shook her head. "There's no string," she said apathetically. "The strings are with the cello."

"After you hear Gabi talking, leaning against the pillar, do you stay there?"

"I mustn't listen," she said. "I mustn't listen."

"You don't stay there?"

"I walk away quickly. On tiptoe, so they won't see that I heard something . . ." Nita writhed in the armchair. She tossed her head from side to side.

"You walk away quickly. Where to?"

"To the stage. Everyone's still onstage," she said, surprised. She was still frowning, but her body had stopped writhing, "They're packing up and talking, and Mrs. Agmon, the violinist, is shouting."

"What is she shouting?"

Nita smiled. A small, joyless smile. Without dimples. "She's shouting: 'It's not right! This is no way to behave! He won't escape me today!'"

"Who's left on the stage?" asked Michael, and he looked at her straining to remember. He listened to her name one after the other, the concertmaster, the woman oboe and clarinet players, the bass and viola players. "A lot of people," she finally said wearily.

"Where's Gabi?" the doctor resumed.

"Not there, he's not there," she said sorrowfully, and she clenched her fists.

"And Theo?"

"He's not there," she said with the same inflection, and her fingers went limp.

"But you're there?" the doctor said quickly.

"I'm there. In the corner."

"And you see Gabi alive?"

"Leaning against the pillar," she said rebukingly.

"Talking. Gabi is talking," the doctor reminded her.

She blinked rapidly.

"Are you standing behind him with a string?"

"No, of course not," said Nita, surprised. "He's there and I'm here."

There it is! the doctor seemed to say with a gesture of his arm. "That's enough for today," he said aloud. "I'm going to wake her up."

"But . . . Just once more ask her who he's talking to . . . At least whether it's a man or a woman!" pleaded Michael.

"I thought we agreed that her welfare was our chief concern. Can't you see how cruel that question is for her? We've gone on too long as it is. And what you wanted to know, you know now. What she herself wanted to know, we also know. This isn't a case of split personality. She didn't kill anybody. That's enough for now," he pronounced and turned to Nita.

Michael listened with half an ear to the instructions issued in a reassuring, authoritative voice by Dr. Schumer. "You'll remember everything, but not the question about who Gabi was talking to," he said twice. "I'm going to wake you up now. You'll be calmer. You'll feel well. Rested. You know now that you didn't do anything bad. You didn't kill anyone. You didn't do anything with a string. Those were only your fantasies."

Michael listened to the countdown, and he tensed as the sound of Dr. Schumer's clapping hand echoed in the room. Slowly, as if reluctantly, Nita returned to the world. She closed her eyes and opened them, and felt the arms of the chair.

"How do you feel?" asked the doctor, and she looked at him with sad, quiet eyes.

"All right," she said wonderingly. "Better, I think." She spoke in her normal voice.

"What do you remember?" asked the doctor.

She looked at Michael, and her mouth relaxed. "I didn't do it," she said, and she rubbed her forehead with a gesture like Ruth Mashiah's. "I only put the cello in Theo's office, went to the bathroom, looked for Theo at the other end of the corridor, and because the light wasn't working, I went back onstage."

10

You Don't Find Babies in the Street

"I don't understand the question," said Theo, pushing his hands into the pockets of his pale trousers. "Do you mean, did I talk to him after the rehearsal?"

"The question seems quite clear to me: After the rehearsal was over, after you went with Nita to your office, after you locked the door and were going back to the stage, did you speak to Gabi?"

"Do you think that if something like that had happened I wouldn't have told you? Or him?" Theo said, nodding toward Balilty, who was sitting next to Michael, studiously examining his bitten fingernails. "Or even the young lady? I would have told her. She was with me for hours!"

"I don't think anything," said Michael in the cold, almost indifferent tone he had used since the beginning of the interrogation. "I have to ask these questions. And so I do."

"And I'm answering." Theo took his hands out of his pockets and sat down heavily. "I didn't speak a single word to Gabi after the rehearsal. I didn't see him at all until . . . until I saw him lying dead."

"How come Nita saw him and you didn't?"

"How should I know?" cried Theo angrily. "How can I possibly answer a question like that? She saw him and I didn't." He rubbed his cheeks with the palms of his hands. Like his sister, he had dark circles under his eyes. His look was haunted and careworn.

"She saw him leaning against the pillar and talking to you."

"She couldn't have seen me," said Theo with irritation. "Maybe she *said* that she saw me! There's a difference between seeing and saying she saw. I don't believe my sister said anything of the kind. She's my sister! And, as you know very well, she's in a terrible state at the moment. Besides, why should she tell such a meaningless lie about me? "

"Meaningless? It's hardly meaningless," said Michael.

"Why? Why isn't it meaningless? What are you trying to say, that I . . . that I was the last person to see him? That I killed him? Where is she, anyway?" Theo demanded as if he were fed up with the waste of time. "I want to see for myself if she said that. Let her tell me herself! Why haven't you brought her here? What is this, divide and conquer?"

"One thing at a time," said Michael calmly, covering up for the vein he felt pulsating in his neck. It seemed to him that the pulsation was visible through the skin to everyone. He couldn't rid his mind of the hypnotist's words: "She's not lying, and it's not an act," Dr. Schumer had said after the session in his consulting room. "There's something that frightens her in what she saw. Frightens her to such an extent that the very memory of it endangers her. She isn't ready to remember exactly what she saw. It's hard to believe how much we're able to repress in order to protect ourselves. Sometimes you really can't believe it, and this is true for everyone, no matter how well educated or intelligent. She must have seen someone or something whose very presence there is dangerous for her. I mean dangerous in the psychological sense."

"All in all," protested Theo, "I don't understand any of this. Why we're talking here about this. One would think that you suspect me. Why are you interrogating me here?"

"You haven't been officially warned yet." Balilty intervened for the first time, crossing his arms on his chest. "Let's simply call it a conversation. Do you object to cooperating with us to help us find the person who murdered your father and brother?"

"Do you think it's the same person?" asked Theo, astonishment in his voice. "Do you think there's a connection between the two murders?"

"What do you think?" asked Balilty. "What's your opinion?"

Theo fell silent and dropped his eyes to his hands. He examined his fingers, long like Nita's, and passed his hand over his face. Once more Michael was surprised, when Theo removed his hand from his eyes, how much brother and sister resembled each other. The eyes, sunk deep in their sockets, were particularly striking now in this regard. Michael's heart skipped a beat when Theo stuck his fingers into his silver mane and raked his hair back from his forehead with the same movement as Nita's when she sometimes dug her fingers into her curls. "Is that why there's a policeman outside Nita's house? Do you think that there's something we don't know? That our lives are in danger, as they say?"

"You were arguing about Vivaldi," said Michael, rolling the cigarette he refrained from lighting between his fingers. He had no intention of telling Theo, let alone Nita, about the new dread that had seized him since the hypnosis. If she had seen something, and if someone knew that she had seen it—he looked now at Theo—he had to make sure that she was never going to be alone from now on.

"Who was?" Theo's eyes darted nervously between the window and the door.

"You and Gabi. About Vivaldi. He said . . ." Michael looked at the notes in front of him as if the few words Nita had overheard were drawn from among many others: ". . . Vivaldi is my field."

Theo's Adam's apple rose and fell. Stiffly he said: "I simply don't know what you're talking about. He certainly didn't talk to me about Vivaldi. Not that day, anyway. We've been arguing about Vivaldi all our lives. About him and about Corelli and about Bach and Mozart and also about Mendelssohn. Vivaldi really was his field. If you're trying to find something significant that he supposedly said to me then, just before he died, first of all he didn't say anything to me because we didn't talk to each other at the time, and anyway, people generally don't say such significant things before they die. Especially if they don't know they're about to die."

"Why don't we go back to what we were talking about at the beginning," suggested Balilty, raising his eyes inquiringly to Michael over the cup of coffee pressed to his lips.

Theo, too, was noisily drinking the coffee Michael had placed before him, and he nodded eagerly. "Do you mean Herzl?"

"You said this isn't the first time. How many times were there before?"

Theo looked thoughtfully out the window. "Maybe four, or five. I don't remember exactly."

"And every time he hospitalized himself?" asked Michael, tapping the point of his pencil rhythmically on the table.

"I think the first time my father signed him in," said Theo slowly, as if he were trying to remember. "We weren't told anything, but I learned about it somehow. It was twenty years ago, or maybe a little less. He hadn't come to work. He couldn't be reached on the phone. Father went to his house. We never visited him there. He didn't like it. Maybe I was there once. It was dark there, with only one dim light. The whole place was cluttered with all kinds of junk he collected. You could see right away that he lived alone, a dog's life." Suddenly he caught himself. "I live alone, too," he said. "But it doesn't have to be like that. My apartment is always clean."

"There was no woman in his life?" inquired Michael, putting the pencil down.

"There was no one. No one. I don't know anything about his parents or family. Only that he came to Israel alone, after the war. As a young man, or even as a boy. I think he was fifteen or sixteen when he arrived here. He came from Belgium. He met my parents during the war and looked them up when he got here. We never spoke to him about the past. That's all I know. We were all the family he had in the world, but we never talked about it. He almost lived in the shop, and he lived for the shop. It was he who found rare scores and unusual recordings. All kinds of music nobody here had ever heard of. I remember . . ." He fell silent.

"And the madness, his illness, began twenty years ago?" asked Balilty, returning to the subject.

"My father took him to a doctor. I remember him explaining it to my mother. I overheard them one night. They thought I wasn't home. I was already grown up, on vacation in Israel with my first wife. They were talking about depression. That was the diagnosis. After that my father took him to the psychiatric hospital in Talbiyeh, to the emergency room, because Herzl wouldn't get out of bed or eat or speak or react to anything. My mother told me this later. It was a long time ago. She spoke in a general way, not going into detail. She couldn't decide whether or what to tell Nita. Nita was always oversensitive, and Mother didn't want to upset her. I think that all she finally said to Nita, who was still a young girl then, was that she needn't be afraid of Herzl, that he wasn't dangerous to anyone, except maybe to himself. To me my mother said that he wanted to die."

"And later?" asked Michael. "After that first attack?"

"Once every few years he would disappear. For a month or more. He was on medication, but I don't know if it helped him. My father told me last year that he was in remission. That his attacks were milder. After that first time he would go to the emergency room by himself. He was afraid he would harm himself. I think he got electric shock treatment twice. And he said that it helped him."

"In other words, you spoke to him about it?" asked Michael. "You said—"

Theo seemed confused. "Two or three years ago, just once," he admitted.

"The doctor told me," Balilty intervened, "that he walked pushing an empty supermarket cart all the way from Hadassah Hospital in Ein Kerem to the center of Jerusalem. He walked down the main road in his white hospital pajamas. He must have been in danger of being run over. He finally ended up in Talbiyeh Mental Hospital." Balilty leaned forward. "The doctor in Talbiyeh said that he was hearing voices. I don't know much about it, but does that sound like more than depression?"

Theo shrugged his shoulders. "Maybe," he mumbled. "I'm not a psychiatrist. From the looks of his apartment you could see he was crazy. Everything was neglected. It was a mess: papers and music and old instruments all mixed up, along with empty bottles, all kinds of debris. And the dirt! There were whole days when he ate nothing. He's a sick man, but I don't think he's dangerous. He wouldn't harm anyone."

"You didn't inform him about the death of your father," said Michael.

"How could we?" said Theo sullenly. "It turns out he was in the psychiatric hospital. As you know."

"But you could have spoken to him."

"In the first place, I had no idea where he was," protested Theo. "It was your job to find him."

"You didn't give us much help. None of you, including your brother, volunteered the information we needed," said Balilty maliciously. "You could have spoken to him after your father died. Didn't you try?"

"I didn't look for him. I had other things to think about. I had troubles of my own. That my father was dead. And the way he died. And my work with the orchestra. I have to work, you know," said Theo bitterly. "You couldn't always succeed in talking with him," he admitted. "He was closer to me than to Gabi, and certainly more than to Nita. But the one he was most attached to was my father. He would have died for Father. Quite literally."

"In that case, what was their quarrel about?" asked Balilty, pulling a burned match from the box lying on the table, and scratching with it on the white paper lying in front of him. The tape recorder vibrated. "And why did they close the shop?"

"I have no idea," said Theo. "My father wasn't prepared to talk about it. He said, 'Leave it alone' whenever I tried to. And I never talked about it at all with Herzl, because I wasn't here. In recent months I've had concerts abroad. I participated in a festival and I never had a chance to . . ." His voice died away. His eyes darted guiltily around the room. "I didn't behave correctly toward Herzl. I should have taken more of an interest in him. I should have pressed him. He's completely alone in the world. He has no one."

"We're searching his apartment now," said Michael.

Balilty stared at him with surprise, which turned to astonishment and then to undisguised anger at this disclosure of confidential information without discussing it with him first. But before he turned his head away there was also a gleam of understanding, and in his nod, which was accompanied by a soundless chuckle, there was also appreciation and admiration of the kind he had not shown toward Michael for a long time. He lowered his head as Theo froze.

Theo's arm held still in midair. His mouth gaped. "But why?" he demanded in a mixture of incomprehension and anger. "Why search there? In that room full of junk? What on earth are you looking for there? You never found anything when you searched my house. I was still too shocked then to ask you what you were looking for. I gave you permission to search my office, and all the musicians' lockers, but now I demand to know. What are you actually looking for?"

"We're looking for a certain Dutch painting," said Michael. "And maybe for something else that will explain things."

"It'll be impossible to find anything there," Theo protested weakly. "You're wasting your time. And anyway, he was in the hospital that day."

"We're not at all sure of that," said Michael.

"What do you mean?" protested Theo. "The doctor said that he was in the hospital. That's clear."

"Yes, he was," agreed Michael. "But precisely on the evening when your father was murdered he disappeared. He isn't in a closed ward. He can come and go. He only returned late that evening."

"How do you know a thing like that?" Theo said, banging his hand on the table. "How do you know? Is that definite?"

"It's definite. No doubt about it."

"And where was he?"

"That's what we're trying to find out. He's not cooperating," explained Balilty. "We thought that you might be able to get him to talk."

"Me?" said Theo, alarmed. "Why me?"

"Well," said Balilty, "there's nobody else. And you yourself said that you're closer to him than the others. Your father is no longer with us. And we don't want to frighten Herzl. We haven't told him yet about your brother. He doesn't read the papers. The psychiatrist told him about your father. He said that it was part of the attempt to return Herzl to reality. But he also said that Herzl didn't react. It was as if he wasn't hearing anything new."

Theo recoiled as if Balilty had slapped his face. "You're wasting your time," he said finally. "It'll take you years to search that place. And you won't find anything."

"We have no choice," said Michael. "And you have to help us communicate with him."

"He's never done anything wrong," said Theo passionately, as if he was trying to convince them.

"But maybe he knows something we don't know," said Balilty coldly. "Like who *has* done something wrong."

"Is that supposed to be a hint?" asked Theo with hostility. He again ran his long hand through his silver hair, and he shook it as if it weighed heavily on his head.

"A hint at what?" asked Balilty ingenuously. "What do you think I'm hinting at?"

Theo was silent.

"You're not prepared to take a polygraph test," Balilty reminded him. "Do you also object to talking to Herzl?"

"I never said I wasn't prepared to take a polygraph test!" Theo protested. "I only said I couldn't do it during the next few days. I've been through a great deal, you know. And tomorrow I have to be in good shape."

"What's happening tomorrow?" inquired Michael.

"I have to be at a music workshop at Beit-Daniel. The commitment was made more than six months ago, and I can't possibly break it. Johann Schenk is coming over specially for one day, and it's the only day that—"

"It's less than forty-eight hours since your brother was murdered!" exclaimed Balilty.

"Do you think I can forget that?" Theo compressed the corners of his lips in the same way Nita did. Only his cheeks, which weren't hollow like hers, gave his face a sulky, cruel expression, rather than her suffering, childlike one. "In my profession such events are paramount. You may not know it, but I'm not just anybody in my profession. That may not mean much to you." It was impossible to mistake the note of conceit accompanying the contempt of his words.

Balilty ignored it completely. His face took on an almost pitying expression. His small eyes sank deep into the chunky folds of his broad face, which shone with sweat. He turned his attention to a tiny stain at the bottom of his striped shirt and examined it studiously.

After Theo had given Balilty time to react, and realized that he was not about to do so, he continued: "Don't imagine that Gabi would have behaved differently. We can't just cancel our engagements or postpone them. There isn't really any reason to do so," he said disdainfully, running his hand through his hair. "Public mourning and all those rites and rituals are narcissistic—they're not serious. Just because someone died, even if he's close to me, even if he's my brother, doesn't mean that I have to drop all my obligations. Should I take a *vacation* because Gabi's dead?"

Balilty sighed and leaned back in his chair.

"It would be insane to cancel a day with Johann Schenk," said Theo van Gelden quietly. "It's an international event, French television is sending a crew, and I'm giving an important lecture to all the gifted youngsters on the Classical period in music that is going to be recorded by our educational television. And Johann Schenk, whose calendar is completely booked up, do you know who he is?" He turned demonstratively toward Michael, who maintained an inscrutable expression. "Why should you have heard of him?" muttered Theo bitterly. "He's not some athlete or pop star."

"Apparently you admire him very much," said Balilty.

"Not only I!" said Theo indignantly. "There are young artists who've been waiting a year for this day, if not more. The best musicians are coming from all over the world. We have some very gifted youngsters here. Johann Schenk is one of the greatest baritones in the world. Maybe the greatest. Nita is supposed to be there for a master class, too. Part of the day will be devoted to song accompaniment."

Balilty eyes blinked rapidly.

"Accompanying *lieder*—art songs—is an art in itself. We'll be working on *Die Winterreise,* a song cycle by Schubert with piano accompaniment." He glanced at Michael again as if he were expecting the nod of a musical connoisseur, and again Michael's face remained expressionless. To betray his familiarity with the Schubert work at that moment would have been to join ranks with Theo against Balilty. "We're devoting half the day to that. And then there's my lecture, which was scheduled months ago. I also have to be there in order to select new singers for an opera production. I'll have my work cut out for me!"

"Isn't this Schenk a human being?" inquired Balilty. "Can't he understand that someone's in shock because his brother was slaughtered the day before yesterday?"

"What should I do instead? Let you poke and pry into my life? Spend my time talking to you? Sit and twiddle my thumbs? Look after my sister? I can't help her. Work, at least, distracts me from these dreadful events. There's been no funeral yet. I don't intend to rot away here and hide from the reporters lying in wait for me at every door to my house and Nita's, or even here. Do you know that they're outside? I saw them when we came in. And the telephone that keeps ringing at Nita's and half the time there's no one at the other end when you pick it up. You can't stop me from doing my work! Am I your prisoner? What do you think you're doing, harassing people like this?" There was now a note of righteous indignation in his attack, as if he were working himself up. "Dora Zackheim, our old violin teacher, phoned me. How can you harass an old woman like that? What can you possibly learn from her? She told me you'd made an appointment with her," he said accusingly to Michael. "What do you want from her? Do you know how many years have passed since she last spoke to me or to Gabi? She can barely walk—"

"Your brother spoke to her a few weeks ago," said Michael. "We can't be selective, we can't make exceptions for anyone. This is about two murders. I'm talking to everyone Gabriel was in touch with."

"What is this Beit-Daniel anyway? It's in Zichron Yaakov, no?" asked Balilty sullenly.

"It's a music center," Theo answered unwillingly. "They do a lot of chamber music there. Festivals and concerts, and master classes for young artists. . . . How do you actually know that Gabi visited Dora Zackheim?"

"Who said that he visited her? I didn't say who visited who. I just said that he talked to her," Michael remarked mildly. "Do you know that he went to her house?"

Theo reddened. "She hardly ever leaves the house," he mumbled. "I just thought . . . "

"Did Gabi tell you about his conversation with her?"

Theo shook his head.

"So is it in Zichron Yaakov?" Balilty demanded.

Theo nodded.

"If he's going to Beit-Daniel," Balilty warned Michael as if they were alone in the room ("Yes? Is that right? And your sister, too?" he asked Theo, who nodded), "then you're going with them."

Michael said nothing. It wasn't the devaluation of his image in Theo's eyes because of Balilty's order, rude as it was, that bothered him. It was, rather, the thought of something strange in the whole story of the mad music shop employee, about whom Nita had never said a word to him. He tried to remember her reactions to his attempts to find out about the quarrel between Herzl and her father, but it seemed to him now that he had been too distracted in the past few days to pay any attention to the evasions, vagueness, unwillingness to talk, and uneasiness the subject had given rise to in her. He had been so busy trying to guard her fragile equilibrium, he scolded himself now, and so intent on not aggravating the crisis into which she had been plunged by her father's death, that even when speaking with her after the hypnosis, he had not asked her what exactly had happened to Herzl and who he really was.

"So you're not taking the polygraph test," remarked Balilty.

"Not now," Theo corrected him. "Not today or tomorrow."

"But you will talk to Herzl for us?"

"To find out where he was on the evening of my father's death? I might be prepared to," Theo said, hesitatingly. "But alone. Just the two of us. Me and him. And then I'll tell you what he said."

"Why?" inquired Michael. "Why is it important for you to be alone with him?"

"He'll talk to me alone in a way he won't talk in the presence of someone else. Especially a stranger. Let alone a policeman!" said Theo, and he looked at Michael as if he had finally caught him out.

"Ah," said Michael, "you're concerned about the success of the investigation. Very good. I just wanted to understand," he said with exaggerated seriousness and ignored the expression of confusion on Theo's face.

"Okay," said Balilty, summing up. "You'll talk to him alone, and report to us." He avoided looking at Michael. "Where do you want to do it?"

"I haven't thought about it yet. Not here, anyway," said Theo, shuddering. "Here he'll panic."

"How do you know?"

"I know him."

"At the hospital, then," said Michael. "We'll arrange for space at the hospital."

Theo looked at him suspiciously, and then at Balilty. "What do you mean, you'll arrange for space?"

"It means that we'll ask them to make a private space available for you, an office with a door," said Michael, "so that you can talk comfortably. Doesn't that make sense to you?" he asked innocently.

"You'll be listening on the other side of the wall," said Theo with a sudden flash of illumination. "What do you take me for, a total idiot?"

"Maybe I do and maybe I don't," said Balilty. "I just want to understand why that should bother you."

"I'm not prepared to talk to him in your presence," said Theo angrily.

Michael leaned forward. "Because of him or because of you?"

"What difference does it make?" grumbled Theo. "Do you want to add it to the list of my failings in your eyes? Go ahead and add it. I'll talk to him alone or not at all."

"No problem," said Balilty indifferently, glancing at his watch. "I understand that you're afraid he may say something we're not supposed to know about. Excuse me a minute," he added, and he left the room.

Theo's gaze followed him suspiciously. They were alone together now, he seemed to be saying to himself when he realized that Michael was still sitting before him, and his body relaxed. "Is Nita feeling a little better?" he asked quietly.

Michael nodded.

"Isn't it strange for you to be so involved in this matter? For example, the fact that you had dinner with me the day before yesterday? Doesn't it bother you?" he asked with some malice. "Or are you one of those people that nothing bothers?"

Michael smoked in silence.

"You're not even answering me," said Theo bitterly. "You're living with my sister and you won't even answer me."

Michael said nothing.

"And what was all that about, all that stuff about me having an argument with Gabi backstage?"

Michael shrugged his shoulders.

Theo shook his head. "She never told you anything of the kind," he said confidently.

Michael didn't blink. He never took his eyes off the green, sunken eyes opposite him. And in order to distract himself from the consciousness of the effort, he compared Theo's eyes to Nita's. He concluded that they were only similar in form, not in color, and especially not in the proportions of the parts. It was this proportion, he consoled himself, that created the expression. "Why should she lie?" he asked, and he feared that he had gone too far.

Now it was Theo who shrugged his shoulders.

"I wanted to ask you," said Michael casually, "if you know anything about an envelope of spare cello strings Nita had at home."

"You've already asked me that," said Theo impatiently, "and I told you."

"No," Michael corrected him. "I asked you about the ones in her cello case. Now I'm asking you about another envelope, which was still unopened."

"How should I know?" complained Theo. "I'm not a cellist. I don't have anything to do with such things."

Michael sank into his chair despondently. The search in the cabinet at Nita's apartment hadn't produced anything. They were going in circles.

"Where is he, your friend Mr. Balilty?" demanded Theo after a few seconds of silence.

"He had to see someone about something else," lied Michael.

"What's all this about Dora Zackheim? Why do you have to talk to her?"

"I told you already. Your brother spoke to her a few weeks ago. We're trying to get to know him."

"You're trying to get to know him? Gabi? Why do you have to get to know him?"

"That's what we do when someone's murdered. We find out everything we can about him and his surroundings."

"Do you really think you can get to know someone in such a short time?"

"That's the question. Who knows if it's possible to know anything at all about anybody?" said Michael philosophically, as if he were oblivious to the cliché. "But we have to try."

"To reach as far as Dora Zackheim!" muttered Theo. "It's been years. And, you might as well know, she can't stand me," he warned.

"That bothers you," said Michael, making an effort to sound sympathetic.

"Yes," Theo admitted frankly, "but she always loved Gabi. She'll tell you that, too."

"Why, exactly?"

"She thought that he was more . . . more serious, I think, as if he was more talented."

"And was he really more talented?" asked Michael. "In your opinion, too?"

Theo looked hurt by the question. He took a deep breath. "Do you really want to know?" he whispered, and Michael nodded.

"And if I answer honestly will you believe me?"

Michael nodded again.

"I think not," said

Theo. "And not just because I'm more, let's say, more famous, if you'll excuse me, but it's a simple fact, and it doesn't mean anything, just that I was more successful, but because I'm more ambitious, apparently."

"More ambitious than who?"

"More ambitious than everyone else. Than Nita, than Gabi," said Theo matter-of-factly. "Gabi was a really great violinist. But the truth is, and Gabi would have told you the same, manners are irrelevant when you're talking seriously about things like this, and I'm not as unserious as Dora Zackheim thinks. Even she doesn't really think so. Gabi is . . . was . . . very gifted. A great artist, but in his own field. He could never have done Wagner. And he didn't want to. He couldn't even listen to the Overture to *Tannhäuser*. The first few bars drove him up the wall. Not that he didn't understand Wagner's greatness, his innovations and contributions to the history of music. Do you know that he was a great revolutionary? Do you understand what was involved in that?" he asked almost contemptuously. "Gabi hated Wagner. And even Mahler, he couldn't conduct Mahler. Bartók, yes, he played Bartók brilliantly. He didn't conduct him, but he played him. And if you ask me, all that obsession of his with period instruments and historical performance paralyzed his libido."

"What do you mean?" asked Michael.

"I mean that with his pedantry, his fanatical insistence on authenticity, he lost all the vitality and passion that even Baroque music is capable of. And as for Bach, if you ask me, in the cantatas and the B Minor Mass, Gabi simply murdered him! As a conductor, I mean. With a chorus of eight singers and a bland articulation of music that should raise the roof!"

"You'll have to explain more to me about this authenticity business," said Michael.

"Let Dora Zackheim tell you about it. Since you're going to see her anyway, she can explain it to you!" Theo said resentfully.

"If you really think that he wasn't a greater musician than you are, why does Dora Zackheim's attitude upset you?" To his satisfaction, Michael heard his voice sounding gentle and fatherly. There was suddenly something childish in Theo's expression, in his pouting lower lip.

Theo shrugged his shoulders. "Unfinished business," he said dismissively. "Are you now playing psychologist?"

Michael smiled. Theo looked at his watch.

"How much alimony do you pay a month?" asked Michael.

Theo looked surprised, thought for a moment, and said: "I don't know exactly. I've got it written down somewhere. Why do you ask? It's a fortune. Almost half my income, and I make a lot of money. You know how it is, Nita told me you're divorced. There's no end to it. How do you manage?"

"With me it's different. My son is grown, and my wife comes from a well-to-do family. Her father left her enough to last her the rest of her life. He was a diamond dealer, and she's an only child. From that point of view I only had a few difficult years."

"Sometimes that's not relevant. Sometimes it's the opposite. The woman who gives me the most problems in that respect is the one who comes from a rich family. It's a kind of revenge," said Theo confidingly, as if they were both in the same boat.

"That kind of trouble at least," said Michael with a sigh, "I haven't really experienced. Not like you, anyway. Tell me," he said as if the thought had just come into his head, "that woman, the one you were with, you said, on the day your father died, the Canadian, does she come to this country often?"

"Two or three times a year. Sometimes we meet in Europe, or else in New York. It's not so far from Toronto. I don't know how to get rid of her."

"And we don't know where to find her."

"It shouldn't be so difficult," said Theo sarcastically. "She's a married woman with children and a house and a permanent address. A pillar of Toronto's Jewish community. She's easy to find."

"There's no one at the phone number you gave us, only an answering machine. Do you have any other way of contacting her?"

"I never contact her," said Theo. "She always contacts me."

"You should try a little harder. She's your alibi for the day your father was murdered," said Michael sternly.

"Why do I have the feeling that you . . . that you're laying a trap for me?" complained Theo.

"If anyone's laying a trap here," said Michael, grinding out his cigarette on the tin ashtray, "it's not us for you."

"What? I'm laying a trap for you?" He laughed unpleasantly.

"Or you for yourself," said Michael quietly.

"Me? For myself? What are you trying to . . ."

The telephone rang, a long, sharp, continuous ring, which made them both jump. Michael picked up the receiver.

"Congratulations! She's had the baby," said Tzilla. "One hour ago, cesarean, and everything went well." It took a few seconds before he realized what she was talking about.

"What is it?" he asked.

"A girl. We knew that already. Just over five pounds, thirteen ounces. But she's not in such great shape."

"Who?"

"Both of them, actually. The baby had respiratory problems toward the end, and Dafna has some complications."

"And Shorer?"

"I haven't spoken to him," said Tzilla. "You're not alone in the room, are you?"

"Not really," said Michael, averting his eyes from Theo. "Is there anything new in that other business?"

"I haven't had time to find out. Where am I supposed to find the time to talk to Malka about babies?" A note of annoyance and resentment crept into her voice. "I'm stuck here with all the orchestra musicians. One after the other, for the second day running. Nobody saw that Herzl on the day Felix van Gelden was murdered. We've talked to all the neighbors. And nobody saw him in the concert hall area or at the rehearsal when Gabi was murdered. As for Izzy and Ruth Mashiah, nobody saw them that day. And there was a whole business here with Mrs. Agmon, the violinist—"

"I know who she is," Michael interrupted her. "What about her?"

"Nothing significant. Fainting, hysteria, weeping. And the concertmaster, Avigdor—another character. They may be artists, but they're also like a bunch of union officials. All they can talk about is pensions and work rules. There's only one of them, a young new guy, who sounds different. All he dreamed of was being in the orchestra, and then he discovered that it's a job, just a job. And now they want me to go with them to search Herzl Cohen's apartment. Balilty's just ordered me to meet him there. He's bringing Forensics, too, for fingerprinting. . . . By the way, what do you think about Dalit finding Herzl?"

"I think this: Some hours went by from . . . if you know what I mean."

"Do you mean that she kept the information to herself?"

"Yes."

"I'm sure she has an explanation for that," said Tzilla.

"I'd very much like to hear it," said Michael, and he looked at Theo, whose eyes were wandering over the walls of the little room. "In any case, thanks for letting me know the news."

"He wants to talk to you," warned Tzilla.

"Who?" said Michael, tensing.

"Shorer. His secretary said that he wants you to get in touch with him toward evening at the hospital. Soon, that is. You can't avoid it much longer," she said gently. "You have to talk to him."

"I'll talk to him."

"And another thing. Have you obtained permission from Theo van Gelden and from Nita to examine their bank accounts? And we also have to get permission from Izzy Mashiah. Eli will talk to him. We have to look at the bank accounts."

"It can be arranged," said Michael in a stiff, neutral tone. "But it won't give us a true picture."

"Why not?"

"Because it's almost certain that most of it is outside the country, especially in this case."

"What case? The van Gelden family?"

"Also individual members."

"I don't understand what you're getting at," said Tzilla slowly. "Who's there with you? Someone from . . . Theo?"

"Exactly."

"Oh," said Tzilla guiltily, as if she had been particularly obtuse.

"Why didn't you say so? Oh, of course you couldn't have said so. . . . Well, when I saw Balilty here I assumed that you'd finished with Theo. Okay, we'll talk later." And she hung up.

Michael and Balilty drove Theo to the psychiatric hospital in Talbiyeh in Balilty's Peugeot and dropped him off there. Then they drove around to the back of the large, low building and parked near a repair van with the Electricity Company logo on it. Walking with Balilty from the car to the van, Michael was assailed by the gray sky and oppressive air, heavy as if the first rain of the season was about to come splattering down. "Doomsday weather," said Balilty.

"Do you still need me here?" asked the technician from Forensics who had installed the listening equipment.

"You'd better stay, in case something goes wrong," muttered Balilty, and he sat down behind the wheel. The technician obediently moved into the back seat and Michael sat down next to Balilty. A gust of wind blew a plastic bag against the windshield. Their brief argument while they were driving around the building still echoed in Michael's head. "Why do we both have to be here?" Michael had asked as they watched Theo, his shoulders stooped, going through the gate and crossing the concrete square in front of the hospital entrance. "Lately I keep feeling that we're like children playing at something. What's to stop me from listening to the recording later?"

"It was you who taught me to be prepared for any eventuality, that anything could happen!" protested Balilty, shocked. "You were the one who always talked about being on the spot in real time and so on. Now all of a sudden you no longer understand that? Do you have something more urgent to do? Some diapers to change?"

Michael said nothing.

"You asked me to head the team. I told you I wasn't going to be a rubber stamp. What do you want? For me just to be your tool? You're free to go, I'm releasing you. But that you should be saying it's a waste of time?"

"Okay, okay," said Michael sourly, raising his palms in capitulation. "It's just that. . . ." He fell silent. The truth was that Balilty was right. He felt very uneasy about the baby, even though he knew that Nita wasn't alone with her. A whiff of the baby's comforting smell enveloped him as he thought of the coming meeting with Shorer. It was as if he hoped to draw strength for the meeting from the infant. He wouldn't even have time today to bathe her. And Nita, who knew something she didn't know she knew, at any moment someone could harm her.

He tensed as the van suddenly filled with sounds: the click of a door handle and the door closing, heavy, dragging footsteps, the creak of a chair, the muffled murmur of an unfamiliar voice. Behind them the back seat squeaked as the technician shifted his weight from side to side.

"Have you ever seen him?" Balilty whispered, as if they could be overheard by those they were overhearing. Michael shook his head. He had never seen Herzl except in a photograph of one of Theo's weddings. Nita had pointed to the edge of the group, where, she remembered, her father had urged Herzl to squeeze in because he was "one of the family." Without bitterness, she was mimicking a foreign accent, presumably her father's. "Some family," she had said the evening after her father died. "None of us even knows where he is."

"Only in an old photograph," Michael heard himself whisper to Balilty, silencing for a moment the creaking of the chairs in the room he couldn't even picture.

As if he was reading his mind, Balilty said: "It's the hospital director's office. He's the one I spoke to, because the others, the doctors, are too busy with the psyche to have any time for real life. The director's owed me one for a long time."

Michael put a finger to his lips, but Balilty had already stopped talking, for he too heard Theo's voice, after the familiar cough, saying: "I brought you some grapes. And also the cheesecake you like, Herzl." Theo's voice, Michael noticed immediately, was submissive. There was an emotion in it he had never heard from Theo before, and he couldn't identify it. His voice was higher, as if produced by strained vocal cords.

"You see how important it is to hear things in real time. That's something I learned from you, a long time ago," whispered Balilty.

"I'm not arguing anymore," said Michael calmly. "I'm just saying that lately I've had a strange feeling about things like this. Maybe it's because of my absence from the job for the past two years.

Sometimes I just say things, not everything has a deep meaning. Anyway, it's clear that we should be here." He himself wondered at the word "clear," because at the moment things weren't clear at all. But there was a feeling of danger and urgency in the air, maybe simply because Herzl was mentally ill. The baby's soft, pink face suddenly turned into Yuval's face. Suddenly he saw his lost and despairing expression, and then the image of Nita's hollow cheeks. The terror in her eyes. The sounds of the Bach Cello Suite she played over and over again in the afternoons as if she were seeking solace in it, while Ido lay as if he were listening, sucking his fist.

"Why don't you eat the grapes?" Theo's pleading voice filled the interior of the van.

Now Michael identified the unfamiliar emotion in it. It was fear. Fear and a panicky eagerness to please. There was the rustle of plastic bags, and again the creaking of a chair. "Okay, save them for later," said Theo's placating voice. "How are you, Herzl? Are you feeling better?"

Silence. Outside the van, a car alarm wailed in the distance, and there was muffled roar of traffic.

"I have to tell you something," said Theo in a different, restrained voice, after a long silence. "I've come to tell you about Gabi. Gabi's dead."

Not a sound.

"Did you hear me, Herzl?" Again the voice was almost falsetto. "He was murdered. The day before yesterday. After the rehearsal."

"At his apartment?" another voice suddenly said, weighty and muffled, hoarse as if the words emerged with great difficulty, struggling through sedation.

"No, in the concert hall building."

"Was he shot?" asked the other voice.

"No," said Theo, and he paused for a moment. "With . . . a knife, maybe."

"Ah, stabbed in the heart," said the voice, as if relieved.

"His throat was slit," corrected Theo.

"A lot of blood," said the weighty voice thoughtfully. Suddenly, clearly and matter-of-factly, it asked: "Who did it?"

"They don't know," said Theo. "They're looking."

"Ah. Looking." Herzl's voice was muffled again. "They won't find him," he said softly.

"Maybe they will," said Theo. "They're working hard at it."

"They won't find anything," promised Herzl. "They never found out about your father. Gabi told me. He was murdered, too."

"Gabi told you about Father?" Theo was flabbergasted. "When did he tell you?"

"When he was here."

"When?"

"They won't find the person who killed your father. They haven't found him up to now. And they won't find whoever killed Gabi, either."

"With Father it's different. It's because of the painting that—"

"Not the painting, not the painting."

"The painting was stolen," said Theo loudly.

"But not because. Not because. There's a lot of evil. Everywhere. There's a lot." The voice died away slowly.

"When did Gabi come to see you? Why didn't he tell me?"

Silence.

"Don't close your eyes. Don't go to sleep now, Herzl," urged Theo. "Help me. We're the only ones left now. We and Nita."

The sound of a contemptuous snort echoed in the van. Michael shivered.

"Herzl," pleaded Theo. "I'm talking to you."

"You didn't tell me about your father. You didn't come to tell me about it," said Herzl accusingly.

"How could we?" Theo's voice sounded despairing and guilty. "We didn't know where you were!"

"Gabi knew. He found me."

"He didn't tell me," pleaded Theo. "If I'd known I would have—"

"They suffocated him, too," said Herzl.

"It's not the same thing," protested Theo. "It was only after Gabi died that they discovered . . . How do you know? How do you know that they suffocated him and that it wasn't an accident?" he asked, alarmed. "Herzl, if you know things like that, we have to . . . The police know that you weren't in the hospital on the day Father was murdered. Where were you that day when you left the hospital, Herzl?"

"Did you find the music?" asked Herzl with sudden animation.

"What music?"

Silence.

"What music are you talking about?" Theo's voice was now cold and tense. "What do you know that I don't know?"

"You know, you know," said Herzl. "Now everything, everything is . . ." The grating of the chair legs masked the rest of the sentence. "Don't touch me!" shouted Herzl. "I can't stand it when you touch me."

The chair legs grated again. "Look, I've moved away," said Theo nervously. "Why are you angry with me, Herzl? I didn't know where you were, believe me."

"I want to go back to my room." Herzl's voice again was dull and tired. "Take me back to my room."

"They're looking for the painting," said Theo, ignoring the request. "The police are conducting a search."

"Take me back to my room," repeated the muffled voice.

"In a minute. Just tell me, what happened with the lawyer, Meyuhas?"

In the seconds of silence Michael felt his jaw muscles tighten. Balilty opened his mouth, Michael shook his head warningly, and Balilty said nothing.

"Your father loved Gabi," said Herzl. "He loved Gabi most. It's a good thing he died before him."

"He left a will. He left you—"

"I don't want anything from anyone. I don't need anything. Only the music," Herzl interrupted him with sudden animation. "Everything belongs to you."

"And to Nita," said Theo.

"And to Nita," Herzl agreed. "She has a baby."

"And he left you something, too," said Theo appeasingly.

"I don't want anything. Is the shop closed?"

Michael could imagine Theo's nod.

"They'll sell it," said Herzl in a broken voice. "Take me back to my room, and then bring me the music."

"I'll take you back in a minute." Theo's voice shook. "What music?"

Silence.

"Why are you looking at me like that?" pleaded Theo. "You know that you're dear to me."

Suddenly Herzl's voice was heard. Hoarse, surprisingly deep, it was humming a sweet melody. It ended abruptly. "Bring me the music," he said in a resolute, threatening manner. "It was your father's and it belongs to Gabriel. He said so. And now I want it. Gabriel's dead."

Seated behind the wheel, his hand on the gearshift lever, Balilty turned the upper half of his body toward Michael, an inquiring expression on his face. Michael shook his head uncomprehendingly and shrugged his shoulders.

"They want to know if you saw Father on the day he died," said Theo.

Silence.

"Did you hear me? Herzl? They say that you left the hospital that day. They want to know if—"

"Take me back to my room," Herzl's voice echoed threateningly. Again the chair's grating masked muffled words.

"Aren't you taking the grapes?" asked Theo.

There was the sound of heavy, dragging feet.

"The police are searching your apartment," Theo's voice announced defiantly. Balilty froze and gave Michael an accusing look, as if to say: I told you so, look what you've done.

The noise of the footsteps came to an abrupt halt. "It's my apartment!" he said with a despairing cry.

"I told them so, and I also told them—"

"They're not to touch my things!" Herzl's voice rose strongly, suddenly clear and lively. "The things I collected, and my music and the instruments and the records! They'll destroy the virginal I built! Those things are all mine! I didn't take anything from anybody!" Now he burst into tears, and Theo's soothing, reassuring voice did not drown out the sobs.

"I only . . . I told your father that he mustn't . . . that he must . . ." His voice was choked. "And I told him not to talk to the lawyer, but he only . . . And afterward . . . I don't want them to touch my things!" There was the sound of a body thudding to the floor and Theo's panic-stricken voice calling, "Herzl! Herzl!" Then the sound of a door opening. "We're going in," ordered Balilty.

Theo, his face white and stiff, his mouth gaping like a mask, stood in the doorway of the hospital director's office. The office was empty. His arm leaning against the doorpost, Theo looked at them. "I don't know if he's dead," he said hoarsely. "You . . . you . . . I didn't do anything to him." The panic in his eyes turned quickly to accusation: "I knew you were lying," he said over the kneeling Balilty's back, which was bent over Herzl.

"There's a weak pulse," he said to Michael. "No need for resuscitation." Balilty gently shook Herzl's shoulders and slapped him on the cheeks. "Call a doctor," he ordered, then stood up himself and ran out of the room.

Theo dropped onto the leather armchair and stared into space. Michael looked at him and at the long scarecrow body beside which he was now kneeling. He laid his fingers on Herzl's wrist. He felt the weak pulse and then put his face very close to the twisted mouth with the whitish foam at its corners, listening to Herzl's shallow breathing. Then he stood up and looked at the white wisps of hair sticking up like a clown's wig, wondering how old the man was. Herzl looked old, but his face was unwrinkled. A few teeth were missing from his gaping mouth, which smelled of tobacco and acetone.

"You told him about our searching his place," Michael said at last.

"To wake him up," explained Theo hoarsely. "He was completely indifferent, apathetic."

"But you didn't ask him what music he was talking about."

"He's sick, he's crazy, he's hallucinating," muttered Theo. "He mixes everything up—the music, the lawyer, everything."

"But you know what he was talking about," Michael gambled.

"Me?" Theo demanded, astonished. "I have no idea—"

"He talked as if you both knew exactly what it was about. He said, 'Bring me the music.' He sang you a bit of it. You're a musician. You recognized it," Michael insisted.

"Can't you see that he's insane? Can't you see that he doesn't make sense? I have no idea what he was singing!"

Theo looked at the shrunken body, and Michael, watching his eyes, said firmly: "He sounded quite sane to me. Even though he's sick. He spoke as if you both knew what he was talking about. Like some family story."

"I knew you were lying to me," said Theo bitterly. "The whole time I had the feeling that you were standing under the window or overhearing us like in a detective story."

"And that's why you tried to distract him. To change the subject whenever he mentioned that music," said Michael. He was about to continue when Balilty returned with a woman doctor and two middle-aged men.

"Take him quickly to the ER," said the doctor to the two men and pushed her glasses up to her forehead after she had knelt next to Herzl, called his name, slapped his face, and listened gravely through the stethoscope. "He's lost consciousness," she said to Balilty. "We have to find out what happened. Maybe he swallowed something. We can't know without examining him. He's not epileptic or diabetic," she said, and put her fingers on his throat again, nodded, stood up, and folded her stethoscope. "We'll transfer him to a regular hospital if he doesn't come around in a few minutes. It could be serious. Are you a relative?" she asked Balilty, who shook his head. Then she turned to Theo.

"I'm the relative," he said.

"Then please stay here," she instructed him, "until we see if we have to transfer him. The pulse is hardly audible, and his blood pressure is very low. With manic depression like his, you can never tell what he might have taken."

They left a police car outside the hospital entrance. Three times Balilty said to Zippo: "And don't move from here. If they transfer him, notify us. And don't let Theo van Gelden make a move without you, stick to him like a shadow." Three times, until he was convinced that Zippo understood.

Theo had stood at the entrance to the emergency room complaining about various things and looking at his watch and at the sky, which was still gray and oppressive. His look remained with them as they left the psychiatric hospital. The radio transmitter had beeped the moment Michael opened the door of the van, to which he had returned to retrieve his cigarettes. The technician handed him the instrument, and Emanuel Shorer's secretary sniffled, sneezed, and apologized before saying: "He's on the phone and he wants to know if you can come see him at the hospital right away. He's already been briefed on everything. He's edgy because he's finally seen the newspapers and TV this morning. And the Commissioner and the Minister have already contacted him," she explained.

The many years they'd known each other, and the motherly affection she felt for him, caused her to speak to him now as if they were old allies. Maybe she liked Michael because of the flowers he brought her from time to time, and to the attentive ear he lent to her problems with her adolescent son. She always spoke to him in a flirtatious manner, to which he spontaneously responded by stroking her hand. And he never failed to praise any change in her appearance, complimenting her on a new dress or hairdo. How little it took to make a woman happy, he would think with the pangs of conscience that sometimes made him feel cheap.

Michael rubbed his cheek and looked at Balilty, who started the car and shifted the gears as if he hadn't heard anything.

"No problem, I'll drop you there," he said to Michael when they reached the end of the street. "You yourself once told me that the fear of being afraid is worse than fear itself. What more can happen? Talk to him and get it over with."

Michael said nothing. He wanted to say something like: Don't let him take me off the case. The kind of thing that he would normally have said to Shorer directly. And now, all of a sudden, Shorer was the one he needed the protection and patronage from. For a moment he even considered asking Balilty to accompany him into the hospital, to be with him at the meeting with Shorer. If only it were possible simply to share his feelings about the baby with Shorer! If not for the investigation, if not for his involvement in the case, he could have done it.

"Your great good luck," said Balilty, "is that he's in trouble. He's worried to death about his daughter." He seemed immediately to realize the poor taste of what he had said, because he began to chatter as he always did in order to efface the impression made by some unfortunate mistake or slip of the tongue, talking about the night his own daughter was born, about his anxiety about becoming a grandfather, about the impossible helplessness of waiting in hospital corridors when fateful things are being determined.

"I'm going to join the search of Herzl's apartment. Maybe we'll find some musical score there or something," he said, making a face and stopping the car in front of the hospital in which Shorer was awaiting Michael. "But how will we know what music we're looking for?" he complained. "We'll have to take everything and bring in an expert. I'll leave a message with Tzilla," he promised. "When you're finished here, get in touch with her. What a figure!" he said, nodding toward a young woman in a tight white smock passing on the pavement opposite them. "Like a movie star. Look, look! You can see everything, exactly where her underpants end. And the way she walks! And that pair of headlights! These nurses are something else! I wouldn't mind a piece of that," he said, sighing. Then he nodded at Michael, who got out of the car, and drove off.

The big window before which they stood burned red and gold. It was not raining. The moments during which the oppressive gray of the sky had turned into the colors of a khamsin sunset had passed unnoticed by Michael. In the distance he could see two bulldozer drivers taking advantage of the last moments of light to go on leveling the hill opposite. The flags next to the huge billboards announcing the luxury apartments about to be built here hung motionless in the windless air. During the hour they had sat together in the corridor, Shorer had told him in detail about the past twenty-four hours. Twice he had wiped his eyes, and Michael had felt anxiety gnawing at him in anticipation of Shorer suddenly bursting into tears. White stubble covered his jaw. The space between his upper lip and his big, hooked nose, where for years now he had grown a thick mustache, was totally gray. His eyes were red, and his complexion, usually dark, was yellowish. The brown spots on his upper cheeks stood out, underscoring the acne scars scattered over his skin. He spoke compulsively, without pause, and it was hard to know when the right moment would arrive for Michael to bring up his own business. For a moment Michael considered avoiding the entire subject. After all, he told himself as he went to get them both coffee from the nurses' room, why burden him now with your conflicts?

The thought developed into a full-scale speech, which sounded completely convincing as he poured boiling water onto the instant coffee powder. The broad back that was turned to the corridor, the forehead pressed against the big windowpane, the eyes that had been staring at the Arab village at the bottom of the hill, and the hoarse voice that said: "Here we are on Mount Scopus, as the song says"—all this and the nod of the head toward the gray hills and the lights blinking in the distance exposed the fatuousness of the hope of sparing him and refuted the possibility of putting things off. On the contrary, he found himself waiting anxiously for the right moment to break in at last and give Shorer the situation report, as he called what he would have to say.

"What does it look like?" Shorer suddenly asked, turning away from the view. "Give it to me briefly. The Commissioner's called here three times. The District Command is bogged down with its own scandals, and at least it keeps them off our backs. But they've got time to phone. Who appointed Balilty to take your place? You?"

Michael nodded.

A moment or two passed before he began to explain, quietly and briefly, the chain of events at the crime scene from the moment he saw Gabriel van Gelden's body. Shorer listened without looking at him.

"Okay. I understand. It's got everything but the kitchen sink," said Shorer. "But why is Balilty the head of the team? Since when have you ever stepped down from a case for him like that? Are you under pressure in your studies? Is it a family problem? Is Yuval okay?"

Sometimes a nod, a little white lie, a possible evasion, a diversion, seems such an easy way out, thought Michael as he said aloud that Yuval was fine.

"You must miss him," said Shorer reflectively. "That's why people need a lot of children, one isn't enough." He added something about the difficulty of being a father, a difficulty that increased grew as children grew older. "What can you do except stand by one and pray," he said, not for the first time that day. Again it crossed Michael's mind, hopefully and fearfully, that the subject could be avoided. It seemed to him that he saw the figure of Shorer's wife emerging from a side door, and suddenly he hoped that they would call Shorer in, distract him. But when he looked again at the man standing next to him, he saw that his eyes were fixed on him. Therefore, like someone forced to jump into a deep pit in the hope that the bottom would be padded with sawdust, he expounded in a few short sentences on what he prefaced by referring—with embarrassment, aware of the stilted attempt to sound objective and restrained—to "special circumstances on the personal level."

First he spoke about the baby and how he had found her, about his desire to keep her, and then about Nita, about how he had received the first call on the radio. He spoke about the objections of the team members to his presence on the SIT, and about his own inability to give up either the case or the baby. He repeated this conclusion twice, wonderingly: "I can't give them up. I want them both," he said to his own astonishment, as if he had just discovered a great truth. "I need both."

Shorer was silent for a long time.

"Let's go sit over there," he finally said with cold reserve, pointing at two empty armchairs. "Let's sit down and talk for a minute," he said, and he took hold of Michael's arm, as if in support of a sick person. He settled into the orange upholstery, patting the armchair beside it. He put his coffee cup down on the linoleum at his feet and turned to Michael, who was still holding the cup from which he had not yet taken a single sip.

With an empty heart and a dry mouth Michael waited, in what seemed to him to be utter indifference, for sentence to be passed.

"You love her, and so you have too little distance from the case," said Shorer. "That's all there is to it."

"She's so small, and sweet, and dependent on me," Michael tried to explain. "If you could only see her—"

"I'm talking about the woman, not the baby," said Shorer, putting his hand on Michael's arm. "About Nita van Gelden."

Michael was silent. He couldn't produce even a meaningless sound. The world began to spin. Shorer sounded confused to him, unexpected, unbalanced. How could he tell if Shorer was right?

"I don't intend to gloss over anything about this," Shorer promised, "but if there's one thing that makes me happy about the whole business it's that you really love her. And it seems to me that you had a dream with her, a dream of a nice, happy family. I know you."

"I'm concerned about her," said Michael. "I care about what happens to her. But the main thing is the baby."

"You'll have to give up the baby," said Shorer severely. "That's absolutely obvious."

"But why?" Now Michael set the full coffee cup down at the foot of his chair and stared at Shorer. A heavy lump began to form in his throat, and he was terrified that it might find its way to his eyes.

"Because she's not yours," answered Shorer simply. "You don't find babies in the street. The world doesn't work that way. This baby has no place now, between the two of you."

"But there's nothing between us! Between us nothing's happened yet. . . . You have to believe me. It's exactly as I told you!"

"I only believe the facts. Calm down. But even you," said Shorer calmly, "don't know everything about yourself."

Michael said nothing.

"How long have we known each other? Almost twenty years. You know that I know you. I've never said anything about any of your affairs. I always knew when you were with someone. Of all your women, including that married one—how long did that go on, seven years?—I liked Avigail best. She had guts, Avigail. And delicacy and charm. And she was no fool. You never told me what happened with her, but I'm sure you didn't really love her, otherwise you wouldn't have let her go. Maybe you wanted to love her, I don't know, but you're such a romantic, God help us! It didn't work out. Why not?"

"She didn't want children. No matter what, she didn't want to have children," said Michael. "Maybe that's why. I think that's the reason. She had a lot of psychological problems about a skin disease she couldn't overcome. Everything with her was complicated. She couldn't trust me. These aren't things you can explain. It's an accumulation of a lot of things. Constant disappointments. It was impossible to achieve tranquillity or intimacy with her. Peace of mind. Maybe if I'd waited a few more years—"

"You didn't love her enough," pronounced Shorer. "Sometimes it's as simple as that. I hear you talk about this woman, this Nita. You're completely taken with her. And that's it."

"I don't feel it," said Michael, embarrassed. "I only feel that I'm concerned about her. I simply want her to come back to life. To start playing the cello again. You have no idea how gifted she is. I want her to be happy again. I don't want anyone else to mistreat her. Before it all happened, I felt that I could make her happy. In a careful kind of way, we had it good together."

"I'm sorry, it can't go on like this," said Shorer with a sigh. "You have to give up the baby and get off the case. Hypnotist or no hypnotist, she remains a suspect until we know otherwise. Is Balilty interrogating her?"

"Why should I give up the baby?" whispered Michael. Something of the total numbness he felt started to melt and give way to anger.

"Once again: Because you don't find babies in the street. You don't find babies in the street. Leaving aside the fact that you're too busy to take care of the baby properly. You want a baby? Very well. Fall in love with a woman and you can have a baby. I told you long ago: The way of the world makes sense. You may deny it, but there's a logic in the natural order of things. For a baby you need a mother and a father."

"Just because I'm a man?" protested Michael.

"Yes. This isn't California, or Hollywood. This is real life," said Shorer without a smile. "I believe that bringing up a child takes a mother and a father. I'm not saying," suddenly the certainty and authority of his voice wavered, "I'm not saying there aren't special circumstances—divorce, death, things like that—but finding a baby in the street? No!"

"You're being completely illogical," said Michael sharply. "All of a sudden you sound like my grandmother. How can you subject a thing like this to that kind of reasoning?"

"What can I do?" said Shorer, sighing. "When you spend two days and nights here, and you see so much trouble, and you turn into a kind of dishrag, into someone who realizes that in a matter of minutes he could lose everything—his daughter, his baby granddaughter—you get a sense of proportion. So I'm being illogical! Or maybe you don't understand my logic. Which is sometimes your logic, too, and which I've often failed to understand. What can I tell you? We've exchanged places!"

"And if—which I don't intend doing, but for the sake of argument—if I give up the baby?"

"What 'if'? There's no 'if' about it! You'll give her up because Mrs.

Mashiah will force you to give her up! So if there's no 'if' about it, what is your question?"

"How do you know Ruth Mashiah?"

"Never mind that now. What's your question?"

"The case. This case."

"If you can stay on it?"

Michael nodded.

"We've never had anything like this. And how do you see it? You go to bed with her and then—"

"I've never been to bed with her!" said Michael in despair. "I told you, I've never even touched her."

"Okay, okay," said Shorer soothingly. "So let's say you sit with her in the afternoon as a friend. You hold her hand, you play with her baby or whatever, you want her to live, to be happy and so on, and then you interrogate her in your office? With Balilty? How do you see it? How did you imagine it? Explain it to me. I'm not making any problems about what's already happened. But I demand an explanation of how you see things in the future. An investigation like this one could go on for weeks and months, who knows?"

"We can work it out. I can concentrate on other aspects of the case," mumbled Michael. "I have to find out," he heard himself saying hoarsely. "I have to find out exactly what happened."

"Yes. You have to," said Shorer, sighing. "And I'm sorry, too. For once I hear you talking about a woman in a way you've never talked about any woman before. Tell me how it could work."

"I won't be in any kind of contact with her until we solve the case," announced Michael. He himself heard in his voice the blustering tone of the disobedient child promising to mend his ways. "No personal contact." Skeptical thoughts arose within him: Are you sure? Be serious. How will you deal with her feeling neglected? You'll have to live with the fact that she hates you. You won't even be able to explain it to her.

Shorer looked at him inquiringly. "How will you do it? You live right below her apartment. Assuming, just assuming, for the sake of argument, that it solves the problem. How would you do it in practice?"

Michael bent his head. He, too, didn't know how exactly, or if, he could do it. Or what it was that was compelling him to continue working on the investigation. He looked at Shorer, he wanted to tell him that he didn't know, to ask for help. But stronger than this was the wish to maintain his self-control, not to betray the uncertainty, the confusion that was overwhelming him. If Shorer were to ask him why he was, for the sake of working on the case, prepared to give Nita up—because for a moment he understood that giving her up for a while would mean giving her up forever—he would be at a loss for an answer. And even if he found the words, Shorer wouldn't understand them. "Put me under surveillance. Whatever you want of me. I'll move out of my apartment," he said in the end, "just don't take me off the case. Please. And I also have to know that she's being watched. She might be in danger. I don't know if I told you how worried I am about her."

"Don't you think that she needs you more now as a friend?" asked Shorer. "Forget procedure for the moment. We're talking personally now."

"I can't be her friend now!" lamented Michael. "Not until I know for sure, until I have proof!" Dryness hurt his throat. He drank the dregs of the coffee.

"Do I have to endanger a murder case that has the commissioner and the minister on my back, and the press and the whole world breathing down my neck—do I have to screw up because of your personal problems?" said Shorer angrily. "I'm through talking personally. Now we're talking about work, what's good for work. I've always told you, for work you need distance."

Michael thought for a long moment. "There are things that only I know how to ask," he said finally. "Or to understand," he added quickly. And when he saw the expression on Shorer's face he made haste to add: "I'm the only one around here who understands anything about classical music. Not much, but something. And this, believe me, is a musical case."

Shorer snorted. "So we've finally arrived at your famous 'spirit of things,'" he said with bitter amusement. "I wondered why you hadn't said anything about it yet. But this time it's not so simple. Do you remember what a mess you got into with Aryeh Klein? And with him you were just his ex-student. You couldn't stop yourself from believing him even when you discovered he was lying. You liked and admired him, you knew him. And here? Can you really be objective?"

"I really and truly believe, ninety-nine percent. To be strictly rational, we'll leave one percent of doubt."

Shorer cut in furiously. "You know our rules. They exist for good reason. As you yourself would say in my place. Emotional involvement disqualifies you automatically."

"But I don't feel like that, not this time. It's not like it was with Aryeh Klein," protested Michael, even though he was well aware that his protests were falling on deaf ears. They didn't even convince him. He was on very dangerous ground, like a gambler betting everything on one card. "Besides, in the final analysis I was right about him. He lied, but it wasn't important."

"Haven't you arrested anyone yet?" asked Shorer in an entirely different tone, as if he could see the Commissioner or the Minister before him. "Or do I have to get hold of Balilty to find out what's really going on?"

"We haven't arrested anyone. All we've done so far is take passports. It isn't that Balilty wanted to arrest someone and I wouldn't let him."

Shorer reflected aloud: "The brother and sister, or maybe even that mental patient, should at least be seriously interrogated. And what about Izzy Mashiah? You haven't dug deep enough there yet."

"And Nita, too?"

"You don't have anything against her so far," admitted Shorer. "Or anyone else, either. About that, you're right."

"So maybe," said Michael in a sudden illumination that almost relieved him, "maybe we should wait a day or two. Maybe tomorrow, after I've talked to Dora Zackheim, and after I've spent the day with the two of them in Zichron Yaakov, we can reevaluate the situation."

"Do you think something will happen and in a day or two the case will solve itself? You're waiting for a miracle, is that it?"

Michael nodded and sank into his chair. He bent his head, and his hands held the arms of the chair.

"Even a day or two comes with a price," said Shorer.

"What do you mean, a 'price'?"

"You can't be alone with her."

"With Nita? She can't be left alone in any event. There's always someone . . . I told you that."

"No, my friend," said Shorer severely. "I'm talking about cutting off relations, keeping away from her completely."

"I thought you were glad that I . . . that I love her. That's what you said," Michael protested. A feeling of panic rather than joy spread though him at this unexpected understanding on Shorer's part. This understanding rather disrupted his train of thought.

"You step down from the case," said Shorer quickly and firmly, "and end this business with the baby. That craziness has to stop," he said, staring straight ahead. "But that, I have to tell you," he said clearing his throat, "is already being taken care of."

"What do you mean, being taken care of?" Michael felt the blood draining from his face and arms, as if it were pouring right out of his body. A great weakness overcame him. His fingertips prickled as if an electric current were flowing through them.

"I have to tell you now," said Shorer, gazing into his eyes with an expression gentler than usual, and even frankly paternal, "that the baby is no longer with you."

"Where is she?" Michael heard himself ask in a strange voice that sounded as if it were coming from a distance, with no connection to his body, to his vocal cords.

"Ruth Mashiah has taken her to a foster family. She found a good place for her," promised Shorer as he gripped Michael's arm. "She said that you could come see her, if you like."

"How could they do that?" said Michael. The lump in his throat threatened to dissolve into tears. "How dare you do such a thing to me without . . . without. . . ." For a long moment he was filled with wordless feelings. Images whirled before his eyes. The worst has happened, he tried to say to himself in order to stop the giddiness, the churning emotions. Maybe it's not the worst, he thought, maybe it's better this way. It was necessary to give her up. It really was conceit and craziness to think that he could do it. How could he? Shorer was right. How sad it would be for him now, to stand before the empty cradle. Facing nothing. Facing the nothing inside him, he corrected, demanding uncompromising honesty of himself. An image of a tiny garment, orphaned. No more running home to hold the baby. He had to give her up. It was right. To return to the old-new loneliness, familiar but different. There was no such thing in the world as that sudden, miraculous salvation. There couldn't be. It couldn't be that she provided it. It wasn't right to concentrate so on a baby. The sudden stab of a great, paralyzing fear now gave rise to the question of how it would be from now on, if salvation was not possible. But another thought arose, with quiet confidence: You'll endure it, because you have no choice if this is the truth that emerges. Shorer was right: You really don't find babies in the street. In this truth there was something great and right. And then there was Nita. With her it might be possible to build something. She could be . . . When her face suddenly lit up with joy. . . . But why? A new torrent churned inside him. Why should he think that it was impossible? Why should he think that it couldn't be done? Who were those others to decide what was best for the baby? What did they know? He wouldn't let them get away with it. He had to fight them. Maybe there was such a thing as sudden, miraculous salvation. Finally, it was no coincidence that it was he who had heard her crying in the cardboard box. Finally, it was no coincidence that he had been open to that crying. No, he wouldn't agree. He wouldn't let them do it.

For a few minutes they sat without talking. Shorer's hand never left his arm. Suddenly the realization struck him, sharp as a knife. "How do you know?"

"How do I know what?" asked Shorer calmly. He took his hand away from the trembling arm, which Michael quickly crossed with his other arm.

"How do you know they took her away? You . . . you knew it all the time!"

Shorer nodded.

"And you never told me . . . You let me . . . How long have you known it?"

"Since this morning," said Shorer calmly. "They came to tell me this morning. I didn't say anything to you because I had to hear what you had to say."

"Because you wanted to see if I would tell you," muttered Michael in a voice choked with anger. "Because you thought I would deceive you. The whole thing was a test. Who came to tell you?"

"What does it matter? I had to—"

"What does it matter? What does it matter?" shouted Michael. Shorer put his hand on his arm again in a soothing gesture, and Michael quickly lowered his voice. "You know very well that it matters. I have to work with those people. If Eli or Tzilla came to tell you without telling me—"

"It wasn't Eli or Tzilla."

"Who was it, then? You can't not tell me who. Did Ruth Mashiah come and talk to you?"

"I promised not to tell, I gave my word," said Shorer, and for the first time a note of hesitation crept into his voice.

"I'm not interested in your promises," said Michael severely. "Do you want me to leave? To resign from the force? I can't work with people who stab me in the back. I understand that if you refuse to say who it was then it's one of us. Maybe I've gone off my rocker, as you say, but I can still think."

"This morning, after your meeting, that girl was here, what's her name?" Shorer shifted uneasily in his seat. "Dalit?"

"The snake," Michael heard himself say.

"An ambitious girl," agreed Shorer. "Not a fool by any means. She was worried."

Michael said nothing.

"It's a delicate question, the question of loyalties," muttered Shorer. "The fact is that neither Eli nor Tzilla nor Balilty said a word. They never talked to me," he went on with increasing uneasiness, as if he had been caught conspiring in an act of treachery.

"You're taking her off the case!" announced Michael.

Shorer kept quiet.

"Yes?" he insisted.

"We'll see." Shorer scratched his head.

"And because of her, of what she said, they came and took—"

"For the baby's well-being," said Shorer sharply. "Ruth Mashiah phoned me. They told her that we're close, so she said, and she asked me to talk to you, to prepare you. When she phoned I already knew what it was all about."

"Did Dalit speak to Ruth Mashiah, too?" asked Michael with grim astonishment.

"She said that she was concerned about the baby's welfare and that you were away from home for hours at a time." Shorer's voice died away, embarrassed.

"Oh, the power of liberal sanctimoniousness. Especially when it's a matter of the baby's well-being, the good of the case."

"But," said Shorer carefully, "when you set personal feelings aside, there's something to it. She wasn't lying," he added, looking quickly sideways. "You really are running around like . . . like when you're working on a case and many things are going on at once. But I have a suggestion."

Michael waited.

"My suggestion," said Shorer, speaking slowly and deliberately, as if he were choosing his words very carefully, "is that you come to stay with me for a while. My wife will be with my daughter and her baby." He glanced in the direction of the maternity ward. "I'll be alone in the house. Move in for a few days. Until we know where we stand."

"I'm not giving up the case," warned Michael.

"We'll see," said Shorer. "We'll see what happens. It all depends."

Michael looked at the wall opposite him. At the patches of color in a pastel drawing of a Jerusalem landscape. I'm not giving up the baby, either, he said to himself. They won't take her away from me so easily. He looked at Shorer.

"Ruth Mashiah told me that she warned you. She told you that the baby wasn't yours, and they didn't even take the baby away from your apartment. She was at Nita's. It's all for the little one's own good. You must remember that. Loving someone means wanting what's best for her. You yourself have explained that to me often enough," said Shorer. "And they took her away for her own good. You'll get over it, and you'll give her up because you know very well that it's the right thing to do."

11

We've Never Had Anything Like This Before

The phone rang as soon as Shorer had locked the door from inside. Like someone fearing the worst, he paled and snatched up the receiver. After a moment his facial muscles relaxed. "He's here," Michael heard him say, letting out a deep breath. "We just came in. I thought it was the hospital," he explained, beckoning Michael to the phone.

Because of Michael's planned trip to see Dora Zackheim in Holon and to the music workshop at Beit-Daniel in Zichron Yaakov, they had scheduled the meeting for seven in the morning. Freshly shaved for the first time in days, Shorer got into the car saying: "We'll have our second cup of coffee at the meeting." And in fact, before he did anything else he bent over to examine the two black plastic jugs standing in the middle of the table.

"It used to be a *finjan*," he grumbled as he struggled with a jug's sophisticated lid. "They'd bring a big *finjan* of Turkish coffee and the smell of the cardamom alone was enough to wake you up. But that's prehistory, before your time." He finally opened the lid and breathed in the smell. "Instant," he said with disgust. "Like in the hospital. Who drinks instant coffee here?" he complained to the room at large as he opened the second jug.

"I do," said Tzilla from the doorway sleepily and rubbed her bleary eyes. She shook her head and her long silver earrings swayed. "Balilty will be here in a minute. He's on his way from Forensics. He was there because of the painting. He wanted to bring it there himself. He wouldn't let even the technicians carry it." She spoke with ostentatious objectivity, as someone who had decided to refrain from judgment, not to betray her true feelings. She pushed her hand into the belt of her trousers. "I made two kinds of coffee because last night I slept only an hour and a half, here in the office." Then, with sudden urgency, she asked Michael: "Do you know we found the painting? He said he'd call you. I told him where you were."

"He phoned last night, the minute we got in," Shorer reassured her.

Michael wondered how Shorer had succeeded last night in making him stay in the car after meekly putting the key to his apartment in Shorer's outstretched hand. All Shorer had said was: "You'd better not go in at all, to avoid any conflicts and regrets. I suggest we go straight to my place from here." There was no hint of suggestion in his voice, which carried the assurance of command. "I'll go in and get you what you need for tonight and tomorrow, and later you can make a list and I'll see to it that the things are brought to you."

Michael had sat by himself in the dusty Ford Fiesta for a few minutes, struggling against the image of Nita's lost face and thoughts of the empty cradle. He mourned the loss of the baby, feeling a sharp, heart-wrenching pain. "Here you are," Shorer had suddenly said, erasing the image of the baby as he opened the car door and put two blue shirts and a bag containing underwear on Michael's lap. "You can get toiletries at my place. I don't have time for details," he had said, sitting down behind the wheel.

Michael had looked at the white and pink room. Shorer had gathered up from his oldest daughter's narrow childhood bed a little row of fluffy koala bears that had once belonged to her and placed them carefully next to the collection of miniature scent bottles standing on the shelf above. Then, with a sigh, he had opened the window and moved it to and fro to introduce some fresh air into the stuffy perfumed room. "This is the guest room now, not that we have so many guests. Children!" he said, savagely shutting the floral curtains. "One day they're here, running around the house. Then the house is empty and next thing you know they're having children of their own."

It was clear to Michael that he wouldn't sleep that night, but he fell asleep the minute he pulled the thin blanket over his head. He woke up in a panic, the vestiges of a nightmare still flickering in his mind.

He had dreamed of a big house, gutted and open on all sides. He walked over smashed-in doors that partly barred his way, until he reached a back room, very big and empty, like a hall, at the far end of which stood a cradle. He went up to the empty cradle, and at its foot, in the corner of the room, lay a huddled, shriveled body, the tiny mummy of a baby. That was all he remembered. He turned on the bedside lamp, which had the figure of a red-capped gnome.

With trembling fingers he lit a cigarette and went over to the window. New streetlamps illuminated the remnants of orchards at the foot of the Bayit VeGan neighborhood. When Yuval was little they had often gone for walks in the abandoned orchards and climbed the hill to the Holy Land Hotel. Now the trees had been uprooted, and bulldozers had leveled the tops of the hills, erasing their gentle curves. The light of the lamps atop the silver poles revealed the frameworks of the houses the developers had begun to build on the land that had been snatched up the minute it came on the market. In the distance, in the midst of what had once been an apple orchard, there was already a four-story pseudo-Spanish castle with rounded balconies and stone columns. There's no hope, he said to himself. He closed the window and went back to bed. He would have to learn that this baby would not be his. He would not change her life. Somebody else would. A foster family. An image of that family immediately came into his head, living in a house with a room like this one, overlooking a garden and with a red tiled roof. But the words "foster family" had a harsh, cruel ring to them. Maybe, however, nevertheless . . . , he thought stubbornly, but he ground out his cigarette in a saucer he had found and switched off the light. No, there is no however, no nevertheless, he thought as he turned from side to side. You really don't find babies in the street. Nita's face, shining, unhappy, lost, called to him until he fell asleep again.

The door to the conference room flew open. "Well, what do you say now?" thundered Balilty's voice, bursting with pride. He repeated what he had said to Michael on the phone: "I can't get over how they could have done that! It's worth half a million dollars! It was lying just rolled up in the kitchen cabinet. Wrapped in paper. That shiny white paper we used to line kitchen shelves with. If I hadn't looked inside, behind the bottles and the cocoa, I would have thought it was just a roll of paper. I thought it would take months until we found it, if we ever did, and all of a sudden, out of the blue!" His eyes were red, and he kept blinking as if they hurt. Stubble a day or two old gave him the appearance of neglect. The striped shirt over his big belly was partly out of his trousers, covering his belt, and behind his broad back stood Dalit.

At the sight of her face Michael was filled with rage. He clenched his jaw and stared at Shorer, who sat next to him examining his coffee cup with great concentration, as if he had noticed neither her nor Michael's look. For a moment Michael thought of getting up. He even imagined overturning his chair, leaving the conference room, slamming the door behind him, and not returning until that pale, shining face under the cropped fair hair had been banished. He dismissed this option and others that occurred to him at that moment as melodramatic and pointless, and chose instead to sink deeply into the padded chair, stretch out his legs, cross his ankles, give himself up to a feeling of hopelessness, watch the movement of the hands of the big clock on the wall opposite him, and then stubbornly rub his finger at a grease spot on the brown formica top of the pale wooden conference table.

Balilty sat down at its head and dished out compliments to himself, to Dalit, and also to Tzilla, and unwillingly added a remark about the good work done by Eli. Zippo looked at him with humble expectation, and lowered his eyes when it became clear that Balilty was not going to mention his name. It seemed to Michael that he could discern signs of relief on Eli's and Tzilla's faces at Shorer's presence and at the apparent resolution of Michael's situation. Tzilla's eyes, when she sat down opposite him, avoided meeting his. Balilty directed his words to the corner of the table where Michael and Shorer were sitting. He devoted a few minutes to recapitulating the course of events "for the head of Criminal Investigations," he said, looking at Shorer, "even though I know that he's already been briefed by Ohayon last night." He then described in detail the state of Herzl's apartment. ("A stinking basement in Beth HaKerem, four inches of dirt on the floor, your shoes stick to it when you walk, if you can find anywhere to put them down, it would take a trowel to scrape it all off. You wouldn't believe what people collect. The guy's under sixty years, and he's got all kinds of stuff piled up. Including musical instruments. I know nothing about it, but it looks to me like there are some valuable ones lying around. The place is like a junkyard.") He had taken the trouble to search the kitchen cabinet thoroughly despite the Forensic investigators' doubts. Yet there the painting was, well hidden. ("Behind bottles of cheap red wine and medicinal brandy. Who drinks stuff like that nowadays? And ancient Dutch cocoa. It looked as if the cabinet hadn't been opened for years, and yet its doors didn't have a speck of dust on them. Whoever hid the painting had wiped them clean. And all this time I'd been talking to Interpol about those Frenchies we caught!") He went on to tell in detail about how every handle of every door in that filthy apartment was clear of fingerprints, especially the kitchen, which was "completely different from the mess and dirt everywhere else, which tells us that it wasn't Herzl who hid the painting there. Why should he wipe off his fingerprints? It's his own place, his fingerprints have a right to be there," he concluded thoughtfully.

"How do you know?" Eli Bahar argued. "Maybe they hid something else there. Maybe he put the picture there, and afterward someone else came in looking for something else, and that one wiped off the fingerprints."

"You could be right," said Balilty, twisting his mouth contemptuously. "But I'm telling you that it happened the way I say."

"What's that supposed to mean, 'the way I say'?" Eli complained. He looked at Michael, who leaned his chin on his hand and said nothing.

"I'm telling you," stressed Balilty, "believe me." He raised his arm and spread out his hand. "Those kitchen cabinets were wiped clean. Why waste time talking about it?" he said. He emphasized that there were no signs of a break-in, and that the handle of the front door, like all the other door handles in the apartment, had not a single fingerprint on it. "After all, Herzl lives there, and he doesn't walk around with gloves on," he summed up with satisfaction. "He doesn't have to wipe off his own fingerprints, right?" He turned to Shorer expectantly.

Shorer cleared his throat and, after crumbling its head to powder over his empty coffee cup, put down the burned match he had taken from the glass ashtray. "It sounds that way," he agreed unwillingly, and he listened attentively to Balilty's vivid description of how he had awakened the art expert in the middle of the night in order to confirm the authenticity of the painting. "Because," said Balilty importantly, "from what I understand from my conversations with Interpol and all kinds of experts, there are a lot of copies—fakes—on the market. We had to be sure that it was the real thing. You should have seen him. He flipped out."

"Who?" Zippo spoke up for the first time.

"The expert, Professor Livnat. His hands shook when he held that painting. If you ask me, the painting's nothing special. If I hadn't been told it's a big deal, seventeenth century and all that, I wouldn't look at it twice."

"In the photograph it looks beautiful," said Tzilla hesitantly, "especially the woman's face."

"And what did Mister Theo van Gelden have to say about it?" asked Shorer.

"Well, the first thing we did was go and get him. Zippo picked him up at the psychiatric hospital and brought him to Herzl's apartment. And by the way, before I forget: He and his sister will be going to Zichron Yaakov in a police car. We're not taking any chances. We're letting them think it's for their own safety," he said, and he looked at Michael. "I can't arrest them, or hold them by force. I don't tell them what I'm thinking, and they don't ask," he added thoughtfully.

"So Zippo brought him to Herzl's place," said Michael gloomily, "and you showed him the painting. What did he say?"

"He nearly fainted," Balilty said chuckling. "Zippo didn't prepare him for it, I asked him not to say anything."

"What could I say to him?" mumbled Zippo, diligently polishing his lighter. "I didn't know anything myself."

For a moment Balilty looked confused. But he immediately recovered and ignored the interruption. "I took him into the kitchen and showed him the picture. He didn't say a thing. I spread it out on a towel. Everything is so dirty there. And after all, half a million dollars! I asked him to identify it. He identified it. This was before the art expert arrived, and after the forensic examination. There were no fingerprints on it. Gloves. Only then did it turn out that van Gelden had a key to Herzl's apartment," Balilty said dramatically. "His father had one, too. I asked him why he didn't tell us that before, and he said: 'You didn't ask me.'" Balilty paused deliberately for dramatic effect, and then he said: "And they're not the only ones who had a key."

"Who else?" asked Shorer when he saw that Balilty was waiting to be asked.

"Gabriel van Gelden had one, too," said Balilty. "We didn't know that before, either. You heard yourself," he said, turning to Michael, "that Herzl was obsessed with his privacy. It didn't even occur to me, but Dalit found it last night. The brothers got the key from their father. Apparently Herzl trusted the old man. And maybe the old man had it duplicated and gave copies to his sons. Maybe Gabriel had it duplicated. Theo van Gelden says he can't remember who gave him the key. It was a long time ago."

"I wouldn't get excited about anything Theo van Gelden says," grumbled Eli Bahar. "I wouldn't take a single thing he says for a fact. Not a single thing."

"Anyway, I asked his sister, too," said Balilty. "And Dalit found that a key to Herzl's place was at Gabriel's—and so at Izzy Mashiah's, too. She found it last night. All that in one night! What do you say to that?" he asked Michael triumphantly. "Nice, eh?"

"Very nice," agreed Michael, looking at the wall opposite him. "Everything's very nice."

"And Nita says that her father had a key to Herzl's apartment hanging behind the refrigerator at his place, on a ring that also had keys to her place and to Gabi's." Balilty passed the tip of his pink tongue over his lips until they shone wetly, and then he smacked them twice.

"Very nice, Danny," said Shorer. "Congratulations!"

"And that's not all. We've got another bombshell."

"Yes?" inquired Shorer.

"I don't know what it means, though. Where's the folder with the photographs?" he asked Dalit.

"In your office. Should I go and get it?" Dalit rose quickly to her feet.

"Never mind, there's no time for that. They'll believe me. We found Herzl's passport. And it's stamped Amsterdam, six months ago."

"Herzl Cohen's passport?" asked Michael. "Amsterdam? What was he doing in Amsterdam?"

"They were all there, so why not him? Haven't you noticed? The old man was in Holland, Gabriel was in Holland, Izzy Mashiah was in Holland. The only ones who weren't there are Theo van Gelden and Nita. Haven't you asked yourselves why all this interest in Holland?"

"We're waiting for you to tell us," said Eli Bahar coldly. "I'm sure you know."

"Not really," admitted Balilty, "but it might be a lead. The painting is Dutch too, don't forget."

"What's the position with Herzl now?" asked Michael.

"They took him to the regular hospital," said Balilty. "We left Avram there. Herzl's recovered consciousness."

"Well?" prompted Tzilla.

Balilty sighed. "Everybody in this case has to be handled with kid gloves. So he's conscious, but up to now," he looked at his watch, "he's not been ready to talk. And since he's a certified mental patient, we can't arrest him. Avram's there, if he happens to change his mind. Avram will call if anything happens. He'll talk in the end," he said hopefully.

"Either he will or he won't," Eli Bahar said, looking around gloomily.

"So where are we?" Balilty began to sum up. "We have a painting worth half a million dollars that was stolen and we've recovered. A painting that maybe nobody intended to sell. We have surgical tape and a cello string, but we don't know where the string came from. We have a pair of gloves, whose owner we know, but those doesn't mean much. We have two bodies, and a lot of trips to Amsterdam. We have a house in Rehavia that's worth millions, and a shop that's worth a lot too, maybe even more than the house. Money and things, and two heirs. And also grandchildren and a queer who stands to inherit from his . . . Do you know that Gabi van Gelden increased his life insurance two months ago and that Izzy Mashiah is the beneficiary?"

"Don't talk like that," said Tzilla.

"Like what?"

"What you said about Izzy Mashiah."

"What did I say? Queer? I beg your pardon, forgive me." Balilty put his hands together as if in prayer. "I beg all liberals and progressives to forgive me, but I don't like queers. That's the truth. What can I do?"

"You shouldn't talk like that!" said Tzilla sharply. "You should keep opinions like that to yourself."

"The ones I really can't stand are the ones who play the woman." Balilty's eyes darted around the room until they came to rest on Tzilla's face. "The ones, you know, that . . ." he said with the suggestion of a wink.

Tzilla tugged at a lock of graying hair at her temple, opened her mouth, and shut it again without saying anything.

"What you want to say," said Shorer, cutting through the oppressive silence, "and we don't have much time," he added, looking ostentatiously at his watch, "is that you're exonerating Herzl? Is that what you want to say? You're concentrating on Izzy Mashiah and Theo and Nita van Gelden?"

"More or less," agreed Balilty. "I spoke to her yesterday, in the early evening. For hours. Two hours at least. During the search of her apartment," he added thoughtfully.

"Spoke to Nita?" asked Michael.

"Uh-huh," said Balilty, and suddenly he looked embarrassed. "It was before Ruth Mashiah, umm, arrived with her team to . . ." he said softly to Michael. "I left before they . . . believe me, I didn't know anything about —"

"Never mind that now," Michael interrupted him impatiently. "What did you find out in your conversation with Nita?"

"I explained to her again that she doesn't know that she knows something, and maybe if she spoke to us, that something could come out, whatever it is. But she really doesn't know, to put it mildly. It's as if she isn't with us at all. She really doesn't know a thing. We gave her a polygraph test," he added quickly.

"When?" asked Michael, trying to keep his voice under control. "Last night?"

"Yes. I couldn't find any inconsistencies. Even when I asked her who was with Gabriel behind the pillar. I tried all the names, and the needle didn't move. Not when I said: 'Theo was standing there with him,' and not when I said: 'It was Herzl.' Nothing. The only new thing I learned from her was that she's been afraid of Herzl ever since she was little girl. Because of the way he looks," he said. "She told me, before the polygraph test, that when she was maybe three years old—it's one of her first childhood memories—she came out from under the big desk in the music shop where they did the accounts. She was playing there, and her father called her to come and say hello to Uncle Herzl. She came out from under the desk and she remembers—you can hear it all on the tape—that she looked at him and his shoes alone frightened her, even though she saw his face and it wasn't really frightening. His hair sticking up frightened her, and now she knows that he, too, was frightened. Not of her, but because he had just arrived in the country, and he was frightened of everything."

"That doesn't make sense," said Michael. "She's only thirty-eight. He arrived in Israel in fifty-one. She wasn't even born when he got here, and she's known him since the day she was born. When you've seen someone from the beginning, you don't suddenly become frightened of him at the age of three, unless he's done something."

Balilty was confused. He did the calculation, and then he said: "Okay, I don't know. It doesn't matter now. Anyway, that's what she said."

"Actually it does matter," said Shorer. "We're talking about Herzl Cohen, her father's employee, in whose kitchen you found the stolen painting. I understand," he said nodding at Michael, "that there are all kinds of mysteries connected with him, and the fact that he frightened her is one of them."

"Okay, so maybe she didn't notice him before. Maybe this was the first time she really saw him. You can listen to the tape yourselves," said Balilty dejectedly. "In any event, what's important is that he frightened her. But she says that she knew very well that he was harmless. That he's a good person. But he frightened her. She's sure that he didn't harm anyone, especially not her father."

"And what about the person who did harm her father? The person who suffocated him? Could he, Herzl, in her opinion, have harmed *him*? In other words, punished old van Gelden's killer?" asked Eli Bahar. "Did you ask her that?"

"You'll be surprised," said Balilty. "I did ask her that. And she said that she really didn't know, but that it was hard for her to imagine him being capable of violence. But we know, and she said so too, that he's had a number of outbursts."

Dalit touched his arm, and he leaned over toward her. She whispered something in his ear, and again Michael was filled with rage at the familiarity permitted to her, at Balilty's dependence on her. "Yes," said Balilty with nearly smug solemnity. "Dalit correctly reminds me about Meyuhas, the lawyer. We haven't managed to get in touch with him yet. He's on vacation. Nobody else knows what that's about. We're trying to find out what old man van Gelden and Herzl quarreled about," he explained to Shorer. "He'll be back tomorrow. We'll be wiser then. But we did find the Canadian woman. Our representative in New York has interrogated her. Dalit spoke to him."

"What Canadian woman?" asked Shorer.

"The one who was with Theo van Gelden the day the picture was stolen and his father was murdered. Theo was with two women," said Balilty, sighing, "on the same afternoon, before a concert in the evening. Some people are made of steel. What can I tell you, all on the same day! And now he has a solid alibi."

"We should keep the guard on Miss van Gelden," said Shorer. "Is someone with her now?"

"Only the babysitter, the policeman outside the building, and her brother," said Tzilla.

"They're getting ready to drive to Zichron Yaakov," Eli Bahar reminded him.

"Okay, so from the minute they leave, if not before. I don't like this knowing not knowing business. It's dangerous. We don't want another corpse today," said Shorer.

"Will do," said Balilty, pursing his mouth. "Within the hour."

"What about that musical score Herzl was talking about? Anything new on that? We should get an expert to listen to the melody," Michael said suddenly.

"To the what?" asked Balilty with surprise.

"To the tune Herzl sang to Theo in the psychiatric hospital," said Michael. "We have to play the tape to a musician."

"Right," said Balilty. "Take that down, Dalit. Do you have anyone in mind?"

"The important part of that conversation was about the score, and we don't even know what score. We have to bring a musicologist into the picture. Ask Nita or Theo, without telling them what it's about."

"What do you think I am?" demanded Balilty, offended. He looked quickly at Zippo, who was covering his face with his hands. "I already asked them, indirectly. Both Nita and Theo. And while we're on the subject," he said suddenly, "you're going to a place that'll be filled with musicians. Why don't you take the cassette with you? Dalit will make a copy for you now."

"I already have," said Dalit.

"Excellent," said Balilty. "Give him the copy, and he'll play it to the geniuses who'll be able to identify it after listening to a couple of notes. Maybe this is another case where you can tell the whole story from part of one sentence."

"I have to go," said Michael, picking up the tape Dalit set before him without looking at her. "You don't keep an eighty-six-year-old lady waiting."

"Once a gentleman, always a gentleman," remarked Zippo.

"And I'll need a cassette recorder," said Michael, "with fresh batteries."

"Zippo's taking Theo and Nita to Zichron Yaakov," said Balilty. "I meant to send Tzilla, but she's too tired after last night."

"Zippo was up all night, too. Send Eli," said Michael authoritatively, just before remembering that he wasn't heading the team. "All we really need is a driver," he said apologetically. He saw that Eli's face, which had suddenly brightened, again darkened.

"I can drive them," declared Zippo, insulted.

"There are a million other things to do here," Michael said, trying to smooth things over. "Why should you have to go all the way to Zichron Yaakov?"

"I've got no problem about driving to Zichron Yaakov. When my grandmother was alive I used to do the trip in two hours. Not actually to Zichron Yaakov, a little before, just after Hadera. I used to do it every two days. Under much worse conditions."

"As you like," said Michael, and he saw Eli's head sink. "I thought that on the way back Eli could stop in at the pathologist's again and pick up the papers," he explained. "Think about it," he said to Balilty. "I have to go."

At that moment Shorer's secretary appeared in the doorway. "Izzy Mashiah wants to talk to Chief Superintendent Ohayon," she said to

Balilty. "He tried to reach you," she said to Michael, "but he can't get through. He has something urgent to say."

"You should use your cell phone, too," Balilty rebuked Michael. "How can I get in touch with you when I need to? Don't tell me you're allergic to them. We can't indulge your allergies when they interfere with your work."

Michael left the conference room and followed Shorer's secretary. His eyes were fixed on her tiny steps. Like a Chinese woman with bound feet, she wobbled in her tight skirt on slender high heels.

At the office door she stopped and looked at him with maternal affection. "You don't look so good," she said. "Are you okay?"

"As far as I know." He produced a smile with effort. "It'll pass," he promised. When he realized that she was waiting for details, and that she would be hurt by his silence, he added: "It hasn't been easy lately." He picked up the phone.

"Is there anything I can do for you?" she asked before leaving the room with ostentatious discretion.

Holding on to the phone, he tried to look grateful as he said: "Thanks, I can't think of anything at the moment." She nodded gravely, completely innocent of the irony of his words. He felt as if they were reciting dialogue from a romance novel.

"Tell me if there's anything, anything at all. I'd be happy to help," she concluded, leaving the room.

"I have to talk to you about a couple of things," said Izzy Mashiah, his breath making a gasping, whistling sound, as if he were fighting for air. "There are a few things that are bothering me. You said I should get in touch with you if I needed to."

"Of course, certainly," said Michael. He wondered if Izzy could possibly have noticed the surveillance, the disguised police car parked outside his house, or that his phone was bugged. "Now? On the phone?"

"No, no!" cried Izzy Mashiah, horrified. "It's a delicate matter."

"Is it urgent?" asked Michael, looking at his watch.

"I don't know how important it is to you," said Izzy unhappily. "It seems pretty urgent to me."

"Is it about the key?" guessed Michael.

"What key?"

"The key to Herzl Cohen's apartment, the one that was in Felix van Gelden's house."

"I don't know what you're talking about." Izzy fell silent, and his breathing grew even heavier, the whistling shriller.

"The key Sergeant Dalit found in your place," said Michael.

"What Sergeant Dalit?" said Izzy, alarmed. "I don't know any Sergeant Dalit."

"The policewoman who spoke to you last night," said Michael impatiently. "Didn't you talk to a woman named Dalit about the key to Herzl's apartment?"

"I don't know any Dalit," pleaded Izzy Mashiah. "I don't understand what you're saying."

"Okay, so maybe it wasn't Dalit. But what about the key?"

"What key? I don't know anything about a key." Izzy coughed up phlegm and gasped for air.

"Take it easy," said Michael, forcing himself to sound calm. "Did you have a visit from the police last night?"

"There was no one here last night," said Izzy Mashiah.

"Are you sure?""

"Of course I'm sure!" he shouted. "I may be going crazy, but not to such an extent," he added bitterly.

"Okay. So what did you want to talk to me about?"

The wheezing in Izzy's voice subsided somewhat as he said: "About all kinds of things, but not on the phone."

"Can it wait until this evening?"

"I suppose so," sighed Izzy Mashiah. "It would be better right now."

"I can't now, it's impossible," Michael explained as if to a child. "Can someone else talk to you instead?"

"I'd prefer to talk to you, if you don't mind. Gabi admired you and I'd be more comfortable with you. If I have to wait till this evening, then I'll wait."

"Late this evening," Michael warned him.

"I'm not going anywhere," said Izzy sadly. "I'll be waiting for you here."

"There's something I don't understand," said Michael at the door of the conference room. "Give me just a moment, please."

"Haven't you left yet?" asked Tzilla, surprised.

"Just a moment," he repeated. "I'd like your attention, please!" They all stopped talking and looked at him expectantly.

He made a point of looking at Balilty, and only at Balilty. From the corner of his eye he caught the movement of Shorer's hand scribbling with a burned match on a sheet of white paper that he carefully flattened with his other hand, as if his thoughts were somewhere else entirely. But Michael knew that he was concentrating intently.

"I've just talked to Izzy Mashiah," he said quietly, his eyes still on Balilty.

"So?" said Balilty impatiently. "What's up?"

"What's up," Michael said deliberately, "is that nobody spoke to him about any key to Herzl's apartment. He doesn't know any policewoman called Dalit."

Balilty's mouth fell open and his eyes narrowed. "Is that what he said?" he asked, astonished. He turned sharply toward Dalit, who looked blank, shrugged her shoulders, spread her arms in a helpless gesture, and said nothing.

"What's this about?" Balilty asked her sharply. "Were you there yesterday or not?"

"Of course I was," said Dalit and opened wide her light blue eyes. Her eyelashes fluttered and seemed to cast shadows over her pale skin.

"And you talked about the key?"

"Of course we did," she said with determined calm. She smoothed a slender eyebrow with her finger, and then clasped her hands together.

"And the key?"

"The key . . ." For a moment something appeared to crack in her self-confidence. "It's with the file we handed over to Forensics along with the other evidence. I bagged the things last night and handed them over myself."

"You drove to Forensics last night?"

"Early this morning, before I came here," said Dalit defensively, looking right at him with a wounded expression. "I left it there, in an envelope," she added.

Balilty's eyes narrowed. He looked at Michael. "Someone isn't telling the truth," he said finally. His words rang in the silence of the room. "Someone, in other words, is lying, in a big way. What's in the surveillance report this morning? They must have reported Dalit's visit. What does he mean, he doesn't know any Sergeant Dalit?"

"We haven't received last night's report yet," said Tzilla uneasily. "It's due at noon."

"They may not have seen me," said Dalit hesitantly.

"Why shouldn't they see you? Were you hiding, or what?" demanded Balilty, and not waiting for a reply he said again to Michael: "What does he mean, he doesn't know any Sergeant Dalit?"

"I'm only telling you what I heard," said Michael, leaning against the door, which he had closed. "You can listen to the tape of the conversation in Shorer's office. Why should Mashiah make this up? What good could it possibly do him?"

"We'll have to talk to him again," said Balilty uneasily. "We've never had anything like this before. There's something completely crazy here. Why should he deny it after he's already handed over the key?"

"Why indeed," said Michael. "I'm wondering why, too."

"I have no idea," insisted Dalit, as Balilty again looked at her. Her face was now flushed. Michael felt at a loss. He himself didn't know what to believe. Now he was sorry he had spoken in front of everybody. Not because he doubted Izzy Mashiah, whom for some reason he tended to believe, but because he felt certain that something ugly and sordid, something murky, was about to be revealed, and he was the one who had exposed it and brought it up from the depths. Without reflection, without thinking of the consequences. In a manner that was uncharacteristic of him. Because he was going to be late for his meeting with Dora Zackheim. And also in order to settle a score with Dalit. But he felt no lust for revenge, or any sense of satisfaction. Where had all the anger he had felt only a moment ago gone? he wondered. How could he not have taken into account his vindictiveness, his desire to get back at her, and admit that it was this which had motivated him? Maybe these things existed in him even though he didn't feel them at all.

"Get me Forensics," said Balilty impatiently to Zippo. Eli Bahar followed Michael out of the room in order to go and get Izzy Mashiah.

Dalit shrugged her shoulders and collected her papers with nervous, jerky movements. "What's going on here?" said Michael to Eli as they stood outside the entrance to the building. "What do you think?"

"I had a bad feeling about her from the beginning," Eli admitted. "But I thought I was imagining it, that it was because of Balilty putting me on the shelf, sending me on errands. Now I'm no longer sure of that. I think," he said, chewing his lower lip, "that we also have to check the matter of our man in New York, too. If she says she spoke to him, how do we know that she really spoke to him?"

"In other words, are you saying it's possible that she's lying?" asked Michael, and to his surprise he felt a surge of anxiety welling up inside him.

"I remember how long it took from the time she found Herzl until she reported it. I'm thinking about that, and I can't find an explanation for it," said Eli Bahar.

"But what could her motive be?" wondered Michael. They were already standing at the car door. He looked at the domes of the Russian church, and again he was moved by its naive beauty, standing there untarnished. It was like an illustration from an old book set among the parking lots, the fence around the police building, the clusters of people, the kiosk at the church's side. Suddenly he noticed the dark brown color of the domes. "Weren't they green?" he asked, astonished.

"What? What was green?"

"The church domes. Before I went on leave, they were green. I'm sure they were green."

"Yes," said Eli, suddenly smiling. "They were green. They've been brown for a long time now. I don't know why, maybe they painted them."

"She must know that we'll find out in the end. Where's the sense of it? Why would anyone do such things, especially when they know they'll be found out?" Michael persevered.

"Once you would have said, 'Wonders will never cease,'" replied Eli, looking at the tips of his black running shoes. "You haven't said that for a long time. If it's true, then she's simply crazy."

"Simple is the one thing it's not," said Michael, listening to the roar of the car engine. "And that's no explanation either, only a description. It's obvious that there's something crazy here. But what exactly? Do me a favor," he suddenly remembered. "You go to Zichron Yaakov with the van Geldens, not Zippo. Insist on it!"

"What?" said Eli sullenly. "You want me to ask Balilty? Why should I? I'm not asking him for anything. If he wants to, he can send me." His face took on a withdrawn expression. He bit his lower lip, his eyes olive green in his dark face.

"Do me a favor," pleaded Michael. "Don't do it for yourself, but for me as your friend. What use is Zippo? First of all, someone has to listen to what they say to each other on the way. Second, it really is too dangerous."

"There'll be a tape recorder. They're going in the Forensics van. It's bugged, which I know for a fact, because it was my job to set it up. So you see what my position has become here. That's all Balilty thinks I'm fit for."

"I need someone there I can . . . someone who understands . . . someone who . . . You know what I mean. I need someone who really won't take his eyes off her. You never can tell what . . . "

Eli lowered his head, again examined his shoe tips, and drew a little circle with his right foot. "Okay, we'll see," he said unwillingly, "if it can be managed."

12

The Right Distance

He arrived in Holon much later than he had intended. Behind the hedge a sprinkler danced over a small strip of lawn. Petunias in red clay pots stained the green with bright pink and purple and white in front of a row of modest white stucco apartment buildings. A paved path, short and straight as a ruler, led to the entrance. Twice he had ignored DEAD END signs as the car twisted and turned in the narrow streets behind the town's main street. He was following the map Theo had drawn for him. "She's still living in the one-and-a-half-room apartment they gave her when she arrived in the country after the war. It's in one of those housing developments from the fifties that look like trains. And in Holon, for God's sake! That should tell you what kind of person you're dealing with," Theo had said, raising his head from the piece of paper on which he was drawing. "Anywhere else in the world she could have been God knows how well off. A musician of her caliber! With so many of the leading violinists in the world owing their careers to her. She's still there in Holon of her own free will. Not that she's never had offers, mind you," Theo said wagging his index finger, "but she always said that those things weren't what was important. She didn't have the strength to move. The apartment was good enough, the one she'd had in Budapest was no better. Even though she was already a very well-known violinist before the war, on the brink of an international career. Then came the war, and after the war she never went back to playing. She was in the camps. I don't know where for sure, I think it was Auschwitz. I remember in our lessons, when she sometimes demonstrated something, she played marvelously. She had a daughter by her first husband when she was twenty. The daughter lives in Cleveland. She's also a musician, a singer. Dora Zackheim had three husbands. She outlived them all," said Theo with a laugh. Then he grew serious again, remarking parenthetically that he thought the first one, the father of the daughter, died in the Holocaust, and he resumed his smile when he came to the third: "The last one she dragged with her to Israel. I remember him. He had a mustache, wore a hat, was always on his way outside. She was soon rid of him. But she didn't want to move. During the war she could only dream of ever having one square yard of her own to live in. And so what she had was enough for her, or as she says, everything's already a miracle as it is. You can't suspect her of any affectation when you see the way she lives. As if there really is nothing in the world except for music, her pupils, and maybe a few books. Gabi also used to try to persuade her to move, but nothing doing."

For a few minutes Michael stood before the closed door of the apartment, having climbed up sixty-four steep, narrow steps to the fourth floor. He marveled at a woman her age making this climb every day. Coming from behind the door he heard the sound of a violin. It was the Sarabande from Bach's Second Partita, the first piece of music that no one had introduced him to, that he had learned to love by himself, and that he therefore felt he had actually discovered. He loved it all the more because of this. The music sounded clear, and exquisitely beautiful. He waited for the player to be interrupted so that he could ring the bell. Once or twice, when it seemed to him that the music had indeed stopped, he raised his finger to the doorbell but left it hovering when the music immediately burst out again.

Finally he dared to ring the bell. The music did not stop, but brisk footsteps approached the door, which swung open. A small woman stood before him. Her hair was a dull chestnut brown, as if a tub of dye had been emptied over it. Her eyes—clear and blue in a face almost free of wrinkles—shone with expectation and vitality, as if every opened door held the potential for a great adventure. His first reaction at her unexpectedly youthful appearance—if he hadn't known how old she was he would have taken her for sixty at most—was amazement. When he introduced himself in a whisper—the violin went on playing—she nodded vigorously and held out a gnarled hand. He suddenly realized that because of Theo's awe he had expected a very tall woman with a lined face and pursed lips. It hadn't occurred to him that she would be so tiny, so full of grace and vitality and even radiating a kind of joy. Only now did he notice the slender brown cigar she held between the fingers of her left hand, and he almost smiled as he recalled old Hildesheimer gravely insisting on calling these little cigars by the correct name, cigarillos. She remarked that he was very late, and a good thing, too, she said in a strong Hungarian accent, because the lesson was not yet over. She exhaled a cloud of bluish-white smoke and turned her back to lead him inside. Now that he could see the small hump between her shoulder blades and, under the brown striped dress, the thin legs encased in support bandages, he had no doubt that Dora Zackheim was an eighty-six-year-old woman.

A black metal partition divided the small foyer from the room where a tall, thin adolescent stood before a music stand with his back to them. He continued to play. Dora Zackheim said nothing, only shaking her head and clucking her tongue disapprovingly as she walked back toward the violinist and indicated a chair for Michael next to the table in the foyer. It may have served as a dining table, but at the moment it was covered with a yellow cloth embroidered with blue flowers. On it also were a very old typewriter and a Venetian glass vase containing three red gladiolus. This room suddenly reminded him of the home, in the little town of his childhood, of a family of new immigrants from Poland whose only child, a boy his age named Adam, he was assigned to "adopt," meaning to help him with his homework in a new language. The father was short and thin, with a shifty, fearful look, the mother tall and aristocratic. Adam soon caught up with the rest of the class and soon, no longer needing Michael's help, became its top student. That family, too, had a table with an embroidered cloth and a vase with red flowers in it.

"The left hand is not free enough, is not strong enough. It is too stiff," he heard Dora Zackheim calling in a voice filled with grim disapproval. And then, almost in a shout: "Enough! Enough! Stop!" The boy lowered the violin and turned toward his teacher. "It is a sarabande," she cried angrily. "What about the tempo? Andante and lively at once! From the beginning!"

The boy started to play again, and she tapped several times. "The left hand is not flexible enough today," she scolded. "The fingers are not strong enough." She took the boy's left arm and shook it until his hand swung to and fro. "Not enough!" she complained. "This is a stupid hand. And you haven't done enough work on the second finger. It probably hasn't practiced enough scales today." The boy whispered something. "We don't go by the clock here," she said, glaring at him. "One hour is nothing today. The hand is stiff and the fingers not strong enough. There is no control! It is a piece of wood! And the tone!" She ground the stub of her cigar out in a big glass ashtray and clapped her hands. "What kind of tone is that? Terrible! It is no good at all," she cried in disgust. She looked at the boy, who stood there as if he were used to it, and then she looked at Michael—who quickly averted his eyes—and in a dramatic whisper said: "Last week, at a memorial service for the composer Paul Ben Haim, my pupil Shmulik played this sarabande much, much better." The boy looked at her without saying a word. "Okay," she said, softening, "he is not Jascha Heifetz either, but much better than what you are doing here today." The boy bowed his head as if waiting for something to pass over him. Finally she fell silent, grumbled to herself once more, put her hand on his arm, and said quietly: "I do not like your mood today. You are sad. Is something wrong at school? Are you getting enough fresh air? You have been like this for some time." The boy remained silent and shrugged his shoulders. She drew a yellow metal container toward her, extracted from it a slender little brown cigar, lit it with a big silver lighter, and, putting her head to one side, looked at the boy. He was silent. Gently she removed the violin from his hand. Now he turned and looked at Michael. Open curiosity burned in his blue, almost transparent eyes, over which dark, thick eyebrows met on the bridge of his nose, emphasizing the white skin of the face with the fair down on its cheeks. "Enough for today. You have a long way to travel. Very far," she said, concerned. The boy put his violin in its case. "Is Zichron Yaakov one hour or two?" she asked Michael as the boy headed toward the door. For a moment Michael wondered whether he was ready to give up the hour of solitude he had been looking forward to, but when he saw the boy's friendly smile he couldn't help announcing that he himself was on his way to Beit-Daniel, and if the young man could wait until he finished his talk with Mrs. Zackheim, he would give him a lift.

"That is wonderful, Yuval!" she cried with delight, wrongly stressing the name's first syllable. "That is very good of you," she said to Michael as though Yuval weren't there. "He works too hard, without enough rest. And it is dangerous these days on the buses," she reflected aloud. "You can never tell what is going to happen. These are very difficult times," she said, shaking her head. "And we began at seven o'clock this morning," she said. She took a deep drag on her cigar, coughed, and added in a confidential tone: "Usually I have to say they do not work hard enough. But him? Too much!" She shook her head. "Too much work, too little life. Children his age also have to live. When will he be sixteen again?"

As if he hadn't heard a word, Yuval looked down at the lower shelf of a big brown wooden bookcase covering the wall and pulled out a magazine. "This is the *Musical America* with the article about you!" he said excitedly, turning to the page with photographs of her. "Shmulik told me about it. Can I read it now, Dora?" She waved her hand dismissively. "Nonsense, a lot of nonsense," she muttered. "Some books fell down," she added, and Yuval bent down and picked up three paperbacks.

"It is very nice of you to offer the lift because he comes all the way from Haifa," she explained. "And this is already the third time this week. Every lesson takes a long time. He left home at five o'clock this morning." Yuval blushed.

"But I do have to talk to you privately," said Michael, and he looked at the big sliding door that divided the room in two. It was partly open, and he could see the bed taking up most of the space in the other half.

"We can close the door," she said lightly. "No problem. No sound comes through," she added, and then she cheerfully announced: "First we have time for fruit juice or coffee."

Yuval sat down next to Michael, where he read the magazine while playing with the fringe of the tablecloth. Dora Zackheim went into the kitchen, and from where he sat Michael could see her determined movements in the small rectangular space as she noisily poured and stirred. Yuval raised his face, which looked as if he were strenuously suppressing a burst of laughter. His eyes twinkled. "I wondered if I'd get hot chocolate today," he teased her when she returned carrying a wooden tray with glasses in silver holders, "because I played so badly, and now I see there are even cookies."

She put her head on one side and looked at him critically, but also with quite a bit of warmth. "It is a good thing you are happy now," she rebuked him, "because yesterday and today I worried that you were too sad."

When they finished their snack, Dora Zackheim beckoned to Michael, who hurried after her into the other half of the room. She vainly tugged at the sliding door, which seemed to be rarely used. "Allow me," said Michael, and she moved aside and nodded her thanks. She opened a small window that overlooked a side street and motioned him to sit down on the only chair. She herself sat down on the bed and put her bandaged legs onto a little stool. Her face grew serious. Her eyes were blue and intense.

"I grieve for Gabi," she said without preamble. "Such a great tragedy, a very great tragedy." He wanted to let her go on talking, but she said no more and looked at him with intent expectation, as if she was straining to lift her wrinkled, short-lashed eyelids. Michael had assumed that she would be suspicious of him, maybe frightened, and was surprised at her failure to make any of the usual stereotypical remarks about policemen. Now he thought with satisfaction that his offer to give Yuval a lift to Beit-Daniel had ingratiated him with the old violin teacher.

"I came to ask you about him," said Michael hesitantly. "I'd like you to tell me about him and also about Theo."

"Theo?" she exclaimed with surprise. "Oh, well, Theo. Theo is completely different. Completely," she assured him. "A great talent," she added.

"Who?" asked Michael.

For a moment she seemed confused. "Gabi," she said, and she immediately added: "And Theo, too. But Theo is different."

"In what sense?"

"Gabi was with me from seven to eighteen. Then he went to New York, to Juilliard. Theo stopped studying with me at fourteen or fifteen, and then *presto*!—straight to New York."

"And you've kept in touch with him all these years."

"With Gabi? Of course, all the time. In very close touch. He always wrote to me, phoned, came when he was in Israel. I have many pupils who keep in touch, but Gabi was especially good about it."

"And Theo?"

"Theo is completely different," she insisted. "A great talent, but not for the violin. He did not have enough patience. He had to be pushed to work. Unlike Gabi, who worked too much. You know Theo, yes?"

He nodded. "Is it impossible to be a great violinist and a conductor at the same time?" he asked.

"It is certainly possible," she said, surprised at the question. "A pianist, too. Barenboim, for instance, has developed very well as a pianist, and he is a great conductor, too. No question, it is possible," she said reluctantly. "Sometimes. There are other examples."

"But not Theo?"

"And you? You are a policeman, yes?" A sudden cloud veiled her brow and her eyes. "Terrible, terrible! So much work and so much talent. And suddenly—gone!"

"You liked him very much?"

"Liked!" she said dismissing the word. "Liked? I loved him very much. My pupils," she said, looking out the window, "are children to me. So many hours, so many years. Ah!" she said sorrowfully. "What is there to say?"

He asked her to tell him about Gabriel's personality.

She opened and closed her mouth once or twice, and then she said: "It is impossible to describe a human being. If you know the person it is even more impossible. He began with me at age seven. Even then he was a pedant, a perfectionist, but with very much talent. So serious. Also naive. With ideals. He was special. Quiet but special."

"Was he already interested in early music when he was young?"

"Gabi?"

Michael nodded.

"Yes," she said, hesitating. "Not as much as in recent years, but yes, you could say so. Even as child he liked Baroque music best."

"And Theo?" For a moment he thought that she would say again that Theo was completely different. But she said nothing, only tightened her lips, and suddenly wrinkles he had not seen before appeared on her chin. She thought for a moment, and then she said: "I am thinking of Thomas Mann when I think of Theo and Gabi, because of the great difference between them."

Michael was silent. It seemed to him that she could hear the tape recorder running in his pocket. But she had withdrawn into herself: "Gabriel was more interested in the inner side of things. He, not Theo, was a kind of Adrian Leverkühn."

"Who?" whispered Michael.

"Mann's novel *Doctor Faustus*. You haven't read it?"

"I tried once, a long time ago," he admitted.

"It is a difficult book if you don't know much about music," she said forgivingly. "Do you know much about music?"

"I don't know anything about it," said Michael. "I only love it."

"Loving it is the most important," she assured him. "Not for an artist, not for a musician," she added quickly. "For him love is not enough. Sometimes it even gets in the way. An artist has to be rather cold. An artist has to be almost a monster," she said, smiling. "He has to send everything off to hell, even love, when he is playing. He must play with feeling without feeling it. Do you understand? He needs—how should I say it?—distance, the right distance," she said finally with an expression of relief at having found the satisfactory words. "But for life he needs . . ." she spread out her arms, tilted her head, and examined his face alertly. "You studied at the university?"

He nodded. "History and law. But I haven't graduated yet."

"What kind of history? Art history?"

"No, medieval history mainly," he said uneasily, and his discomfort increased when he saw her nodding politely.

"Is that related to the police?" The question was polite, but it contained a note of surprise.

"That was before . . . before I knew that I was going to join the police force," he tried to explain briefly. It was hard for him to tell how much interest, if any, she retained in him from the moment she realized that he was neither a musician nor knowledgeable about music. If only he could tell her his life story, tell her the combination of circumstances that had caused him to find himself in the police rather than pursuing his historical studies, if he could make her understand that he wasn't just another policeman, that he, too, longed for things of the spirit. He felt a childish need to be valued at his true worth. How could he penetrate the barrier erected by a person who was simply incapable of understanding the point of a life that was not filled with music, and who therefore found him of no interest at all? If only she knew about his relationship with Nita, about how moved he was by her playing, maybe she would value him more. Maybe she would even like him. Something about him would get through to her. He felt much respect for her, and a deep desire for her to feel a little respect for him, too. At the same time he was ashamed of this very desire. He suppressed the urge to explain himself and said nothing.

"What were we talking about? This old head!" she said, tapping her forehead. "Ah yes, *Doctor Faustus*. Yes, there is a composer in it who sells himself to the Devil. Gabriel didn't sell himself, but he felt as if he had sold his soul. He was not a composer, but he always wanted purity, purity—he was crazy for purity. I asked him, when he was still a boy: 'What is so impure about Mendelssohn?' Even Mendelssohn he didn't like." She smiled sadly and lightly slapped her hands on her thighs.

At first he hesitated a bit, but when he looked into her eyes he decided there was nothing to fear. "Did you know that he was a homosexual?"

She didn't even blink. "I thought so. It is too early between twelve and eighteen to know for sure. The person himself doesn't always know at this age. But I always thought he might be. Then he married, and I thought I had been wrong. But as the years went by, when he came to see me, I saw that it was so. I also heard things."

"But you didn't talk to him about it?"

"Never," she said, shaking her head and biting her lip like a young girl.

"And he always came to see you alone?"

"Always alone."

"And he came to see you a few weeks ago?"

"Is it a few weeks already?" she said, surprised. "I cannot remember when exactly. It was very hot. I think it was in August. The beginning of August. Yes, it is a month and a half already since he was here."

"Was there anything special about the visit?"

She seemed to be straining to remember. "No, the father was still alive. Gabi was very excited, very happy. He had a surprise for me, he said, but he would not tell me what it was. He would tell me in a couple of months."

"And there was no hint? Nothing out of the ordinary that he said?"

She thought for a moment, and then she murmured: "He was happy, but there was also a lot of—what is the word?—tension."

"And that's it?"

"Well," she said, seeming to lose patience, "he was here only for an hour. He brought me presents from Europe. He always came with little presents. Chocolate, cheese from Holland, where he had just been, a pretty scarf. I am still happy with LP records," she said with a childlike smile. "I said to him I will go to the next world without such things, and yet he brought me a CD player and some Heifetz CDs. He did not always like Heifetz's playing, but he brought them for me. Sometimes he brought me his own recordings. Bach's B Minor Mass, which he conducted three or four years ago in Jerusalem. I did not like the way he did it, but it was interesting."

"Did you have the feeling that he had come to ask your advice about something? That he was in some sort of crisis?"

She hesitated. "He always came for advice. Before an important concert, when he was working on something new. We would talk for hours, talking and thinking. He was very clever, Gabriel, a true musician. We spoke a lot about interpretation. For example, how to reconstruct Baroque music. We did not always agree."

"You've known him since he was a child," Michael pressed her. "Wasn't there anything special, out of the ordinary, about that last visit?"

"Well," she said with evident uneasiness, and a profound sorrow welled up in her eyes. "Of course we did not know that it was the last visit. We also did not know that he would go before me. And in such a way."

Michael was silent.

Again her face looked strained. "I do not know anymore if it was really that way or if it is because I want to help," she said apologetically. "But maybe . . . I remember that we talked about Vivaldi. He always talked about Vivaldi in recent years. This time even more than usual. And there was something that seemed particularly . . . yes, happy in him about it."

"What about Vivaldi?"

"He asked me," and again she smiled, "if I believed that Vivaldi wrote a requiem." Now she laughed aloud, a brief, low, mirthless laugh. "That is funny," she said.

"What's funny about it?" asked Michael.

"That there could be a requiem by Vivaldi is funny! It is impossible! It is absurd! Do you know Vivaldi's music?"

"Everybody knows Vivaldi. *The Four Seasons*, a lot of concertos you hear all the time. But I don't really know—"

"Vivaldi did not write funeral music. He wrote maybe the most cheerful music in the world, in all of human history. Vivaldi never wrote a requiem. It is a paradox to say that he did. Do you understand?"

"When Gabi said that, did he mean that Vivaldi wrote one that's been lost? Like a lot of Greek tragedies?"

"It is well known," she said dismissively, "that many of his compositions are lost."

"And have some of them been found?" asked Michael alertly.

"They find things all the time," she said. "Including pieces by Vivaldi. A few, and not recently."

"So he asked you if you believed that Vivaldi had written a requiem?"

"Yes," she said with a sigh. "And I laughed. I said: 'I believe it the way I believe Brahms wrote an opera.' The same likelihood."

He felt that if he asked for an explanation of the analogy she would despise him utterly. And so he asked her if she would be willing to listen to a passage from a musical composition and identify it. So that no one would hear anything they shouldn't, he had located in the car the exact spot on the tape, the seconds when Herzl had sung the snatch of music during his conversation with Theo.

She asked to hear it again and again. She frowned. "It is hard to tell what this is," she finally said and fell silent.

"Could it be Baroque?"

She shrugged her shoulders.

"Could it be Vivaldi?"

She hesitated. "It is hard to say. It is not anything I ever heard before. And it is very brief."

"But it could be Vivaldi?"

"It could," she reflected aloud, "but what is so important about it?

It is brief, and the tape does not give us any chords—the harmony—so it is hard to say what it is. It could also be Scarlatti or Corelli. It could even come from a Classical or Romantic piece. It could be anything, maybe even just an ordinary song."

"What do you make of Gabi's question about Vivaldi?"

She pursed her lips in puzzlement. "I really don't understand it," she confessed.

"And there's no requiem by Vivaldi?"

"None," she declared.

"And if one had been found?" he ventured.

"We would know about it," she said dryly. "Such a thing would not be overlooked as if it were nothing."

It seemed to him that he had reached a dead end. "I understand that there was some jealousy between Theo and Gabriel even when they were children."

"And how!"

"Theo was jealous of Gabriel?"

She hesitated. "And vice versa," she finally said. "When they were children—two brothers, two violinists. It was very difficult. And there is a sister, too. Named Nita after a member of the very musical Bentwich family. Do you know any of this?" She glanced at him and he nodded. "Beit-Daniel belonged to the Bentwich family," she explained with satisfaction. "The sister is a good cellist. She also studied at Juilliard. The van Geldens are also a very musical family." She fell silent and withdrew into herself.

"But at a certain stage Theo stopped studying with you. He stopped before Gabriel did."

"He thought I did not appreciate him enough." Her eyes narrowed reflectively. "That is . . . I am not an easy person," she said apologetically.

"He told me that it was you who suggested he stop."

"I do not remember anymore," she apologized again. "It is more than thirty years ago. But it could have happened that way. Why waste time with something that was not working?"

"Was working with Theo a waste of time for you?"

Again she hesitated. "That is a brutal way to say it. A large part of being a good violinist—or any instrumentalist, but maybe it is hardest for violinists—is the matter of character. It is a matter of strength. It is also important what the strength is used for. It is not only talent. There can be much talent and nothing is done with it. Or something bad is done with it. With me pupils do not learn to be international successes. I teach only how to work. International success is not really interesting."

"Mrs. Zackheim," said Michael delicately. "The greatest violinists in the world today studied with you. Names known all over the world."

She looked at him angrily. "Known all over the world?" she seemed to spit the words out, and she breathed heavily. "Fame? Success? What does it matter?" She was silent and she glared at him. "Nonsense!" she suddenly shouted, and she removed her feet from the stool and waved her arms furiously. "It is an accident! They learned to work! To work! And to work more! Day and night, summer and winter. All the rest is nonsense. So someone is famous. It means nothing, nothing!" She breathed hard, composed herself, smiled, and said quietly: "To tell the truth, success does no harm if it does not corrupt. Sometimes it goes to the head. What can you do?" The last words were spoken in a murmur. She averted her eyes and stared at the wall with a sad, stubborn look.

"And Theo?"

"Theo had no patience. He was talented. Very talented. But he immediately wanted to be a conductor. If he was not a violinist like Heifetz, then he would be a conductor like Bernstein. That was Theo. You know, he is also an important analyst of music. I heard him on television talking about Romantic music. It was first class. But Theo, with all his talent, had too little patience, too much appetite for everything. For international fame, for money. Also, I hear, for women," she said smiling, and her eyes twinkled mischievously. "But the strength to work and patience with the violin?" She shook her head and clucked her tongue loudly, rattling her teeth. "You saw Yuval?" Her breathing quieted, subsiding slowly as if she were reminding herself of where she was. Her chest rose and fell as if with a great effort. "He has discipline and patience. The potential of being a great artist. You need a strong ego. Lots of ego. There are people with endless appetite. Never satisfied with what they have. Artists," she said, leaning forward, "need a great appetite, an appetite for perfection and discipline. But they also need a sense of humility."

"And Gabriel had it, this sense of humility?"

"Yes, he did," she said. "Two children in the same family. Such a difference—day and night. You don't know if genetics or psychology is behind it. People are born with personalities, they have them before there can be any outside influence. One like this and the other like that. Gabriel was very close to his father. Theo was the mother's favorite. She was a good pianist."

"Do you know if there was anyone who hated Gabriel?"

Again she shook her head violently. "Certainly not," she said in a choked voice. "You do not know Gabriel. He was hard, but hard on himself. He was also at a new high point of his career in rethinking Baroque music. He was starting a historical performance ensemble in Israel."

"Did you ever meet his companion?"

"Never," she said sadly. "Some pupils talk about their life, family, everything. Gabriel was discreet about his private life. We were very close, but we did not talk about such things. I never even met his wife. Theo, on the other hand, was like a child. Very open. For Theo it is very important that people like him. He has a lot of libido, as they say."

"Wagner," Michael reflected aloud.

"Wagner," she agreed. "I hear Theo wants to make a Bayreuth festival here in Israel. It is maybe a move, I think, also against his father."

"Well," Michael reminded her, "his father is no longer with us."

She sighed and shuddered. "So brutal," she said, "so frightening. For a painting? It is better to have nothing. Look," she spread out her arms, "I lack nothing. But also there is nothing worth stealing here."

"Would you say there was a difficult relationship between Theo and his father?"

"No," she said confidently. "I knew Felix van Gelden for many years. He was a very good father to Theo. And Theo also loved his father, but he was not the favorite. And Theo, if I understand him correctly," she said with hesitation, "did not give way easily. There was tension."

"Could he have killed him?"

"Who?" she asked astonished.

"Theo, his father?"

"Ah!" she dismissed the question contemptuously. "Certainly not! Impossible!" She put her feet back on the stool, and gave him a penetrating look.

"But the business with Wagner," Michael said stubbornly.

"That is complicated. Felix van Gelden was for boycotting Wagner. I do not feel like this, but as long as there are people alive that it disturbs, it is impossible as yet to play Wagner live here. But he was a great composer." A shrewd glint flashed in her eyes as she continued: "And yet the radio boycott has ended. Lately we hear Wagner all the time on the radio. But it is all on the quiet. Theo understands the erotic in Wagner's music, and for him this is very important from the musical point of view. Thomas Mann says that Wagner's anti-Semitism is nonsense of course, but his music is another story. And that is what Theo also believes." Her lips trembled. "After fifty years people forget. This is good and also bad."

"What did Wagner mean to Gabriel?"

"Ah!" She waved her arm and smiled. "For Gabriel, Wagner was not interesting at all. Of course he knows the music, but it means nothing to him. Not only because of his father, but because his path was completely different, toward much earlier music."

"Could you explain this matter of historical performance to me? And Gabriel's obsession with it?"

She nodded energetically. "Certainly, why not?" And then, remembering: "But Yuval is waiting. Do we have time?"

"A little," he said, silencing the anxiety that had been gnawing at him all morning. If only he could phone to make sure that no one had harmed Nita. But to phone now would be to lose the moment with Dora Zackheim, who at any minute could simply stop talking.

She planted her feet on the floor in front of the bed, leaning heavily on her hands to support her thin body. "It is not a simple matter. I will explain it a little, yes?" And not waiting for him to respond, she began to talk.

In the great emptiness that had overwhelmed him and never left him since Shorer had told him what had happened with the baby, Dora Zackheim's stream of words and the need to concentrate on them offered a distraction. From not knowing how Nita was, from the simple longing for her voice, her movements, her presence; from wanting to touch her skin, to embrace her. And the whole time he was uncomfortably aware of how brief and precious Dora Zackheim's time was.

Her old woman's voice was lower now, almost choked, and she went on chain smoking the slender cigars she pulled out one after the other from the yellow metal container with a picture of a panther on it. "You must remember," she said, pulling the hem of her long, narrow brown dress down over the bandages on her legs, "that historical performance began just recently. The rediscovery of Renaissance and Baroque music has already been going on for generations. But when they began to play Baroque music again, in the nineteenth century, they played it in the Romantic fashion of the time." She then spoke of the revival, in various countries early in this century, of the harpsichord, which had been superseded a hundred years before by the newly invented piano. Now performers like Wanda Landowska and later Ralph Kirkpatrick began to play Bach and Handel and Scarlatti on the instrument these composers originally wrote for, and to play it with greater and greater fidelity to what scholarship revealed not only about instrument making but also about tempo and the minutiae of old musical notation and performance of the time. She ground out the stub of her cigar and stared reflectively at her bandaged legs before resuming. "Then, after the Second World War, the world was no longer what it used to be. Nothing from before, nothing that people had been used to could be any good now," she said in a cloud of gray smoke and with a deep, dry cough. "So, when things are very bad, people look to the distant past. And finally in the last twenty years, we have orchestras with period instruments—violins with gut strings, trumpets and horns without valves and pistons, wind instruments that are exact copies of old ones, timpani not with plastic but with animal-skin heads—playing not only Monteverdi and Rameau, Corelli and Vivaldi, Telemann, Bach, and Handel, but even Haydn and Mozart, Beethoven and Schubert. All in proper authentic tempos and with authentic dynamics, and with the authentic number of musicians. And so on," she concluded.

"Would you say that to play Baroque music as it was played originally you have to play it in a smaller, more limited way?" Michael asked, embarrassed.

"That is too simple," she said didactically. "But it seems so. Everything was different then. The halls were small, the instruments were very different. Only after Beethoven were trumpet valves invented."

He felt in his shirt pocket, seized with horror at the thought that the tape recorder might stop working. It was clear to him that he would have to listen several times in order to understand fully what she was saying.

"There are big problems," she went on, "in actually realizing the music."

"In what sense?" he asked, feeling his shirt pocket.

"What, for example," she said with satisfaction, "does Bach mean when he writes a trill? That is, a symbol for a certain sound. The same thing Schubert means?" And she asked sharply: "Do you know what a trill is?"

He shook his head despairingly. She stood up with astonishing agility, opened the door with an effort, and called: "Come here a minute, Yuval, bring the violin."

Yuval stood in the doorway, holding his violin case and looking at her with bewildered expectation. "Play a few bars of something with a trill in it, yes?"

Michael could not identify what he played. She stopped the boy as soon as he had finished playing two rapidly alternating neighboring notes.

"That is a trill." She looked at Yuval as if remembering his existence. "What are you doing in there? Take something to eat if you want."

"I'm reading, it's okay," said Yuval, putting his violin away. "Are you . . ." he hesitated, "are you going to be much longer?" His eyes were downcast.

"No, not very long," Michael reassured him. "Another few minutes, and then we'll be off."

Dora Zackheim sat down on the edge of the bed again. "That was a trill, an ornament, decoration. But you can play it many different ways—slower or faster, beginning on one of the two notes or on the other, and so on. The written notes do not tell you how. And then there are decisions to make, such as whether or not to add ornaments, and if so, all the time or only at repetitions. It is a very complicated matter, Baroque music. There are many arguments these days about how to play it now and what it really sounded like in the past. And even whether you should play it the way it was played then."

"And Gabriel thought it should be," concluded Michael.

She nodded vigorously. "And not only with Baroque music. The authentic music people are now working on Schumann and Berlioz and Brahms, even."

"Did Gabriel do this, too?"

"Yes, sometimes," she said disapprovingly. "Like everything else, it is a matter of degree. How much makes you a fanatic?"

"Was Gabriel a fanatic?"

"Sometimes," she admitted unwillingly. "And sometimes he did things I did not like much at all, like the Bach B Minor Mass with the tiny chorus. On the other hand, Gabi's recording of Vivaldi's Opus 8 Concerti is very fine, you can hear this is Vivaldi and not some kind of Elgar. There is a real Baroque style to it, and it is full of life."

"Was Vivaldi his favorite composer?"

She frowned. "It is impossible to speak in such terms of these things. Did he like Vivaldi better than Bach? No. But this," she said, pulling a compact disc from a shelf and putting her finger on the picture of Gabriel van Gelden adorning the box, "is excellent. It is Vivaldi's wonderful concerto *La tempesta di mare—Storm at Sea*—and you can hear in Gabi's performance, both as conductor and violinist, what lyrical melodies Vivaldi wrote. And how much invention there was in his music, what a magician he was of form as well as of atmosphere." She put the disc down on the bed. For a moment her lips trembled, and she passed a finger under her eyes to wipe away a tear. "I think," she said after some seconds of silence, "that Gabriel was on the right road. If he had not been . . . if he were still alive, he would have become truly authentic, and not at all fanatic. He was sometimes a wonderful combination, deep down, of an artist of the end of this century and an artist of the eighteenth. In him there was a real, beautiful dialogue between periods. You must listen," she said, touching the CD box again, "to *La tempesta di mare*, because the Venetian Antonio Vivaldi knew and wrote about the sea not only with Baroque grandeur but also with a feeling of intimacy with it. Gabi would have created a musical renaissance here in Israel. Gabi still had a lot to say," she said in a dry, forcibly restrained voice.

"What surprise could he have been talking about? Do you think it really had anything to do with Vivaldi?"

"I really do not know. It could be so many things."

"Is Vivaldi so important and significant for you, too?"

"Well, of course," she said, surprised. "All Baroque music is important. But the Classical period—Haydn, Mozart, Beethoven—is equally important. As it was for Gabi, too. It is very hard to know what he meant exactly. For me," she said, smiling with a conspiratorial air, "to tell you the truth, I feel closest to the Romantic period. To the nineteenth century—the concertos of Mendelssohn and Tchaikovsky, as played by a Heifetz or Erica Morini. Do you understand?"

"He never prepared any surprises for you before?"

She smiled and lowered her head. When she lifted her face to him again, it was hard, and her voice was low and cold: "I have lived so many years, seen so many things—everything is a surprise to me. Every visit of Gabi's was a surprise. A good recording or concert by a pupil is a surprise. To wake up in the morning and breathe is a surprise." She looked at her watch, stood up with an effort, and almost hobbled to the sliding door, which Michael hurried to open for her.

13

Et Homo Factus Est

"Three years ago," said Yuval as they were reaching Zichron Yaakov, "I won first prize in an important violin competition. I played the Mendelssohn concerto. At my first lesson after the competition, I played the piece for her. When I finished she said: 'All right, but you know Shlomo Mintz played it much better.' I laughed, and she said: 'What are you laughing about? You should play it as well as he does.' I didn't understand why she had to tell me that Mintz played better. I thought it was silly. I was only thirteen and Mintz had worked on the Mendelssohn for years."

He looked at Michael for a reaction. When none came, he went on: "A lot of people are offended by her. I was never offended. She makes me angry sometimes, but I don't feel insulted. For instance, we were listening to Bach together, and suddenly she said: 'Who plays better, Milstein or you?' If I'd said something critical about Milstein, she'd have cried out and said something like: 'Who do you think you are, how dare you criticize Milstein?' And if I'd said Milstein was wonderful, she'd have shouted: 'What did you say? You shouldn't say that! You have to think that you're wonderful, that you're better than Milstein.' Stuff like that. Obviously," Yuval said, turning to him and smiling innocently, "I can't play like Milstein on the one hand, and at the same time not like everything he does. I have to think really hard about what to say when we listen to something together. Not compromise and not worry about what she wants me to say. Sometimes she seems really out of it," he said and immediately took fright at his own words. "Not because she's old, you shouldn't think that. There's nothing wrong with her head," he assured Michael. "She was always like that, even twenty years ago, old students have told me. She can tell a student one day he played better than another one and the next day tell the other one the opposite. Sometimes you feel she's trying to break you."

"She did tell me that it takes a strong ego to be an artist," murmured Michael as he maneuvered the car into an empty space between two big olive trees and turned off the engine.

"Then I must have one," said Yuval simply as he swung his legs out of the car. "She's never succeeded in breaking me, even though I'm not yet seventeen. She complains about the way I play, I practice from morning till night, and the next time I always play better. And I also know," he said, standing beside the open car door, "that it prepares you to face all kinds of difficulties. There's a lot of pressure and uncertainty in a musical career. I've already felt it. I've already made one recording. I've heard a lot from even great violinists about all the problems, and being with her prepares you for them."

"Do you think she does it consciously, on purpose, to prepare you?" asked Michael as he bent over the lock and opened the door again to make sure that he had switched off the radio transmitter.

"I don't know if she's always aware of what she's doing, if it's all part of some overall plan. Sometimes it can really be destructive. One of her students, a famous violinist, had terrible stage fright because whenever he was on the stage he remembered all her lectures and yelling and lost his confidence."

"So it's hard for you with her," said Michael as they walked toward Beit-Daniel's main building, and he looked down at the pine needles covering the heavy, dry earth and up at the tops of the cypress trees. His eyes came to rest on the familiar van with the Electricity Company's logo on it. He felt a sense of relief knowing that Theo and Nita had already arrived. It seemed to him that here, in this place, no harm could come to her. But he knew that he would be unable to relax until he saw her with his own eyes. There was a stab of pain, too; because if you spread a blanket exactly here, under this pine tree, you could put a baby on it, on her back, so that she could see the sky and the tree. You could lie down next to her and listen to her contented cooing. You could, if only you could.

"It's not too bad," said Yuval. "Without her it will be a lot harder for me. She's the most important person in my life now. If she weren't here . . . I think . . . I'm afraid I won't be able to come to any musical decision without her approval. If she dies I'm sure I'd be completely lost."

"Tell me, Yuval . . ." Michael enjoyed saying the name this boy shared with his son. During the ascent to Zichron Yaakov—maybe because of the view of the sea from the top of the hill on the way to Beit-Daniel—he had imagined for a moment that it was his own Yuval sitting beside him. It was already a week since he had last spoken to him, and the conversation had been brief and frustrating, filled with "How are you?" and "Is everything all right?" These were the only questions he had ever succeeded in asking him, repeating them over and over again during the months of Yuval's wanderings in South America. His postcards were brief and matter-of-fact. He hadn't mentioned the baby. He couldn't tell him something like that in a telephone call whose main purpose was to notify his father that his son still existed. ("Hi, Dad, I'm alive," Yuval had announced in his most recent call. "Alive and well?" asked Michael. "Just fine," Yuval assured him without going into detail. This conversation had taken place with the baby in Michael's arms. Her head rested between his neck and shoulder, and she was snoring lightly into his free ear. He had wanted to say something about her to his son, and now he no longer needed to or had to.) Yuval, he calculated, should be leaving Mexico for the U.S. any day now. But where exactly in the States he would be Michael had no idea.

"Tell me, Yuval, don't you think that's a weakness of hers as a teacher? Can you become independent when you're so dependent on her?"

Quietly, with no hesitation, Yuval said: "I think it'll be all right. I know that when I leave her to go and study abroad, or when I begin to play all over the world, I'll be independent. It'll be hard at the beginning. I talk to her old students, and that's what I see. In time they free themselves from her. . . . It's hard to explain. . . . It's as if you have to take her as she is, with the yelling and everything."

"Apparently education doesn't work without some terror," said Michael, smiling as he opened the brown wooden door to the narrow entrance, and he looked at Yuval ascending the broad steps before him, swinging his violin case.

There was nobody else in the entrance hall of the big building. On a long formica-topped table was a large bowl with a few apples, paper plates with apple cores, and styrofoam cups containing coffee dregs.

"The break is already over," said Yuval. "I've missed the first lecture, but it doesn't matter. I have to run to the other building," he explained, and thanking Michael for the lift, he hurried outside. Michael stood in the entrance hall and looked out the big window at Yuval running down the dirt path until his figure disappeared around a bend. In a narrow corridor leading off the entrance hall, next to the toilets, he found a pay phone. As he rummaged in his pocket for coins, he peeped into a big room. From where he was standing he could only see some wall and a wide brown bookcase, in which a few books and magazines lay scattered. Suddenly he heard the sound of a piano, soon joined by a singing voice and then a cello.

"Where the hell are you?" demanded Balilty angrily at the other end of the line. "Why didn't you take a cell phone? Why did you turn off the radio transmitter? We've really been looking for you!"

"I arrived at Beit-Daniel just this minute. I'm calling from a pay phone," said Michael, examining a photo on the wall beside him of two men standing in front of an orchestra. The caption read that they were Arturo Toscanini and the violinist Bronislaw Hubermann, founder, in 1936, of the Palestine Philharmonic, as it was then known. He stepped back to look again.

"Have you talked to Eli yet? Talk to Eli! And don't take your eyes off them. I told Eli exactly what to tell you. The van Geldens are there with him, and instead of . . ." Balilty swallowed something. "Instead of Dalit I sent someone new, a young guy. Have you seen him?"

"Not yet, I just arrived."

"You'll like him," said Balilty with a chuckle. "He looks a bit like you looked twenty or so years ago. Tall and thin, with those eyes, and full eyebrows, the kind the girls like, only he's not . . . he hasn't . . . he's less . . . he's more ordinary," he finally pronounced. "He's a rookie from a *moshav*, with no bullshit about him. You've got enough people there to keep a constant close watch on them. I don't want your maestro to be alone for a second. Or to have any long conversations with his sister, either."

"Has something new happened?" asked Michael, and he turned his face to either side, thinking he heard footsteps. But there was no one there, and the music had stopped, too. Instead, from a nearby room he heard a loud voice speaking in English.

"A few things have happened. Eli will fill you in. I don't want to go into it now. Not on the phone. But what I can tell you now is that we've found the Canadian woman. She denies being with him on that day. She admits she was in the country, at the Hilton or whatever it's called now, but she wasn't with him. You can get the details from Eli."

"So she actually lied about that, too?"

"Who? Dalit?"

Michael said nothing.

"Yes," said Balilty curtly.

"We'll have to go over everything she touched with a fine-toothed comb," warned Michael.

"It's been done," said Balilty without an argument. "We checked on the Canadian. I spoke to our man in New York myself. Dalit never talked to him at all. She made up the whole thing. I don't want to hear another word about it now. The guy in New York, Shatz, knows you. He says he met you a few years ago. He's sending me a fax of the transcript of the Canadian woman's interrogation, and a cassette of it by express. It'll be here tomorrow."

"It's hard to believe that somebody could . . . that things like that could . . ." muttered Michael. "It seems you can never tell what surprises are waiting for you where people are concerned." Since Balilty remained silent, he added: "We all make mistakes."

"You said it," confirmed Balilty indifferently. "Let's not talk about it anymore. Is there anything else you want to tell me? How was your meeting with the old lady in Holon?"

"Very interesting," said Michael. "And in the light of the facts, yours and mine, I want you to get a search warrant for the concert hall offices. The administrative director's and the artistic director's. And for Theo van Gelden's apartment. Also the papers from Felix van Gelden's safe—in short, everything. All the papers, Gabriel's, too. I want to go through all of them."

"Theo's apartment too? Maybe he'll agree without a warrant, like last time—"

"No, we can't take anything for granted anymore," said Michael severely.

"Because of the Canadian woman?"

"That and some other things. What about the other woman?"

Balilty smacked his lips loudly. "We're being very mysterious today," he said mockingly.

"Only because of the telephone," Michael apologized. "I'll explain as soon as I see you. But what about the other woman? We have to talk to her again too, after—"

"She's already here, waiting outside," Balilty interrupted him. "I may make one or two mistakes, but my brain's still working, you know. Get Eli to bring you up to date on the rest, because over the phone I don't . . ."

Michael missed Balilty's last words because of the young woman in the black pants suit who looked out of the entrance hall into the passageway where he was standing: "Are you the one the two men who came with Mr. van Gelden are waiting for? They told me to expect you."

Into the receiver Michael said only, "I'll phone again," and paying no attention to the stream of new instructions Balilty began to issue, he hung up and turned to the young woman. He smiled back at her, declined the coffee she offered him, accepted a glass of cold water, and followed her into the big room. He made his way between rectangular tables covered with white tablecloths laid for lunch and an open grand piano, a floral armchair, and a footstool standing in the aisle, stumbled over the ragged corner of a Persian carpet, and glanced at the pair of black-bound music scores lying on a brass tray next to the piano. "I'm looking for Miss van Gelden," he said to the young woman.

"She's at Mr. van Gelden's lecture."

He almost asked her if she was sure, but he restrained himself and even lingered at the bookcase, fingering the volumes of an old-looking edition of Voltaire in French and then turning to a pamphlet in Hebrew about the settlers' movement on the West Bank. Then he realized that the young woman was waiting for him. He apologized and followed her out through a side door. They went by a number of empty offices in one of which flies buzzed around an open jar of jam.

Then they went outside and down the path where Yuval had disappeared from view.

Sitting on a white plastic chair on a neglected, yellowing lawn next to the gnarled, crooked trunk of a gray olive tree not far from an old iron bedstead someone had apparently abandoned there, was Eli Bahar. Behind him was a little porch leading to descending stairs, from beyond which came the sound of a piano accompanying a good-size chorus. The young woman in the black pants suit smiled pleasantly, asked if she could leave them to look after themselves from now on, and said that there would be places for them at lunch. It would be best, she said, if they were to go into the lecture separately so as not to disturb it.

"The master class on singing with cello accompaniment has been canceled, and instead Mr. van Gelden and the singers will be working with piano accompanists alone. And, at Mr. van Gelden's request, Educational Television has also been canceled, and there will only be audiotaping," she said as if the two men were among the regular participants. The word "police" was not mentioned. Michael wondered what she had been told about them.

Eli Bahar waited for her to leave, and with a lazy movement pulled up a second plastic chair, set it upright from the upside-down position in which it had been lying on the yellowing grass, and patted the seat. "I waited for you here outside, so we could talk. It's impossible to talk in there, and nobody can do any harm while he's lecturing," said Eli. "There's really no need to sit in there."

Michael sat down and lit a cigarette.

"I've never been here before," muttered Eli. "I didn't even know such a place existed. It's so beautiful here, but look how neglected it is."

Michael tried to remember what Nita had told him about the Bentwich family, and he nodded.

"They began trying to renovate the place a few months ago," Eli explained, "but that young woman, she's the manager here, told me that they had to stop in the middle of it. The workmen put the old windows back in instead of putting in new ones, and look how the plaster's crumbling and so on. It's a shame, no?"

Michael nodded.

There was a patch of sunlight on the lawn in front of him. In his mind's eye, he again spread a flowered blanket on the grass and laid the baby on it on her stomach. Who was carrying her around now? Who was breathing in the fragrance of her cheeks?

"They have concerts and things here. Have you ever been here?"

"Once, a long time ago," murmured Michael, and he turned his head toward Beit-Lillian, the building not far off, where he had been with Avigail more than two years before, on an autumn evening during the Succoth holiday, a few months before they split up. They had played Schubert's *Trout* Quintet. Avigail had stared straight ahead with a blank face half hidden by large sunglasses, immobile, unsmiling, showing no reaction to the music being played inside the hall. She had insisted on staying out on the lawn. It wasn't true, as they said, that sorrow left no marks. The thought of Schubert's joyful piece would always be linked in his mind with Avigail's dejection and sorrow. She had refused to take off the sunglasses even after the sun had set. All that could be seen of her face was the narrowed pretty mouth and the dry lips. Her long white sleeves were fastened at her wrists. During the night, in the inn, she had wept. His love for her was helpless to save her.

"Where's Nita?" he roused himself to ask Eli, who shrugged his shoulders and said: "Inside, in the lecture hall. Her body's inside—where her soul is, God knows. All the way from Jerusalem to Zichron Yaakov her brother talked and she didn't say a word. Just looked out the window. And he never shut his mouth. He talked and talked to her, as if she were listening. I had the feeling she didn't hear a word. Part of the way she slept. It looks to me as if they doped her up completely. And her baby—it wasn't so easy to get her to agree to leave him! I don't understand why she . . . But her brother insisted on her coming along. He put it into her head that they have to be together now. At least till the funeral. Now she's inside. The manager woman told me that they canceled some master class Nita was supposed to give here. And they're waiting for some big star, some singer."

"Balilty said he's sent a young guy here instead of Dalit."

"He's inside. I don't know him, but he seems okay. He's inexperienced, but at least he's not a psychopath. His name's Ya'ir. Tzilla worked with him on the Arbeli case. They've changed that whole team, so they transferred him to us, on Tzilla's recommendation. He doesn't have much experience, but at least he's not a liar. And he hardly says a word."

"I understand that the report on the Canadian woman was an invention, too," said Michael.

"Can you believe it?" Eli sat up in the plastic chair and turned the upper half of his body toward him. "When I said that to you this morning I was just talking, I didn't really believe what I was saying. But by the time I returned to headquarters Balilty was already on the phone with our guy in New York. She hadn't spoken to him at all!"

"Who?"

"Dalit, to our man in New York. She never contacted him at all. Can you understand it?"

"To tell the truth, no. I can't understand it," said Michael thoughtfully. He listened absently to the sound of the chorus rising from the building. Another part of him concentrated on the signs of disintegration on the wall opposite him, where the paint was peeling. There were gray and yellow patches of sunlight on the tall, golden-yellow grass. "You can talk about an illness, but that doesn't explain anything. It isn't necessary or possible to understand everything in the world," he said, reminding himself. "There's a limit."

"And then there's the key. Dalit never talked to Izzy Mashiah at all, and there's no key," said Eli. "He knows nothing about a key to Herzl's apartment. It really freaks me out, but one good thing came out of it."

"Yes? What?"

"Balilty. He's come off his ego trip a bit. He's not so sure anymore that he's the king of the world. And Shorer, who stayed on after you left, he's the one who sent me here. He suspended Dalit on the spot. And he said something to her that sent her packing."

"What, are they just going to let it go?" Michael was scandalized.

"I have no idea what they're going to do about her, and it isn't our business any longer," said Eli Bahar, narrowing his eyes against the sun. "They sent her to Elroi. They always send people to the psychologist first. . . . But they're sure to haul her over the coals. There'll be an inquiry, disciplinary proceedings, and in any event, she's finished. I thought that maybe she had the hots for Theo. Maybe that's why she . . . But if that's the reason, it doesn't explain why she found Herzl and so on. She's not only mad. There's no method to her madness."

"Yes, there is. The wild ambition to succeed. And to sabotage, no matter what. To obtain power and recognition, on the one hand, and to destroy herself and everything else on the other. And even to be punished for it, because she didn't even try to cover her tracks. What did Theo say about the Canadian woman?"

"He hasn't said a word to me about her. He still thinks he's got an unbreakable alibi in her," said Eli with satisfaction. "I leave that to you. We'll be here with him all day, so what's the hurry? He's not going to run away. We can arrest him tomorrow."

"We don't have enough on him to arrest him. Not yet. First of all, there's still the other woman. Second, we don't have a motive. It's not clear why, even if we say it's for the inheritance, why precisely him and why precisely now. I always like to wrap things up tightly before making an arrest. If possible."

Eli Bahar made a face. "I've never agreed with you about that. There always comes a moment when you drag things out too much. I've always told you that. Why can't you arrest him and release him later if we're wrong?"

"And I've always explained to you that there's something to be gained by not arresting at this stage. He still trusts us, and I haven't got enough from him yet," contended Michael. "There are a lot of things we haven't wrapped up yet. We don't even know where the string comes from—"

"There are things that are impossible to wrap up," said Eli Bahar philosophically. "Just as there are leads that don't take you anywhere, that only waste your time. Like with that painting and all the experts Balilty had on it. He investigated the entire underworld, and it didn't lead anywhere! Then it's found in a kitchen cabinet behind the cocoa. And the whole thing might be—we don't even know that for sure—a red herring. And Balilty was stuck for weeks with experts from here and there. Is there anything new at your end?"

"Maybe," said Michael, and he hesitated. "But it's still so up in the air, and so complicated and maybe even absurd, that it's better not to discuss it yet."

Eli Bahar maintained an expectant silence for a few seconds. His eyes followed Michael's hand as he ground out his cigarette at the edge of the lawn, stood up, and went over to the wastebasket at the building entrance.

"As you like," he said at last, rather sulkily. "When are you going to confront him about the Canadian woman?"

"Later," said Michael. "He's giving a lecture now, isn't he?"

"Yes, for about another hour, and then there's lunch. Maybe that would be a good time . . ." he said hopefully.

"Maybe," Michael agreed. "I want to go inside. Are you staying out here?"

"There's nothing for me in there," said Eli glumly. "I'll wait here. I had a long night." He put on a pair of sunglasses. "Wake me up if I fall asleep."

"Hand me a fresh cassette. I've pretty much filled up the one in my recorder," said Michael.

He opened the door into a room smaller than he had expected. Exactly across from him, at the other side of it, in front of French windows opening onto a flagstone porch, sat Nita in a deep, shabby brocade armchair. Her limp body slumped into the chair as if it would be an enormous effort to raise her limbs up again. Her eyes met his. He felt a great sense of relief at seeing her alive. A warm wave of feeling overcame him, a great urge to touch her, to hear her voice, to be at her side. For a brief moment she looked at him, her eyes dull and expressionless. A flicker of shock passed over their blue-green depths, and then they narrowed and almost closed. Her face was very pale. She didn't move. And not only did she not smile at him, but she also tightened her lips and turned her head to look at her brother. There were about fifteen young musicians, boys and girls, in the room, all with their eyes fixed eagerly on Theo, who was sitting in front of them on the bench at an open baby grand piano, his legs crossed, and talking. When Michael closed the door behind him and sat down on one of the chairs at the back of the room, Theo looked at him, surprised, nodded his head, and went on speaking with the same relaxed voice as before. Maybe the hint of a blush crept onto his cheeks. His eyes glittered, their deep green emphasized by the dark circles beneath. He folded his hands but could not hide their trembling. He leaned against the piano. Instrument cases lay at the feet of some of the youngsters. Yuval was sitting not far from Nita next to a swarthy young man who was sitting erect with his arms crossed, and who, Michael was sure, was the new man on the team.

"A precise definition of all the aspects of the Classical style—that is, the style brought to its maturity by Haydn and Mozart," said Theo with a small, forced smile, "is impossible." The young faces looked at him with anxious expectation. The boy sitting close to the piano on its other side monitored the big tape recorder on the floor next to him.

Michael looked at the slats of the torn blind beside the French windows and at the vestiges of masking tape, remnants of the Gulf War, still stuck to the glass.

"Because, like everything else," said Theo reflectively as he looked outside, "such a definition would not be restricted to the music alone, but finally also to its social surroundings—the way people, rich and poor, lived from day to day. Just as it's impossible to understand rock music without knowing about the world we live in, it's impossible fully to understand the Classical style in music without a sense of the context."

Michael looked at Yuval's face. The boy was listening intently as he leaned forward on his hard chair. A single sunbeam lit up the fair down on his cheek and then glinted on the silver flute lying in the lap of a girl playing with a lock of her straight hair. Nita's eyes were closed. Michael felt that she was bearing a grudge against him, that she was ostracizing him, that she regarded him as her enemy.

"We're dealing here, as you already know, with the second half, more or less, of the eighteenth century," said Theo, "and the Classical style seems to be the most orderly, most restrained musical style that has ever existed. To us, in this century of ours, it sounds mainly charming," he said sardonically. "Sometimes too charming. Charming unto idiocy." He suddenly started to whistle the beginning of *Eine kleine Nachtmusik*, broke off, and said: "Sometimes we ask ourselves: What are they so happy about?" Again he whistled sharply and clearly. "There's an incomprehensible gaiety here, and where it isn't cheerful, there's a beauty that can sound exaggerated, a beauty too beautiful. I know people who abhor the Classical style because this makes it seem false, like a museum of wallpaper from a world that is dead and gone."

Yuval smiled at these words, and the girl with the flute burst into loud laughter, which stopped abruptly. Michael had noticed the ingenuous and somewhat theatrical tone with which Theo spoke, as if he were constructing a convincing argument only in order to refute it.

"The Classical style in music is seen as having emerged after the Baroque period, and that it relates to the Baroque as if it came into being in order to oppose it, to develop in confrontation with it, making the transition from polyphony and complex contrapuntal works to the simpler world of homophony. And the most important form," he said, pausing to rake his hand through his hair, as if making an effort to concentrate, "perfected in the Classical period is sonata form. But you already know all this, and so I intend to talk about an intrinsic matter, about style itself," said Theo, taking off his glasses, rubbing his eyes, and then putting the glasses down on the piano. "What kind of human metaphor, what state of mind, what kind of feeling was expressed by Classical music? That is our ultimate question. The Romantics considered the music of the Classical period abstract music. But when we listen to it today, the first question that comes into our minds, if we're honest about it, is: Is it sad or happy? We know that minor keys, then as now, were regarded as expressing sadness, and *that* is no longer abstract."

He paused, as if awaiting confirmation. The youngsters' faces looked thoughtful, and some nodded in agreement. He put on his glasses again. "There is, however, a way to discover what feelings composers thought they were expressing in their music, and that is to examine what music they wrote when they were setting words to it. Even single words. If we look at masses and requiem masses composed from late medieval times down to the present day, we find that the very same Latin words are set to very different kinds of music, and this, of course, reflects the very different worlds in which these works came into being. Every mass opens with a prayer for mercy, the Kyrie, then comes the Gloria, and after these two comes the all-important central section, the Credo." The audience of young people sat still, in respectful and suspenseful silence.

"The Credo is the central statement of the core of Catholic Christian faith," Theo explained. "The text begins with an affirmation of belief in one God but also—and this may sound absurd to us—in the two other persons of the Trinity: Jesus Christ, the son of God, and the Holy Ghost, who incarnated Jesus through the Virgin Mary. Jesus descended from heaven for our salvation, and he was crucified and resurrected from the dead. He ascended to heaven and sits at the right hand of God. This is what the Credo of every mass in every century says."

A freckled young man smiled. Nita clasped her hands and stared at a point in the distance. It seemed to Michael that she was making every effort to avoid his eyes, and for a moment he thought that she was about to get up and leave the room. What harm have I done you? he pleaded with his eyes, as if he were trying to clear a path to her, but her eyes would not meet his. He went on looking at her. Not that he didn't know what he had done to her. He knew very well that he had suddenly disappeared from her house, and that, just as suddenly, the baby girl had disappeared, too. And that since yesterday he hadn't spoken to her. But somehow he believed, for a moment he was even sure, or maybe only hopeful, that she would have faith in him. Enough faith to understand that he had no alternative, that in order to remain part of the investigation he had to keep away from her. He had thought that the estrangement between them would only be temporary, that it would end in a few days. But now that he had seen her, he realized that he hadn't allowed himself to think it through. He had considered neither the situation nor her possible reactions. He hadn't taken into account what her immediate response to the fact of his absence would be, preferring to cling to a vague conviction that she would understand what was at stake as if she could read his mind, as if she could understand on her own everything there was to understand.

Suddenly she looked at him, and a faint blush spread over her pale cheeks. As if against her will something approaching a smile appeared at the corners of her lips. Maybe he only imagined that he saw a spark of understanding in her eyes, and maybe even a kind of relief that he was here now.

Theo went over to the stereo system on a shelf in front of a red brick wall next to a fireplace and a pile of logs, took a compact disc out of the player, and examined it closely. "What I want to do now," he said absently as he put the disc back into the player, "is to compare Mozart's setting of a passage we heard a few minutes ago in the Credo of Bach's B Minor Mass, the words *Et homo factus est*—'And was made man.' And in particular to compare how the word 'man' is set by each composer. With that, intentionally or not, each composer expressed what it meant to him to be a man, and what's more," Theo waved an arm enthusiastically, "with their settings of this one word they also show they think about what happened to God when he turned into a man, whether it was something bad or good."

Michael noticed Yuval's half-open mouth and the gaze fixed on Theo's face.

"The more interesting setting, from this point of view, is Mozart's. Listen to the *Et incarnatus est* of his C Minor Mass, K.427, written in the early 1780s, after he had left Salzburg for Vienna and began working freelance." He pressed the button and the room was filled with the sounds of a soprano and a flute, oboe, and bassoon. To Michael it seemed that everyone was holding their breath. As Theo sat down to listen demonstratively, the new man sent by headquarters kept his eyes on him as if by magnetic attraction.

"How would you describe the mood of this passage?" asked Theo with curiosity after he stopped the music. Michael listened absentmindedly to the answers, which dwelled, among other things, on the beauty and optimism in the flute part. He found himself listening proudly and attentively when Yuval said that for him the soprano, especially in this performance, which he had never heard before, was "the essence of purity." He went on to say that "this means that, for Mozart, man is something pure and beautiful, a source of hopefulness, especially if we compare it to Bach's setting."

Theo seemed surprised, but he hastened to say: "Not all of the Mozart Mass is like this." He waved his index finger admonishingly. "It is also a harsh and bitter piece. See the very opening, for instance. In the *Et incarnatus est* the style is really different." Theo's voice rose dramatically and fell to almost a whisper as he added: "In Bach's Mass that and the *Crucifixus* are very slow." He paused as if to give them time to remember. "That is how Bach composed the passage where God becomes man."

Michael's eyes strayed from the ancient, gnarled olive tree whose gray leaves touched the window to a blue violin case lying not far from Nita's feet, which rested closely together on the floor.

"In Bach the incarnation is a cause for mourning," said Yuval loudly. Theo smiled. He praised Yuval's observation, and then began, again with the tone of a storyteller, to explain: "What produces the feeling of grief, and also confirms that this was Bach's intention, is the presence of a *basso ostinato* in the style of a lament. The lament," he continued with somewhat strained enthusiasm, "which developed in Italy over a period of three hundred years, is an imitation of weeping. From the Renaissance to the Romantic period, opera heroes and heroines die in this style. When Bach thinks of God coming down to earth—he thinks of it as an a priori bad thing. For him, when the Holy Spirit descends, it keeps on going deeper and deeper down, creating a metaphor in sound for something very dangerous happening to the Deity. For Bach the incarnation is the immediate prelude to the Crucifixion. For him *Et homo factus* leads straight to the Crucifixion. In his eyes the descent of God to the world is in itself the cause of the Crucifixion. The moment in which God becomes man is connected to catastrophe, lamentation, tragedy. In Haydn's *Nelson* Mass, you'll remember, the *Et incarnatus est* is also given to a soloist. The word 'man' is heard," his voice rose almost to a shout, "but everyone has his own choice of man, and Mozart chooses a soprano, a woman."

Again Theo paused before the eyes gazing at him with undisguised admiration, and he smiled.

"A Romantic would say that the kind of virtuoso music Mozart gives his soloist here is completely unsuited to the text. It sounds like some kind of multiple-instrument concerto. But look at what kind of a concerto blossoms here at the words 'and was made man.'" Theo told them that they would now hear the passage again, and as he pressed the buttons he declaimed the words *Et incarnatus est de Spiritu Sancto ex Maria Virgine, et homo factus est.* He held his hand up in the air and exhorted them: "And now listen, here begins the *ho . . . mo,* stretched out in a slow coloratura, and finishing with the words *factus est.* And after that the opening words are repeated. Right?"

Without waiting for a reply, he pressed the button, the passage was heard again, and before it ended was switched off. "And then, after the chord under the sustained *fa-* of *factus,* comes the astonishing, concertolike cadenza for the soprano, accompanied by the three wind instruments. Do you understand what this means?"

There was silence in the room. An embarrassed silence, because it was clear that the audience did not know what it meant. The young new detective relaxed his arms and recrossed them on his chest. Nita's eyes were closed, and her face was immobile. She looked as if she were sleeping.

"From the moment the word 'man' is uttered," said Theo with undisguised excitement, "the music takes on an ideal form, becomes a kind of idea of beauty. There are all kinds of echoes here, symmetries, everything that Mozart knew. This passage is one of the most distilled examples of the beauty of the Classical style. Mozart sees the descent of the Holy Spirit as liberating the world, unlike Bach, who sees the descent as activating it. Either way, man is the solution, as it were, to the Divine mystery."

Nita's eyes opened. She gave Theo a look of concentrated sharpness, as if she was wondering about something she had just remembered. As if he felt her look and wanted to distract her, Theo raised his voice, stressing every word: "The idea of music as beauty is contained in the word 'man' here, not architectonic beauty but the ways in which types of beauty are symbols of the activities of life. The syllable *fa* here is both the F-major key of the aria and the Italian verb for 'to do,' or 'to make.' Do you remember where else Mozart used this *fa*?"

Not waiting for an answer, he hurried on: "At the end of the Catalogue Aria in *Don Giovanni*. Do you remember what Leporello says there? He sings: *Voi sapete quel che fa*—meaning, 'You know what he did.' Meaning, if you'll forgive the expression, 'He fucked.' So there you have the full sense of the way in which Mozart relates to *fa*, and this sense he introduces into the C Minor Mass in another context: conception, birth, becoming man, incarnation. He sees the transformation of God into human as entry into the most beautiful thing there is. And for its sake he employs the human voice and the instruments into a kind of soap bubble of what seems to him, and not only him, the perfect idea of the beautiful. That is what Mozart did here."

Perhaps it was the words "conception" and "birth" that brought back the stab of pain, thought Michael as he placed his hand on his chest and tried to imagine where the baby was now, who was feeding her. He interrupted himself when he heard a kind of collective sigh, as if the audience had let out its breath all at once. No one spoke, but the tension in the room again diminished for a moment. Theo waited and looked around. His eyes gleamed when they met Michael's. Then he turned his head to Nita, who looked like a wax figure.

How could she sit there in the same position for so long, Michael wondered. But for an occasional blink—and he had hardly taken his eyes off her—he would have thought she had lost consciousness. He was certain now, as she opened her eyes wide and he saw how enlarged her pupils were, that she was heavily sedated.

What harm have I done you? he said bitterly to himself. Why can't you understand that this is the way things have to be for now? But he knew that he would not ask her these questions today.

"Now I want to turn to something that may sound strange, but in the end you'll see that it's relevant. It's about the slow movements in Classical-period compositions. Some people feel like falling asleep during the passages when the music becomes slow and wearying; that, by the way, is how Haydn could write a *Surprise* Symphony. In other words, at certain moments some people fall asleep. Classical-period composers often begin their andantes and adagios with a marvelous melody, second and third themes follow, and then there suddenly arises from the background a note that is repeated over and over in a literally monotonous manner that is perceived as wearying."

The girl with the flute giggled. "Here's Mozart in the A Minor Piano Sonata. Let's listen to it for a while." He turned around and picked up a CD.

"Who's playing?" asked the girl. "Murray Perahia," said Theo, and he pressed the button. "The slow movement." After a few minutes he halted the music, saying, "Let's stop here, where the repeated notes begin yet again, along with a trill."

He put the CD back in its box and picked up another. "This time, the andante of Mozart's *Haffner Symphony,*" he said, and after a while: "Here they are, the same obsessively repeated notes." Again the music was turned off. "There's a vast number of slow movements whose central internal episode is built up against the background of a single repeated note that acts as a kind of tonal horizon. I've tried for a long time without success," confessed Theo, "to find another musical style, among any of the world's traditions, that uses repeated notes in this way. I've never found one. It exists only in the Classical style, and often in rapid movements as well." The youthful musicians all looked as if they, too, were searching their memories. Someone shifted in his seat, the girl with the flute frowned, Yuval put his finger to his lip. They were wondering if Theo was right.

After a pause he went on: "Anyone who plays an instrument, as you all do, knows how difficult it is to properly repeat one note again and again. And what is this monotone anyway? Is it a line? Is it a horizon? It isn't isolated, because it has a rhythm and a tempo, but it isn't much of a melody because the next note is its twin. And it isn't a pedal point, which is its congealed cousin. It's a place of stillness in the very center of the work. If we miss that," he said, his voice again rising dramatically, "we fall asleep. But when we feel it, we find ourselves at a point of minimal being, confronting this monotone, and I think . . ." and again he paused for a while, "I think that it's intimately connected with the body's pulse."

Yuval opened his mouth.

"I really do think that it's directly connected with heartbeat," Theo added. Yuval sat up straight in his chair, very agitated.

"From the end of the Renaissance to Mozart's father's time," announced Theo, "many musicians set andante tempo by the human pulse—seventy-two beats per minute."

A kind of relief flooded Michael for a moment, as he remembered Dora Zackheim talking about Baroque tempo. Suddenly the words sounded familiar to him, but he was surprised that it was Theo saying them. Surely, Michael thought, it would have been more fitting for him to be giving a lecture about Wagner. It was surprising to hear him talking of Baroque music with such respect and passion. Dora Zackheim had spoken of his brilliance as a music theoretician, but Michael had somehow failed to take her seriously. "The pulse defines the tempo of this line of notes, this thread of life! They dared to construct entire movements with accompaniments based on repetition," cried Theo. He sat down again on the piano bench.

"In the Classical period, music for the first time is no longer abstract. It is now exclusively an activity of life itself! Think about Zerlina in *Don Giovanni*, how she puts Masetto's hand on her breast and in the accompaniment you hear precisely the heart and its rhythm. Think about it! Do you know that Mozart cribbed this? This isn't my idea," said Theo modestly. "H. C. Robbins Landon discovered that Mozart got it from Haydn, who, by the way, wrote some wonderful operas." He suddenly cleared his throat, as if he were about to choke. "One of them . . . excuse me," he said, and he coughed lengthily, "*Il Mondo della luna*, contains many passages built on the pulse beat, because one of the characters has a heart attack in the finale, accompanied by a series of scales. It isn't always the heart in the sense of a pump," he said, smiling, "it's pulses that might be called molecules of the soul."

Michael wondered if he should believe this stuff about molecules of the soul, and, overall, he wondered how, if his intuitions about Theo were correct, he could possibly say the things he was saying here today. In any event, he said to himself as Theo asked the audience to listen again to Mozart's A Minor Sonata, the things he had said about man were . . .

His train of thought was interrupted when Theo, bending over the CD player, said: "Classical-period music is the first music that takes place entirely within the 'soul.' And the heart, the pulse, the most basic activity of life, is the hidden, constant voice of this music, the music that gave the beat such a dominant place as to grant it the status of an independent voice. Where this happens is the 'divine' place, and therefore it puts some listeners to sleep." Now he put the CD down and stood up again.

"They become giddy because this place is in essence mystical, as in a kind of return to the womb they suddenly hear their mother's beating heart, and on it depends the whole world, all of sounding existence. When Haydn and Mozart come to this ta-ta-ta-ta"—Theo pronounced the syllables with deliberate dullness—"to this apparent monotony, they are at the very core of their style, the focal point of the myth of Classical music. From then on it becomes clear that music is no longer an image of the cosmic order, as in Bach, but a matter of mind and mood."

Theo pressed a button, and Nita closed her eyes again. A vertical line appeared between her eyebrows. Had Theo really invented all these things, or were they accepted truths? How lucky these gifted youngsters were, Michael thought with a pang, to really understand, to have it all at their fingertips, while he . . . Everyone was silent when the music stopped. And slowly they rose to their feet. Some clapped, others went up to Theo. Michael pricked up his ears, but he only managed to catch the name Wagner and a few words of Theo's: "Of course not in *The Flying Dutchman*. . . ." As soon as he saw Michael looking at him he averted his face and lowered his voice. The boy at the tape recorder switched it off. The young man with his arms crossed sitting between Yuval and Nita still didn't move. Nita, too, remained seated. Michael stood up, approached her, bent over her, and put his hand on her arm. She opened her eyes. The pupils were really dilated. Something flickered in the eyes of the young police detective.

"They took her away yesterday," said Nita in a flat, hollow voice, as if the act of speaking was difficult for her. "And you disappeared, too."

The young detective stood up. Suddenly Michael felt that it was not Theo and Nita the man had been sent to watch, but he himself, that he was not to be left alone with Nita. Along with the rage that surged up in him there was also a feeling of shame. He clenched his teeth, furious with the young man and with the procedures responsible for this humiliation. He almost demanded to know exactly what the man's instructions were when he sensed with his body that the man was too close, that he was listening to every word they were saying.

"That was an amazing lecture," he said to Nita, just to say something. Her lips parted and closed. "No? Wasn't it amazing?"

She shrugged her shoulders. "Not to me. It was nothing new," she said in a heavy, tired voice. "I've often heard it before."

"From Theo?" asked Michael, and as if to remind himself that they were brother and sister: "At home?"

"Not only from Theo. From his arguments with Gabi," said Nita haltingly. "He worked all that stuff out in those quarrels. Part of it they agreed on. I used to love listening to them," she mumbled and immediately put her hand over her mouth and looked at the young detective standing silently near them.

Michael looked at her steadily, hoping that he could convey with his eyes what he could not say now in words. He wanted to tell her that he was under orders, that it wasn't by his choice. He wanted to ask her to trust him. He wanted to remind her of moments they had shared. Even to tell her about the baby, and about his efforts to renounce her because it was, however cruel to himself, the right thing to do for the little girl. And about the other times, when he had been determined to fight for her. But the detective did not move away, and so all Michael said, in a very low voice, was "Nita," and he pressed her arm and looked into her eyes. It seemed to him that for a second they were illuminated by a great, gray pain, that she knew exactly what he felt, that she felt as he did, that she understood everything. Then he dared to give her a questioning look, asking for confirmation with his eyes. And she nodded. Very slowly she lowered her head, raised it, and then lowered it again.

At lunch the three policemen sat at a separate table. It was only then that Eli formally introduced him to Sergeant Ya'ir. They spoke little. Michael sat in a chair with his back to the red bougainvillea creeping around the window, a portrait of Lillian Bentwich on the wall beside him. At a nearby table sat Theo and Nita with a tall man with flushed cheeks and wavy, graying fair hair whose horn-rimmed glasses glinted so as to hide his eyes, but whose halting English, loud voice, and booming laughter they could hear very well. Having once seen his photograph, on an old record jacket, Michael had no doubt that this man, who had embraced Nita and stroked her curly head when she entered the main building, and who had warmly shaken Theo's hand, was Johann Schenk.

Since they barely spoke—inhibited by the presence of the talented youngsters seated at the tables surrounding them—Sergeant Ya'ir busied himself with his food, helping himself to more of the boiled cabbage and willingly accepting a second portion of the dried-out turkey. And since Eli looked tired, and seemed preoccupied by questions raised by what he called the team's division of authority, about which he muttered to himself from time to time, Michael was free to eavesdrop on what was being said by Theo and Nita and the great singer Johann Schenk himself. It was not Schenk on the recording of *Die Winterreise* Becky Pomeranz had sent to him twenty-three years ago when Yuval was born. But hearing the work on the new CD he had bought himself a few years ago, he had been captivated by this man's warm, thrilling, and occasionally frightening voice, especially in the last, desolate song.

A few minutes passed before Michael grasped that Johann Schenk was talking about a production of *Don Giovanni* in Salzburg. "The Commendatore's head is smashed to bits!" he cried out loudly and with a bellow of laughter. "And Donna Elvira! What he did to Elvira!" Here he sketched a swaying figure in the air with his big arms to depict the singer floating over the stage tied to a trapeze. Then he bent over his soup, polished it off, and went on talking. Now Michael heard him mention the city of Dresden and the STASI, the East German secret police, and some people's names. Finally Michael heard him saying loudly that he had demanded to see his own secret police file.

"Why?" asked Theo, also very loudly. "Why did you want to know? Weren't you afraid of what you might find there?"

Johann Schenk banged his fork on the edge of the table, his face grew very flushed, and in the big room, where everyone else was talking in whispers, the answer was clearly heard. He could no longer live without knowing, he cried, which of his friends had betrayed him. He wanted to know exactly what was there about him in the STASI files, he said in his booming voice, his eyes on the dessert tray of Jell-O gleaming redly in small glass dishes. Theo bent over and whispered something. Johann Schenk looked with alarm at the policemen's table. Nita pushed away her dessert. She hasn't tasted a thing, thought Michael as he saw her stretch out a trembling hand for the water pitcher, and he wondered angrily how he could have allowed her to be here today.

"Because there was nothing you could do about it. That's what she wanted, and the funeral won't be till the day after tomorrow," said Eli. Only then did Michael realize that he had unwittingly spoken aloud. He looked around apprehensively. Eli studied his face. "How long is it going to take here today?" he asked.

"I have to be alone in the room with them when Theo and Nita are working with the singer," Michael whispered urgently. "And I have to talk to this Johann Schenk by myself." He looked out of the corner of his eye at Ya'ir, who maintained his silence.

"As far as I'm concerned it's okay," muttered Eli uncomfortably. "But you'd better talk to Balilty first, because Shorer told us, and especially him," he said, jerking his head in Ya'ir's direction, "that at least two of us have to be with them all the time," he said apologetically with increasing discomfort. He stood up heavily, went over to the counter, and came back to the table with a pitcher of water and sat down again. So uncomfortable did he appear, his torso twisted toward the grand piano in the corner of the room in order to avoid looking at Michael, that Michael felt sorry for him and fell silent himself and stared at the side door and at the portrait of Lillian Bentwich.

"Don't worry, I'll phone him now," he finally said. He rose to his feet. "I myself don't want Nita to be left alone for a second." Michael saw Johann Schenk's side glance as he passed his table, wondering what Theo had told him. And then he reminded himself that a policeman nearby was enough to alarm a former citizen of the German Democratic Republic.

And it was apparently this deep fear, from which Johann Schenk could not free himself, that was the main reason for his outburst at the beginning of the master class. Only a young pianist and Theo and Nita were present in Beit-Lillian's big hall. While the others enjoyed a post-lunch rest period, the pianist was working on lieder accompaniment with the great singer. Nita sat at the back of the hall, in the right-hand corner. The interior of the hall was unlit, in contrast to the bright light shining on the lawn outside the open doors, where Michael stood with Eli Bahar and Sergeant Ya'ir. Theo sat at the piano, turning pages for the pianist, a boy of about Yuval the violinist's age, who was starting to play *Die Winterreise*.

For some minutes he repeated the opening chords again and again, the great baritone stopping each time to explain something. Theo spoke to him, too—it was impossible to hear their comments from outside the hall, only the echoes of their voices and the sound of the piano—and finally they allowed him to play the chords without interference.

Johann Schenk began to sing.

Michael stood on the lawn listening. "A stranger I came here, / And a stranger I shall leave it," the words echoed inside him. "I cannot plan my journey, / Nor can I choose the time, / I alone must show myself / The way in this night's darkness." It was broad daylight outside. The yellow sun glared on the grass, and inside the hall was shrouded in a heavy gloom. Theo turned the page quickly.

"I pass through the door . . . /I write and hang a little note on it: 'Good night,' / So you will know I thought of you," sang the great baritone standing next to the piano and looking at the young pianist. He paused for a moment.

Michael felt that he was singing for him alone. And standing there on the lawn outside the hall, he felt a cold hand clutching at his heart and tightening its grip on it. He felt drawn to the darkness inside and entered the hall. And since Johann Schenk was facing the piano, he did not notice Michael as he sang of the frozen tears. Only after the lament on the tears flowing from the burning heart, after singing the words "the whole winter's ice," did he pause, take an ironed handkerchief from his pocket, wipe his face, and turn around.

When he began to shout, the boy, alarmed, stopped playing. Theo spread out his arms. "Out of the question!" shouted the great man in his German-accented English. "Out of the question!" he upbraided Theo. Then he turned to Nita. "Them I did not invite and with them I will not sing. This is a private matter!" he shouted, banging on the side of the piano. "This is not a concert, and it is out of the question that people from outside, and *Polizei*"—the German word rang out amid the awkward English—"are present here!"

Michael retreated, breathless and filled with consternation, to the corner of the lawn where Eli Bahar and Sergeant Ya'ir were standing. He composed his features and calmed his now noisy breathing. At that moment he felt as if there was nothing to him but a curse. As if his very existence, here on the lawn, represented brute force and oppression, besmirching the music. None of them, except for Nita, knew how much he loved *Die Winterreise*. And in the eyes of the great artist the presence of a policeman at the doorway of the hall was a desecration.

Minutes passed before the baritone's singing voice was heard again, and over half an hour before Johann Schenk finished the penultimate song of the cycle. Then there was silence.

When Michael approached the doorway again, he heard him explaining to Nita, who had not moved from her place, that he would not sing the last song, *"Der Leiermann,"* now, because if he did he would be unable to sing it again at the concert that evening. This song, said Johann Schenk—who now was speaking to the accompanist—should never be sung more than once a week. After it there could only be silence.

But it was precisely this song, the saddest of all, the song of the living dead man, that Michael wanted to hear now in the darkness of the hall. There was something absolutely right about it for the way he felt today. About the chilling despair and renunciation of the sad, almost frozen voice with which the protagonist asks the old organ-grinder to accompany his song. How empty his own arms were now. Someone else, he thought, is now stroking my baby's smooth skin. But then, defeated, he reflected: My baby? Why mine? How mine?

Michael bravely reentered the hall. To his astonishment the singer descended rapidly from the wooden podium, came up to him, and began to apologize.

"A rehearsal is a very intimate thing," he said, embarrassed. "And for me this lesson with a young artist was a kind of rehearsal. Later there will be a master class, but that will be for television and not a problem. But this time!" And again he mentioned that no one had prepared him for the presence of police while he was singing, although he should have known, he said with a sigh, because of what had happened to Gabriel van Gelden. He had heard the details that morning. "What a terrible tragedy!" And now he was perfectly willing to devote a few minutes of his break to the police, if he could be of any assistance. The late Mr. van Gelden was so talented, and he had seen him not long ago in Amsterdam.

Not far from Beit-Lillian, in a corner from which the tiled roof of a tiny house was visible, Michael asked Johann Schenk if Gabi had asked him to take part in performing a Baroque work. The man looked completely taken aback, and also frightened, with the characteristic fear of contact with the authorities felt by people who had grown up under a totalitarian regime. Again he wiped his broad face with his handkerchief, cleared his throat, and said that Gabriel van Gelden had indeed, over a month ago, at their last meeting, shown him two pages, written out in a modern hand, of a work unfamiliar to him. Although Gabriel had refused to say what and by whom it was, he assured him that it was a Baroque masterpiece of inestimable importance. The part was written for a bass, but since there were no really serious basses today, he had offered it to him, even though Schenk was a baritone. Now he asked how Michael knew about it, since its existence was so strictly confidential that he had even been asked to sign a document to that effect.

Instead of answering his question, Michael asked him whether he still had the two pages. The singer, alarmed, said no, he certainly did not. Gabriel van Gelden had refused to leave them with him.

Michael asked if anyone else knew about his meeting with Gabriel.

Schenk shook his head. But he trusted Gabriel. Everyone knew what a serious musician he was. And he had worked with Theo a number of times on Wagner, and also on Mozart operas. He had the highest respect for him, too. And for Nita as well. For the whole family, a wonderful family. And whenever they performed in Europe, even when the Berlin Wall still stood—he himself was allowed to travel freely for concerts abroad because of his international reputation—he had been in touch with them. They had forgiven him for being German, he said with a half-smile, and so he was prepared on trust to undertake the commitment before he knew what it was all about. He only knew that someone had found something that would create an unprecedented sensation. Gabriel van Gelden had assured him of it, and Gabriel was not a man who made wild statements. He was a reserved person, and totally reliable.

Michael made his way back to Eli Bahar and Sergeant Ya'ir, who had remained standing on the lawn outside the hall. "Some bat must have spat out a seed here," said Sergeant Ya'ir to Eli, and he pointed at a nearby loquat tree: "You can see that it wasn't planted here on purpose. We have these trees on our *moshav*, too."

"And what's that tree there, the one like a Christmas tree?" asked Eli, who had not yet caught sight of Michael.

"It's a fir," said Sergeant Ya'ir.

Michael raised his eyes to the crest of the tree, saw the flags above the electricity wires, and coughed. They both turned at once to face him.

"How much longer are we going to be waiting here?" demanded Eli. "How long is this thing here going to last?"

"It's supposed to go on till six," said Michael calmly, "but I'm not staying here with you. I'm going back now. I arranged it with Balilty. There are some things I have to take care of at headquarters, and the two of you will come back with them later."

Eli took off his sunglasses and was about to say something. But he changed his mind and put the glasses on again without saying anything.

"I want to leave with you a few questions for Nita," Michael said to Eli. "I want you to put them to her later, but not when her brother's around."

"Why don't you ask her now yourself?" said Eli with a generous wave of his arm.

"Because . . . it's complicated. I'll leave them for you in writing, and I want you to record them and her answers."

"You can ask her yourself," said Eli, "and record the answers yourself, right now." He looked at Sergeant Ya'ir, who dropped his eyes. "Tell her to come outside for a minute," said Eli to the sergeant.

Nita emerged from the hall and closed her eyes against the sun. She looked slender and fragile to him as she stood in the doorway. He hurried over to her. Behind him he heard Ya'ir's footsteps, but the sergeant did not dare come close to them.

"I can't talk to you now," said Michael in a choked voice, "but there's something I have to ask you."

"Why can't you talk to me?" she asked expressionlessly as she shaded her eyes with a big hand. Her face hardened.

"I can't tell you that, either. Just tell me if Gabi ever spoke to you about a requiem mass by Vivaldi."

She took her hand down from her forehead and looked at him as if he had disappointed her in every way. "What?" she asked blankly.

"Gabi, a requiem by Vivaldi. Did he ever say anything to you about it?" he asked in a choked voice, looking at her extremely dilated pupils.

"Vivaldi never wrote a requiem," said Nita, averting her eyes as if she was too embarrassed to look at his face. "Don't you know there's no Vivaldi requiem?"

"In other words, Gabi never said anything about it to you?"

"How could he say anything about it to me if there's no such thing?" said Nita in her dead voice. She raised her hand again to shade her eyes. "Is that all you wanted?"

He bowed his head.

"They took the baby, they took her away."

He nodded.

She looked into his eyes as if she were seeking a sign. "And that's it?" she asked, and she stared at him for a moment as he stood silent. "So now there's nothing," she mumbled, starting to walk slowly back to the hall. He watched her. A few steps away stood Sergeant Ya'ir, and not far from him stood Eli Bahar, he, too, watching her walking away.

"It's a very nice theory. Not that I understand the first thing about it, but it's very nice anyway. And why should I understand all of it? It's enough that you understand it, because you know about such things. Aryeh Levy would have remarked about your university training by now," said Balilty, referring to the retired district commander, "but me? I'm not bothered by all your education. It's very nice. But, with all due respect," said Balilty, making a mincing gesture with his arm, which sketched an exaggerated flourish in the air, "in the meantime everything's up in the air, a mirage."

"That's why I asked you to get the search warrants for me, and to make all the papers available. And that's why I'm asking for additional manpower now, to conduct the search."

"And I did," said Balilty, taking a pile of papers out of his desk drawer. "If you hadn't stopped at your place on the way and then spent half an hour talking to that Sergeant Malka, you would have been finished with Izzy Mashiah by now."

"I didn't stop at home," protested Michael. "I haven't even passed by it since—"

"I thought you'd changed your clothes," Balilty apologized. "I thought you were wearing a different shirt this morning."

"I wish," muttered Michael. "I came straight here from Zichron Yaakov and I found Sergeant Malka waiting for me in the corridor.

You saw it yourself." He fell silent and looked out the window, fighting a sudden impulse not to satisfy Balilty's curiosity. "She's been found," he said finally.

"Who?"

"The mother. She's been found. That is, they didn't actually find her. A friend of hers talked her into telling a social worker who deals with new immigrants."

"She's a new immigrant?"

"A nineteen-year-old girl. A Russian, all alone in the world."

"And they're going to give her back the baby?" exclaimed Balilty, astonished, and he immediately added: "No, they won't give her the baby. They'll put her on trial. She committed a crime, abandoning a baby in some stranger's basement."

"I don't know what they'll do," said Michael hesitantly. "I understood that they're prepared to take her circumstances into account. In any event, she arrived in Israel all alone, and somebody took her for a ride . . . I don't know exactly how. Meanwhile, the baby's with a foster family, Malka tells me, and nothing final has been decided yet."

"Does she want the child at all? If she gave her up for adoption, with all the demand for babies we have here, she'd stand a good chance of getting off. But if she makes trouble . . . I don't know. They'll probably close the file in any event. But let's leave that now, okay?"

Michael nodded.

"You'll have to testify if it gets to court," Balilty suddenly said. "And you too didn't exactly stick to the letter of the law either, right?"

"We'll see," said Michael vaguely. Now there was suddenly nothing to fight for and no one to fight against. He had never really believed that the mother would be found.

"Don't worry," said Balilty. "We won't leave you in the lurch, we'll provide you with character witnesses," he said with a giggle. "And now, do you want to go to the concert hall first, or do you want to talk to Izzy Mashiah? He's been hanging around waiting since this morning."

"Izzy Mashiah first, I think, but we can have our people start looking through all the papers in the meantime."

"That would be a little difficult," said Balilty sardonically, "since nobody but your majesty knows yet what we're looking for."

"We're looking for a score. A music score."

"Aha," exclaimed Balilty, and he leaned back in his chair, his bloodshot little eyes making him look like an old boozer. "What are you saying? A score? Just a score? Did you see how many scores there are there? Are you totally crazy now?" He leaned forward and said almost in a whisper: "You'll have to be a little more specific, if you don't mind."

"After I've talked to Izzy Mashiah," said Michael. "All I can say now is that I don't know what it looks like. Only that it's paper almost three hundred years old, with notes on it."

"No one . . ." Balilty swallowed and coughed at length. "No one, do you hear? No one but you could ask me to send anyone on such a wild goose chase. Maybe you'll be good enough to explain. . . . Ah, what's the use?"

"Certificates of authentication," Michael reflected aloud. "Maybe you should bring in someone from the documents lab, to have an expert on the spot."

"I won't bring in anyone until we find something!" shouted Balilty. "I'm not going to keep anyone hanging around there for nothing! It could take all night, it could take days! If we ever find anything at all!"

Balilty looked at his empty coffee cup, banged it on the table, and then said more quietly: "For me what the girl said is enough. Ten minutes was all it took to break her. And then she said that he was supposed to be with her, you hear? *Supposed to*! She waited for him for an hour, and then she left. He arranged to meet her in a café, and he didn't show up. He ended up coming to her apartment. A quarter of an hour before they both had to leave. She, too, she plays in the orchestra, she's an extra violinist. He asked her not to tell anybody that he came to see her so late. He promised her the world if she kept her mouth shut. What is he, an idiot? Why should she lie for him? All I had to do was tell her I was going to arrest her for lying, and she broke. I can't understand what he thought he was doing, making a date with a woman before a concert, and then turning up for fifteen minutes. Anyway, as far as I'm concerned, we have enough. Now that he has no alibi, we can arrest him right away!"

Michael felt like saying: Then arrest him and be done with it! Instead he only said: "Do me a favor. I know you're the head of the team, but trust me, and if I'm wrong I'll never argue with you again. Even if you think I've gone off the rails, as you keep on saying, just trust me on this. Believe me, it's better to talk to him before we arrest him. Everything's still too vague, and with the kind of lawyers he'll have, we should get a confession out of him first. And only then —"

"You'll get a confession out of him?" said Balilty, snorting. "When hair grows here!" he cried, slapping the palm of his hand. Then he recovered and continued in a normal voice: "Izzy Mashiah's waiting with Tzilla." He rose heavily and pushed his chair back. "I'm going now to the concert hall. The scores from his house will be brought here, to your office. The ones in the concert hall I'm not moving from there. I've already wasted the whole morning on that other business," he said, turning his face to the window and rubbing his cheeks.

"What business?"

"You know, with that girl who . . . with Dalit," he said, openly embarrassed. "Elroi's taking care of it now. He's already spoken to me. She . . . It's a sickness. Do you know that? She's sick," he said, puzzled. "How could anyone tell?" he said after a moment, sighing. "She seemed completely normal. God knows what's going to happen to her now," he concluded as he walked toward the door with his hands deep in his pockets.

The conversation with Izzy Mashiah took far longer than expected, even though it contained few of the details he had hoped for when he imagined the man unburdening himself of everything he knew in an attempt to gain sympathy and trust.

Michael ignored his doleful expression, the slackness of his limbs, the undisguised fear in his eyes. Impatiently, he asked him: "What did you want to talk to me about?"

"There's something I haven't told you," confessed Izzy Mashiah.

"What is it?"

"You already know that for the last month or two Gabi and I were . . . had difficulties . . . That man," he said, jerking his head toward the corridor, "said that my polygraph was irregular."

"It was very regular," Michael corrected him, "but it gave rise to a number of questions, precisely because it was so regular. The regularity showed that you were lying."

Izzy Mashiah sighed. "Some time before . . . about two months ago, I sensed that Gabi was involved with something."

"What do you mean?" Michael said, tensing.

"I mean I felt that he wasn't really with me. His mind . . . his heart . . . were preoccupied with something he wasn't telling me about."

"Did you talk to him about it?"

"He denied it. He said that maybe he was under stress about the new ensemble he was setting up. But I had a bad feeling about it. And around two months ago he went to Europe and he didn't want me to come with him. I was looking forward to that trip so much." He covered his face with his hands.

Michael tapped a pencil impatiently on his desk. In the ensuing silence he forced himself to overcome his impatience. Izzy Mashiah uncovered his face. Michael was relieved to see that there were no tears on it.

"Ever since Passover we'd been talking about going to Europe together, and then he went alone. Twice! And he wasn't even prepared to tell me why!"

A good while was wasted on a detailed description of Izzy Mashiah's mental agonies. ("I was having all kinds of difficulties at work, too, and questions about my life, and every spring I get depressed." And: "It was a time when I needed him most, and when I told him that I needed him he only got annoyed.") Then he came out with a simple statement of jealousy: "I thought he had someone else."

Michael lit a cigarette. "And what did you do about it?"

"I began searching through his papers, following him, checking up on him," said Izzy Mashiah, blushing. "I know it sounds awful, but I was desperate."

"How did you check up on him, exactly?" asked Michael, holding his breath and trying to look indifferent. "What did you find out?"

"I looked in his date book, I opened his mail," whispered Izzy Mashiah. "And in the end, I went to Holland to see who he was with . . . I thought he had someone in Delft."

"Why Delft?"

"There were two letters from there, and . . ." He fell silent.

"And was there someone?"

"It wasn't what I thought at all," said Izzy Mashiah, groaning. "I was sure, almost sure, I was so afraid. There were phone calls from

Delft. Two. And a fax. And there was a name in his date book with a phone number."

"What did you do with his date book?"

"I took it away," Izzy Mashiah admitted. "I hid it among my papers at work, and he thought it was lost. I had no other way to check. I had to . . . actually steal it, and afterward I couldn't put it back."

"And after he died? Did you keep it there?"

Izzy Mashiah shook his head. "I burned it," he said guiltily. "I was afraid that . . . after the polygraph, and the way the other policeman looked at me, I panicked."

"You burned it? How?"

"What does it matter? I burned it."

"Where exactly? When?"

"Well, I didn't exactly burn it." Izzy Mashiah looked embarrassed and his eyes shifted uneasily. "It sounded better to say burned, but where could I have burned it? I tore it to pieces."

"When?"

"After I was here at the police station the first time. I tore it into little pieces and . . . "

"And . . . ?"

"I flushed them down the toilet," he admitted. His face flamed. "I know it sounds awful," he stammered. "I know it looks as if I don't care about Gabi's memory. As if I despise his belongings. But it isn't true." Now he looked into Michael's eyes. "It really isn't true. Believe me, it only looks that way. It's just that I was so frightened, and also ashamed. It goes against all my principles about privacy. I've never done anything like that before, believe me."

"And what was written in the date book?"

"There were those names in Holland. All names of men. And they sounded so . . . Hans and Johann, they sounded so foreign, so German or Dutch . . . I thought he was tired of me. That he'd fallen in love. Finally I went there myself," he said with a groan.

"You were in Holland. We knew that. You told us so. You were there just before Felix van Gelden was murdered."

"And I was in Delft, too," admitted Izzy Mashiah, "and I went to Hans van Gulik's address."

"Van Gulik—isn't that the name of the man who wrote the

Chinese detective stories Gabriel read?" Michael asked in a deliberately pleasant tone.

"Right," said Izzy Mashiah, surprised. "But it's not the same van Gulik."

"So you went to his address," Michael said, bringing him back to the subject.

"It's an antique shop. I went in. There were two saleswomen inside. It's a fairly big shop, bigger than Felix's. Filled with all kinds of old furniture, and there was an old man there, too. About Felix's age."

"Did you speak to him?"

"I told one of the women that I was looking for Hans van Gulik," said Izzy hoarsely. "And she pointed at the old man and said: 'This is Mr. van Gulik.' "

"And then?"

"And then I suddenly realized that it was something else entirely, but I went up to him anyway. And I asked him . . . I told him that Gabi had sent me. He suddenly sat up straight and gave me a look as if I'd committed some terrible *faux pas*. As if . . . I quickly told him that Gabi had recommended him to me as a reliable dealer. That he had sent me to him to help me find an old harpsichord in need of renovation. I talked a lot, and I saw that his attitude toward me was completely different from what it had been before. At first he had been really tense, but as soon as I mentioned the harpsichord he became courteous, and I understood that there was something going on here. Not that he wasn't nice. He asked me if I knew Felix. And he even asked about Herzl."

"He knew Felix and Herzl?"

"He told me that he was a childhood friend of Felix's. I wanted to tell him that I was part of the family, that Gabi and I . . . But I didn't say anything."

"And the other man?"

"All it said in the date book was 'Johann—Amsterdam,' and the name of a café I don't remember."

"And did you tell Gabi about it when you returned?"

"How could I?" demanded Izzy Mashiah. "After his father died like that, how could I bother him with my fears? And I wasn't even with him when it happened. I only arrived a few days later."

"So you never went to a conference?"

"Yes, I did, of course I did. You checked it out yourselves. I had to bring that girl all the documentation . . ."

"What girl?"

"The blonde one with the short hair. I gave the policewoman all the documents the day after I gave you my passport. I was at a conference in France and then I went to Holland only about Gabi. I phoned him from Paris and told him I was going somewhere to rest for a few days. I was vague about the details. I was afraid to tell him the truth, and I also wanted him to stew a bit," he admitted, embarrassed. "I didn't know that while I was away his father was going to be murdered." Again he buried his face in his hands.

"And how did he react to your vagueness? Was he as jealous as you were?"

"No." Izzy Mashiah sighed. "He wasn't. It was always a waste of energy to try to make him jealous. I told him long ago that he didn't let himself be jealous, that he was defending himself because he was afraid of being hurt. But he only laughed and said: 'I'm completely confident that nobody can mean to you what I do. And if you do find someone who means more to you than I do, then it's a sign that that's the way it has to be.' I envied him his strength. I felt so weak and vulnerable next to him! Confidence like his is completely beyond my powers. But now I think that it was a defense. That he didn't allow himself to love me as I loved him. That's what I think."

"In your opinion jealousy is a sign of love," concluded Michael. "Is that what you really think?"

Izzy Mashiah nodded after a certain hesitation, and he said: "Look, I'm not so simple-minded. I understand that my fears aren't necessarily a function of love. My vulnerability is my own problem. Possessiveness needn't necessarily have anything to do with love. But these are human feelings, after all. Almost part of human nature, and they emerge in relation to our deep encounters with other people. Otherwise why should we be afraid at all?"

Michael was silent.

"This rationality of Gabi's never convinced me. The power he had over me, as if he knew that for me he was . . ."

"Did you hate him when you went to Holland?"

Izzy Mashiah looked at him with alarm. "Hate him? How could I hate Gabi? I was afraid. I tell you I was afraid that he wanted to leave me. That he had someone else. You know," he said with an insightful air, "maybe I also hated him. I suppose I also did hate him. Anyhow, I suffered terribly."

"And after you met Hans van Gulik?"

"In a certain respect it calmed me. But not completely," Izzy Mashiah admitted, "because I thought that maybe through this Hans he had made a connection with someone else. Like Johann, for instance. But late at night, when I couldn't sleep, I thought that maybe he had some other business with him. Something very important. So important that he made two separate trips he wouldn't tell me anything about. And suddenly I was furious at him for keeping me out of it. But then his father was killed, and after that . . ."

"You had no idea what was preoccupying him?"

"I wish I had. It would probably have saved me a lot of heartache."

"Tell me," Michael said, passing the pencil from hand to hand, "how much would an old manuscript of a musical work be worth?"

"An important one?"

"Let's say it is."

"It depends on how old it is. Really old?"

"Let's say a Baroque manuscript."

"It could be worth millions. Somewhat less if it's not the composer's autograph manuscript but a contemporary copy. And most important, of course, is who the composer is."

"Do you know," said Michael quietly, "that the plumber you said you were waiting for actually turned up? At about noon?"

Izzy said nothing.

"And you weren't home. On the day Gabriel was murdered. Do you know that there is something very unclear in the polygraph at this point?"

"I didn't kill Gabi. I loved Gabi, believe me," said Izzy Mashiah in a flat voice. "But if you suspect me anyway, I don't care anymore. I've got nothing more to lose. As far as I'm concerned, you can arrest me right now."

"I'm talking about whether you left the house," Michael reminded him. "You said that you didn't leave the house all day. So did you or didn't you?"

"I was near the building," said Izzy Mashiah in a whisper.

"Near what building?" asked Michael for the sake of the tape recorder.

"In front of the concert hall."

Michael lit a cigarette.

"I didn't go in. I swear to you that I wasn't inside."

"But you were outside."

"I wanted to know if he was really . . . I . . . I was following him." Izzy Mashiah spoke with downcast eyes. "I wanted to see if the car was there."

"And was the car there?"

"No," said Izzy Mashiah miserably. "It wasn't there. I'd completely forgotten that Ruth was supposed to take it. And I thought, He's lying to me. He says he's in one place when he's somewhere else. My imagination started working overtime, there was a movie playing in my head until . . . until you came and told me he was dead," he said in a broken voice.

"Why didn't you tell me all this before?" asked Michael in a kindly, paternal tone. "Because you were afraid? Were you afraid we'd suspect you of the murder? Is that why you didn't tell us that you were outside the scene of the crime?"

"No," whispered Izzy Mashiah. "It had nothing to do with that. I'm not afraid of being a suspect. I feel now as if I've got nothing more to lose. It wasn't out of fear."

"What then?" asked Michael.

In a choked voice, from behind the hands that were covering his face again, he blurted out: "Out of shame." Now he was crying aloud. "Only out of shame. I was so ashamed," he said, and he sobbed and uncovered his face, which now was bathed in tears.

For a long moment Michael waited for his weeping to subside. He had plenty of time in which to formulate his next question, which he posed in an authoritative tone: "Could you identify an old manuscript of a musical composition? Of the Baroque period?"

"What do you mean, identify? Say who wrote it?" he asked, confused.

"If you saw the original score of a work by Vivaldi, for example, could you identify it as a manuscript from about that period?"

"Of course I could," said Izzy Mashiah confidently. "There's no way of mistaking such things. In Salzburg, for instance, you can see autograph scores by Mozart. I've seen a lot of such scores in museums and photographs of them in books."

"So you could do it?" Michael interrupted him. "Even if the identity of the composer isn't certain?"

"I can tell if it looks like an old manuscript," said Izzy carefully. "But there are a lot of forgeries around. You really need an expert. But I could certainly tell if it looks old. And so could you, believe me. It's not hard. For one thing, the paper is very different from ours."

"And do you know Vivaldi's music?"

"I certainly do."

"Everything he wrote?"

"Everything?" Izzy Mashiah laughed. "'Everything' is going a bit too far. He wrote hundreds of pieces. But I'm very familiar with Vivaldi. Like any serious musician."

"In that case," said Michael, "come with me now."

Submissively Izzy Mashiah picked up his shoulder bag and car keys and, without asking where or why, followed Michael out of the room.

At the entrance to the psychiatric hospital Michael asked him to wait in the car. After a short battle with a nurse ("There's already one policeman here," she argued. "We have to think of the welfare of all our patients, not only of your interests."), and after Zippo came out of the room to remain in the corridor, Michael was allowed to go in to talk to Herzl.

Once again he found himself sitting close to someone under the influence of powerful medication, someone whose eyes were closed and who refused to cooperate. After a number of failed attempts at beating around the bush, he decided to change tactics and go straight to the point. He touched the skinny arm, and Herzl quickly opened his eyes. Before he had time to snatch his arm away, Michael asked: "Who brought that score to Israel?" Herzl opened his toothless mouth, fingered the white hairs sprouting from his scalp, and something very lucid, lucid and terrified, showed in his eyes. He looked around, made sure there was nobody else in the room, sat up in bed, and looked at Michael. Suddenly he asked for a cigarette. Michael made haste to offer him one, bent over to light it, lit one for himself as well, took a puff, and asked again: "Who brought the score?"

"You're from the police, right?" stated Herzl matter-of-factly. He sounded totally sane.

"I'm from the police," agreed Michael. "And who brought the score?"

"You don't even know what that music is," muttered Herzl with suspicion and contempt.

"You'll tell me," said Michael pleasantly, and he offered him a plastic cup for his ashes.

"They don't let you smoke here," complained Herzl, and with the same breath he added: "Felix wanted it for Gabi. He said Gabi should have it. That it would bring him the recognition he deserved."

"Did he bring it from Holland?"

Herzl nodded. "Not Felix, me. I brought it. He couldn't go, because of Nita. She was just about to give birth. He only went later. To check the authentication. But when the first telephone call came I flew there. Felix sent me. I'm the one he sent. Felix and me," Herzl crossed his fingers, "we were like that. I understood him. But later he made a mistake." Herzl shook his head. "He made a very big mistake."

Michael listened for a long time to the torturous speech, with its digressions, detailed descriptions, associations, and regressions, until he grasped the nature of the argument between them. ("I said to him, Why Gabi and not Theo? Why don't you tell Theo? He's entitled, too. He was furious. He was so angry because I told him that if he was only going to tell Gabi, I would tell Theo first. I was angry, too. In the end I didn't want to speak to him anymore. That's why we closed the shop. And after that—after that he was dead," he said almost with surprise.) In a stream of words that included a very detailed description of the city of Delft and its great church, and of Felix's childhood friend, an antique furniture dealer, he described the old church organ this man had bought for Felix, who wanted to restore it. Herzl told about the dismantlement of the organ, about its double layer of wood, and about the manuscript.

"Inside the organ? The score was inside the organ?" asked Michael in a businesslike tone as he steadied his trembling hand.

"The antique dealer realized right away that this was a matter for an expert. He could see that the papers, which were tied up in a bundle with a cord, were old. But what they were he didn't know. He only knows about furniture," explained Herzl. "That's why he phoned Felix. Felix couldn't go. And we didn't know how very, how very—"

"What's the Dutchman's name?"

"I'm not naming names," declared Herzl. "You're not family," he explained in a friendly tone. "No names."

"Did Nita know about this?"

"We didn't tell Nita. What for?"

"And you killed Gabi, so that Theo would have the score." Michael hoped that this gamble would shake Herzl into revealing more details.

Herzl looked at him astonished, as if Michael had taken leave of his senses. "Me?" he cried out amazed, and he gave Michael an almost pitying look. "Why should I do that? I'm against killing. I would never kill anyone."

"But you left the hospital on the day Felix died."

"Of course I did," said Herzl proudly as he raised his skinny neck. "There was a concert. How could I miss the first concert of the season? When all three of them were performing?"

"You were at the concert?" Michael overcame his astonishment and asked: "How did you get in? Did you have a ticket?"

Herzl waved his hand dismissively. "I don't need a ticket. I went in through the side entrance, like always."

"Through the musicians' entrance?"

"Up the stairs, at the end of the corridor in back," he said he said as if it were self-evident.

"Did anyone see you?"

"Who?" asked Herzl indifferently.

"Do you remember the flutist?"

"She played Vivaldi," Herzl recalled. "The concerto *La notte*. It was all right."

"Only all right?"

"I've heard the piece a few times in my life. She wasn't anything special," he said impatiently.

"Do you remember what she was wearing?"

Herzl looked at him incredulously. "You're a strange person," he said distantly. "What do you care what she was wearing? It wasn't a beauty contest."

"But she was beautiful," said Michael, immediately regretting it. Why don't you stop treating him like a child, he said to himself, and ask him outright for proof, for witnesses.

"A blue dress, kind of shiny," murmured Herzl. "Like a fish." And he suddenly shivered.

"It was also on television," Michael reminded him.

"In the hospital they don't let you watch so late. At home I don't have television."

"Did you see Felix there?"

"No, I didn't," said Herzl angrily. "And even if I did, let him look for me! Why should I look for him? He was in the wrong."

"But was he sitting in his regular seat?"

"No. There were two other people sitting there," said Herzl, offended. "They gave our seats to other people. That's why I sat in row seventeen. But it was all right there, too."

Michael offered him another cigarette, and he grabbed it eagerly and sucked on it like a nipple. He leaned back in bed, lowered his long white face, and plucked at the blanket. "How could I know he would die?" he lamented. "For six months I didn't speak to him. I said to myself, If he wants me he can come to me. After the mother died there was no one to care about Theo. Only about Gabi. It's not right to give it all to one child. You tell me. Am I right or not?" He raised his head.

"We found the painting at your apartment," said Michael very quietly.

"What painting?" asked Herzl innocently.

"The *Vanitas* that was in Felix's house. The Dutch painting."

"With the skull? At my apartment?" asked Herzl, surprised. With open curiosity, without a hint of fear, he asked: "How did it get there?"

"We found it in the kitchen cabinet behind the cocoa and the brandy."

"Who put it there?" asked Herzl.

"I thought you might know."

"I really don't know," said Herzl, puzzled. "That's not a good place for a painting. Those cabinets are sometimes damp. They're never opened."

"Who had a key to your apartment?"

"Just Felix," said Herzl resentfully. "I wanted to take it away from him, after he wouldn't agree about Theo, but I decided not to talk to him. He would have thought it was an excuse to speak to him," he explained.

At any moment, Michael knew, there could be an unexpected outburst. At any moment the clear and indifferent flow of words might suddenly be cut off. As if treading in a minefield, he took care not to say the words "Vivaldi" or "requiem," and Herzl, too, named no names. Something told him to keep the subject vague until he understood the particulars.

"Gabi came to see me," Herzl suddenly said with great weariness, and he laid his trembling head down again on the striped pillow. "He came to see me here. That's why I was so angry with Theo. He didn't even look for me to tell me Felix was dead. Only Gabi came. He wanted to know what you want to know. Felix had told him about the manuscript some time before he died. They went to Meyuhas because he's a copyright lawyer. I already knew that Felix had told Gabi. Felix told me everything. He didn't lie."

"And Theo? He didn't tell Theo about it?"

"I told Theo," Herzl confessed, and he looked around fearfully.

"When? When did you tell Theo?"

"Before . . . the last time he came to see me. After we closed the shop. After Felix refused to agree. Two or three or four months ago, I think."

"After Gabi already knew?"

"I told him because Felix took Gabi to see the lawyer. That's why I told him."

"A manuscript like that is worth millions, right?"

Herzl shrugged his shoulders. "Of course," he said indifferently.

"Did you tell him it was by Vivaldi? What exactly did you tell him?"

Herzl sat up at once, and he looked at Michael as if he were just realizing that he had been poisoned. "I'm not talking to you anymore," he announced. "You know nothing and understand nothing. I'm not saying another word. Not another word. Not even if you kill me. What can you do to me?" he demanded defiantly.

"Where is the manuscript now?" asked Michael.

Herzl lay down with his eyes closed, and he clamped his mouth shut.

Michael put the pack of cigarettes down next to the bed. Herzl opened his eyes, looked to the side, shook his head, pretended not to see the cigarettes, and closed his eyes again.

"You know that Gabi was murdered," Michael ventured. But Herzl didn't move. "Do you want Theo to be murdered, too?"

Herzl only tightened his narrow lips and breathed rhythmically.

"Have you got a tape recorder here?" Michael asked Zippo, who was standing in the corridor reading the notes pinned to the cork board hanging on the wall near the nurses' station.

Zippo felt in his pocket. "Sure I have. I took it along this morning. I never move without it."

"So switch it on and go sit next to him. Does he talk to you?"

"Sure. All the time."

"What?" Michael was amazed. "What do you talk about?"

"All kinds of things," said Zippo. "About his childhood in Bulgaria. Did you know that he was in an orphanage until he was six?" Zippo clucked sympathetically. "Poor guy. He hasn't got a soul in the world. We talk about everything. About women, about why I won't let him have a cigarette. He's actually a very nice guy. And he's not stupid. He understands everything you say to him. I tell him about Jerusalem in the old days. You know, in the days when—"

"And did you tape it?" Michael interrupted him.

"No, actually I didn't." Zippo bowed his head. "I didn't know it was relevant—"

"Everything's relevant!" Michael said in a choked whisper. "Do you hear? Everything!"

Zippo tugged at the ends of his mustache in evident discomfort and looked at Michael nervously. "Believe me," he pleaded, "it was all just ordinary talk, like between ordinary people."

"You're going back in there now," said Michael.

Zippo nodded quickly.

"And you'll start talking to him again. Get him to talk about the van Gelden family, about Theo van Gelden and about Theo and Gabi. Get him to tell you about his trip abroad. Ask him about Holland. Have you ever been to Holland?"

"Not Holland," Zippo admitted. "A year ago my wife and I went on a group tour to London and Paris. It was very nice. Two weeks. We saw everything. But we didn't go to Holland. We thought maybe next year. . . ."

Michael recovered his composure and restrained his impatience. "Very nice," he said. "So ask him where in Holland you should go on your trip. Things like that. Get him to talk to you about the city of Delft."

"Delft," repeated Zippo.

"Get him to tell you about his last visit there. You'll have to be very cunning," Michael warned.

"No problem," said Zippo, beaming.

"And get him to tell you in detail about the church there, and about any antique dealers he knows in Delft. Record every word, do you hear?"

"No problem," Zippo again assured him. "Delft," he repeated to himself. "Funny names they've got over there. Delft!"

14

A Torso

Izzy Mashiah trailed obediently after Michael until they reached the administrative wing of the concert hall building. But as they passed the row of musicians' lockers, he hurried past him and stopped at the locker that still bore Gabriel van Gelden's name. He touched it, swallowed hard, and walked on ahead to the orchestra manager's office. At the door he stepped aside and let Michael go in first. Inside, Balilty was already waiting. He sat in an uncharacteristically erect posture opposite the nervous-looking manager, studying tables and columns of figures on a long computer printout, which had fallen to his feet and snaked across the green carpet, ending up in the hands of Sergeant Ya'ir, who raised his eyes at their arrival and solemnly explained: "This is the detailed balance sheet for last season. Income, expenses, subsidies, losses."

"What are you doing here?" asked Michael, alarmed. "Where are Nita and Theo?"

"She isn't feeling well," explained Ya'ir calmly. "She couldn't stay in Zichron Yaakov. We had to take her home. We even thought of getting an ambulance, but finally I brought her in the van."

"And Theo?"

"He stayed there. He's with that German singer. Eli will bring them back later. They'll need transportation, but . . ." he nodded at Balilty, "the chief said he'd take care of it."

"And where is she now?"

"Miss van Gelden? She's at home. I took her there. She could hardly walk. Tzilla was waiting for her at her apartment. A babysitter's there, too. She's not alone," he added quickly when he saw Michael's eyes. "At Beit-Lillian they called a doctor. I wanted to call an ambulance to take her to the emergency room, but she wouldn't hear of—"

"What exactly is the matter with her?"

"The doctor said it's a virus," said Ya'ir. "There's one going around now, lots of people have it, with nausea and weakness. She suddenly had a high fever and she vomited. They tried to get her to lie down there, but she wouldn't. The doctor . . ."

Balilty lifted his eyes from the computer printout, raised his eyebrows, and pushed his small reading glasses halfway down his nose. "Do you think that . . . Well, it's not important. There's another doctor at her place now. And Tzilla's with her. She's in good hands. Ya'ir says Theo put up a big fight about her leaving. I suggest we start with his office now, before he gets here."

"Excuse me, I just want to help. What exactly are you looking for? I don't quite understand," the orchestra manager said nervously. He stood up from his seat behind the desk, hunched his shoulders, sank his narrow head between them, and rubbed his hands. "Not that I'm entitled to, of course. You certainly don't owe me an explanation, perhaps you're not at liberty to give me one, but I'd really like to help. If you'll just tell me exactly what you're looking for, I'm sure I could . . ." His eyes shifted from one to the other of the three policemen. None answered him, and he fell silent.

Balilty stood up with a heavy sigh, stretched his limbs carefully, and rested his hand on his hip. "There are another two men in the basement. There's a room down there where they keep the music scores," he said to Michael. "But you have to give me a more detailed description, so I can tell them exactly what to look for," he said as he left the room with Michael behind him.

Izzy Mashiah followed them without a word. Ya'ir closed the office door behind him. But the manager quickly opened the door again and hurried after them. "I don't want to make any demands," he said. His eyes darted in all directions, deliberately avoiding theirs. "I understand your position, but the last time your men searched the premises they left such a mess that it took us two days to clean it up. I have to ask you, if possible—"

"Don't worry, we'll do what we can," Balilty promised him. Then he waited for the manager to go back into his office and shut the door.

"What does an original manuscript of a Baroque score look like?" Michael asked Izzy, who was leaning against the corridor wall. In the fluorescent light his face had a yellowish tinge. He twisted his ring. The green stone glinted.

"It usually comes in the form of sheaves of paper, sometimes sewn together, sometimes not," Izzy said hesitantly. "Large sheets folded in two and with music notation written on both sides. The paper is usually heavy and fibrous, and is often rust-stained."

"Did you hear that?" Michael asked Balilty. "Tell them to look for something like that. But I don't believe it'll be in the storeroom with all the printed scores. Tell them to put everything in boxes," he decided after some hesitation, "and we'll do Theo's office now."

"You!" Balilty addressed Izzy Mashiah. "Wait outside! There's either a bench at the door or we'll bring a chair out for you. Wait outside and we'll call you if we find anything!" he said with demonstrative skepticism.

Michael started to say something. "Don't argue with me," said Balilty. "I can't work with people from outside getting underfoot. And besides," he added when they were inside the room, "you keep telling me not to say anything to him about whose handwriting it's about, to wait and see if he identifies it by himself, to see if it really is what it's cracked up to be. So what do you need him in the room for?"

"You're right," Michael apologized.

"Not that I believe we'll find anything here," complained Balilty. He tucked the ends of his shirt under his broad belt and felt his back. "We already searched this room. For a whole day."

"But then we were looking for a string," Michael reminded him.

"Which we didn't find here. And we also looked through the papers," muttered Balilty.

"But we weren't looking for a manuscript. You don't find what you're not looking for. How can you find something when you don't even know that it exists?"

"Bullshit," retorted Balilty. "All my life I've found what I wasn't looking for. Most of the time exactly when I'm not looking for it. And you—who found a baby when he wasn't looking for one?" he asked provocatively and immediately looked abashed and changed the subject. "Look, I've thrown my back out," he said, making a face. "I hope to God it isn't going to be like that time last year. . . . Why do you have to do everything yourself? Why are we the ones conducting this search?" he complained suddenly. "We could have put a few men in here to take the place apart. All you had to do was tell them what to look for."

"You don't have to do it. I can do it with Ya'ir. And you—"

"Not on your life, my friend," said Balilty, kneeling in front of the bookcase. "I'm not missing this, not that I really believe we'll find anything. But for the two and a half percent chance that we will, I'm prepared to put up even with the pain in my back."

"It's going to rain," said Ya'ir, sniffing the air after opening the big window. "I can feel it, there'll be rain by this evening. Maybe that's why your back hurts. On days like this my father's leg hurts."

Balilty gave him a wrathful look.

"I'm never wrong about things like this," the sergeant insisted. "Just look at those clouds."

"You know," said Balilty as he pulled a pile of books from the bookcase and dumped them onto the floor, examined the bookcase's exposed wooden back, and began to page through the books. "When I was busy with that painting I learned a lot about forgeries. Even if we find this music—which I don't believe we will—it'll take ages before we get the authentication."

"According to what Herzl Cohen said, I have the impression that they've already taken care of it," said Michael. "That's why Felix van Gelden flew to Amsterdam twice after Herzl brought it here. And not long ago Gabriel van Gelden flew there on the same matter."

But Balilty, on his knees and with one hand supporting his back, was not ready to let it go at that. The expression of demonstrative concentration on his face, a kind of grimace that involved the narrowing of his small eyes, which were fixed on an invisible point in the distance, indicated that he was about to deliver a lecture.

"I still don't believe that Zippo got him to talk," said Balilty. "It shows you. Like my late mother used to say, in the end God finds a use for everyone. You can never know who'll do what and where. Who'll succeed at what and where. My back hurts like hell."

"It'll pass after it begins to rain," promised Sergeant Ya'ir, who was still standing at the open window. "It's going to start coming down in a few minutes. Do you want me to begin looking here?" he asked, and he crouched down beside a long alcove set into the wall under the window. Without waiting for a reply, he opened the thin white sliding wooden door and began to pull out music scores in black bindings with red labels stuck to the spines.

"The Malskat case, for instance," said Balilty self-importantly, "is the most interesting. Have you ever heard of him?"

"No, I haven't," said Michael, and he emptied the top drawer of the desk onto the carpet, where he began going through every piece of paper and rummaging through photographs. In one of them Theo stood next to Leonard Bernstein among a group of people dressed in evening clothes, in another, an old black-and-white snapshot, he immediately recognized little Nita, with a smile exposing the gaps in her front teeth and dimpling her cheeks. She was holding a cello as big as she was. How sweet she looked, he thought with a sudden pang at the sight of her fair curls and bright, serious, innocent gaze. He put the snapshot into his shirt pocket. Among the key rings, matchboxes, a pack of toothpicks, aspirin, notes, and receipts, he found (and read) love letters, letters of complaint, clippings of concert reviews, old concert programs, greeting cards, and a document that turned out to be a faded copy of a divorce agreement.

"It was in Germany. They were restoring an old church. A local restorer named Malskat worked on it for a whole year. He wouldn't let anyone see what he was doing. He worked all by himself on a scaffold specially built for him. When he was finished he gathered everybody to see what he had found—pictures on the ceiling, incredible things from the thirteenth century. You like that period, don't you?"

Michael grunted from the depths of the second drawer.

"But, like I've always said, the trouble with all these people—forgers, frauds, and also cold-blooded murderers—the trouble with them is that they don't understand that no man can think of everything. You know what I think?" he said, paging through a music encyclopedia. "Have a look at this picture, just have a look," he said, reading something with interest. "It's Beethoven. Look at what he looked like." He turned the pages rapidly and then set the book aside with the rest of the volumes he had already checked. "I think," he said emphatically, "that fools are people who think the whole world is too stupid to see what's really going on. Am I right or am I wrong?"

Michael grunted again. Out of the corner of his eye he observed how carefully Sergeant Ya'ir was taking the scores out and slowly turning the pages.

"So that's what also happened to this Malskat. There were eight turkeys in his painting on the ceiling of that church. But in the thirteenth century there weren't any turkeys in Germany, because Columbus only brought them to Europe from America at the end of the fifteenth century, understand?"

Michael contented himself with another grunt. In the third drawer there were only boxes of cigars and more concert programs. He moved on to the wardrobe.

"So what happened? It came out that Malskat had painted the picture on the ceiling himself. And because of the scandal all kinds of other things he did came to light as well. For example, the saints in the cathedral. Did you ever hear about that?"

"No."

"When Lübeck was bombed during the Second World War, a Gothic cathedral was hit, and the plaster fell off its walls in layers. A restorer was called in, and he announced that under where the plaster had been there seemed to be frescoes from the Middle Ages. And in 1951, after three years of renovations, there was a gala reception in honor of this wall, which showed saints from the New Testament standing in a row, each one three meters high. There was nothing like it anywhere else in Germany. It caused a sensation. The German postal authorities even issued a series of stamps with the pictures on them. They must be worth a fortune today, those stamps," he mused gloomily. "Are you listening?"

Michael grunted from inside the wardrobe, from which he removed some printed scores and rummaged mechanically and apathetically through the coats and tuxedo jackets, even going so far as to unfold a cashmere sweater, as if its folds could provide a hiding place.

"And everyone praised the restorer who had found and cleaned the paintings. But that wasn't the end of the story. Later, when Malskat was exposed for painting the turkeys, it turned out that he had been the restorer's assistant in the cathedral. He confessed that he had painted the saints and that for years he had also been making fake French Impressionist pictures. There are dozens of stories like this all over the world. The most famous forger was a Dutchman, van

Meegeren. And even the most important art museum in the world, the Uffizi in Florence—have you ever been there?"

Again Michael contented himself with a grunt as he carefully examined a set of suitcases that had been stored in the wardrobe, while Sergeant Ya'ir raised his head from the alcove and said: "I've never been to Italy at all. Only to the United States, with a high school group."

"Well, even the Uffizi bought a portrait by Leonardo da Vinci, and two hundred years later it turned out that da Vinci couldn't have painted it because when they examined it with lasers they discovered that in every brush stroke the hairs on the right side of the brush sank deeper into the paint than the hairs on the left side. Do you get it?"

"No," said Michael, who stuck his head out of the wardrobe and looked at Balilty with surprise.

"Then I've got news for you!" cried Balilty triumphantly. "Leonardo was left-handed! He didn't paint with his right hand! You didn't know that, did you?"

Michael meekly shook his head, and Balilty said to the sergeant: "Come here, young man. You've got nothing wrong with your back. Pick up this pile of papers, there's nothing in them. And bring down what's up there. You'll have to climb up and open those glass doors. And see if there's a lock, because my eyes aren't what they used to be, either." He sighed and watched the sergeant as he climbed carefully up onto the table and reached for the glass doors.

"They're locked," said Sergeant Ya'ir. "But that's no problem," he muttered. "Should I open them?" he asked. When Balilty nodded, he took a pin out of his pocket, leaned carefully against the glass doors, and after a few seconds pulled the door open. "I'll pass the things down to you one by one. They're heavy," he warned.

"What have we here?" muttered Balilty as he looked at a big book.

"Let me see," requested Michael. He glanced at it and said: "Just another printed score."

"Look at the fancy binding. Black velvet, no less. What does it say here? I can't read these letters at all."

"*Der Freischütz*," said Michael after examining the Gothic print. "It's an opera by Weber. In Hebrew it's called *The Marksman*." His finger hovered over the elaborate letters.

"Weber, who's he anyway?" Balilty felt the binding. "This isn't an ordinary book, it's something special. Take a look."

"I'm looking," said Michael, and he carefully turned the heavy pages. "It looks like something historical, with pictures of the sets," he said as if to himself.

Sergeant Ya'ir got off the table and placed another large volume bound in black velvet on the desk. "It's heavy," he said with a sigh, "and it's so thick. It says here that it's an opera."

Michael turned his head and glanced at the volume. "It's *Les Troyens* by Berlioz, I've heard about it, but I've never seen or heard it. It's very rarely performed because right at the beginning you need a whole navy on the stage."

Sergeant Ya'ir opened the book and began to leaf through it. He turned the pages carefully. This score, too, was a special illustrated edition. "We're not in the public library here," Balilty scolded him. But he rose from his crouching position and stood next to the sergeant, looking over his shoulder at precisely the moment when the young man turned a few pages at a time to reveal the large vertical rectangle that had been cut into the middle of the page they were looking at and all the pages below it.

For a few seconds the three men were silent. It was the first time, entirely by chance, that all three were standing together at the desk, Michael and Balilty on either side of Sergeant Ya'ir, looking at the same book. Balilty heaved a loud sigh and sat down.

Very carefully, Michael lifted a parcel wrapped in tissue paper from the hollowed-out space inside the book and laid it on the desk. He unwrapped it and revealed a bundle of heavy, stained pages. His hands trembled. "Millions," whispered Balilty. "It's worth millions, right?"

Sergeant Ya'ir cleared his throat. "It's like a story," he marveled. "In the Arbeli case all we found were a few fibers in the car, some of which belonged to the victim and some to persons unknown. And here—we look and look and in the end we find this."

"Good for you," said Balilty loudly, and he slapped the sergeant on the back. "Very nice work."

The sergeant blushed, lowered his head, held it down for a few seconds, raised it again, sniffed the air, looked at the window, and cried:

"I told you it was going to rain! And only two days ago we finished harvesting the cotton. What luck! Just before the first rain."

And it really was raining, loud and heavy. "It's coming down hard for the first rain of the year," said Michael, hurrying to close the window. "All of a sudden, without any warning."

"They said on the radio," said Balilty as he looked at the bundle of paper, "that the first rain is always like this. It's Succoth now, and there's always a flood now. We had a few drops last week already. Why don't you call him in, so he can look at it?"

"I'll call him in a minute," said Michael and he sank into a chair. "It's just hit me, that it really could be. I just can't take it all in," he mumbled as he looked at the first page, at a spot of ink above a word between the staves that he couldn't make out.

"Wait!" cried Balilty, alarmed. "Put these on!" He pulled a pair of thin gloves out of his trouser pocket, handed them to Michael, and watched him putting them on. "It's just the way he said it would be," he marveled. "Heavy, fibrous paper. Feel it, feel the corner! Right? We have to alert Forensics. Isn't this something, life is really . . . I was sure we wouldn't find anything here. Go and tell them to stop searching the basement," he instructed Sergeant Ya'ir.

Izzy Mashiah was sitting on the chair in the same position they had left him in when they closed the door: his body bent over, his face buried in his hands, his fingers spread from halfway up his cheeks to the top of his forehead. He slowly lowered his hands and looked at Michael blankly.

"There's something we'd like you to see," said Michael casually with a tinge of reluctance, as if he were speaking of some tedious and insignificant matter someone had obliged him to deal with.

Izzy Mashiah rose heavily to his feet and followed him into the room. "Sit down," said Michael, offering him the black executive armchair, "and take these." He handed him the gloves he had stripped off his hands.

Izzy Mashiah looked at them with surprise.

"So as not to blur any existing fingerprints," Michael explained. Izzy nodded, removed his gold ring, put it carefully down next to him, and pulled on the gloves. Behind him Michael heard Balilty moving heavily, and he knew that he was switching on his little tape recorder.

From the first moment, when Michael laid the bundle of paper down in front of him—he had lifted it with his fingertips and laid it down with reverent care—Izzy Mashiah's face remained expressionless. Seconds passed before he raised his eyebrows and said with astonishment: "It . . . it looks like an authentic old manuscript." He bent over the pages.

"How can you tell?" asked Balilty behind his shoulder.

"Look here." Izzy Mashiah pointed to the staves, which were not printed but drawn in ink. He fingered the edges of the paper. "This clearly is old paper, heavy and fibrous. The handwriting style is old. And here," his finger hovered over something, "is the stamp of a library. We need an expert to tell us exactly which library, but it looks Italian to me. Maybe even Venetian. I need a magnifying glass to . . . And look at these rust stains! Is it a fake?"

No one answered the question, and he repeated it.

"Let's assume it isn't," said Michael finally.

"Do you have a magnifying glass?"

"We'll get you a magnifying glass," said Balilty, and he hurried out of the room. The sound of his feet running heavily down the corridor made the door shake.

"If it's what I think it is," said Izzy Mashiah in a trembling voice, "and if it isn't a fake, and if it really is from a Venetian library, it could . . . it could even be . . ." He looked at the pages with anxiety. "And if it's eighteenth century, which it seems to me to be, it could even be . . ." he repeated anxiously and raised his eyes to Michael, who maintained an inscrutable expression. Very carefully Izzy Mashiah turned the pages. "If it's authentic," he said as he did so, "it's not complete. The beginning is missing, but that's typical of such manuscripts, because they consist of a gathering of folded sheets of paper. Here, you see?" He picked up the corner of a sheet that was separate from the one lying underneath it. "Anyhow, I'm not a manuscript expert, and anything I say here is limited."

"You've never seen this music before?"

Izzy Mashiah looked at him with astonishment. "This music? Me? Where could I have seen it?"

"How should I know? Maybe at Gabi's?"

"It was never in our apartment," Izzy Mashiah assured him.

"Believe me, I wouldn't have forgotten something like this. Not that we didn't have some old manuscripts at home. Once Felix even bought a Baroque manuscript, but it was some instructional music, exercises. But something like this? If it's authentic it's worth a lot. Priceless," he blurted. "Where did you get it?"

Michael did not reply.

"Is it Theo's?" Izzy persisted. "I want to know if it's Theo's."

Balilty flung open the door, out of breath. He put a magnifying glass down in front of Izzy. "Here you are," he said, and he dropped onto a chair. Sergeant Ya'ir came into the room and stood in the corner at the door, as if on guard.

Izzy looked at the stamp through the magnifying glass. "Yes," he said in a tremulous voice, "it's the seal of a Venetian library, and below a rust stain the year 1725 is written. See for yourself."

He offered the magnifying glass to Michael, who took it, held it with a steady hand, and looked. Izzy Mashiah paged reverently through the second sheaf, then the third and fourth. "It's a requiem," he said suddenly. "The torso of a requiem, since the beginning's missing," he said to himself. "And the end, too. But the middle, the middle!" He stood up and started walking around the room. "If only Gabi could have seen this!" he said in a strangled voice. "He's the man you need now. It would have been only right for him to have seen and heard this. He would have gone out of his mind about this!"

"Maybe he did see it," said Michael calmly.

Izzy stared at him. "Do you think he would have known of something like this and not told me?" he demanded. And he went on furiously: "You don't understand anything! There's no chance that he wouldn't have told me about it. He told me everything, especially in this area! Even if it's a fake, a fake on such a high level! Music like this! He wouldn't have been able to sleep at night!"

"And had he been sleeping well recently?" asked Balilty.

Izzy recoiled and froze. His face reflected confusion, terror, illumination, and terror again. "Is this what was in Delft?" he asked Michael in a whisper. "Was it this?" he demanded threateningly as he took hold of Michael's blue shirtsleeve. "Is this the business he had with that antique dealer in Holland?"

"That's what we think," said Michael.

Izzy Mashiah dropped his hand from Michael's arm, looked at the manuscript, sat down, and stared blankly in front of him, his face very pale. "He didn't tell me anything about it," he whispered. "Not a word, not even a hint. How can that be?"

"How can we find out who the composer is?"

Izzy Mashiah pushed the score of *Les Troyens* away, put his arm on the desk, and laid his forehead on his arm. "I'm going to faint," he warned, and with great difficulty he took shallow, whistling breaths.

Michael pulled him to his feet and dragged him to the window. He opened it. The rain wet their faces.

"I need my medicine," said Izzy Mashiah. Drops of sweat gathered on his brow.

"What medicine?" Balilty barked.

"It's an inhaler. I have asthma."

"Don't you have it with you?" asked Michael.

"In my pocket," said Izzy in a stifled voice. "In my jacket pocket."

"Where's your jacket?" demanded Balilty.

"Outside, I think."

Balilty opened the door. "There's no jacket on the chair," he announced from the corridor. "Where outside?"

"Maybe there in the office," said Izzy, his chin trembling. "In Zisowitz's office."

"Who's Zisowitz?" said Balilty.

"The orchestra manager," replied Michael, and Balilty charged down the corridor to the manager's office and returned with a light-colored jacket. He rummaged roughly through the pockets and produced a small box. "Is this it?" he asked, and at a nod from Izzy Mashiah he took out a small inhaler.

Izzy sprayed and inhaled. Michael now remembered Ruth Mashiah's warnings about his asthma. The thought of her brought with it the image of a tiny face and the sound of running feet he might have heard some day. And a stab of pain in his heart. She's gone, he reflected sternly. Gone. It's over. Finished. They've even found the mother. There's no point in even thinking about it now. He resumed poring over the manuscript.

Little by little Izzy Mashiah started breathing regularly again. He didn't look at the policemen as he put the inhaler away in its box. He also avoided looking at them when he sat down on the chair again, and pulled the manuscript toward him. Whistling with every breath, he continued carefully to leaf through the second sheaf. "The Introit is missing, this is the Dies Irae," he said apathetically, "and if it's authentic, it's Vivaldi. It certainly looks like his work."

"What's that you said?" demanded Balilty, and Michael remained silent so as not to antagonize him.

"Dies Irae . . . It means Day of Wrath, the Day of Judgment. It's a standard part of the Requiem Mass," said Izzy Mashiah, his voice tremulous and remote. "And it's always the most stormy part. You can hear that in Mozart's and Verdi's requiems. But in the Baroque period they liked it especially stormy. They liked to stress the drama. And the greatest creator of musical storms at the time—what the Italians called *temporale*—was Antonio Vivaldi. Anyone who has heard his *La tempesta di mare* concerto can see that this Dies Irae is by him."

"You can tell how it sounds just from looking at the notes? You don't have to play it to know?" Balilty asked doubtfully.

Izzy Mashiah looked at him with astonishment. A few seconds passed before he understood the question. "I can read music," he said, gripping his soft, trembling chin. "I can't understand why he didn't tell me," he murmured. "And I'll never forgive him," he vowed, bursting into tears.

Balilty inflated his cheeks and expelled his breath noisily. He looked at Michael with a vexed expression and rolled his eyes at the ceiling as if to say, What do we do now?

"If you don't feel up to it," said Michael paternally, "we can bring in an expert. We have experts we can call on, and there's no problem about bringing in someone from outside—"

"There's no need." Izzy Mashiah roused himself. He blew his nose, dried his tears, and stopped crying. "I can deal with it. I can examine the manuscript right now and give you a definite answer."

"Are you sure?" asked Michael, ignoring Balilty's warning look. "We can easily have it examined by someone from the university and by our lab."

"There's no one in Israel who knows any more about the Baroque than I do," said Izzy Mashiah, his breath whistling again. "Now that

Gabi's gone, there's no one. And besides, I'm entitled to see it before anyone from outside . . . I'm sure that I . . . You're not just simply going to take it outside," he cried out, horrified. "Outside in the rain!"

They waited for a few moments while Izzy Mashiah leaned back in his chair and used the inhaler again. Then he carefully turned pages once more. His lips moved occasionally like the lips of a person silently praying.

"It's a requiem. And the whole of the Kyrie is missing because the first pages are missing. Apparently the first sheaf is lost. The second section is here, and so is the third, and we have part of the fourth. The last section is missing. Altogether we have three sections—the second, the third, and part of the fourth, which begins with the Offertorium and breaks off in the middle. Do you see?" He turned the pages carefully. "In every sheaf there are eight leaves written on both sides. In other words, sixteen pages. We have here thirty-two pages from two sheaves and another four of the Offertorium. There's no title page and no composer's signature. There are signs that it's Vivaldi. You can see his stylistic fingerprints and also his wit."

Again he sank back. "It's simply inconceivable that he didn't share this with me," he muttered. "Maybe he intended to tell me when he got back from Holland," Izzy said, staring at the music. "Maybe if I'd picked him up at the airport he would have told me. But I didn't go because I was so hurt. And that hurt him, and . . ."

Once more he turned pages. Wiping his face and rubbing his eyes under the lenses of his glasses until they reddened, he suddenly said: "I see that he didn't complete everything, some parts have been left blank." His finger hovered over the manuscript and came to rest on the desktop. "I can explain that as follows," he said with undisguised excitement. "Vivaldi had a number of patrons. One of them was a certain cardinal whose name I don't remember. In the sources there are references to a mass written in 1722, possibly for Ferdinand de Medici, the Grand Duke of Tuscany. Although we don't know exactly what kind of mass it was, it was apparently the kind where certain parts are left unwritten. In other words, in a mass for the dead the composer wrote part of it and the rest the priest would intone in traditional chant.

"And here, in the Sanctus, is one of your proofs," he went on.

"Proof of what?" demanded Balilty severely, in a hard voice.

"That it really is by Vivaldi. The music of this Sanctus is an exact replica of the music in a passage of Vivaldi's *Gloria Mass*. And it's logical that he should have taken it from there because the number of syllables is the same in both texts and both passages are in the same key, but maybe . . ." He fell into a reflective silence.

"Maybe what?" demanded Balilty.

"Maybe we're only seeing part of the score and in the original there were also parts for trumpets and drums."

"I can't see how that amounts to any kind of proof," said Balilty sullenly. "That you know it's from somewhere else. Isn't that what you said?"

Izzy Mashiah was gazing at him absently, and suddenly he roused himself. "What don't you understand?"

"What it proves."

"At that time they all quoted one another. Bach did it, and Handel also took things from other composers. But Vivaldi was famous all over Europe during his lifetime, and none of his contemporaries would have risked taking something of his and putting it into a work of his own."

"How did something like this end up in Holland?" asked Balilty. "You say he lived in Italy."

"Vivaldi traveled a lot, both in Italy and abroad. Long journeys to all kinds of places. We know that he was in Holland in 1738. He was very famous, and Bach himself and his son Carl Philipp Emanuel Bach arranged works by him. I'm sure that this manuscript circulated. There's documentation of a performance, in 1722 or 1728, of a piece that subsequently was lost. Though it has never been identified as a requiem, this could well be that piece."

"You know a lot about it," said Balilty from behind Michael's back. He spoke with reluctance tinged with respect.

"About Vivaldi? I'm an authority on Vivaldi," said Izzy Mashiah bitterly. "And that's why I simply can't understand how Gabi could have . . . He always discussed everything to do with Vivaldi . . . I know everything that's known about Vivaldi. Every date, every quarrel, every woman he slept with, and . . ." His lower lip trembled and he wrung his hands. "I don't understand it. And I thought he had someone else.

Maybe when I was suspicious, when I was angry with him, he was busy with this."

He paused for a moment and took a deep breath. "Well, I suppose you could say this was the someone else." He fell silent for a moment. "Gabi told me that he was going to his father's place. I called there and there was no answer. I thought he was lying, and when he came home I made a scene. Maybe they were together consulting. . . . I wish . . . How could he have kept this from me?"

"Maybe he was sworn to secrecy," Sergeant Ya'ir suddenly suggested from his place at the door.

Michael turned around quickly and gave him a threatening look. He was afraid that this interruption would cut off the flow of Izzy's talk.

"Who? Who could have . . ." Izzy began loudly, the hurt growing in his voice, and suddenly he stopped.

"Yes?" Balilty's small eyes narrowed as he asked: "Yes? What were you going to say?"

"Only Felix could have . . ." said Izzy Mashiah with his head bowed. "He was the only who had such power over Gabi, to make him swear not to tell me. But I can't understand why. I'm just the person they should have asked. It's not possible that Gabi didn't know about it and Theo did. And if Theo knew, why didn't they tell me, too? I don't understand it."

"So you're an authority on Vivaldi," said Balilty, bringing him back to the subject. "Aren't we lucky," he added joylessly. "You were in the middle of your explanation. You were saying," he said, rolling his eyes toward the ceiling and then looking at Izzy Mashiah from behind Michael's shoulder, "you were talking about the sources. The word 'requiem' isn't mentioned there."

In a monotonous voice, as if his mind were somewhere else, Izzy Mashiah said: "The Dutch had better printers than the Italians. There was a big demand then for Italian music in Northern Europe. Vivaldi was most popular in Germany. As early as 1711 a Dutch publisher, Etienne Roger, printed one of the most important musical publications of the first half of the eighteenth century, Vivaldi's *L'estro armonico,* twelve concertos for solo violin, two violins, and four violins."

"You're absolutely positive that this is by Vivaldi?" Michael asked.

"I'm more or less certain. Even if it's not his autograph manuscript, it's definitely his composition, in a copy made from his original draft. It can't be by an imitator, because no one in Venice would have dared to perform in public a piece so characteristic of Vivaldi. A piece with the Sanctus taken from Vivaldi's *Gloria Mass.* And the style, too. I wish I weren't so sure. I wish it weren't Vivaldi. How could he? Not a word. He didn't tell me anything!"

"Would you please describe to me the special features of Vivaldi's style?" Michael asked. "Briefly."

"Now?"

Michael nodded, and Izzy Mashiah leaned back in a demonstrative display of exhaustion.

"He had a weakness for what, during the Baroque period, they called *bizarrerie*. In other words, whimsicality or oddness or the fantastical," he said, looking out the window as if his eyes were swallowing the darkness. "It's there even in the *Four Seasons*, which is full of surprising, novel effects. He was extremely original, and here, in the Dies Irae," he said, tapping wearily on the desktop, "you can see it clearly."

"That's it? Is that enough?"

"Another thing," continued Izzy Mashiah after a long pause, "which appears here in the choral parts, is Vivaldi's abstractness. It's true that when we speak of particularly fine Baroque melodists we often think of Corelli, but Vivaldi, too, had a lyrical gift. But his specialty was constructing entire movements without a single melody, merely recurring motifs repeated in a variety of keys, as in the concerto *La notte.*"

"And that's enough proof of a style? That would be enough for musicologists to establish Vivaldi as the composer of this work?"

Izzy Mashiah sighed. "Even if it's not a composition of Vivaldi's, it's still worth a good deal," he said apathetically. "But I'm convinced that it is by Vivaldi. The musicologists would agree with me."

"And something like this could really be found out of the blue in an old organ in Delft?"

"Berlioz's Mass was found lying on the top shelf of an organ loft in a Belgian church. It was a bundle of paper tied up with string, covered with dust," said Izzy Mashiah. "These things are sometimes involved with inheritances and other kinds of complications. You know, musicians keep their music in all sorts of peculiar places. Why not in an old organ in Delft?"

"I don't know if you realize this," said Balilty slowly, "but if it belonged to Gabriel van Gelden, you're the heir. He left you everything."

Izzy Mashiah's face turned pale. He stared blankly at the manuscript and quickly took his hands off the desk. "Gabi didn't tell me anything about it," he lamented again, shaking his head from side to side. "Not a single word. He couldn't have wanted it to be mine. It isn't mine if there's nothing official registered about it anywhere. And maybe I really don't deserve it, because I didn't trust him and I accused him of . . ." His lips pouted in an aggrieved expression. "And if he didn't intend me to have it, I don't want it."

"How could he have intended you to have it?" said Balilty, almost with pity. "He thought he was going to publish it, he didn't know that somebody was going to behead him because of it."

"Because of it?" Izzy Mashiah recoiled, and he looked around. "Because of it? Who?"

"Theoretically it could have been you," Balilty reminded him.

Izzy Mashiah looked at him uncomprehendingly. "I didn't even know that it existed! He didn't tell me about it!"

"Such things have happened before," said Balilty sententiously. "And for far less than this."

"But I didn't know anything about it!"

Nobody spoke.

"I don't want to look at it anymore," whispered Izzy Mashiah. "I don't want to touch it."

Balilty put his head to one side. "I can promise you that you'll get over it. A million is a million, after all. Anyway," he said dryly, "can you attest in writing to everything you've just explained to us?"

Izzy Mashiah nodded miserably. "I didn't kill Gabriel," he said as they were standing at the door. "I didn't know anything about the manuscript. And I wasn't in the concert hall building."

"You lied on the polygraph," Balilty reminded him.

"But I didn't kill Gabi," he pleaded.

"If you didn't kill him," said Balilty, opening the door, "then we shouldn't let you out of our sight. With what you know now, your life is in danger."

"And Nita? Is Nita involved in it, too?" Izzy Mashiah whispered, horrified, to Michael in the corridor.

"And now I want to bring in a documents expert from Forensics," said Balilty to Michael in the car. "Even if we find the Dutch authentication certificate. Was there nothing like that in the safe?"

"It could have been put in a bank abroad," said Michael.

"But he hasn't left the country since his father's . . ." said Balilty, almost too late to catch himself in time.

"Maybe the papers were left in Holland, and there hasn't been time to retrieve them. What . . . ?" Michael turned around in his seat.

Izzy Mashiah was looking at them as if he had suddenly realized something that made him say, with a tremulous voice: "Stop here quickly!" He covered his mouth with his hands. Sergeant Ya'ir quickly opened the back door, waving his hands and shaking his head at a woman who stopped to stare as Izzy Mashiah vomited onto the curb.

"No forensic expert will want to touch it," said Balilty, drumming on the car window. "They'll be afraid to damage it. I know them. They'll say that the examination might ruin it. We'll be better off trying to get the authentication papers out of him."

"Go wash your face and have something to drink," said Michael to Izzy Mashiah when they arrived at the parking lot in the Russian Compound. "We've got a long night ahead of us," he warned Balilty as the operator announced over the transmitter that Eli Bahar was looking for them.

"Where is he?" asked Balilty.

"On the Tel Aviv–Jerusalem highway. In a traffic jam. There's a demonstration, he's trying to get onto the shoulder. He wants you to contact him on the cell phone, not the radio."

Izzy Mashiah looked at his face in the cracked mirror in the bathroom at police headquarters. Michael stood at the door with his arms crossed. "After you sign your statement," he said, "I'll explain to you what we want from you in connection with Theo."

Izzy Mashiah turned on the faucet. The water spurted out noisily.

"Theo's coming here? He'll be here and I'll have to see him?" he whispered with his head under the tap.

"Not just yet. He'll be brought here, but it'll be a while, and until then we'll have time to. . . ."

Water streamed from Izzy Mashiah's face and hair, and he passed the palms of his hands over his head. "I can't see Theo now," he said, and he sat down on the floor. He raised his knees and rested his head on them. His breath whistled. The faucet dripped. "I can't," he pleaded.

"You loved Gabriel," Michael reminded him, feeling as if he were talking to a child who at any moment might throw a tantrum.

"He never told me anything about it," moaned Izzy Mashiah from between his knees. "Not a word, not a hint, not a thing."

"Let's go," said Michael gently, helping him up. "We've made some tea with lemon for you."

15

A Matter of the Dynamics

Very carefully, and without his usual patronizing "Very nice, Zippo, good for you," Balilty removed the cassette from the small tape recorder. The tape that Zippo had brought back from his conversations with Herzl Cohen was stopped at the point where the name of the Belgian expert Felix had met in Amsterdam was mentioned. Balilty's face remained fixed and frozen. It had taken on the baffled expression of someone unable to accept that reality had refuted his prejudices. It was evident around the mouth and in the slackness of his lips, and it also dominated his eyes, which followed the mechanical tapping of the pencil in Michael's hand. He was on the phone, speaking at length with Jean Bonaventure, a distinguished scholar of Baroque music and manuscripts, who had drawn up and signed, more than six months before in Brussels, the documents that confirmed Izzy Mashiah's suppositions. To Michael, Bonaventure's musical explanations—in French with a Belgian accent—sounded familiar. The Belgian gave reasons nearly identical to Izzy Mashiah's for considering the work a torso of a requiem by Antonio Vivaldi. The musicologist added that, having promised Felix van Gelden to keep the discovery a secret and even signed a notarized statement to that effect, he was now disturbed over the delay in announcing the existence of the Vivaldi requiem and in performing and publishing it.

It took the intervention of the first secretary at the Israeli embassy in Brussels ("A friend of mine from the army," Balilty had said as he promised "to take care of the problem in no time") to persuade Bonaventure to talk to the Jerusalem police and to sign a statement.

Averting his face from Balilty in order to concentrate on the conversation, Michael sensed Balilty's efforts to take down some of Michael's hurried translation of the stream of French coming from the speakerphone. Out of the corner of his eye he noticed Balilty diligently writing, licking his full lips as he did so, phrases like "dating the paper," "age of the ink," "different watermarks," "fine Venetian paper," and "techniques of . . . ," at which point Balilty touched Michael on the shoulder. "What was that word? Techniques of what?" he demanded.

Michael apologized to the musicologist, switched off the speaker, and replied to Balilty: "Techniques of staff printing." Balilty nodded and Michael switched the speaker on again. Once more the room resounded with the loud, hoarse voice of a suddenly awakened elderly man explaining that he had compared the handwriting in the newly discovered requiem with that in confirmed Vivaldi autograph manuscripts and that his examination clearly indicated that the manuscript in Felix van Gelden's possession was the work of a copyist, all but some measures that had been added later by Vivaldi himself.

"I still can't believe what Zippo got out of Herzl Cohen!" said Balilty as he again listened to the tapes of the conversations with the Belgian musicologist and the copyright lawyer Meyuhas. "I should say something to him, no?" he added guiltily.

"Are you ready to go in?" asked Michael. He was nervous, with a knot in his stomach and the feeling that fateful events were still in store. "They've been waiting for us for over two hours already."

"What am I doing, playing bridge?" said Balilty sulkily. "It's better to get all this stuff wrapped up beforehand."

In the conference room Eli Bahar was standing behind Avram, who was sitting at the table looking at papers. Tzilla, who had come in after Michael and Balilty, said, breathing heavily: "I've brought Nita here. They're waiting in separate rooms. I put her in your office, because of the sofa," Tzilla said to Shorer. "She doesn't know Theo's already here. She's lying down. She really is sick. And Theo," she turned to Michael, "is waiting in your office. We thought we should put him in a small room. And, as you ordered, he's not alone. The duty sergeant is with him. Theo doesn't know anything yet either, including the fact that Nita's here too. Izzy Mashiah is talking to the woman from the Forensics documents lab now. What's her name?"

"Sima?" asked Balilty. "The one with curly hair and big glasses?"

"That's right, Sima," Tzilla confirmed.

"She's okay, she knows what she's doing," said Balilty, sitting down to the right of Shorer, who was absorbed in the pathologist's report, going rapidly though the papers in front of him. At the far end of the table, his head also down, Sergeant Ya'ir, too, was absorbed in copies of the same papers. His finger hovered over the lines and he frowned in concentration, as if he didn't want to miss a single word.

"Great strength," murmured Shorer. "Do you hear? It says here that whoever did it would have had to exert great strength. If it was a woman she would have had to be enormous. Look," he said to no one in particular, "it says: 'low probability.'" He took off his reading glasses.

"So it really looks as if she's out of the picture," remarked Balilty. "If that's so . . ." he said thoughtfully and fell silent.

Michael looked at him anxiously, as if he were reading his mind, and quickly said: "Forget it."

"Forget what?" asked Balilty innocently.

"Forget what you're thinking. I can do it myself. I *want* to do it myself."

"Did you get her inside without the reporters noticing?" Eli asked Tzilla.

"There was only one of them still waiting. All the rest have given up. He keeps nagging me about the Japanese knife."

"What Japanese knife?" asked Eli, surprised.

"He got it into his head that Gabriel van Gelden's throat was cut with a Japanese knife. You know what they're like. If you don't tell them anything they make up some nonsense and then—"

"You can't do that to her," Michael warned Balilty.

Shorer looked from one to the other and then asked impatiently what they were talking about.

"He thinks he knows what I'm thinking. Now he's a mind reader." Balilty raised his eyes to the ceiling.

"We don't have time for these games," said Shorer with some irritation. "Tomorrow I have a meeting with the commissioner and the minister. It's already one A.M. They want to transfer the case away from us. Please get to the point, Danny."

"Look," said Balilty with ostentatious patience. "We have a serious problem here, which we've often had in the past. I'm not saying that nothing like this has ever happened before, but this time it's particularly serious. You know it yourself, sir," he said to Shorer. "We learned it from you, and from him, too," he said, and nodded in Michael's direction. "It's a matter of the dynamics of the kind of interrogation awaiting us now. Almost everything we have in this case is circumstantial. I don't believe we can break him."

"But he doesn't even have an alibi!" cried Eli Bahar. "What do you mean, circumstantial? He lied about his alibi. We've talked to the Canadian woman and we've talked to the musician girl. He wasn't with the first, and he wasn't with the second at the right time! And we have a motive, too, now. And an opportunity. We have everything. It's an open-and-shut case!"

"We want a confession and a reenactment of the crime," pronounced Balilty. He leaned forward, spreading his hands out on the table in front of him as if he were about to transfer his weight to them. "We've done a great job. We've even got the lawyer's testimony about the meeting that was supposed to have taken place, and about Gabriel van Gelden's visit to him. Not to mention the Belgian and the copies of the authentication documents that will arrive by express tomorrow. We've done a hell of a job. It would be a shame to throw it all away without trying to get a confession out of him. Otherwise it'll drag out for months in court."

"What's the problem?" asked Avram.

"The esteemed maestro," said Balilty slowly, "doesn't give a damn about any of us. He has no respect for us, and no fear of us, either."

Only Zippo spoke. "Why do we need him to give a damn?" he asked, undeterred by the sour expression on Balilty's face. "I want to understand," he persevered. "How will I learn if I don't ask?"

Balilty looked around with the weary expression of someone asked to explain the obvious. "Well," he said reluctantly, "it's a matter of the dynamics of the interrogation."

"I don't understand," said Zippo with uncharacteristic determination. "Please explain it to me."

"You know how an interrogation like this is conducted," said Balilty with a sigh. "It can take days, at least hours."

"Yes?"

"And you know that there has to be some kind of relationship between the interrogator and the subject?"

"So?"

"I don't know anything about this music," Balilty said, squirming, "and even our friend Ohayon, who knows something about it, even if he knows a lot about it, this maestro with his international reputation and all doesn't give a damn about him."

"He doesn't?" said Zippo, surprised. Eli Bahar sighed loudly.

"He thinks," said Balilty, and he looked at Michael, "forgive me, but he thinks that we're all stupid. Including you. Isn't that so?"

Michael lit a cigarette. His hand was trembling.

"So what?" said Zippo. He polished his silver lighter with his thumb and smoothed his mustache. "You thought I was stupid, but that didn't stop me from bringing you that Herzl Cohen cassette, right?"

Balilty removed his hands from the table, wiped his brow, looked at Michael and Shorer with a helpless expression, and admitted uncomfortably: "That was a very nice bit of work. But it's not the same kind of thing."

"If I'd been put in the picture from the beginning," said Zippo mildly, "if he didn't always prefer to work alone," he said, nodding toward Michael, "I could have helped even more."

"Let's stop wasting time," said Shorer. "Just tell us what you think and why Michael's opposed to it. We aren't, as you can see, mind readers."

"He wants a confrontation with Nita," Michael burst out. His face flamed. "He wants her to talk to Theo. For us to be behind the glass. She won't be able to get through it. And anyway, she'll never agree."

Shorer gave Balilty a questioning look, and Balilty nodded and blinked as if he was disappointed by Michael's good guess, which prevented him from expounding his plan in full.

A tense silence descended on the conference room. It was as if no one was prepared to reveal his position one way or the other. Sergeant Ya'ir folded his arms and examined everyone's faces with a serious, interested look.

"What do you say?" asked Shorer finally, looking at Tzilla. "You've been with her all these hours. What do you say? Can she get through it?"

"She's really sick," said Tzilla doubtfully. "She's delirious half the time. But she's not so weak. Her body has been weakened, but she's . . . I don't know how to say it, but it's as if she's got some kind of strength. She's not an ordinary person."

"What can we lose by trying?" demanded Balilty. "If everyone agrees, if we stage it properly, we can get a recorded confession out of him in no time and then confront him with it. If not—if she doesn't agree to participate, or if he doesn't say anything to her—what have we lost? We can't worry now about what's good for her and what's not."

"A recorded confession isn't admissible in court. And if he recants afterward?" said Avram.

"She won't agree," said Michael, his armpits becoming damp.

"We don't have to put it to her like that," said Balilty sharply. "If you weren't . . . If it were about a stranger, you wouldn't have any problem with it. Where are we here? Have we sworn always to tell the truth during interrogations? You know that doing it is right for the dynamics."

"Of course, the dynamics," muttered Michael. "The sacred dynamics."

Balilty gave him an accusing look. "You're the one who introduced the term in the first place, and you didn't have anything against it when it was a question of interrogating strangers," he said maliciously. "But here? Here it's about family."

Shorer coughed. "That's enough, Danny, you've made your point," he said, crumbling the burned match he had fished out of the ashtray in front of Michael.

"Maybe . . ." Sergeant Ya'ir said, hesitating. Everyone turned to look at him with surprise, as if they had forgotten his presence. "Maybe we could come back to the point raised by the chief. I once heard Ohayon give a lecture on the dynamics of interrogation," he said, gesturing toward Michael, "and I don't understand why he can't interrogate the suspect himself. She really does have fever and chills and nausea. She really isn't in good shape. I personally think that she's too weak for something like this." His brown eyes met those of Michael, who suddenly noticed him as if for the first time, remembering Balilty's mocking remark that Ya'ir reminded him of the Michael of twenty years ago.

"You know as well as I do," said Balilty impatiently, "that interrogating Theo van Gelden would take dozens of hours, without the dramas you see in the movies. It's no secret that we have to get him on technical issues. The whole thing demands . . . a kind of chemistry with the suspect. You're not going to get that kind of chemistry between Mr. Theo Van Gelden and any of us here."

"I don't agree with you," said Sergeant Ya'ir pleasantly. "I actually think that there could be chemistry between Theo van Gelden and Chief Superintendent Ohayon."

Shorer pushed the pathologist's report aside. "Do we really have to go into the psychology of interrogation now?" he grumbled.

"I don't know if he's right," said Michael, glancing at Sergeant Ya'ir. "I really don't know if I could get him to the point of needing me to listen to his self-justifications. Even if he doesn't really think I'm stupid. For him I'm just an object. If he doesn't need something specific from me, I barely exist. But that's something that could change during the course of the interrogation."

"No such situation could ever exist between the two of you. This guy's much too full of himself," protested Balilty. "You'd never get on the kind of footing with him that you did with that Air Force officer, Colonel Beitan. And that wasn't murder, only embezzlement, but there you really did . . ." He shook his head with reluctant admiration. "There you did a really nice job. When you listen to the tapes of the interrogation you can see exactly where you were leading him and what was going on between the two of you. The whole thing really depended on his trust in you, and on how important it was to him what you thought of him."

"I'd like to hear those tapes myself," said Sergeant Ya'ir fearlessly. "I'd like to know exactly how it happened. I came across Colonel Beitan myself, in the early stages of the investigation, and he, too, as my father says about him, was one of those 'born unto trouble, like the sparks that fly upward.'"

Balilty looked at him in astonishment mingled with incomprehension. He leaned back in his chair, opened and closed his mouth, rolled his eyes, sat up, and cocked his head as he did when he was about to say something particularly caustic. "What kind of sparks?" he said nastily. What really bothered him was not the biblical reference but the unusual combination—also impressive to Michael, even in these moments of extreme tension—of naiveté and assertiveness.

But before Ya'ir could go on, Shorer interrupted, saying firmly: "In that case—how should I put it?—Chief Superintendent Ohayon succeeded in becoming for the subject, at least in that particular context, a figure with moral authority. One capable of granting absolution. After you've worked for years in our profession, as we have," he explained, "you see that people have a great need for moral justification in general. And sometimes, with some luck, the interrogator can turn into someone who in the suspect's mind's eye can insure forgiveness, pardon, or moral legitimization. He becomes an authority figure. It doesn't always work, but in that particular case it worked very well."

"Sometimes you have to do terrible things," said Balilty, sinking into reflection. "You wouldn't believe the things I myself have done. I've even cried with suspects. About their lives and mine. And about their crime. Once I even told someone . . ." A gleam flicked for a moment in his eyes as he lowered them and said: "Never mind that now."

"And Michael," Eli suddenly intervened, "during the interrogation of Colonel Beitan, spent hours talking about their divorces and their relationships with their children! A quarter of the interrogation was spent on that. Remember?"

Michael bowed his head. Even now he felt uncomfortable remembering those interrogations and the enjoyment with which his colleagues had listened to the tapes. He remembered only too well the moments when there was no pretense in those dialogues, and it seemed to him now that everyone had sensed the exact moment when he had been tempted to really open up, that they knew it as well as he did. And as if he had read Michael's thoughts, Eli added: "And it isn't just a trick, it isn't only cunning, it's a relationship between two people coming into being."

Michael shifted in his chair. He had to say something now, to put an end to the embarrassment and shame overwhelming him. Especially at the memory of sharing with the colonel a crisis in his relationship with his son, Yuval. So he quickly brought the discussion back to the theoretical level: "What prevents criminals from confessing isn't fear of imprisonment," he heard himself explaining to Sergeant Ya'ir. "They don't always have enough imagination for that. They don't really see themselves in prison. What frightens them, surprising as it may sound, is actually the moral aspect. Their difficulty in living with moral guilt is what enables us to communicate with them. They long, most of them at any rate, to attain a state, a sense, a confirmation that from a moral point of view they're in the right. In this case before us now, getting moral support for the right to have a father's love. That's how one can get through to Theo van Gelden. And if the interrogator is prepared to accept the suspect's position, he's on the way to getting a confession. In other words, if Theo van Gelden feels that, from the moral point, I accept his motives, understand them, maybe even justify them, we have a chance with him. The question that bothers Danny is whether I can be a significant enough figure for Theo van Gelden to grant him legitimization."

"We haven't got much time," Balilty suddenly warned. "We haven't got time for philosophy now."

"In this kind of interrogation," said Shorer, "you always wonder about what kind of person you're up against. You suddenly find yourself talking about yourself. You look for points of contact. Just as you would with anyone. One of the reasons Michael gets such surprising results is that he's really prepared to open up and understand the person opposite him."

"Not always," Michael heard himself saying. "Not with Tuvia Shai, for example, and not in other cases, where I simply had to lay a trap."

"Murderers," said Shorer, "have to be understood just like everyone else. Their motivation, how they think, how they feel."

"What makes them tick," said Balilty in English.

"Why do you think he can't do it this time?" persevered Sergeant Ya'ir. "Ohayon is even connected with the family, if I understood correctly. That might give him an edge."

"That's exactly the problem," said Balilty, pounding the table with his fist. "He's introducing irrelevant personal considerations. We should work in two stages, her first."

"What have we decided?" demanded Shorer impatiently. "Can you put it to her in a way that will make her want to do it, or not?"

Michael nodded and stood up. He couldn't speak.

"Take Nita to the blue room," he heard Balilty call after him. "We'll put him there first."

The blue room was as gray as all the others. Rumor had it that its name came from a blue curtain that once covered the one-way mirror behind which witnesses sat to identify suspects.

Three times Michael was on the point of jumping up and bursting into the room to rescue Nita. Each time he sat down again between Balilty and Shorer, gripping the metal frame of his chair and looking around without otherwise moving. From the moment he had touched her arm and led her into the blue room, he felt as if he had put her on a path that would make her incapable of surviving. For a few moments he even had the feeling that she was in actual physical danger, that she would not emerge from the blue room alive. He had submitted meekly to her accusations of cruelty, accusations she had made in a cold, unfamiliar, openly hostile voice in Shorer's office. Now, through the one-way mirror, he again was struck by the flush covering her face. He had expected to find her in a state of collapse in Shorer's office, to which he had hurried from the conference room. But he hadn't expected this face, radiant with a rosiness he had never seen on it before, the deep gray eyes glittering with fever. She had listened to him attentively when he told her about the requiem and its discovery, about the conversation with the Belgian expert, about Theo's exploded alibi. "There's no such thing," she said firmly. "I simply don't believe it."

Michael sighed. He picked up the phone and asked for Izzy Mashiah and the Forensics documents expert to be sent in, along with the manuscript.

"Is it true?" she asked Izzy Mashiah, after she put the manuscript down on the sofa. "He says . . ." she said in a choked voice that she then raised somewhat. "He says it was found in Theo's office."

Izzy bowed his head.

"He says that Theo . . . Gabi . . . Father . . . is it true? Do you know anything about it? Do you believe it? Do you believe him, Izzy?"

Izzy Mashiah looked at the manuscript and at Michael. His breath came in short, rapid gasps. "Gabi didn't tell me about it. He didn't share it with me. But it's by Vivaldi. It's definitely by Vivaldi. And it was in Theo's office, inside a score of *Les Troyens*."

"What he seems to be implying," insisted Nita, "he doesn't say it directly, but the implication is that because of it Theo murdered Father and Gabi." She averted her eyes from Michael, to whom she referred coldly and caustically, as if he were her worst enemy.

Izzy Mashiah turned pale. Beads of sweat broke out on his forehead. His breath whistled weakly.

"What do you say about it, Izzy? You loved Gabi, what do you say about it?" Her voice was cold and resolute.

"I didn't mean him any harm," said Izzy fearfully. "They showed me the Vivaldi. . . . Who could have known where it would lead?"

"He says that Theo didn't meet the woman before the concert that day. He says that Theo . . . the string . . . he says that . . ." Her voice broke. Now she looked at Michael. Pain and hatred were mingled in her look.

It wasn't me, Michael wanted to say, I only happen to be here. But he maintained his reserved expression and said nothing.

As if she had heard his mind, she said: "It's not your fault. You didn't cause anything. You just went behind my back and . . . It doesn't matter," she said, waving her hand dismissively. "You're only doing your job."

Izzy Mashiah sat down, dropping into the chair next to where Michael was standing. "I don't know," he whispered. "It really is hard to believe. I don't know what to say."

"For this! For this?" She pointed to the manuscript. "For this, Theo, Gabi's neck with a cello string? Father, for this?"

"Nita," Izzy Mashiah whispered, panting for breath. "It's a requiem by Vivaldi!"

"It's not really because of that, not only because of that," said Michael.

"He says," she said, ignoring Michael, "that Theo was always sick with jealousy of Gabi. Always. And of me. And he couldn't forgive Father for loving Gabi more. He also says that Father loved me, too. And then he says nothing. He lets me reach the conclusion by myself that Theo could kill me, too. As if he's a dangerous lunatic or something. Some kind of Macbeth. What do you think, Izzy? Is that possible?"

"There's only one person who can answer that question. And of all of us the only one he really owes an answer to is you. He owes you an answer," said Izzy in a clear voice. "And from the minute the question's been asked you won't have any peace anyway, and neither will I, and neither will anybody else."

"I wish I were dead. I wish the earth would swallow me up," said Nita.

Izzy looked at Michael helplessly, Michael gestured, and Izzy quietly left the room.

"Don't treat me as if I were crazy," Nita warned him, raising her head as the door closed behind Izzy. "There are families with curses on them. It's a fact and you don't have to be crazy to believe it."

"I don't believe in family curses," said Michael Ohayon. "I always assume that anyone is capable of anything. I've learned that lesson in my life. Do you think there's no hatred in families? Think of the accounts of the Black Plague in Europe in the Middle Ages. How mothers abandoned their babies, running away from them the moment they recognized their children's symptoms. Do you think they didn't love their babies? Husbands left their wives, wives their husbands, lovers their beloved, children their parents—they all ran away in order to survive. Even if they themselves no longer had a chance to survive. Everything fell apart and all bonds were broken because a great horror threatened them. Greater than any love or devotion or responsibility. There's nothing certain in the world. It's impossible to think that anything in it is eternal. I'm very sorry to have to be the one to bring you the news. But believe me—you can't live in the world without knowing this truth."

"I wish I'd never met you," she said suddenly in a lamenting voice. "I wish I were dead."

He was silent.

"All you want is to . . . to impose order. To be right."

He was silent.

"I have no choice," she said suddenly, with less hatred. "I have to talk to Theo, but alone. And before you do. Before you talk to him. I don't want you there when I talk to him," she said threateningly.

He nodded.

"I want to be alone with my brother. Even . . . even if . . . He's still my brother. He doesn't stop being my brother. And if you're right, if there's anything, anything at all, to what you say, he's still my brother. And you can't have a relationship with the sister of . . . of a murderer. It's the end for us. If you're right, and also if you're wrong. You left me alone in this and went over to their side."

He sensed how pale he was and how shallow and rapid his breathing. Every word she said was like a stone aimed straight at his chest, straight at the inside of his head.

"After I've talked with him, even if you're right, I'll never see you again. Even if you're right. And now I can't even ask you if you want me to talk to him. I can't not talk to him. That's what you've done. And even if you didn't do it, it's the way things are."

He wanted to ask her if things would have been different if he hadn't told her, if he had questioned Theo himself, on his own initiative, if he had only faced her with the facts afterward, if he had spared her. He wanted to touch her and tell her how much he had actually been at her side, and how there simply hadn't been any other way. He wanted to explain to her that it wasn't the way that mattered here, but the facts. But even as the thoughts shaped themselves into words he knew that he wouldn't say anything. At this moment he had no right to divert attention to himself. She and the interrogation were the main thing. And there was no point in saying anything to her, since the facts couldn't be altered. If she chose to see him as chiefly responsible for the need to acknowledge them, there was nothing he could do. Now, the thought suddenly surfaced, that's how she sees it now.

"You could have helped us," she suddenly said in a despairing, childish voice.

He spread out his arms in the gesture of helplessness he hated so much.

"Your work and your achievements are what's important to you now," she said bitterly. "You chose them."

He wanted to protest, he longed to tell her that there was no other way, but there was no point in talking. With his head bowed he saw how she was evading the main issue, outflanking it, circumventing it as if she were circling a ring of fire. How intent she was on hurting him, how her lips were sucked in, how her teeth dug into her lower lip, how finally her facial muscles and her body relaxed, and she leaned back with her eyes closed. Her lips moved, over and over again saying soundlessly, as in prayer: "I wish I were dead." Until, suddenly and unexpectedly, she sat up, straightened her back, and said: "I have no choice. I have to know. I can't go on living like this. After I know the truth from Theo, and only from Theo, we'll see if I can go on living. If there's anything left at all."

• • •

The first time Michael wanted to rush into the blue room was when Theo put his hands on her shoulders. At that moment he suddenly had a horrifying vision of those hands encircling her neck and squeezing with all their strength. But Theo only looked into her eyes—again Michael was amazed at the discrepancy between the identical structure of the siblings' eyes and the complete difference of their expressions. Theo's face conveyed only remoteness and coldness, without any fear, while Nita's blazed with a terrible knowledge, with a pain that was hard to look at even from behind the glass. Theo took his hands off her shoulders. For a moment Michael closed his eyes. When he opened them he heard her say: "They found the requiem."

He saw Theo recoil and look around in terror.

"We're alone here," said Nita, "you have nothing to fear, Theo. They found it in your office."

Theo sat down with a thud in the chair next to him.

"You didn't tell me anything about it," said Nita frostily. "Now you have to tell me everything."

Theo shook his head from side to side. Then he raised it and raked his hand through his mane of silver hair. In a strangled voice he said: "They're listening to every word."

"There's nobody here," said Nita. "He promised me."

"He's lying. They're all lying," said Theo. "You were always naive."

Michael stood up and approached the glass wall so closely that his breath left a mark on it. He saw her eyes narrow for a moment and then open wide again.

"Maybe I was," he heard her say simply, and he saw the pink spots on her cheeks darkening, "but I'm not anymore. I can't afford to be."

Theo grunted unintelligibly and looked at her in silence.

"You can tell them whatever you like, Theo," said Nita, putting her hand on his arm. They were sitting opposite and very close to each other. There were only two other chairs and a green metal table in the blue room. "But you have to tell me the truth. Everything."

Theo's eyes darted from corner to corner. He raised them to the ceiling as if looking for hidden microphones. At last he stood up and surveyed the room, as if he were about to begin pacing from wall to wall. But when he realized how small the room was, he sat down again.

"Everything. You must. About Father, too."

"Nita," said Theo angrily. "What can I tell you about Father? You heard yourself that I was with . . . a woman, two women, that day. I feel uncomfortable talking about such things with you."

Her face suddenly turned pale, as if all the blood had drained out of it. For a moment Michael was afraid that she would faint, fall off her chair and hit her head on the dusty stone floor. But she sat up straight, and in a very choked voice she said: "Listen, Theo, listen to me and listen hard. First of all, as you know, I'm not exactly a virgin. Your womanizing is no secret. Second, I'm no longer a child. And if I was still a child not long ago, I'm not one anymore. I had to grow up fast. And third, the Canadian woman you were with at the Hilton, or wherever, says that she wasn't with you."

Theo smiled. For a moment he even looked cheerful. "Naturally she denies it," he said almost relieved. "What do you expect? She's a respectable married woman, a pillar of her community. She has four children."

"Don't talk to me like that," Nita suddenly said with vehemence. "I'm your sister, not some policeman. I'm talking to you because I'm your sister! When will you understand that? You're all I've got left. Even if you . . . Even if you're a murderer," she added in a whisper. "There, I've said it," she muttered in disbelief. "I love you even if you are, unconditionally. But you have to tell me the truth. Don't lie to me anymore. That woman said she was with another man at the time. She gave his name, he confirmed it, they have her on tape and in a signed statement. And Drora Yaffe, too, the violinist you were supposed to be with after that, broke down under interrogation. She said that she waited for you and you didn't show up. So don't tell me any more tales."

"What other man?" asked Theo, his eyes darting. "What other man did she have? She's not even pretty, that Canadian."

"Is that what's important now?"

"So why haven't they arrested me?"

"I don't know," Nita admitted. "Maybe you're already under arrest. But I asked to talk to you, and they let me. I have to know, for my own sake and yours, too. From you and not from them and their interrogations and trials. I have to hear it from you."

"You asked to talk to me? They didn't tell you to?" There was surprise and relief in his voice. "Are you sure?"

"I asked. Nobody told me to," she said in a broken voice. "Don't you understand that you owe me an honest answer? Don't you understand that you have to tell me?"

Theo was silent.

"Only if you tell me might I be able to stand by you. Even though . . . even though Father and Gabi . . . I might be able to . . . I don't know how, but you know I don't tell lies. If you want to be close to me now, if you tell me, if you trust me."

"What does it matter now?" mumbled Theo. "Nothing matters anymore. Believe me. Not if they found the requiem. Did Herzl tell them about it?"

"I don't know. They found it in your office. Inside the score of *Les Troyens*. The one bound in black velvet. The one Mother gave you. The one with the pictures you used to show me when I was little."

Theo was silent.

"I'm not asking you why, Theo. Right now I'm not asking you why, I'm asking you if you did it or not. That's what I'm asking. The why I understand by myself. If anyone can understand it. The why can wait till later."

"You understand it by yourself? How can you?" Theo shouted and stood up. This was the third time Michael was afraid Theo was about to fling himself on her and beat her to death. He stood over her and shouted uncontrollably. In his neck, long like hers, the veins stood out. "How can you understand when all your life you were everybody's darling. They gave you whatever you wanted. You were adored by Father and by Gabi, too. How can you understand what it was like for me to hear from Herzl and then from Father about the requiem and to know that I wasn't going to be allowed to touch it? That it would be the key to Gabi's well-deserved fame? You hear? Gabi's *well-deserved* fame! That's what Father said. Nothing I ever did, in my whole life, all my efforts, all my fame, all the innovations, all the praise for my brilliance—nothing changed the contempt Father felt for me. And his preference for Gabi! Whatever I did, whatever I did was a lost cause. And he talks to me about well-deserved fame. About what Gabi deserves! About his being a *really* serious musician. To me he never said anything like that! Not a word! The first time I conducted the New York Philharmonic, do you remember? Mother came by herself. He couldn't leave the shop! And not even a phone call after the performance. And you can understand that? You with your naiveté? You with the family myth you insisted on cultivating? You . . . you . . . with your fairy-tale life?"

Nita sat frozen. Her arms, like Michael's own, rested stiffly on the arms of her chair, taut as if all her weight were concentrated on the palms of her hands.

"Never a word of praise. Never anything about my talent. Only Gabi, Gabi, Gabi." His voice suddenly fell and became dry and apathetic. "And I wanted so much for him to appreciate me a little, too."

Nita didn't move.

"After Mother died there was no one who had a kind word for me in that house. Herzl told me about the requiem, not Father."

Again Michael saw to his great surprise that a man of over fifty, an acclaimed conductor wearing a suit and tie, was turning before his eyes into a child of three. His lower lip was extended as if he had just been grievously insulted. As if he had been deprived and treated with outrageous injustice.

"Did you ever think about that?" Theo yelled. "That Father's miserable assistant was the only one on my side? What do you have to say about the fact that your father didn't even intend to tell me?"

"You intended to kill Father," said Nita in a hollow voice. "Did you really hate him so much? So much that you could plan to kill him?"

"I hated him? How can you say I hated him? I wanted so much . . . so much . . ." His voice broke. After a few seconds he recovered. "Don't be so melodramatic," he said severely. "I didn't plan anything. I went to the house to talk to him. He was so . . . so cold, and so full of contempt. He was preoccupied by Herzl's having told me about the requiem and that I'd be unable to keep it secret. The whole time he was thinking only of Gabi, and of what Gabi deserved. We were in the bedroom. He was lying on the bed. I saw that he had no idea of what I was going through, of what it meant to me. All of a sudden the blood went to my head. And I picked up the pillow to throw it at the wall. I didn't mean—I really wasn't thinking. And then his face suddenly looked to me like a monster's face, like . . . like the way Kafka talks about his father. That's what he looked like. With that clicking of his dentures and that certainty that I was nothing. I didn't plan it. How can you plan a thing like that? I wanted it, I often felt like killing him, like shaking him with all my strength, but I didn't plan it in cold blood."

Now Nita's face was bathed in tears. Michael heard Balilty rub his hands and breathe a sigh of relief.

"I didn't mean to . . ." Theo bent toward her and held her hands. "I don't even know how the pillow, instead of hitting the wall. . . . I can't remember how it ended up on his face. I only wanted not to see his face, with that contempt, that callousness toward me, never thinking of me for a minute. I wanted not to see his face. To cover it. Not to see it anymore. I put the pillow on it. I don't know how much time passed before I realized what I was doing. And I can't even tell you how I knew he was dead. He must have been a lot weaker than I thought. I didn't mean to do it, Nita. I, I loved him, too. I wanted . . . I couldn't get through to him. Whatever I did was no use. Please understand. You said you wanted to understand."

"And the painting? And Gabi?"

"Afterward I got into a panic. I don't know where the idea of the painting came from. I didn't plan that either. Believe me. Everything was in a fog. I didn't think of what was going to happen next. I myself can't tell you how or why I moved him to the chair and gagged him, and how I got the picture out. I took the frame apart. I took the canvas to Herzl's place. I didn't think of the consequences. I didn't think of anything. It was . . . like a dream."

"And then at the concert you looked the same as usual. And we all waited for Father!"

"I . . . it was as if it was someone else, not me," said Theo in a dreamy voice. "It's impossible to explain, and I'm not asking you to forgive me. All my life I've been driven, haunted. This is the first time I've ever talked about it to anyone. About the hurt that never stops. About the despair you feel when you realize that whatever you do is no use."

"And Gabi."

"And Gabi." Theo bowed his head.

"Everything was planned."

"You can't really say that either," said Theo.

"What are you talking about, Theo?" She buried her face in her hands. "You took the package of strings from my wardrobe. In advance. And the gloves, they tell me, from the locker. You took the strings I'd forgotten all about. And you know that they're concert strings. And that nobody else had ones like them. As if you wanted them to think that I . . . I did it with you. You let me find him!" she sobbed. "I don't know if you even saw him after that. How much hatred you must have felt to do what you did! How much hatred to give you such strength!"

"I had no choice," said Theo. "He would have found out that I . . . He would have found out what I did. . . . He would have found out about Father. He wouldn't have given an inch. It would have become a sacred principle for him to carry out Father's wishes. I couldn't go back anymore. I couldn't."

Behind the glass wall there was only the sound of Nita's sobbing.

"What are we going to do now?" asked Theo in a small voice.

Nita wiped her face and blew her nose. "First of all, we'll get you a lawyer," she said hoarsely.

"No lawyer is going to get me out of this," said Theo. "For the rest of my life, whatever's left of it, I'll be locked up somewhere. You must realize that's not for me."

Nita looked at him in silence.

"You said you would stand by me," Theo reminded her like a child reminding its mother. "You said you would help me." There was something cunning in his voice. It was apparently this that made her stand up, trembling, and put her hand on his arm, as if he really were a small child. "I have to think about it," she said. "I still have no idea of what to do now."

"Ask your friend," whispered Theo, and he raised his eyes to the ceiling.

"Now," said Balilty, tugging at Michael's sleeve. "Go in there now."

She stood facing the door. Her arms hung limply at her sides. "He'll tell you whatever you want," said Nita on her way out. "Get him a lawyer, and whatever else he needs," she added and collapsed. If Michael hadn't supported himself against the doorpost, he wouldn't have been able to bear her weight. Danny Balilty carried her into Shorer's office and called an ambulance.

The interrogation of Theo van Gelden continued for five days. During those days Michael never left the building. The world ceased to exist. Sometimes Balilty and Eli Bahar joined in the interrogation. "So he'll appreciate you more," Balilty joked to Michael. During those days—in a bare, windowless little room on the fourth floor—Michael sometimes felt the boundary between his skin and that of the man opposite dissolve. During those days, he sometimes thought as he retired to Shorer's office for a few hours' rest, he was living as if he had lost himself and his own life, as if he were truly inside the mind of Theo van Gelden, who was becoming increasingly dependent on him.

Even when he closed his eyes in Shorer's darkened office, the voices went on echoing in his head. Things were mixed up. Every day Balilty cursed the press and tried to calculate precisely when the right moment would be for the reenactment of the crimes. Continuing to complain about Michael's attachment to the suspect, Balilty would also give him a brief report about the state of Nita's health, assuring him that she was never left alone. Izzy Mashiah sat by her bedside, and there was a hired nurse and the babysitter Ruth Mashiah had engaged. Once he also said something about Nita's baby: "Ido stood up today, he doesn't know yet how to sit back down, and he cries a lot."

Theo, too, was never left alone. Michael was always on the alert during those days, and Balilty took care never to leave the building without making sure that there was someone standing outside the door when they let Theo sleep for a while, and that there were no sharp or blunt instruments within his reach. "No tie or shoelaces," Balilty would repeat to the policemen on guard, "no knife or fork, just a spoon."

Sergeant Ya'ir walked in front of Theo when they climbed the stairs from the improvised detention room on the second floor to the interrogation room on the fourth. Michael followed a few steps behind Theo, who walked to the end of the corridor with his head bowed like an apathetic old cart horse. And this slow, submissive walk of his in the narrow corridor was the reason both Michael and Sergeant Ya'ir allowed themselves to be distracted from the possibility that hovered day and night in the air of the building and were taken by surprise when Theo suddenly leaped aside with astonishing agility and lightness and threw his body over the balustrade into the black void of the stairwell.

Michael's scream was heard throughout the building, and dozens of policemen were already in the basement by the time he got there. They stepped aside so that he could see for himself the smashed, broken-necked body.

Weeks passed before he was allowed to see Nita. During those weeks Ruth Mashiah would knock at his door every day on her way out of the apartment building. Her wrinkled little face became the sight most precious to him. Every day she would tell him something about Nita and Ido. He would sometimes see the baby from the kitchen window, when the babysitter took him out in the stroller. He didn't dare go out to see him. Ruth Mashiah made it clear that he could not see Nita until Nita agreed to it.

"At the moment," she said to him gently, "your name can't even be mentioned in her presence. But I believe," she added compassionately, "that one day, with a lot of patience . . ."

She didn't finish the sentence, but Michael clung to it nonetheless, week after week, by day and by night.